"You are the most stubborn, bull-headed man I have ever met. Why I would even try to make this marriage real is beyond me! I don't know why I was thinking you—" cried Hallie.

Kit gripped Hallie's wrist. "What were you thinking?"

"Nothing! Let go."

Kit wasn't going to let her go, not until he heard her say exactly what she meant.

Hallie pulled her hand away, and he wrapped his arms around her. Her hair fell over his arms. She looked up at him, glaring, and he was lost . . .

Her lips parted, an invitation. He tasted her, and sweet desire bolted through him. "Tell me you want me," he whispered. "Tell me you're not afraid."

Hallie moaned and pressed against him.

"Tell me with words. I need to hear the words," he breathed.

"I want you . . . but I didn't know how to show you. I . . ."

"Show me now . . . "

The Heart's Haven

Jill Barnett

POCKET BOOKS

New York   London   Toronto   Sydney   Tokyo   Singapore

An *Original* Publication of POCKET BOOKS

POCKET BOOKS, a division of Simon & Schuster Inc.
1230 Avenue of the Americas, New York, NY 10020

ISBN: 0-671-68412-4

First Pocket Books printing July 1990

10 9 8 7 6 5 4 3 2 1

POCKET and colophon are registered trademarks of
Simon & Schuster Inc.

Printed in the U.S.A.

To Meagan McKinney,
who believed in a stranger's story.

Chapter

One

A patch of faded blue gingham hovered in the lofty branches of Abner Brown's precious apple tree. As the branches shuddered, dropping the delicate pink blooms onto the grass below, Haldis Fredriksen stopped. Her gray eyes narrowed when she recognized that familiar swatch of cloth—the same cloth that was becoming more and more visible with each quiver of the tree. Grinding the heel of her boot into the soil, she turned and crept slowly toward the tree.

Hallie edged closer, using the furrow of lush rosebushes for cover. As she peered through the roses, she could see the checked fabric, now waving like a flag in the gentle spring breeze. She glanced from side to side, assuring herself that her nemesis, that priggish Mr. Brown, was nowhere in sight. When she was three feet from the tree, she straightened and planted her hands firmly on her hips. "Liv, get down out of that tree, now!"

There was a frantic rustling in the upper branches of the tree, followed by a heavy shower of apple blossoms. As the floral curtain thinned, a mass of gingham skirts and blond braids tumbled to the ground. Sitting indignantly on a bed of crushed apple blossoms was Hallie's nine-year-old sister, Liv.

"Thunderation! Hallie, you scared the spit out of me!" Liv stood up, carelessly slinging a knotted pair of black stockings over a shoulder before attempting to dust off her debris-covered behind. "A person could get hurt, having a body creep up on them like that."

"I know a person who'll be hurting—and soon." Hallie turned Liv around and swatted the dust off the girl's skirt a bit harder than necessary. "You swore you'd stay off Mr. Brown's property. Here it is only two days later and you're back in his tree again. Why?"

"I don't know," Liv mumbled. She gave Hallie a quick, guilty glance before she sat down and started fumbling with the knotted hose.

Hallie looked down at Liv. The young girl was tugging on a stocking over her bark-scraped leg and muttering something about crossed fingers. The sight struck a familiar chord in her. It seemed that all she did lately was lecture Liv. Was she being too hard on her, or was Liv just testing her limits? She'd been a handful for as long as Hallie could remember, but in the three years since their mother's death, Liv's belligerent attitude had worsened. Hallie had tried reasoning with her, but that hadn't worked. The young girl kept defying the rules. With Liv, you never knew what to expect next. But Hallie loved her, and because of that she couldn't let Liv's disobedience go unpunished. The child needed a lesson in keeping her word.

"Well, young lady, it seems you don't know why you're doing anything lately, doesn't it?"

Liv was silent.

Hallie tried to infuse a stern tone into her tired voice. "A day spent inside might improve your memory. And while you're trying to remember why you broke your word, you can do that stack of mending sitting by my bed."

"But Hallie—"

"And if you finish before supper, you can give the boys a bath." Hallie watched Liv's face contort into a grimace of distaste. They both knew from experience that bathing the four-year-old twins was like being thrown from Noah's Ark—only forty days and nights of rain was probably dryer.

Liv scrambled to her feet, this time ignoring her dusty derriere in an urgent effort to make a last plea. "A person could get sick, stuck in a stuffy house all day, breathing that stale air." Her eyes grew big as she added dramatically, "And then, if she got wet, a person could get lung fever and die!"

"You're going to wish you were dead, young lady, if you give me anymore backtalk. Now get!"

The angry flush staining Hallie's neck sent Liv scurrying toward home. As she rounded the corner, Hallie noticed Liv's shoeless feet. She started to call the girl back, but didn't want to risk alerting Mr. Brown. They'd been trespassing in his prized garden long enough, and if children's shoes weren't so hard to come by in San Francisco, she would have been sorely tempted to just leave them. But the memory of the last interminable wait for the very shoes Liv had so carelessly abandoned now sent her searching for them.

She looked around the base of the tree and found nothing. Poking in a few nearby bushes only resulted in disturbing a few bees. As she swatted the bugs away, she looked up and found what she was seeking. Dangling from one of the uppermost branches of the apple tree were Liv's new shoes.

Now what? Hallie thought, hoping some solution other than retrieving them herself would pop into her mind. For as long as she could remember, anything steeper than a flight of stairs had sent her into an attack of vertigo. Her one prideful attempt at overcoming this weakness was burned into her memory, along with the humiliation she had suffered when *she*, the captain's own daughter, had to be cut down from the tangled rigging some thirty feet above the ship's deck. The endless five minutes she had spent helplessly swaying from the ropes convinced her to accept her weakness.

Of course, that had been six or seven years ago. Maybe it

had only been a childhood fear. Didn't one grow out of such things? She *was* much taller now. What could be so frightening about climbing one fair-to-middling-sized tree? Besides, she reasoned, how else was she going to get those shoes?

Hallie glanced around self-consciously, knowing she really shouldn't do it, but now she was convinced that retrieving those shoes somehow symbolized her emergence into womanhood.

The lowest branch was right above her head, and for once thanking her Nordic ancestors for her majestic height, she pulled her five-foot-ten-inch frame onto the branch. By throwing her right leg over it, she managed to get into a sitting position. Feeling secure on her perch, she sat there grinning, surprised and proud of her newfound skill.

Fortified with confidence, she reached up and grasped the next limb, pulling herself into standing position. Then she made a mistake. She looked down.

The ground appeared to rise like yeast on a hot day. Her vision blurred and she wrapped her arms around the limb, holding on for all she was worth. Sucking in great breaths of air, she managed to calm her fluttering heart. Her sight cleared and she glanced around the tree, hoping to somehow recapture her nerve. It was gone.

Stuck in her precarious position, Hallie glared at the shoes. The blasted things were hanging high on the branch, and their mocking challenge egged her on. With one arm gripping the limb, she very slowly stretched her free arm toward the shoes. She was still a few inches shy.

She searched around for a twig to help extend her reach, found one, and tore it from the branch. Standing bravely on her tiptoes, she hooked the forked end of the twig around the knotted shoelaces. Gradually, she lowered the boot enough so she could grab its toe. With a quick tug, the leather half-boots came free, along with most of the blossoms on the high branch. Clutching the shoes in one hand, she waited for the drifting petals to clear, and then she turned slowly, trying to get a better grip on her security limb. Just as she started to squat, the wood cracked under the pressure of her weight. The branch tipped sharply toward the ground and Hallie slid down the limb, stripping it of twigs and blossoms before she skidded abruptly to the ground.

"My tree! My tree!"

The high-pitched wail pierced the air, penetrating Hallie's rattled brain. She brought one stinging hand up to brush the pale hair out of her face. There, with arms waving like the semaphore atop Telegraph Hill, was a raving Abner Brown. Clad in his usual black undertaker's garb, he was hopping up and down while he whined his tree litany.

"Mr. Brown, I . . . uh," Hallie stammered, unable to voice aloud any feeble excuse as she watched his apoplectic reaction.

His pallid skin was unnervingly lifeless for a man in his thirties, and its sallowness made his brown hair appear lank. The huge hook nose that dominated his homely face was his only bit of color. It was bright red. And as his jaw worked in and out, it looked to Hallie as if the man had finally grown a chin. The anger that emanated from his cold, penetrating eyes had a sinister quality that made her spine itch, and her eyes widened as she watched his long, skinny fingers form claws which she could picture wrapped around her throat—squeezing.

"Mr. Brown, I know I've damaged your tree." Hallie swallowed, noticing that as his anger became more rabid, the knotty Adam's apple in his long throat began to twitch. "I'm sorry—"

"Sorry! You're sorry?" he cried, walking over to stand directly above her. "I'll tell you what's sorry! You and those rowdy children. Don't have any respect at all for other people's property!" He paused and his pale blue stare turned into icy assessment.

Hallie sat frozen and fearful. But her fear subsided when he turned his calculating eyes away and began to pace back and forth in agitation.

"Do you realize I had this tree shipped from New Hampshire? It made it all the way around the Horn, enduring stormy seas and traveling with that gold-seeking riffraff. It survived the last three San Francisco fires, and what destroys it? A blight known as the Fredriksen family!" Abner stopped directly in front of her.

Hallie looked up at his accusing finger. "I know how you feel about that tree." *Oh do I know,* she thought, feeling an unexpected affinity with poor Liv. She watched him raise his spindly arm and shake one finger at the sky, a gesture she knew from experience preceded one of his lectures.

"Girlie, do you realize this is the only apple tree in San Francisco?"

Oh no, Hallie groaned inwardly, here it comes.

"It produces only the finest fruit. Back East, people pay the highest prices for the succulent apples from this strain of tree. They come from township after township to taste the crisp, luscious, red . . ."

Hallie stood while the man droned on. She knew the story well enough from the times he'd come to the house, dragging out Liv or the twins and accusing her of letting the children run wild. He called them vandalizing little urchins and said she was too young to control them. Agitated at the memory, Hallie shook out her skirts. She wasn't too young; she was almost nineteen.

Since her fifteenth birthday her father had left her in charge; he trusted her. As captain of a whaler, he was gone so much of the time that Hallie was left to rule the roost, and her roost consisted of her two younger sisters and her twin brothers. She tried to give the children a normal home, but with no mother, it hadn't been easy. And their home was changing.

In the last three years San Francisco had grown from a sleepy little village to a wild and sprawling port. Hallie had watched the city fill with men who were lured by the tales of gold. And now many of those same men were so disillusioned that they had become as savage as the criminals who had also swarmed West. It was hard, living in a place where gold fever drove even the best of men crazy.

Was that part of Liv's problem? Could she expect a young

girl to behave when grown men showed so little restraint? Maybe they needed to get away from the violence of this city. She would talk to Da when he came home.

Hallie realized that Abner wasn't even looking at her, he was so enthralled, having reached the pinnacle of oratory bliss. As she bent over and picked up the troublesome shoes, her long blond braid flopped over her shoulder. She flung it back and began rummaging through the broken foliage in search of the large hairpins that held her heavy braid in a tight bun. She only found two. Shoving them into her shirt pocket, Hallie straightened.

Lord, that man loves to hear himself talk. She shook her head in disgust and then, out of boredom, turned to survey the wreckage. She wanted to cringe when she saw the damage. There were only a few dozen blossoms left on the fractured fruit tree, and its biggest base branch was angled down toward the ground. It was almost laughable the way the broken limb looked like a crutch. No doubt there would be little if any fruit ripening on that tree this year.

She knew she was at fault; she *had* practically destroyed his tree. But the way he was acting—well, it was unnatural. Of course, Abner Brown was pretty strange himself, kind of picayunish. And he was always talking. But then, his job was dead people, and since the dead don't talk, it was little wonder he would rattle on whenever he came across a warm body.

Suddenly aware of her own warmth, Hallie looked up at the sun. Its position high in the sky indicated that most of the morning was already wasted. "Mr. Brown," she interrupted. "I'll pay for the damage."

"You sure will, girlie. Someone your age climbing trees when you ought to be watching those—those brats!" He sneered. "I'm going to report this vandalism!" With that pronouncement, Abner Brown raised his gump of a chin, crossed his gangly arms and waited.

Hallie considered his threat, knowing it was made to intimidate her. The authorities hardly had time to keep peace, much less cause her any trouble. But Abner Brown

7

had influence. He knew Sheriff Hayes well, since he was the only undertaker in the city, and what with the lack of law and order, heaven knew San Francisco had enough bodies to be buried lately.

"I said I'd pay for the damage," Hallie repeated. "How much do you want?"

Abner's eyes took on a larcenous gleam. He looked at the nearly naked tree and then toward its remains, scattered like flotsam all over the grass. He bent down, picked up a blossom and began to stroke it affectionately. "Oh, I think five hundred dollars ought to do it."

Five hundred dollars! Hallie swallowed, hard. The greedy pirate had her trapped, and they both knew it. He could claim to have been able to sell the fruit to the miners for that much and he was most likely right. With so much gold exchanging hands, prices, especially for eggs and fruit, were outlandish. Men had been known to pay ridiculous amounts for scarce items.

Since she had damaged the tree, she felt responsible, but it stuck in her craw that he could legitimately extort that kind of money from her. She didn't need any trouble with Da gone, and on the slim chance that Mr. Brown could make trouble for her and the children, Hallie didn't call his bluff. She was mad at this chiseling weasel, mad at Liv, and even madder at herself for getting into this mess.

Feeling the heat of her anger bubbling forth made her anxious to get away. Giving in to it would only make things worse. "I'll have the money for you by Friday." She forced the cowardly words past her lips and briskly walked away. Just before she reached the perimeter of the yard, she heard his nasally voice.

"See that you do, girlie. See that you do."

Kit Howland crumpled the letter into a tight ball and pitched it across the room. Reaching over his cluttered desk, he lifted the brass lid from an ornately carved tobacco holder. His strong, dark fingers disappeared into the depths of the wooden jar as he filled and packed his pipe before jamming the bit between his teeth. Striking a flame, he lit the leafy blend and began to puff, hoping that a smoke would ease the tension he felt knotting inside.

His father's letter had been apologetic. He had tried to dissuade Kit's mother and his aunt from their plan, telling them Kit was a grown man and doing fine on the West Coast. But his mother worried anyway.

Kit remembered her tearful pleading a few years ago, when he had announced his plan to move to San Francisco. His wife had died and her death had finally put an end to their disastrous marriage; and he'd wanted, needed to get away. As much as he loved his family, he couldn't stomach the pity he saw lurking in their eyes. Staying in New Bedford would have only served to remind him of his failed marriage and of the love/hate he still perversely felt for his unfaithful and now dead wife.

Now, he drew deeply on the pipe, holding the rum-tainted smoke in his mouth before expelling his breath. The bittersweet taste heated his mouth like the bitterness of his wife's betrayal burned in his hollow heart. Slamming his fist on the desktop, Kit stood and walked over to the wad of paper he had angrily thrown to the floor. Picking it up, he pressed it open and stared, hoping maybe he had misread its contents. Two words loomed from the page. *Aunt Madeline.*

Groaning in reaction, Kit felt like the black cloud that had been shadowing him had just unloaded. It was bad enough that he had to pay exorbitant storage fees while he cooled his heels waiting for the cursed merchant ship, but now his father wrote that his aunt Madeline was on board— something his family conveniently neglected to tell him until now. No doubt they assumed that the ship had docked and Maddie would already be billeted in his house, philanthropically mothering him. According to his father, Kit was her latest lost cause.

He swore loudly, relishing the release he felt at uttering a vulgar word. Where the hell was Taber's ship anyway? The clipper should have docked weeks ago. It wasn't unusual for merchant vessels to arrive a few weeks late, and battling anything from fierce storms to windless seas made the long voyage from the East Coast arduous and unpredictable.

Having once captained his own ship, Kit knew how nervewracking it could be, stranded in a doldrum sea, dependent upon the whims of the ocean current as the only mode to propel the ship, waiting for the wind to once again catch the sails and speed the vessel toward its destination. Picturing his aunt on that journey brought a smile to Kit's lips. He could imagine his domineering relative ordering the crew about like a seasoned master. Spending those endless hours with her would be unbearable to the men on board.

Kit chuckled. She could nag the weather into changing. But if Charles Taber were real resourceful, he would use Maddie's flapping mouth to help blow the ship to port.

With that thought, a smiling Kit returned to his desk. He picked up the last quarter's market prices, forwarded by his father, and checked the figures against his current contracts. His smile faded. Prices were dropping, which was not good news to an agent who had a leased warehouse full of whale oil and baleen, waiting for shipment to the factories back East. He had promised his friend, Captain Jan Fredriksen, that he'd get top dollar for the *Sea Haven*'s last cargo. They had agreed to wait for Kit to sell the goods to the highest bidder.

Kit leaned back in his chair and chewed on his pipe, wondering when the clipper would arrive. Once the ship docked and unloaded, it would reload with Jan's goods, already consigned and waiting. What a relief it would be to have those accounts settled and get out from under the warehouse lease. His own warehouse would be built with the agent's share of the profits, alleviating the need to pay the huge warehouse rents that were now eating up his profit.

Of course, now he had another problem. Although the ship's arrival would eliminate his business problems, it would also bring a new one—his aunt. Kit cursed his luck, knowing with his aunt's arrival, his heretofore peaceful existence would be no more.

Hallie's foot sunk into the oozing mud that masqueraded as a San Francisco street. With last night's spring rain, the sandy dirt had turned into a reddish-brown clay that made the flat section of the road almost impassable. Hallie lifted her skirts and she trudged through the boggy stuff.

In her rush to get away from that greedy rat of an undertaker, she had missed the wood-paved street, and now she had to plod her way down the unpaved section of one of San Francisco's narrow streets. Reaching the plank walkway, she stomped her feet in a futile attempt to dislodge the gunk from her shoes. The gritty mud was seeping through the eyelets on the inside of her leather boots, adding fuel to the fire of her already heated temperament. She banged her shoes a bit harder, imagining it was Abner Brown's knobby throat lying on the gray, weathered boards.

Pacified somewhat, Hallie dropped her skirts and marched down the walkway to the Adams Bank and Express. The door opened suddenly and she stopped. A petite, raven-haired woman emerged, dressed in an expensive-looking plum taffeta gown. The woman pulled the strings of her embroidered purse closed and drew a silk parasol cord off her gloved wrist. As she eyed Hallie up and down, her features filled with haughty disdain. She snapped open her parasol, and as if it would ward off some unseen plague, wielded it in Hallie's face, forcing her back to avoid the lace contraption, whose sharp peak bobbed so perilously close to her nose.

"Well, of all the nerve!" Hallie muttered, watching the woman and her frilly armament scurry away.

As Hallie started toward the door, she caught her reflection in the window. *Lord, what a mess!* Thick strands of pale blond hair had escaped from her long braid and hung from her head like Medusa's snakes. She glanced down at the baggy flannel work smock covering her dark woolen dress. It was littered with petals and twigs. She swiped off the debris and critically eyed her clothing. Dazzling it was not.

Hallie had taken to wearing the concealing smocks almost two years ago, when, in a matter of months, her boyish thinness had blossomed into womanly proportions. When she had dressed this morning, she hadn't intended to go anywhere, but she couldn't find Liv, and so left her sixteen-year-old sister Dagny in charge of the twins and went off to track down her precocious nine-year-old sister.

Hallie frowned at the dreary smock; it made her look dowdy. Little balls of wear speckled its front, and the dour shade of gray drew the color from her face. Throwing caution to the wind, Hallie stepped into a nearby stoop, unbuttoned the overblouse, and pulled the wretched thing over her head. She looked around and spotted an old spittoon. Wadding the garment into a tight ball, she crammed it into the brass urn, holding her breath and doing her best to ignore the urn's rancid contents.

She grabbed a handful of hair, pulled the two hairpins out of her pocket, and placed them between her teeth while twisting her braid into a lopsided bun. Jabbing the pins into her knotted hair, she tucked a few scraggly wisps behind her ears and glanced down at her dark dress. The soft wool didn't hide her deep bust; instead, the fabric clung to her torso before it flared downward in draping gores. No, plum taffeta it was not, but she'd make do. Hallie squared her shoulders and, with a determined step, entered the bank.

Miners were gathered six deep in front of a mahogany counter, and behind it stood two men, dressed in crisp white shirts and absorbed in weighing bag after bag of gold. When the din occasionally lessened, she could hear the clink of gold nuggets as they spilled into the scale's dish.

Another line formed at the counter to Hallie's right. She figured that this was the express station, by the bellowed names of various cities and by the men who groped their way forward so they could arrange to send funds.

Three desks were jammed into the room, their tops smothered with papers and empty chamois bags. The path to one of the desks was open, and the man behind it appeared to be immersed in a stack of papers, oblivious to his chaotic surroundings.

Hallie walked up to the desk. "Excuse me, sir?"

The sound of a distinctly female voice rendered the room suddenly quiet. The young man behind the desk looked up, and startled, he quickly rose. "Can I be of service, miss?"

"I am Miss Fredriksen. My father is Captain Jan Fredriksen of the *Sea Haven*. He said he made arrangements for me to have access to his funds, if need be." Her voice seemed to echo in the room's sudden silence.

"Just a moment, Miss Fredriksen. I'll get Mr. Adams." He walked over to a large door at the back of the room, knocked briefly, and entered.

Hallie could sense the attention she was receiving, and she felt as conspicuous as a nun in a bawdyhouse. She could feel the heat of the miners' eyes blatantly staring at her, and it was frightening. After a few long seconds she crossed her arms protectively over her chest and forced herself to stare straight ahead, wishing she still had the concealing security of her lackluster smock. She felt movement around her, but before she could panic, the door behind the desk opened and an older gentleman walked toward her.

"Miss Fredriksen, it's a pleasure." He stepped around the desk and grasped her still trembling hand. He must have felt her shaking, because his expression changed to one of concern. He assessed the situation, then quelled the ogling miners with a stern look. Placing her hand on his stocky arm, he led her to the safety of the room beyond.

After seating her and closing the door, he walked around the massive oak desk and sat down. "Now, what can I do for you?"

Hallie looked at his kind, round face and felt reassured. "I need five hundred dollars."

"I see," he said, his expression unchanging.

He opened a leather-bound ledger and began thumbing through the pages. Appearing to have found what he needed, he perused the page, and during those awkwardly silent seconds, Hallie's curiosity got the better of her. She stretched her neck, trying to decipher, upside down, the figures on the page. She was beginning to rise from her chair in her craning effort when she caught his sigh and quickly settled back down into her seat.

He looked up. "It seems we have a problem."

"But Mr. Adams, my father assured me he made arrangements for me to withdraw from his account. His voyages have been getting longer and longer, so he felt there might be a time when I would run short of funds. This is an emergency. I must have—"

"Excuse me, Miss Fredriksen," he interrupted. "Captain Fredriksen did give me the authorization. That's not the problem. There isn't five hundred dollars in the account."

Hallie was stunned. "I don't understand, there should be at least fifteen thousand in that account. The cargo from my father's last voyage was worth that much."

He looked back at the book. "There haven't been any deposits for eight months."

"But my father's agent should have transferred the funds over two months ago."

Mr. Adams looked concerned. "Who is his agent?"

Hallie fidgeted slightly. "Howland and Company, across the street."

"Oh yes, I know Kit Howland. A fine young man. There must be some mistake. Kit is as honest as the day is long."

Kit Howland. Her stomach lurched at the mention of that name. *Oh Lord, I don't want to face him.* She could feel the heated blush of embarrassment flood her neck and face. Just the thought of facing him again sent tension speeding from her stiffened shoulders down to her fingers, pressured white from clutching the arms of her wooden chair.

"I'm sure Mr. Howland can straighten this out," he said, oblivious to the turmoil bubbling through Hallie. The banker rose from his chair. "In fact," he said, flipping open an ornate pocket watch, "I have an appointment, so I'll be happy to escort you over to see him right now."

Tucking the watch back in his vest pocket, he grabbed a

low-crowned hat off a peg behind him and helped a stunned and subdued Hallie from her chair.

He whisked her out of his office and through the racket of the bank before Hallie had a chance to regain her composure and find some excuse not to see Kit Howland.

Once outside, the bite of the air released Hallie from her stupor. Her eyes locked on the bold black letters of the Howland and Company sign, watching them grow larger as they neared the opposite side of Montgomery Street. The banker led her along the board walkway that dissected the muddy street, and he chattered about how easy it would most likely be to straighten this matter out. He assured her that Mr. Howland was a reasonable man, a gentleman.

Ha! Hallie thought. She remembered their last meeting vividly. The "gentleman" wasn't very reasonable then; "livid" was a more appropriate description.

He had been the handsome whaling agent her father had befriended, and sixteen-year-old Hallie had taken one starry-eyed look at Kit Howland and fallen deep into the throes of puppy love. When the men sat down to dinner, Hallie had been so busy staring at him in adoration that she had accidentally ladled hot chowder onto his lap.

Horrified at her clumsiness, she had tearfully fled to her room, barring the door, and refusing to come out until the next day. While her father had been sympathetic, saying that Kit wasn't too angry and he'd be fine in a day or so, Hallie knew otherwise. Kit had looked as if he wanted to smack her. She had seen his face redden in anger just before the tears of humiliation blinded her vision, so thereafter she made sure that she was never around when Kit was. Luckily, most of her father's business was conducted in Kit's office, so Hallie hadn't had to do too much hiding.

Mr. Adams led Hallie to the Howland and Company office door and gave her hand a fatherly pat. "Now, my dear, once those funds are transferred, I'll see that you get your money. You just go right on in there and I'm sure Mr. Howland will clear this up." He opened the agency door, and a pale Hallie reluctantly stepped halfway inside.

Thinking quickly, she used the door to shield her from any occupants inside and she forced a polite smile to her lips. "Thank you, sir."

Hallie watched as he doffed his hat and turned to walk up the street. She had stepped back outside, planning to run as fast as she could in the opposite direction, when she noticed that the banker had stopped and turned back around. She quickly stepped back inside, peering around the doorjamb with a false smile and lifting her hand near her dimpled cheek as she wiggled her fingers at him in a farewell gesture. He stood, watching her with a puzzled look on his pudgy face.

Resigned to her fate, Hallie shut the door. Taking a deep breath, she turned slowly, preparing to meet the man she had astutely managed to avoid for the last two years.

Chapter

Two

The sound of the bell over the door drew Kit's attention away from his papers. A hand curled around the wood portal as the rustling flounce of a dark blue skirt appeared around the bottom edge of the door. The skirt rested quietly for a minute before it suddenly whipped into full view as a female figure stood, apparently hugging the door protectively to her breast while her head peered outside.

From the woman's stance, Kit assumed she was hiding from someone, so he stood and walked toward her, hoping to be of assistance. He was a few feet from the door when his eyes locked on her woolen-draped derriere—an enticingly rounded derriere despite the bits of crushed leaves clinging to it. His gaze traveled up her statuesque figure to the flaxen knot of hair lopsidedly skewered to her uncovered head. He stopped suddenly, for its unusual color was hauntingly familiar. No, it can't be, he thought, with a shake of his head.

Then the woman turned, taking a deep breath that made her exquisitely full bosom appear to grow even larger. Relief washed over him, for the silver-haired young girl he remembered certainly didn't have a body like that.

With a smile of greeting, he met her gaze. His look of

disbelief moved back and forth from her face to her bust. It *was* her.

Startled by his closeness, Hallie's hand sprung to cover her surging heart, but her eyes feasted on his features. His hair was still dark and curly. It had been the first thing she noticed about him, those pitch-black springy curls so different from her own straight pale hair. She watched the slashes in her cheeks deepen in one of his rare and slightly crooked smiles. They were wedged into his square jaw, below a set of prominent cheekbones so noble in angle that they should have been on an ancient warrior in one of Dagny's beloved mythology books.

She died a little inside as his heavenly smile faded when he recognized her. *What am I doing here?* she berated herself, noticing that he kept looking from her bosom to her face. In her dazed and downhearted state, she glanced down and examined her bodice, trying to determine what it was on the front of her dress that shocked him so. Then it registered.

Hallie quickly crossed her arms over her breasts, wishing for all the world that they were small and delicate like Dagny's, and not so . . . so pronounced. She read his shocked reaction to her changed figure, and with no way to hide her growth, felt doubly exposed. When he swore angrily, she cringed, certain that her appearance was the reason for his bad temper. Her insides were crumbling, but she defensively raised her chin, hoping that a suitably haughty look would bluff him into thinking she wasn't the least bit intimidated.

Kit was having trouble dealing with the fact that the gawky and shy daughter of his friend Jan Fredriksen was so developed. Well developed. Jan had laughingly told him that all anyone had to do was mention Kit's name and Hallie would disappear faster than rum in a drunkard's cup. His friend had painted such a vivid picture of her escape antics that Kit assumed she was still a young adolescent.

Good God, what the hell was wrong with him? he thought. She's still nothing but a kid, not much over eighteen. Of course, Jo had only been seventeen when they had married. They'd spent her eighteenth birthday locked in the cabin of his whaler, and it had been the most sensual experience of his life. He spit out a pithy oath. Would he never forget that bitch?

He looked at Hallie. She was giving him the same insolent look that his wife used when she wanted to wound him. That snotty little tilt of her chin that proceeded one of Jo's tirades on why she couldn't care less what he did. That image pushed him to his limit.

"Who are you hiding from now, Hallie? Another unsuspecting victim unmanned by your culinary skill?" The insult hung cruelly in the tension-filled air. Her wounded gaze had Kit feeling thoroughly disgusted with himself.

He turned away sharply and went back to his desk, where he filled the silence by shuffling through some papers before he slapped them back down and rubbed his fingers across his forehead.

"Look kid, I'm sorry. Just forget about that stupid accident. I have." He looked up at her pale face. "Oh, for Christ's sake, sit down." He fairly shouted the command.

She stood there, still giving him an injured look that made him feel as if he had just told her there was no Santa Claus.

Hallie was crushed. He'd called her a kid. To him she was nothing more than an irksome brat. Did she really expect him to view her differently? Two years ago she had run away, blubbering like a baby. Then what does she do? She avoids him like a green girl.

She sat. What's wrong with me? she asked herself, realizing she had been acting immaturely. She had never been so lily-livered before. Every time she was around Kit Howland she did something stupid! Her hands would get all clammy, her head foggy, and she'd panic. When the fog cleared, she'd do the first thing that flitted through her mind. That was what always got her into trouble. Her first reaction was usually all impulse and no forethought.

Her self-derision was broken by the sound of his voice. He had been asking her something. She forced herself to look him straight in the eye, knowing that she must learn to harness her dithering reaction to this man. "Pardon me, what did you say?"

"I asked you what you're doing here."

His aggravated tone irritated her. He acted like she was intruding on his precious time. *He* was the one who had made a mistake. Where was the money from the sale of the *Sea Haven*'s last cargo? He was trying to intimidate her. Well, she would show him; the green girl had grown.

"Let me set you straight on a few things. You seem to have the ridiculous idea that I've been hiding from you. I have not. In fact, it seems to me to be the other way around." Hallie realized that turning the tables on him wasn't so hard; in fact, she was lying beautifully. "I don't know how you managed it, but you only showed up when I was busy elsewhere." Hallie ended this last corker with a huff, and the indignation on her face rivaled her sister Liv's.

He leaned forward. "Now wait a minute—"

"And as to the reason I'm here," she interrupted, "I've been to the bank." Hah! she thought, take that. She leaned back against the oak slat of the chair, waiting to see him squirm.

"So?" His looked was puzzled.

He really did think she was stupid. *"Mister* Howland, I realize you think me a clumsy, ignorant child. I am not. My father has trusted me to check on his account." *Once this fibbing started, it was hard to stop. It was little wonder the twins told such whoppers.* "I just left Mr. Adams. Where is the money from my father's last cargo?"

Had he heard her right? Was this the same girl who had been acting like a frightened rabbit? Now she was accusing him of evading her, and suspiciously questioning his business methods. What could a kid like her know about his business anyway? Nothing. She was acting just like a woman, twisting everything around. Did they all, even the young ones, have the ability to convolute reality on a whim? Hell, he and his brothers grew up watching his mother and aunt hone word-twisting to a fine art. It took about fifteen years to realize that when all else failed, women would usually confuse their victim with an illogical statement. And here was Jan Fredriksen's skittish young daughter honing her craft on him. At least the girl had developed some . . . gumption. The first term that had popped into his head would have been anatomically incorrect. He could imagine her face if he told her, in man's terms, exactly what he was thinking. The image made him laugh.

"I find nothing funny about the money you owe my father," Hallie huffed. "That money should have been deposited months ago."

Kit couldn't suppress his grin, especially when it seemed to spur her on. Her eyes glittered and that exquisite skin of hers tinged pink. He shook his head to clear it. Thoughts like those would only get him into trouble.

"I'm here to see that the funds are transferred *now,* Mr. Howland."

"Relax, Hallie." Kit waved his hand in a gesture that suggested she should calm down. It seemed to only make her angrier. "Your father's tonnage is stored at the DeWitt warehouse. It's consigned to a merchant clipper that's late."

"You mean the cargo hasn't been sold yet? Her wide eyes reflected her surprise.

"I expect it'll dock any day." Kit hoped he sounded more confident than he felt. In truth, he was worried himself. If the clipper didn't arrive by the end of the week, he would have to begin to make his own inquiries.

"I don't understand. Da's cargoes have always been consigned and sold within a few weeks of unloading. That load was from a voyage that ended last November. This is April!" Her eyes narrowed suspiciously. "Why the delay?"

"For your information, Miss Fredriksen, your father and I have an agreement. I held back the shipment to wait for an increase in the price of oil, not that I have to answer to you," he added testily. "The clipper that's overdue is owned by a . . . relative." Kit didn't divulge that Charles Taber had been his brother-in-law or that he had purposely held out to get the satisfaction of scalping his in-laws.

"They need the oil and are willing to pay more per barrel

than the other merchants." Then Kit realized that he was feeling defensive and making excuses to the young daughter of his friend. She was really too young to understand the economics of his business, so why was he trying to explain?

"You needn't worry over it. I'm sure this is too much for a kid like you to understand. Your father trusts me to do what's best." Jan was a trusted friend who never questioned his motives.

But Hallie did.

"Are you telling me that my father's cargo has been sitting profitless in a warehouse for five months just so you could line the pockets of your relatives? You're right, my father did trust you, and he worked hard for that load—too hard to let it sit virtually abandoned for all this time."

She ran on, unaware of the desperation in her voice. "I have the children to take care of. I need that money!"

Kit knew instinctively that something was wrong. Her voice sounded too frenzied.

Hallie caught his knowing expression and realized she had given herself away. Oh, no, she couldn't tell him about the tree. It was too embarrassing. To admit to being caught up a tree would make her look like a recalcitrant child. And to this man, who she wished would think of her as a woman, the tree incident would just confirm his opinion of her.

He leaned back with a sigh, "Okay, Hallie, let's have it." He laced his fingers together behind his head. "And none of this nonsense about lining my family's pockets either. Believe me, they don't need it. Now what is going on?"

How could she get out of this? Maybe she could convince him that she needed the money for the household. Although, if the cargo was still in storage, she stood little chance of getting the money to Abner Brown. Still . . . he might consign it to someone else if he thought she was desperate enough, or even advance the funds into their account. He was waiting for her answer. Not wanting to meet his penetrating gaze, she stared at her folded hands.

"Da's been gone since the first of the year, and he hasn't been gone this long since Mama died." Hallie sighed, for emphasis. "The household money is gone, so I went to the bank, and the account is almost empty." She was purposely vague in her explanation.

"That is odd." Kit frowned. "I understood you had an account at Oatt's. Is there some problem?"

Oh rats! Her father must have told him about the account. He looked sincerely worried, and it made Hallie feel guilty, but not guilty enough to admit to Kit Howland that she needed five hundred dollars because she'd been caught up a tree. He was too sharp, and she felt cornered. She needed to confuse him.

Hallie covered her face with her hands and promptly feigned some surprisingly realistic-sounding sobs. Cracking her fingers a smidgen, she saw Kit stand quickly and pat his pockets, obviously in search of a handkerchief.

Her whimpers grew to wails as she began to get into the spirit of things. All the while, her mind rapidly plotted a way to get him to transfer the money early.

Kit pulled out his handkerchief, and as he walked toward her, Hallie heard him mumble something about being a brash idiot. Now what was she going to do? Here she'd gone and done it again. With her rash actions, she'd dug herself into another hole.

Peering through her fingers, she caught sight of a piece of white linen hanging from his proffered hand. She kept her head down and added a few wails to prevent him from seeing her dry eyes while she grabbed the hankie. With a couple of loud sniffles, she covered her eyes and nose with the fabric. His masculine scent radiated from the cloth, and Hallie felt suddenly light-headed.

Kit was consoling her with gentle words. His strong voice softened as he told her she was a spunky thing and that he knew it must have been tough, raising the younger Fredriksens since the death of their mother.

A bit dreamy, she wavered and forgot to add some more wails. Luckily, she was saved from revealing herself when he pulled her into his arms. She buried her face in the vee of his vest and wrapped her arms tightly around his upper back.

The action pressed her full breasts flush against him, and she thought she felt the rumble of a groan.

Hallie clung to his back, still attempting to hide. The hard button of his shirt was pressed against her nose, which began to itch from all her phony sniffles. She turned her head quickly in an effort to keep from sneezing, and her chest rubbed against his. It felt so good, she was contemplating twisting again when she let loose with an indelicate sneeze. Her cheeks, unmarred by tear blotches, and her guilty dry eyes gave her away.

"Why you little faker!" He grabbed her shoulders and began to shake her.

Hallie's jostled mind screamed *run,* but his grip held her tight. She drew her foot back and cracked it against his shin.

"Ouch, dammit!"

His grip loosened while he hopped on one foot, blocking the path to the door. Hallie spun around and ran to the other side of the desk. He turned, and for a moment she was motionless. Anger flared from his eyes, and it seemed as if his dark pupils had disappeared. All she saw was the deep, green gleam that chained her gaze to his.

Kit leaned forward. She stepped back.

He placed his hands on the front corners of the desk and moved his taut-featured face even closer. The desk somehow shrunk.

Hallie locked her knees to keep from shaking, and she grabbed his wheeled chair. Her hands gripped its tufted leather back like a shield, inching it back and forth in readiness. Watching him like a cornered mouse, she suddenly felt chilled. The silence iced her blood.

His wide shoulders shifted to the left. Hallie and the chair slid right. She didn't dare gauge the distance to the door, because his feline movements signaled that he would take that instant to pounce.

Kit, and his menacing glare, edged right. Hallie rolled the chair left. Her wary stare moved to his body, hoping to get a clue to his next movement.

"Jan should have laid his hand to your backside, Hallie."

"Da never hit me!"

"That's obvious."

His words broke her concentration, and Hallie shifted her weight to her right foot.

Kit shot around the desk. She shoved the chair straight at him and ran, but his long reach clamped on the back of her dress. Her buttons pinged as they bounced on the wooden floor, and her bodice gaped open. Cool air pierced Hallie's thin camisole. She felt another tug and looked over her shoulder. Kit sat in his chair, one hand anchored to the desk and the other clutching the back yoke of her dress. His smirk was triumphant.

Hallie tried to jerk forward, but she could feel the seam threads of her dress pop. If she ran to the door, she'd arrive without her bodice. Before she had a chance to think further, Kit rolled the chair, and his hard knees, into Hallie's skirted legs. She fell backward into his lap.

"A bratish act . . ." Kit grunted as he struggled to pull her, facedown, across his knees, "deserves a brat's punishment."

He was going to spank her! She felt his thigh muscles tighten against her ribs as he tried to restrain her flailing arms and legs. Hallie yelled for all she was worth.

She kicked; she fought; she screamed.

One powerful leg clamped over the backs of her knees, pinning her kicking legs between his, and before Hallie could blink, she was staring at the wooden floor. When she felt the first smack on her already-battered behind, she tried to swing upward, but his arm held her down. She struggled some more and realized that her squirming kept him too busy to smack her again.

And then she saw it—the perfect spot.

Her hand shot up to the tender flesh behind his knee and she pinched as hard as she could, twisting her fingers just for good measure. She heard his grunt of pain, and wanted to smile, but she was flung upward so fast she didn't have time.

He held her inches away from his angry face. Hallie glared right back. She could give as good as she got.

"Da would never hit a woman! He's a gentleman and doesn't get perverse pleasure from violence," Hallie taunted, lifting her chin a notch higher. "He knows how to treat a woman."

"Perverse pleasure?" Kit's lips thinned. "A woman?" His look spoke volumes. "So, Hallie . . ." his words grated through his teeth, "you want to be treated like a woman? Let me show you some 'perverse pleasure.'"

His right hand shot out and spanned the back of her head. She felt the hard knot of her hair as it crushed into the well of her nape. His mouth engulfed hers.

Hallie was pinned by his legs and his lips. Her wedged forearms pushed against his chest in a fruitless effort. His lips parted and his teeth lightly scored her upper lip. She gasped, and Kit's tongue delved into her open mouth, foraging its depths and taking away her life's breath.

Her nose inhaled the cool air. The contrast of its chilling bite against the walls of her throat intensified the burning scorch of his plundering tongue.

Her mouth was aflame.

Kit tongued her sweet depths, lessened his driving force. As he swirled his tongue around hers, his gripping hold relaxed and her arms entwined themselves around his neck. The movement left a space between their upper bodies, and he moved his hands to her waist, possessing her lightly and drawing her torso forward to rub the tips of her breasts slowly, back and forth across his cloth-layered chest. Her nipples hardened. So did he.

Hallie's head spun. Her body felt light, except for her breasts. Deep inside, they were blooming with a warm heaviness that sped in concentric swirls and crested at her tight nipples. Her breasts and mouth were intensely alive and her head was so dizzy she actually heard bells.

"Glad to see you're not working too hard, old friend." The deep voice echoed in the steamy silence of the room.

Kit pulled back suddenly, releasing Hallie and cursing under his breath.

A handsome man with a devastating smile leaned casually against the doorjamb. "So this is what whaling agents do. I always wondered what made the job appealing enough for you to give up the sea."

"Shut up, Lee." Kit stood abruptly, blocking Hallie's view. Immediately she stood on her toes so she could peer over his shoulder.

The man lifted his red-bearded chin in an attempt to see around Kit. "Maybe I'll retire and give you a little competition." He kicked the door shut with his heel. The bell peeled a late warning. Removing his cap, he combed his fingers through the wealth of reddish-blond hair that framed his strong-featured face. He walked toward the twosome, stopped a few feet away, placed his hat over his heart and bent in a dramatically gallant bow. "Leander Prescott, ma'am, the incredibly handsome and wealthy captain of the famous ship, the *Wanderer*, at your service. I also happen to be this devil's friend, but I'm sure you can overlook that bit of bad judgment in my otherwise flawless and charming person." This eloquent speech was delivered with a smile warm enough to melt even the coldest female heart.

"Stuff all that rot, Lee. You already know her." Kit spoke the clipped response before he stood back to give Lee a clear view of Hallie.

"Hello, Captain Prescott," Hallie said quietly, still shaken from the kiss. She was embarrassed. Lee Prescott was another friend of her father's, and he'd seen them kissing.

Lee was speechless, almost. "Hallie? Hallie Fredriksen?" His mouth gaped and he looked back and forth between the two of them. After a seemingly endless few seconds, his eyes locked on Hallie's chest. "You've grown." The words stumbled out.

Hallie grabbed the front of her dress.

"Up," he added lamely.

Hallie was so uncomfortable that all she could think

about was getting away fast. "Well," she said, her voice rushed as she began to scoot toward the door, clinging to her dress like a child to its mother's skirts. "I'm sure you gentlemen have plenty to talk about, so I'll just be on my way—"

"Sit down now!" Kit bellowed.

Lee and Hallie plopped down simultaneously in the two chairs facing Kit's massive desk.

Hallie knew she was in for it. Kit looked mad enough to grow horns. And he had every right to be, too, since she'd tried to bamboozle him. She should have told him honestly why she needed the money. She had waged a mental battle, quick as it was, between swallowing her pride or lying. Lying won.

Was it her fault she couldn't think when he was around? Her brains turned to oatmeal and she did the most childish things. There was no way she could continue to lie. Besides which, she couldn't think of a good story when her mind and stomach were all queasy.

Kit sat down behind his desk, afraid to take his glaring eyes off Hallie, for he knew that, given the chance, she would be gone in a flash. He noticed that Lee appeared to have recovered and was watching Hallie, chest level, as she squirmed.

"Lee, I suppose I should tell you what was going on before you arrived." Kit had the sudden urge to draw Lee's attention away from Hallie's attributes.

Lee's face took on a knowing gleam. "Oh, you needn't do that, my father told me all about it when I was twelve. In fact, he took me to this—"

"Oh, stop it!" Kit saw Hallie flush bright red at Lee's inane teasing. "This is serious. She needs money for something, and Jan is still gone." He turned to her. "Tell us, Hallie, and no more theatrics."

"I need five hundred dollars," she mumbled.

"Speak up, girl, I didn't hear you." His voice was so loud that she cringed. Good, he thought, a little fear should wrangle the truth out of her.

"I need five hundred dollars," she said in a voice loud enough to be heard in Sacramento City.

He ignored her impertinent tone, although his spanking hand began to itch. "Why?"

"Because of the shoes," she answered vaguely.

"What shoes?" Kit and Lee questioned together.

"Why, Liv's shoes." Hallie's tone was inflected with reason.

Kit scratched his palm.

Lee leaned over and patted her hand gently. "Don't be upset, my dear." He smiled reassuringly. "You just take your time and tell us the whole story."

Hallie took a deep breath and blurted out the whole tale. When she got to the part where Abner Brown demanded his money, she paused, for Kit's neck was turning a dark red. Attributing it to anger for her foolishness, she rattled on, "I know it was stupid to climb that tree, but I had to get those shoes. I never thought the limb would break and I know five hundred dollars is a lot of money but he said he was going to report me. I try so hard with the children and all and Da's been gone and I'm—" She could feel tears of humiliation rise as she bit back the words *I'm scared*.

"Hallie." Kit spoke her name quietly. "You should have told me what happened in the first place. Abner Brown is taking advantage of you. Let me take care of him."

"But *I'm* the one who should take care of it. It's not your problem, and while Da's gone, I am the head of the family. I have to learn to deal with these things. I'm an adult." In a scornful voice she added, "I'm not a child."

"Your father is our friend. He would want us to watch out for his family. You're a woman, Hallie, and a young one at that." Kit smiled. The poor girl needed some masculine reassurance. "This is something that is better handled by a man."

Hallie looked at Lee, who was nodding in agreement. Neither of the thickheaded men appeared aware of the condescension that echoed from Kit's statement. She wasn't some frail little woman. Did they really think men were so superior? They probably thought she was too young to handle her own problems. Well, she couldn't change her gender or her age, so that didn't leave her anything to argue with. Men and their stupid egos!

Lee rose and helped an agitated Hallie from her seat. "You go on home and don't worry about Mr. Brown. Just leave him to us."

Kit stood, plucking his hat and coat off the rack behind him. "That's right, Hallie. Just run along and don't worry your pretty head about him."

Hallie knew she had been dismissed. She and her pretty head.

She stomped angrily to the door and opened it with a jerk. Turning back to look at the two baffled men, she said, "You're right, I should have come to you first. After all, if a smart woman needs water to clean up a mess, she doesn't haul it from the river herself. She finds two asses to do it for her!"

The door slammed shut.

"I think she's mad." A perplexed Lee turned toward Kit. "Why do you suppose that is?"

Kit shrugged on his coat. "Who the hell knows? That kid is a hellion. Nothing she does makes any sense at all. She hides from me for all this time, and then comes right in here out of the blue and accuses me of cheating her father. She tells half-truths, fakes tears, and then gets violent when I try to teach her a lesson." Kit rubbed the back of his knee. The soreness served as an unwelcome reminder of what had happened after she pinched him.

Lee listened but appeared to have trouble suppressing his grin. "Is that what you were doing when I came in? Giving lessons?"

Kit had the grace to blush, especially since his mind was on the same track as Lee's. He was thinking of how his body reacted when he kissed Hallie—uncontrolled. He didn't like feeling out of control. Jo had taught him that women weren't to be trusted. The pain of the lesson was severe enough to keep him from ever allowing a woman to get the better of him. He always controlled himself where they were concerned. But with Hallie he had acted on pure instinct. Lusty, carnal instinct. And he felt guilty.

To relieve his guilt, he glossed over the incident. "Get your mind out of your pants, Prescott," Kit said, arrogantly ignoring the fact that his own mind, at least during the kiss, had been in the very same place. Then he justified his actions, both mentally and vocally. "I was trying to scare the kid."

"Why do you keep calling her a kid?" Lee's look penetrated right through Kit. "She's not, you know."

"Not what?"

"A kid."

"Of course she is. Just because her body has grown doesn't mean her mind has. While we're on the subject, I don't think Jan would like the way you were ogling his daughter. I know I didn't." Lee raised a questioning brow at Kit. But before he could say anything, Kit added, "I mean, if she were my daughter."

Lee had the good sense to be quiet, although from his wry expression, Kit knew he was jumping to all kinds of wrong conclusions. His thoughtful silence made Kit uncomfortable. Lee was very perceptive—perceptive enough to realize that Kit was confused by his own unusual behavior. Blast it all, he had enough pressures right now. He sure as hell didn't need to stand here trying to buffalo his own friend. He settled for distracting him instead. He opened the office door. "Come on. Let's pay a visit to good ol' Abner Brown."

Hallie walked into the dim house. Though the days were getting longer, a blanket of fog covered the town, dulling the afternoon sun with its damp mist and blocking the light through the narrow windows. The house was quiet.

Too quiet.

She walked out of the foyer and down a narrow hallway

that ran alongside the steep staircase. A scream of frustration pierced the air. Hallie reached for the paneled door of the kitchen and pushed it open.

Inside there was a large tub half filled with water. Standing next to it, drenched from head to foot, was Dagny.

"You little monsters!" Dagny swiped her dark, dripping hair back and rubbed the water from her brown eyes.

Two identical white-blond heads popped up from the deep metal tub. "He started it," accused the boy on the left.

"I did not," came the indignant reply.

"Did too."

"Did not," Knut whined. "Gunnar kicked me first!"

Gunnar took offense and spit water all over his twin brother. "Tattletale."

"You two stop it! Right now." Hallie walked toward the soggy group.

Both wide-eyed, freckled faces turned toward her. Each pointed a finger at the other and spoke at the same time. "But he started it!"

"And I'm finishing it," came the stern reply. Hallie glanced at Dagny. "Let's get them dried off, Duggie. Then you go change into some dry clothes yourself."

"Stand up, boys." Hallie grabbed a large piece of cloth, wrapped it around one of them and lifted his wiry body out of the tub. She rubbed his head vigorously and inspected his oversized ears. "Where is Liv?" she asked.

"Not in there." The smart comment was followed by a bunch of giggles.

"Hush," Hallie scolded at their silliness.

"Upstairs, brooding," Dagny answered. "You know how she's been lately. All grumpy and gloomy." She drew a flannel nightshirt over Knut's head, picked up a pair of gray pants and held them out for him to step into. "You think she's like this because Da's been gone so long?" She pulled the pants up around the youngster's waist, tucked in the shirt, and buttoned the pants closed.

"I don't know," Hallie replied. "I found her up in Mr. Brown's apple tree again."

Dagny shivered. "Ooh, that man gives me the willies! Everytime he comes here he's always staring."

"Well, hopefully Liv's latest punishment will keep her away from his prized garden. She hates sewing almost as much as she hates being indoors, so I told her to do all that mending that was stacked upstairs."

Dagny smiled. "No wonder it's been so quiet up there. It takes her half an hour just to get a knot in the thread."

Gunnar was dressed and Hallie gave his backside an affectionate swat. "You two go up and tell Liv to come down and set the supper table."

As the boys raced through the door, Hallie straightened. "Mr. Brown caught me in his yard after I'd sent Liv home." She saw her sister shiver. "You go on and change before you catch a chill. I'll tell you the whole story after supper."

Hallie bent down and pushed the sloshing tub to the back door. Well, maybe not the whole story, she thought. A girl didn't talk about her first kiss. Besides, Dagny would want to know what it felt like, and Hallie wasn't sure she could put it into words.

She leaned against the wooden frame with her eyes closed, trying to relive the feel of his lips on her own. They had been hard at first, pressing the sensitive inner flesh of her lips against her teeth. Then he bit her upper lip, and it should have hurt, but before she had a chance to think, his tongue filled her mouth. His tongue! Imagine that! Never in her wildest dreams did Hallie think you used a tongue to kiss. She always thought you just puckered up and pressed.

It felt good, though, once she figured out that she should breathe through her nose. She'd felt so light-headed, and when he pumped his tongue in and out of her mouth, her body started to tingle in all sorts of odd places.

She was getting all warm again at just the memory. She opened her glazed eyes and shook her head to clear it. Forget it, Hallie! she reprimanded herself. That is probably your first and last kiss from Kit Howland. He calls you a kid, remember? He thinks you're a silly child. You should be angry at his superior attitude.

She shoved the tub outside and emptied it over the side of the back steps. Why did he kiss her if he only thought of her as a kid? For a moment before his lips descended, he'd looked at her so strangely. He's a hard man to figure out—doesn't make any sense at all.

The sound of the children barreling into the kitchen broke Hallie's reverie. With a sigh, she turned to go back inside and see about supper. Later, she would have to think. Maybe she could find a way to get Kit to see her as a grown woman. She would have to use her head. Her pretty head.

Chapter

Three

The funeral parlor was empty, but as the two tall men entered its draped darkness, a loud hammering echoed from the next room. Kit moved past the false light of a flickering wall lamp and looked through an archway into the adjoining room.

A pensive Abner Brown stood in the doorway of a workroom, watching a huge blond man drive nails into a pine box. The giant's beefy hand repeated the motion, continuing around the edge of the wooden coffin with efficient but noisy strokes. Abner shut the workroom door and stepped back. His bony hand rummaged through the wealth of heavy, tasseled draperies until it found a gold-braided pull. With a tug on the thick cord, he drew the drapes closed and turned. At the sight of the two tall men, his pallid face colored with surprise.

Kit knew the minute the scrawny undertaker recognized him, for an ingratiating smile lit the man's pinched features. As the youngest son of a prominent and wealthy family, Kit had been the recipient of that sort of smile many times; and it never ceased to annoy him. Experience taught him that the person bestowing the smile was usually what the whalemen called a windsucker—someone who attached himself, leechlike, to another in order to milk the wind from his sails. Considering the undertaker's treatment of Hallie only reaffirmed Kit's estimation, and he couldn't resist the urge to toy with Abner just a bit.

"Mr. Howland, forgive me. I had no idea you were here." Abner's falsetto voice scraped the air as he rushed into the front room. "Please have a seat."

He gestured toward a pair of ornately carved chairs separated by a rosewood lamp table. The matching settee and an inlaid tea table sat upon a raised dais; and like a throne, their position allowed Abner to sit regally above whomever occupied the Moorish chairs. Ready to hold assembly, he sat on the settee, crossing his stringy legs foppishly and looking so engrossed with his image of self-importance that he didn't notice that Kit and Lee were still standing.

Kit gave Lee a scheming look and sauntered up to the dais, where he hitched his hip nonchalantly on the arm of the settee, calmly rested an elbow on his thigh, and stared down silently at Abner.

The air chafed with enough tension to penetrate the undertaker's self-concentration. He glanced up and found his eyes trapped by Kit's piercing green gaze. "Wh-what's wrong?" The startled words whirred from his mouth.

A feral smile lit Kit's face as he watched the man squirm. He nodded toward the right side of the sofa, and Lee parroted Kit's earlier movements. Kit knew Lee's predatory stare also mirrored his own.

A sharp stench of fear saturated the briny air inherent to the mortuary. Abner looked back and forth at the two men. He licked his thick lips, and Kit had to squelch the satisfying urge to smack his own.

"Business bad?" Kit broke eye contact with his prey and surveyed the gaudy room. Looking past several dark marble bust stands, Kit found his attention captured by the ungodly amount of gilded cherubs that molded the room's cornice. He resisted the urge to gag.

Abner, who looked as if the red-flocked walls were closing in around him, stammered, "Why . . . n-no . . ."

Kit leaned an inch closer. "Then why are you trying to filch five hundred dollars out of a helpless young girl?"

The eyes of the sniveling undertaker darted back and forth between Lee and Kit. Like a snake coiled and cornered, he bit out, "She destroyed my property! I have every right to claim damages. Maybe that group of young vandals will learn a lesson. They ought to be turned over to the orphan society. Uncontrollable brats, that's what they are! Practically abandoned by that father of theirs, and the one in charge, that chit you call helpless? Ha! She's about as helpless as Delilah with a pair of scissors. What that family needs is a firm, male hand."

Not more than an hour earlier, Kit would have heartily agreed with Abner's assessment of Hallie. But hearing her described as such by the obsequious twit whose snide face made Kit crave to rearrange it, struck a protective chord in him.

Being unfamiliar with Kit's explosive temper, Abner foolishly ranted on, "Why, the only one that's civilized is the dark, pretty one—"

The whiny tirade changed to a gurgle as Kit grasped the man's collar tightly in his white-knuckled fist. "Leave the Fredriksens alone." The words clipped from Kit's lips like shot from a rifle.

"But the fruit from that tree—"

Kit lifted Abner by his collar. "How would you like that tree to become part of your anatomy?"

Abner, who had opened his mouth, managed to gulp down whatever he was going to say.

"Leave it be, Kit. He's not worth the trouble." Lee nodded toward the other room, where the blond giant stood, hammer in hand. Although his expression was blank, his eyes were locked on his employer's flushed face.

"You want to get out of here or do you feel in the mood to break heads?" Lee asked.

Before Kit could answer, the front door opened and Sheriff Hayes swaggered in, followed by a procession of men carrying two dead bodies.

The twit slipped through Kit's loosened grip.

"Got a couple more for ya, Abner," the sheriff hollered into the room before he spotted Kit. "Oh, how ya doin', Howland?"

Kit gave Hayes a nod of recognition. During those brief moments, Abner wrenched his collar back into place and gave his coat hem a precise tug. He pushed his shoulders back in a gesture of authority and stepped forward.

The sheriff rambled on. "Will ya look at these damn idiots? Tried to fight a friggin' duel." He gnawed on his cud of tobacco and shook his head in disgust. "That tight-assed Methodist, Will Taylor, was givin' one of them fire-fangled preachin's of his. Damn fool got 'em all riled up with his flapjawing, and next thing ya knowed, this pair's shakin' hands with St. Peter."

As Abner pranced toward the group, the sheriff pushed the chaw to the other side of his mouth and searched the room with a frown. A look of relief crossed his face, and he walked over to a rare oriental urn perched on one of Abner's marble stands. He expectorated the wad.

Abner sputtered to a stop.

The sheriff wiped a sleeve across his stained mouth and blessed the group with his relieved smile. "Where ya want these carcasses, Abner? In the back room?"

Kit choked back a laugh as he watched Abner try to mask his horror. Lee convulsed in a phony coughing fit, and to Kit's right, he was sure he heard a snort. He turned toward the blond giant, but all he saw was the man's back—and a slight quiver in those massive shoulders.

Abner raced to a door in the corner, half dragging the sheriff with him. "I'll show you. Bring them through here." Abner all but shoved the sheriff through, and then he paused, eyeing the giant as the motley band of pallbearers filed by. "Duncan! Come in here. I'll need your help."

Kit watched Duncan lumber to the corner door through

which Abner had just disappeared. The huge man paused and turned back, surprising Kit with the sparkle of intelligence that lurked in those sharp eyes. The man winked and was gone.

"Come on." Lee stood and clapped Kit on the back, breaking his assessment of Abner's assistant. "I think Abner Brown will think twice before he bothers Jan's family again. That Howland temper of yours is not a pretty sight, and from the way his eyes bulged, I'm sure he's sufficiently intimidated."

Lee's stomach growled like thunder and he made for the door. "I'm so hungry my equator's shrinking. I'm off to Millie's. For weeks I've been dreaming of one of those knuckle-thick steaks, smothered in red onions. And the bread pudding, Lord, I can taste that sweet ambrosia now."

Kit followed Lee outside. "Fine, but first I need to check at the custom house for any news of the *Abigail.*"

"No need. They were repairing her rudder when we put into del Cabos for sup—" Lee was a good five feet away when he stopped abruptly. He turned back and gave Kit a thoughtful look. "I understood that you steered clear of your former in-laws despite their friendship with your family. Why would you want news about one of their clippers? Especially one captained by your wife's brother?"

Kit trudged past his friend and sloshed through the mud-mired intersection. "Apparently, my aunt Madeline's on board. She and my mother got it into their obstinate, maternal heads that I need coddling. It's likely they could pull strings with the Taber line to book her passage immediately. Once my mother makes a decision, she'd never let a little thing like a year-long waiting list postpone her plans. My aunt Maddie's even worse. That harridan is, without a doubt the most—" Kit turned, jolted by Lee's bellow of laughter. "What's so all-fired amusing?"

Lee was leaning against the pole of a makeshift street sign, consumed by one of his obnoxious fits of horse laughter. Sometimes his bizarre sense of humor could really get to Kit. This was one of those times. He didn't think his problems were the least bit humorous, and if Lee had any idea of what Madeline could be like, he'd be a hell of a lot more sympathetic. Thoroughly irritated, but determined not to let it show, Kit crossed his arms and waited.

He was about to comment on his friend's asinine behavior when Lee finally controlled his braying.

"Is your aunt an orange-haired shrew about so high?" Lee raised his hand to about chest level.

Kit nodded.

"You needn't worry," Lee assured him. "When last I saw your aunt, she was brandishing a deadly looking parasol around the head of Taber's first mate and demanding to know where that scalawag of a captain was hiding."

"So much for wishing she'd washed overboard," Kit commented sarcastically. "I don't suppose I could hope that you got a taste of the shrew?"

Lee only grinned.

"I didn't think so. You look unscathed. The Prescott charm wouldn't work on her. If you'd been within a fathom of my aunt, you'd be wincing instead of grinning." Kit walked on.

Lee, following close behind, tried to look contrite. He failed miserably. "I can make you feel a tad better, you know. I remember thinking that you should have been there later when I ran into Taber, swilling tankards of rum in a San Cabos cantina. Your Presbyterian brother-in-law was wrapped in strands of Juanna's rosary beads and babbling into his mug about cursed she-demons from the depths of Hell. Ah, that was a sight, it would have done your heart good."

Kit couldn't resist a smile at the thought of such a satisfying picture. "So there is some justice in the world." Kit quickened his step.

"Now that I've relieved your troubled mind," he said, "how about coming with me to Sausalito for a few days? I've got to get the *Wanderer*'s mizzen repaired, and now you have a reprieve. It should be a week before Taber docks, and that perpetual frown you've been sporting tells me you could use a break." Lee's stomach grumbled again, and he eyed his flat belly.

Kit knew his friend was right, he needed a break. Time spent with Lee usually cleared his head, and besides, they always had one hell of a good time. He grinned. "Come on, let's get something in that groaning belly of yours before some hog hears all that racket and mistakes you for its mate."

The crash of a tin plate captured Hallie's attention. She looked up from the pan's simmering contents and gave Liv a disgruntled look. The younger girl quickly turned and picked up the plate. Hallie watched Liv's white-bandaged thumbs fumble with the wobbly stack of dishes.

"It won't work, Liv."

Liv thunked the plates on the wooden table, and with her thickly dressed thumbs strained upward she assumed an air of innocence. "What?"

Hallie stared pointedly at Liv's hands. "Those thumb wrappings of yours."

"But with all that mending, the sewing needle—"

"Could not," Hallie interrupted, "have possibly caused enough damage to need those cucumber-sized bandages. You'll get no sympathy from me. You shouldn't have been trespassing, and you know it. Now unwrap those silly things before you have half the table setting on the floor."

Liv plopped down on a thatched chair and began to gnaw the bandage knot loose with her teeth. The twins were in a corner, playing with their most prized and fought-over possessions—a set of whalebone animals, hand-carved by their father.

Hallie turned back to the stove, savoring the moment of quiet. She closed her eyes, but instead of peaceful darkness, her eyelids seemed to be etched with the image of Kit Howland's face. She felt sure that he wasn't indifferent to her. Although a novice when it came to kissing, she could see that he hadn't been completely in control. He sure didn't push her away, at least not until Captain Prescott arrived, and then for a moment Kit looked awfully uncomfortable, almost embarrassed.

He'd called her a kid, but if he'd really been trying to intimidate her, and hadn't been affected, would he have been embarrassed? Hallie didn't think so. Men wore their feelings on their sleeves, at least Mama always said they did, right out in the open for any woman to see. A smart woman would know the signs. She'd know that a man would instinctively cover up any slip of emotion that might make him look weak. Men didn't like to be thought of as emotional; it wasn't manly. Of course, men thought anger was a man's emotion, so they'd use it as a cover. Mama said a perceptive woman looks past a man's anger to the feelings he's trying to hide. She also said it was a woman's duty to train a man in the art of emotion, especially in matters of the heart.

If Kit could see her as a woman instead of a little girl, surely she could win his heart, or at least start his training. She remembered how tender he'd been when he thought she was upset. Hadn't he said something about the responsibility of raising the children? Men thought that child-rearing was woman's work. If he saw her with the children and saw how well she handled them, maybe he would realize that she was a woman.

Hallie knew from Da that when Captain Prescott came into port he would get his friend and head for The Grotto. When Da was home, he'd always eat with them instead of the family.

She looked down at the sizzling meat and at the almost full barrel of salted beef sitting against the wall. A half-guilty, half-calculating glance told Hallie that the children were still busy, a good distance from the hot stove. Using her apron as a pot holder, she tilted the iron skillet to its side, allowing the hot grease to spill into the stove fire. Flames shot up, charring the meat and spewing smoke into the air. But Hallie was ready. She dug a bowl into a nearby salt bag and quickly smothered the blaze.

As the acrid smoke smell filled the kitchen, Hallie wedged

the back door open and turned her sooty face toward the wide-eyed children. "Guess I ruined supper," she said. "I'll get cleaned up and we'll eat at Millie's."

The twins immediately whooped up and down, and Liv wasted no time returning the dishes to the cupboard. Millie always gave them huge helpings of dessert.

Hallie, anxious to begin her plan, sped from the room. Her long legs took the narrow stairs two at a time and she burst into the bedroom she shared with Dagny, racing to the oak wardrobe. She grabbed her pink dress and flung it on the bed. Scurrying to the washstand, she began to vigorously scour her sooty face. As she glanced in the mirror, she caught Dagny's questioning stare.

"I burned supper, so we're all going out," Hallie explained, ducking back down and hiding her excited face over the china washbowl. She splashed the cool water over her flushed skin and hoped Dagny would leave the room— and soon, before she had a chance to read the anticipation Hallie knew was plastered all over her face.

Kit and Lee stopped in front of a narrow wooden building that stood a few blocks up from the wharf. A rusty tin sign was nailed to the eave at a cockeyed angle and the air, thick with fog, condensed into henna-colored rivulets that trickled over the painted letters:

THE GROTTO
P. Millicent Dockery, Proprietor

Kit opened the door and they entered the dining house. The succulent scent of steak and onions seeped through Kit's senses. A pungent odor, it flowed from his tingling nose and damp eyes to his salivating taste buds. His stomach contracted, making him acutely aware of its hollow sensation.

"Well, God love ya, Kit Howland, what storm finally blew this friend of yours into port?" An older woman, barely five feet tall but almost that wide, greeted the two men.

"I tell you, Millie, it wasn't a storm. I found him under a rock during last night's full moon. He's been howling that he's half starved." Kit found an empty nail and hooked his hat onto the crowded wall. He turned and grunted when Lee crammed his elbow into Kit's midsection.

"Now what kind of a welcome is that? The only thing that's kept me going all these months, Millie, was the thought of your sweet cooking." Lee enveloped the aproned woman in a hug that lifted her clean off the floor.

Millie waved a long, wooden spoon in Lee's face. "Put me down, ya handsome oaf! Before ya break your back and have half the women in San Francisco after me for ruining their sport!"

"Millie, me love, those women don't hold a candle to you." Lee heaved her higher, ignoring her command. "When are you going to marry me?" He looked at her rosy cheeks as if he were pleading. "I like to starve to death when I'm at sea."

Unfazed, Millie looked at Kit, who was lounging against the edge of a homespun curtain while he watched the bantering. "I sure hope ya brought a shovel with ya, Kit, 'cause this rascal's full of more muck than Cookson's Livery Stable."

She bopped Lee on the head with her spoon, and he set her down. Then she turned to Kit. "Get your backside off them there curtains." She emphasized each word by poking her wooden spoon into a metal button on Kit's chest. "Didn't yer mama teach ya nothin'?"

Kit laughed, rubbing his hand across his prodded chest. "Yeah, she taught me that women whose names begin with M are harpies. *M*ama . . . *M*illie—"

Kit dodged the spoon.

"*M*adeline," Lee added with a devious grin.

"You two boys need some harping to keep ya in line. Now enough of this horseplay!" Millie turned and yelled, "Hey, Maria! Clear off a table for these two peacocks before the bearded rascal dwindles away to nothing but a dung pile."

From the back room the men heard a sudden clang of pots and pans mixed with a string of Spanish curses. The cacophony ended with the shout of one English word: ". . . slave!"

A buxom Spanish girl stormed through the kitchen door. She glowered at Millie, but her look changed to one of delight when she saw the two men across the room. Scampering to a table, she rushed to clear off the dirty dishes.

Kit smiled at Lee, and they both said, "*M*aria."

Mumbling something about that gal needin' mouth slappin', Millie aimed her wooden weaponry toward the table. "Plant yore setters over there if ya want to eat. I gotta get back in that there kitchen."

A few moments later the blood-warming aroma of potent, black coffee wafted up from their just-filled cups. Kit breathed deeply before sipping the hot brew. He glanced at Lee, who was busy flirting with Maria. He envied his friend's finesse with women—his ability to keep his affairs casual. Women didn't cling to Lee, although he drew them like flies to a grub mule.

Kit didn't have that skill. After his soured marriage, he'd vowed never to let a woman get so close again. His experience taught him that when you loved a woman and placed your heart in her feminine hands, you gave her power. Too much power. Jo's powerful little hands had changed to claws that shredded any illusions he had about love and marriage.

But Lee was untouched. A virgin heart. Kit had seen him breeze into port and literally charm the clothes off a woman—make that women—and to Kit's amazement, when Lee left, those women were smiling instead of clinging.

Kit raised the thick-bowled cup and drank. The few encounters he'd had since he moved to San Francisco had not been worth the trouble. His brief affair with a widow was physically satisfying until she began to cling like a burr. He'd made it clear from the start that he would never remarry, but she'd sought to change his mind, and failed.

After that, well, it was easier to hire a woman for the night. No illusions and no chains, just physical release. Only lately, women left him cold, until today.

He straightened his left leg and felt a twinge behind his knee. Unconsciously, his hand rubbed the soreness. The friction of the fabric heated his palm and reminded him that he hadn't been cold this afternoon. He'd been hot—singed by a passion he'd thought was lost. His run-in with Hallie had reignited his blood. For those few moments, he had been alive again.

The memory warmed him. And he didn't like it. He purposely pressed the tender flesh, hoping the pain would change the direction of his thoughts. His traitorous mind flashed instead with the feel of Hallie's warm mouth against his thrusting tongue.

A commotion in the doorway thankfully claimed his attention. Standing inside, surrounded by smaller, cloaked figures, was Hallie Fredriksen, and her warm mouth. She removed her cloak and bonnet and reached upward toward the high peg that sat empty. Kit sucked in a deep breath. The dress clung to her torso, and when she turned, her magnificent chest was draped with lace, a sheer, fine lace that let the soft pink fabric of her dress whisper through. For a brief moment Kit thought the fabric was her skin.

She stooped to untie the cap strings on the fidgeting boys, and the bending action caused the lace to angle to the floor, unveiling the outline of her breasts as they swelled with her downward movement.

Kit's blood burned.

Grasping after the water pitcher, he dumped the cool water into a mug and gulped it down, thinking that he should have dumped it on his horned head.

"Two years," Kit grumbled. "For two years she's invisible, and now I get two doses in one day."

He rubbed his fingers against his pounding temples and wondered briefly if his previous thoughts had conjured up the blond witch.

"Doses?" Lee peered around Maria, who was sprawled

like a napkin in his lap. "Sounds vile, like cod-liver oil." Lee looked at Kit's scowl and then toward the group near the door. "My, my, if it isn't just what the doctor ordered."

Kit couldn't stop himself. He stared at Hallie, whose gray eyes met his, and held.

Lee lifted Maria off his lap. "You had better get back to the kitchen, *querida*, before Millie flays my skin." He gave her an affectionate swat and a wink. "I want to watch my friend here while he tries to swallow his medicine."

Chapter

Four

Hallie was scared. She could feel the pounding of her heart all the way up to her ears. As Dagny helped her herd the children through the dining-house door, Hallie wondered if maybe this wasn't such a good idea.

When she'd stood in the homey security of her kitchen, aching to think of some way to spur Kit Howland's interest, her plan made sense. The walk down to The Grotto had given her creative imagination a chance to unfurl and to limn her beguiled heart's dream in her furtive head. In vivid color she'd envisioned the whole scene. They would arrive early enough so she could get the children fed and calm before the place overflowed with hungry diners. Since Da always met the men after six, her plan gave her plenty of time to set the stage. Kit would walk in, see the children—they were always well-behaved after their stomachs were full—and then he would turn those deep emerald eyes toward Hallie, the woman.

It was the perfect plan.

So it seemed. But now, when she stood in the foyer of the dining house, something didn't feel right. She removed her bonnet and the boys' caps and coats and hung them on the wall, chiding herself for her silliness and blaming her uneasiness on the excitement of executing her brilliant plan. She looked around the room for the perfect table and saw Kit.

Her stomach dove like a sounding whale.

Hallie closed her eyes briefly, hoping that when she reopened them the table would be empty, that Kit was only an apparition. But he loomed before her. She felt a tug on her hands and realized that Knut and Gunnar had pulled her into the room and they were heading straight for the large, empty table next to Kit.

Recovering quickly, Hallie remembered why she was there. *A woman, prove you're a woman in control!* She pulled them back, knowing that she could not allow them to drag her across the room. She had to show how well she could control them.

Her grip tightened on their fingers and she bent down to whisper a bribe. "Behave yourselves and I'll let you have my dessert too."

As Hallie straightened, she missed the boys' expressions. Their gleaming looks might have forewarned her of the destined outcome of her latest plot.

With a twin in each death-gripping hand, Hallie strolled toward the empty table, every inch the poised lady, while Liv and Dagny trailed behind. The men stood, Lee smiling a greeting and Kit looking as if he'd been sucking a lemon.

"Evening, ladies." Lee pulled a chair away from the neighboring table and, with his usual charm, indicated that one of the girls should be seated. Hallie nudged Dagny toward the chair, and with an expectant air she turned toward Kit, determined not to let his sour expression deter her. When he pulled out an empty chair, Hallie sneaked a peek over her shoulder. His vinegary expression had changed. In its place was an intense look, and it wasn't aimed at her face. His gaze rested somewhere below her chin, and she had a good idea exactly where he was looking, for she felt a tightening at the crests of her bosom. Her regal composure slipped a notch, until it dawned on her that a man didn't leer at a child's chest.

It's working. She took a deep breath and sat, reworking her course of action and trying to figure out what he was thinking. He was quiet, and it worried her.

When no new plan came to mind, Hallie, raised a good Christian, turned to a higher source. *Please let him see the real me, not the foolish girl he has known.* She was so busy trying to ensure her plea by mentally reciting the Apostles' Creed that she missed the twins' reaction. Faces filled with awe, they had watched the two tall, godlike men. Gunnar, always the quicker of the twins, raced to an empty chair near Liv and mimicked the grown-ups. Not to be outdone, Knut also grabbed the chair—the same chair, just as an unsuspecting Liv began to sit.

Hallie looked up and her expression turned to horror when, as if in slow motion, Gunnar and Knut both tugged the chair back at the same time.

Like an anchor dropped at sea, Liv's blond head disappeared from sight. The blue oilcloth that covered the table slid with her, sending the dishware clattering to the floor. Hallie and Dagny bolted out of their chairs, each grabbing a twin before Liv, who had murder in her eyes and a plate in each hand, could retaliate.

Holding Gunnar by his braces, Hallie hauled him into an empty chair.

"Sit!"

She pointed at Knut.

"You too!"

Liv stood up, sending a lapful of silverware clinking to the floor. The tinny sound shimmied through Hallie's gritted teeth.

"Apologize to your sister!"

"But it was a accident."

"Now!"

The boys mumbled an apology with shaky voices. Their huge brown eyes welled with a four-year-old's tears of humiliation. Each pale, little face was mottled with pink splotches, and they hung their heads in a child's dramatic gesture of shame.

It worked.

Although Hallie knew she had no reason to feel guilty, she did. When Dagny gave her a sweet smile of understanding, Hallie couldn't take any more, and she stooped down to pick up the scattered place settings. If she looked at those two imps any longer, she'd be apologizing, and that wouldn't teach them a thing.

So much for showing off your motherly control. Here she was, crouched under the table where it was safe, picking up scattered dishes. And hiding. *This wasn't the way it was supposed to be.* She ducked under the cloth, shoved her petticoats and the braid-stiffened crinoline from underneath her knees, and crawled on all fours, her skirts billowing around her like the sails of a pink armada. Her hand grasped a fork and she caught a flash of movement on the other side of Liv's empty chair. She looked up, table level, and spied a headless chest, encased in white linen and an all-too-familiar dark vest. She caught her breath.

Kit squatted, barely two feet away, with a pile of dishes on his bent knees. The tight fabric of his trousers stretched taut over the muscles of his flexed thighs. Hallie watched the dishes teeter a bit on those bulging ridges. Before she could blink, the oilcloth lifted and his handsome face invaded her refuge. When he caught her gape-mouthed stare, his dimples deepened into an infuriating grin.

Oh, rats! I'm caught, she thought, and averted her eyes. She needed to look busy so he wouldn't see she was hiding down here, even though she was. Her salvation came in the form of a lone plate, sitting by the table leg.

She reached for it, but so did he.

Salvation changed to damnation. Their hands touched, each holding an edge of the plate, and her heart thumped so hard in her chest that reflex made her glance up to see if he'd heard the ardent thudding. His grin faded. He was looking right at her, and the look was familiar. It was the same one she'd witnessed right before he'd kissed her. It wasn't a look

51

of amusement or anger, but one of power, nature's power, and for the first time in her innocent life, Hallie felt subjugated.

A strange kind of thrill rippled in her bones, like melting marrow. The loud throb in her ears drowned out all the surrounding sounds. Her neck warmed and she held her breath, waiting for something, anything, to happen. For infinite seconds Hallie and Kit were fixed, their faces locked across the space of an empty chair, their hands fused by a flat piece of glazed pottery that was acting like a conduit, channeling the flood of magnetism between them. The air pulsed around their stunned bodies, and their faces inched closer, lips parted and breath almost fettered in unchecked anticipation.

Then Liv sat down, forcing Hallie back. Her hand released the plate, breaking the illusory bonds so swiftly that she wondered if the moment had been real. When her awestruck breath finally escaped her dry lips, the world around her resumed.

But she didn't stand up, although Kit had, for she needed time to regroup. Wasn't this what she'd wanted? She'd prayed for him to stop treating her like a child, but she had no idea that setting out to win a man's heart could be so consuming. She felt devoured and weak. Like yesterday's tea leaves, she was drained of her freshness and that naive surety of youth that colored her plans foolproof.

Of course, fear changed all that. It relegated her dreamy wishes to the background, and her sensibility lunged into the foreground. And crawling around under a table was not exactly mature, womanly behavior.

Despite her awkward skirts, Hallie backed out from under her shelter, determined to act as if nothing unusual had happened. She butted right into a hard column. She scooted forward to try to move back out at a different angle, but her skirt was caught. She wiggled her behind sideways in an effort to dislodge the fabric, but apparently it was still caught. Aggravated, she turned around to better see the problem.

Her behind rested against a dark, leather boot. She stopped wiggling and made the mistake of looking up, way up, into Kit Howland's laughing eyes.

Lee Prescott pushed his chair back and looked from Kit to Hallie. "What's going on over there?"

Kit glanced at Lee and then looked pointedly at Hallie's behind. Suppressed laughter threaded through his voice when he answered. "I think Hallie's polishing my boots."

She wanted to die, but only for a moment, because the sound of their laughter made her too doggone mad. "What are you doing back there?" she snapped. "You're right in my way!"

"I thought you needed something . . ." Kit paused meaningfully, "a moment ago . . . under the table."

Something? His words hit home. He was making light of the soul-singeing moment that had passed between them. That arrogant ass! *He* had started it with that . . . that randy look of his. But before she could tell him a thing or two, he dumped salt into her wound.

"After our conversation this afternoon, I knew you couldn't possibly be hiding . . ."

He knew darn well she had been hiding.

"So," he continued, with exaggerated innocence, "I thought you might be stuck and need some help."

"I am stuck, under your muddy boot!" Hallie sat back on her heels and pulled fruitlessly on the pinned fabric. He wouldn't budge. She looked at the fork, still clutched in her sweaty palm, and a wicked little smile teased her own lips. Knowing he watched, she eyed his thigh, slowly, up and down, contemplating exactly where to plant the fork.

Kit prudently stepped back, releasing her muddy hem. She swiped at the rusty dirt marks stamped into her favorite dress. The mud wasn't all that dry, so instead of flaking off, the grit smeared into the fine weave of the fabric. That made her madder, and as much as she hated to admit it, she was still embarrassed. Both emotions made her breathing ragged.

She sat there fuming, clutching the fork, daggerlike. A

small hand gently patted the bare skin of her collarbone. Knut leaned over in childish innocence. "Did you lace your gussies too tight again, Hallie?" he asked.

The picture of honesty, he looked up at Kit. "When Hallie huffs and puffs, Da says it's because she laces her gussies so tight she can't move," he announced.

"It's not gussies, silly," Liv corrected with an authoritative tone. "It's gussets."

"I'm not silly! Girls are silly."

"Are not."

"Uh-huh!"

Hallie rose to her knees and slammed the fork on the table so forcefully that both Liv and Knut hushed. Suddenly, two large hands grabbed her waist and lifted her to her feet. Kit's hands squeezed her waist, making Hallie intensely aware of the sparks that flickered through her whenever they made physical contact. She blessed him with a scowl.

"I was checking your gussets, Hallie-girl," he whispered in her ear. "They do feel a little tight."

"They are fine! Just fine! Absolutely perfect!" She twisted out of his grip, having long ago lost her sense of humor, and feeling indignant at being the brunt of his.

Kit shrugged and returned to his table, looking overly pleased with himself. Hallie swished into her own seat, flushed and angry. But soon her anger subsided, replaced by a desolate feeling of failure. *Oh God, this wasn't what I meant. I didn't want him to laugh at me. And he's back to calling me girl!* All she wanted was for Kit Howland to forget the existence of that frightened, silly, clumsy young daughter of his friend.

Knut's chattering little voice caught her attention. He was grilling Lee for whaling tales, but at Hallie's frown he returned to his seat. Millie barreled out of the kitchen carrying a steaming pot which she placed before the men.

She turned her aproned girth toward the twins. "Well, lookee here! These here two musta growed a foot. Gonna hafta feed 'em a whole passel of food jus' ta fill'm up."

"Y'know what, Miz Dockery?" Knut asked.

"What?"

"Hallie burnt supper! Y'shoulda seen it." Knut waved his small arms in the air. "Smoke was everywhere and it smelled something awful! An' Hallie's face got all black an' everything, just like Rufus Jefferson—only his is black 'cause God made it that way—I knowed 'cause he told me so. An' y'know what?"

"What?"

"Hallie promised we could have her dessert if we were good." He looked around the table. "She did. She really did. Remember, Hallie?"

Hallie closed her eyes. *Gunnar was right, he is a tattletale.* But Hallie looked into those guileless eyes and gave up. There were no secrets with chatty four-year-olds. They didn't understand discretion.

"I'm good, huh?"

"Yes, love," she answered, "you're good." *And I'm ruined.*

Knut turned to the steaming pot. "What's that?"

"Jus' the thing ta warm yore vitals," Millie boasted. "Maria will be bringin' ya some real soon."

Knut rose to his knees and craned over to see better.

Millie removed the lid and lifted the ladle. Creamy, thick liquid spilled into Kit's bowl, and she grinned. "It's hot chowder."

Hallie froze; but her blood didn't. It surged to her face, and she knew that anyone who looked at her could see she was mortified. Refusing to venture a glance at Kit, she sunk a little lower in her chair, wishing she could fade away, but knowing that instead she would have to suffer through the longest, most uncomfortable meal of her entire adult life.

"The boys are down."

"Shhh," Dagny warned.

Hallie pressed their bedroom door closed as quietly as she could. A rustle from the single bed across the room drew her eyes. Liv snuggled farther under the heavy, wool blanket, and within seconds the youngster's breathing was slow and even.

Hallie tiptoed over to the double bed she and Dagny shared. Her sister sat cross-legged on top of the woven coverlet, and both of the feather bed pillows were wedged between her back and the iron bedstead. It was a stance Hallie recognized. Dagny wanted to talk, or, more than likely, her perceptive younger sister had decided that Hallie needed to talk.

"What was going on tonight, Hallie?"

"What do you mean 'what was going on'?" Hallie sat on the edge of the bed, giving her prying sister an excellent view of her back as she bent to untie the ribbons on her shoes.

"I'm not a simpleton," Dagny whispered, "although even a moron could have figured that our little family outing tonight had all the earmarks of one of Haldis Fredriksen's famous schemes gone haywire."

"Unbutton my dress."

"Don't change the subject."

"Dagny!" Hallie whispered heatedly, "I'm the oldest in this family and I don't have to answer to anyone." So much for the talk, she thought; a talking *to* is more like it.

"You have to answer to your own conscience." Dagny pushed a covered button through the tight hole on Hallie's dress. "And to Da, when he gets home. Look, Hallie, I'm just worried about you. I love you and I don't want to see you do something stupid and spend another two years having to hide from Kit Howland."

"Are you through?"

Dagny freed the last button. "There, all done."

"That's not what I meant." Hallie shucked the dress, petticoat, and crinoline. "Are you through lecturing me?"

Kicking herself free of the clinging, flannel underskirt, Hallie tore at the knots on her corset ties. They were tangled tighter than a madwoman's knitting. She *had* laced them too tight. She turned toward the light, to better see the knots, and saw the hurt on Dagny's face.

"Oh, Duggie, I'm sorry. I'm not mad at you, just at myself." Hallie had to accept the blame for this evening's downfall. It was her own cockamamy idea. It was dumb, stupid, and as Dagny reminded her, so typical.

"The man has no manners," she grumbled.

"Why?"

"I don't know why! Maybe his mother didn't teach him. If he even had a mother. He was probably spawned from ragweed or a witch or . . ." Hallie's eyes sparkled, "a mule!" She laughed, and then saw that Dagny looked at her as if her attic were batty.

"I meant, why are you mad at yourself?" Dagny clarified.

"Oh." Hallie flopped back on the bed. "You're right. I really did something stupid tonight."

"From your comments, I assume it had something to do with Mr. Kit Howland?"

Hallie nodded.

"So tell me. You always worry over nothing. It's probably not all that bad." Contradicting her words, Dagny snuggled deep into the pillows, as if she were expecting a long story.

Hallie poured out her whole tale, starting with the apple tree and ending with her plan to impress Kit.

"Oh, Hallie."

"I know . . . I know . . . It was a dumb idea."

Dagny leaned real close. "Did he really kiss you?" she whispered.

"Uh-huh."

"What was it like?"

"Oh no!"

"How am I supposed to help you figure out what to do if you won't tell me everything?"

The Fredriksen look of righteous indignation suffused Dagny's face.

"That's personal. Besides, no one can help me now. You heard him, he practically jumped at the chance to go to Rancho Sausalito with Captain Prescott. He looked as if he couldn't get away fast enough." Hallie finished undressing and slipped on her nightgown. "I doubt if I'll have the chance to see him again soon. That's why tonight was so important to me. I foolishly thought that maybe I could make him care for me."

"Were his lips all wet?"

"Duggie!"

"Were they?"

"Well, no. They were kind of dry—"

"Oh yuck!" This muffled expression of disgust came from beneath the blanketed lump in the opposite corner.

"Go to sleep, Liv!" Both Hallie and Dagny ordered in unison.

"How is a person supposed to sleep with you two yakking like a gaggle of geese?"

Dagny pulled a smashed pillow from behind her and flung it at Liv. "Here, cover your big ears with this!"

"All right, I will, but then I can't tell Hallie what *I* saw. And it had to do with Mr. Drylips too."

"What was that, Liv?" Hallie sighed, sick and tired of reliving this disastrous night.

"He stared right at you."

"Really?" Hallie perked up.

"Yup. And when he came out from under the table and put those dishes down, he looked real strange."

Dagny looked at Hallie. "Liv's right. He looked dumbstruck. You know what I mean?"

Hallie knew exactly what Dagny meant. Dumbstruck was mild for what she had felt. Branded in her memory was that moment they had shared under the table. It was the only positive thing that had happened tonight. "He looked dumbstruck?"

"Um-hm," Dagny answered thoughtfully. "You know what else?"

"What?" Hallie scooted to the edge of the bed.

"His ears got red," Dagny stated, as if those four words unlocked all the mysteries that existed between man and woman.

"Red ears? What on God's green earth are you talking about?"

"When Mama was alive and Da would come home, he'd look at her in this special way and his ears would get red. I always wanted a man to look at me and get red ears," Dagny added dreamily.

Hallie pondered that thought until she noticed Liv's nosy little face, toothy grin and all, gleaming from the corner. It was as if her nine-year-old sister could read her mind.

"Let's get some sleep. It won't do to have us all wake up weary-boned." Hallie tuned down the wick in the bedside lamp and laid back in the soft-ticked bed. *Don't get your hopes up.*

But some little ray, deep within her mind's eye, tried desperately to picture Kit Howland with bright red ears.

Kit pulled his crowned cap lower to protect his icy ears from the bite of the wind. One booted foot rested against the sturdy, oak frame that housed the cooling tank of the whaler. His long, lithe body swayed naturally with the undulant ship, and he tapped his pipe gently on the shellac-coated railing.

Stark, white smoke curled upward from the smoldering meerschaum. The chalklike swirls captured his attention as they danced and weaved, waltzing upward into the night sky. The faint glow of San Francisco nestled off the port side, and one lone star winked high in the west, glittering silver gray and conjuring up the image of a certain madcap female, half little girl and half woman.

An unbidden smile played at his lips when he remembered Hallie's antics, and he shook his head at the mental replay. She gave new meaning to the term *trouble.* Of course, he wasn't quite sure who was the recipient of most of it. He just knew it was a hell of a lot safer to laugh at her than to take her seriously. One lesson he'd learned today was that by teasing and provoking her, he maintained the upper hand whenever he was near her. It was a lesson he'd been forced to remember, since the whole day had been filled with strange lapses in his normally strong-willed control. That little exchange at The Grotto was a prime example. He was thirty-one years old, and he'd almost succumbed to rolling around under a table of a public dining room with the daughter of his good friend. Luckily, she was Jan's worry and not his. The thought made him breathe a sigh of immense relief.

The clapping sail above his head buffeted, joining the others in what sounded like applause. *No doubt they'd met Hallie.* The ship pitched slightly and groaned. *Right, bad joke.* He pulled the pipe from his mouth and turned into the wind, letting the salty spray work its catharsis.

"Do you miss it?" Lee stepped out from the shadow of the sheltered tryworks.

Kit didn't move, didn't acknowledge Lee's presence. It wasn't necessary, for both of them were well aware of the powerful lure of the sea. Lee still existed in the thrill of her realm, while Kit had divorced himself from her in order to survive.

"There are times when I do. The sea was my home for a long time. You can't erase that, just like you can't erase the memories, good and bad. It's hard to believe, but the keen taste of her, her smell, can still ignite something deep within me." Kit leaned casually against the ship's rail. "Standing here, feeling her movement under me, it almost seduces me into thinking I can come back."

"You could, Kit. Bury the past. You were a whaleman long before you married Jo," Lee prodded.

"Oh no. I've other responsibilities now. I vowed I'd make this agency work, and I will. As for my past, it's going to haunt me no matter where I am." Kit couldn't conceal his sarcasm. "The Tabers, my former in-laws, are now the largest buyers of oil and baleen on the East Coast. They've taken over Leviathan Enterprises, both the boneworks and the refinery."

Pipe smoke spurted into the night air, signaling Kit's irritation. "I've consigned Jan's last cargo to them."

"Any particular reason? I heard Nantucket needs oil."

"Leviathan is so low on baleen that they've doubled their price and guaranteed to beat anyone's price on oil. I passed up a chance to sell the *Sea Haven*'s load elsewhere when I heard what they were offering."

Lee knew him well, and he asked the question Kit hoped he wouldn't. "Is it Jan you're thinking of, or couldn't you resist gouging the Tabers?"

"So speaks my conscience."

Lee was silent, and Kit knew he was ignoring his sarcastic evasion.

Kit sighed. "I've asked myself the same question. I'd be lying if I said it didn't feel good to have the Tabers eating out of my hand, especially when the price of the meal is so dear. But Jan came to me before he left. He'd had it. The past few years have taken their toll, and since his wife died he's lost his drive. He's tired of leaving his family alone, and he asked me to get top dollar for this last load, even if I had to sit on it."

Both men were quiet, each dwelling on his own thoughts and those of the man they called friend.

"Jan sponsored my master's papers," Lee confessed in a tone filled with quiet affection.

"He did?" Kit was surprised. They were both good friends of his, but this was something neither of them had ever mentioned.

"I wouldn't have the *Wanderer* if Jan hadn't helped me. I think I'd deal with the devil himself for Jan. Didn't he bring you your first commission?"

"First, second, and third," Kit answered.

"We both owe him. Hell, if all those whalemen hadn't run off to the gold hills, you'd probably own all of San Francisco. Lord knows it's a damn sight easier to consign the load here and strike out again than to spend weeks sailing back East, only to unload and have to sail back again."

Kit turned and emptied the remains of his pipe. "That's why I came here. The Atlantic grounds were nearly empty when I was still whaling in 'forty-six. Since the supply is here, I figured that's where a new agent ought to be." Out of habit, Kit put the pipe back in his mouth and chewed on it, as if the motion helped him think more clearly.

He removed it and looked directly at Lee. "You're right about the mining, though—it has affected things. All you have to do is look out in the harbor. Eight hundred ships abandoned. Jesus, what a waste."

"Some of us are still going strong. Give me the sea any day over a maggoty mule and a pickax."

"I wonder what Jan will do."

"Do when?"

"He wants to retire, Lee, and he vowed he'd stay out as long as it took to find some gris. With all the upheaval across the Atlantic, the market's switched to the Orient. I've had bids as high as four hundred dollars a pound."

Lee whistled. "Sweet Lord, that's one helluva lot of money. The last batch of ambergris I found weighed over a thousand pounds, and that was over three years ago, which doesn't bode well for Jan's chances of nabbing it, although I wish him luck."

"Jan intends to ensure this is his last voyage."

Lee scratched his red beard. "So my friend, fate served you your revenge on a platter."

"What are you talking about?"

"Jan's supply and the Tabers' demand clicked right into place."

"So . . . ?"

"That's a bit too convenient for me."

Kit pondered Lee's comment as he watched his friend walk back to the helm. He'd thought he'd made the best deal for everyone concerned, but now Kit questioned his motives. Maybe he'd made a big mistake.

Chapter

Five

Aye, mate, ya got till dark on Sat'rday ta have the quid. Ah warned ya wot happens ta them wot don't pay. The blokes gets thumselves burnt out. Ya pay an' ya like m'partna. The Ducks, they protect ya like. Ah'm ah mon o' my word, mate."

The short, burly Aussie bared his riddled teeth into what might have passed for a bestial grin. Pulling his floppy-brimmed hat low over his pocked face, he turned, purposely running his filthy finger along the rich grain of Abner's burl desk.

"Be a right shame ta have this foine piece a pile o' ashes. G'day ta ya," he added before he skulked from the funeral parlor.

Abner sagged back in his chair and willed his knotted fists to unclench. He hated this. Pushing his chair back, he rose and went to the window. Taking his handkerchief out of his pants pocket, he swiped the sweat from his forehead and then rubbed the damp haze from the windowpane. The burly man, current leader of the Sydney Ducks, joined his fellow miscreants, and Abner stood in silence, watching as they disappeared through the fog, leaving only the echo of threatening laughter in their wake.

This was Wednesday. He had barely three days to come up with the money. Damn! He'd never been caught so short before. When he caught the older Fredriksen girl in his tree, he thought he'd found the perfect way to get that last bit of money. Her father captained a whaler. It was a lucrative business, and the captain got the largest share. With her only parent at sea, he'd assumed he could get the money out of her. He had no idea that someone like that Howland fellow would get involved.

As Abner gazed about the richly appointed room, he tried to come up with a way to get that last five hundred dollars. The vases and sculptures alone were worth twice that amount, but San Francisco had no market for them. He couldn't even sell them, because the fools who could afford them didn't have the class to know their value. The only things that brought top dollar in this gold-mad town were chamois skins to bag the ore dust, food to feed the hordes, and whiskey and whores to feed another hunger. No one cared for the sustenance of art or beauty. Aesthetic value was unknown in a place that slapped together a goulash of canvas and wood structures.

He'd been a fool. When the newfangled metal caskets became available, Abner had to have them, despite that huge number the manufacturer forced him to order and pay for in cash. It was the prepayment that put him in this predicament. The cost had all but emptied his bank account. The company had such a huge amount of orders that they demanded cash. He'd planned on getting the money back quickly, knowing he could charge twice as much for a metal burial casket, though the actual cost was only about a quarter more than the wooden ones. He wouldn't need a carpenter anymore, so he could get rid of Duncan. The man was an idiot anyway, hardly ever spoke, but he did good work. Lately, though, there'd been an insolence about the huge man that rubbed Abner wrong, and he'd just as soon rid himself of Duncan's irritating presence. But he couldn't until that shipment arrived.

Abner ran his finger across the wood of the windowsill. It

was rough, although the mortuary building was considered one of the city's best. Like many, it had been prefabricated in France, shipped to the West Coast, and thrown up in a single day. Although he'd paid for the elaborate moldings, it still was not a suitable encasement for what was left of his heritage. The Lowestoft urns and fine Chinese porcelains had once graced any number of rooms in the Moffat-Brown mansion. He'd been allowed to keep so little in the settlement. His father had repeatedly challenged fate with his gambling, until he'd lost it all. Then he'd put a bullet through his cowardly head rather than face his only son. The only positive thing for Abner was that his mother had died two years earlier and hadn't been alive to see all she loved and cherished sold like paupers.

Those memories stirred Abner's gut, awakening the sharp, burning, recurrent pain that had burgeoned in his belly from the first moment he'd found out what his father had done. He wiped his dripping nose with the crumpled cloth still clutched in his tense fist.

What time was it? Glancing at the inlaid tall clock, Abner saw that only five hours had passed since his last laudanum dose. Lately, his runny nose served as a warning that the tincture was wearing off, and the doses were lessening in effect. He'd increased his intake repeatedly over the last half a year or so, but he wasn't getting any better. The searing agony in his stomach came back along with the most excruciating headaches he'd ever experienced.

He walked outside, then up the narrow stairs to his room, each step now reverberating through his skull like a hatchet lacerating wood. As he sat on the edge of his bed, his belly-burning twisted into a gripping cramp. He reached for the large, rusty-brown bottle on the bedtable and began to count the drops as they plopped into the small, water-filled glass. His hand shook. The strong scent of cloves and cinnamon permeated the air, and with each drop the water deepened to ruby red.

By the time he reached the count of thirty, his usual dosage, the pain was so bad that he had rolled to his side and had drawn his knees to his chest in an effort to control the ache. Recklessly, he counted ten more drops from his fetal position and poured the liquid past his cracked lips, draining the glass. He squeezed his watery eyes closed, feeling the moisture cool as it trailed across his clammy skin to pool onto the already damp pillow. He rolled to his other side, his body's turmoil not allowing him to lie still. As he writhed atop the bed, his mind waited for the numbness to set in, for it was then that Abner regained euphoric strength, wrapped in the soothing, but addictive arms of his opiate.

Hallie stared at the ceiling, her eyes now accustomed to the dark of the room. And she played the game—the one where the burnished knots in the wooden ceiling took other form. The cocoa-brown splotch right above her head looked exactly like a peanut, or a pear, or maybe, she turned her head to the side, a footprint.

Like the muddy imprint on your pink dress.

"Humph." The annoyed sound slipped past her pursed lips. She held her breath, listening for her sisters' breathing. It was smooth and even. At least someone in this family could sleep. Of course they didn't have the ponderous weight of their foolhardy actions on their minds like she did.

The entire evening had been nothing but a joke, at least to Kit, who she desperately wished would take her seriously. Instead, she played the court jester, fumbling, mumbling and tumbling, right in front of her prince. Every time she looked at Kit, he had appeared to be fighting his laughter.

After Millie'd served the chowder, Hallie had waited, then sneaked a look at the men. Kit ate but Captain Prescott caught her look, and he'd sent her a kind smile. She'd assumed he was trying to make her feel better, but knowing that he was aware of her acute discomfort just made her feel worse. Her whole plan had fallen flat. Instead of gaining respect, Hallie was positive she had sunk to the level of infancy, at least in Kit's mind. Her antics tonight sure wouldn't change her childish image. Captain Prescott probably knew it, too, and that's why he was so kind. He must have felt sorry for her. Kit was no doubt laughing all the way to Sausalito—laughing, and relieved to be rid of Jan Fredriksen's cockeyed family.

"Hallie?"

"Duggie, what are you doing still awake?"

"I'm worried."

"Why?"

"Do you think Da will be home soon?"

Hallie turned over, cradling her head on one bent arm. She watched her sister. The same concern and fear she heard in Dagny's voice furrowed her sister's face. It was like looking in an emotional mirror, for whenever Hallie thought of Da, she boiled in the same oil of feeling. "I don't know."

"He's never been gone this long before. You don't think something awful's happened, do you?"

There it was. The oft unspoken question that lurked like a prowling cat around those who waited for the return of an overdue whaler. The clawing thoughts of what might have happened flashed through Hallie's fervid mind but were quelled by her need to douse that kind of thinking from Dagny's head.

"Da's been at this for too many years to make any mistakes now. He knows we need him, and he'll be careful. Let's not go expecting trouble. He's probably found one of those famed whale-filled inlets we're always hearing tales about. I'd bet he's so busy flensing all those whales that he doesn't realize how long he's been gone. Remember, Duggie? He made those arrangements at the bank, so he must have known this might be a longer voyage. Everything will be fine, you'll see. Da will bring the *Sea Haven* in before you know it. Just go to sleep. Everything will be fine," Hallie repeated, also trying to convince herself.

"You're right about the bank. I guess I'm being silly." Dagny turned away from Hallie and pulled the covers high over her narrow shoulder. "G'night, Hallie."

Within minutes Dagny was safely back to sleep. And Hallie, who had been intimidated, angered, embarrassed, kissed, spanked, discouraged, humiliated, and now frightened right down to her supposedly strong, Nordic bones, closed her eyes to lessen the burn of her erupting tears.

Crammed along the sloping streets, the flat-roofed buildings sat, choking one another. Identical in silhouette, like the planks along a clapboard fence, each structure melted into the next, with only their hastily scribbled signs giving an inkling as to what lay inside.

As Abner passed each hitching post, he squinted, trying to read the letters in the faint flicker of an occasional oil lantern. He rounded the corner and was relieved to see that at least this section was better lit. The drifting sounds of laughter against the tinny twang of a piano spurred his pace. He must be getting closer. Drawn by the racket and an eerie glow, he crossed the street and made his way down a narrow alley.

It was like walking from a cemetery into a circus. Activity teemed from every square foot, and clusters of men blocked the walks and doorways of each building. From the low-slung eaves, lights hung every few feet. As Abner weaved his way through the rollicking men, he could hear the distant sizzle of whale oil dripping from the swaying lanterns onto the fog-soaked ground. His nose tingled from the native smells. The strong stench of sweat and whiskey fought for supremacy with that of horse dung and the briny odor of the nearby wharf.

For Abner Brown, the decadence of the city's seedy side was foreign—and stimulating. He found an empty stoop and leaned in its corner. His breath came in exhilarated pants, sending his blood coursing to his galloping heart. The pain in his head and gut was gone, all but forgotten in the drug-supplanted confidence that replaced it. In the past, fear bred from his father's downfall had forced him to avoid anything that remotely resembled a gambling hell. But now he was here, and he would win.

The door splintered as a huge, red-shirted body catapulted through it. The miner hit the walk and tumbled under the rein-tangled rail onto the mucky, horse-filled street. Another man suddenly loomed in the broken jamb.

"You dirty, cheating son of a bitch! Stand up so's I can knock that shit-filled mouth of yours clean out to the privy!"

With a meaty paw, he shoved Abner aside and dove after the other man.

"Fight! Fight!"

The call echoed through the tight stoop as a swarm of men poured outside, elbowing and pushing until Abner had to squeeze inside to escape the ruckus. The place was still packed. Makeshift tables were thrown together out of splintered crates and old pine doors. Every size barrel, from nail to pickle, served as stools, and the noise was deafening. Moving to the sound of shattering glass and ribald voices, Abner edged his way around the perimeter of the room to a broken crate sitting forgotten in a dank corner. He sat, as unnoticed as the damaged crate, and watched the betting and the card games, absorbing each move of the players, learning the only skill he thought might bail him out of his financial bind. While the table nearest him shuffled a new deck, Abner's mind flashed with the cynical thought that he could catch on to the game fast. After all, the techniques were surely inbred. They were a gift from his father—a genetic shortcoming of the Brown bloodline.

Dagny awoke to a cold, empty bed. Sitting up sleep-startled, she eyed the dark room. Liv was asleep but Hallie was not in sight, so she listened quietly to try to hear if her older sister was downstairs. *Probably went out to the privy, silly!* So she waited.

Finally she gave up and slid from the bed onto the chilly floor. She shrugged on her dressing gown while her foot scooted softly under the bed ruffle, looking for her warm, knitted slippers. Finding them near the foot of the bed, she used her finger for a shoehorn and wedged them onto her half-frozen feet.

Tiptoeing to the door, she pushed her free hand down on the swollen doorjamb to prevent it from creaking when she opened it. The hall was black. She felt her way toward a narrow lamp table, picked up the tinder, and lit the oil lamp. She waited for her eyes to become accustomed to the light. The sound of muted voices drifted up from below.

With the way now visible, she walked down the first few stairs. Ducking her head past the floor extension, Dagny had a clear view of the foyer. She could see Hallie's back as she whispered to the man who stood in the shadow of the open door. Chilling fog slunk into the house, but its draft was not what caused the pop of gooseflesh on her skin.

It was the man.

He had a light-colored sea cap crushed in his nervous hands and he wore the heavy, woolen coat of a whaleman. The top of his graying head barely reached her sister's chin. Dagny stopped.

"Oh, my God . . . no . . . pl-please, God . . . noooooo," Hallie wailed, grabbing the newel post for support.

Dagny continued down the stairs, and as she reached the bottom, the man spoke. "I'm sorry, miss." He backed out the door, and before it closed she heard him repeat, "So sorry."

Hallie sagged backward, sobbing. "Da's dead . . . Da's dead . . ."

Chapter

Six

"That looks fine, sir." Hallie turned to her sister. "What do you think, Duggie?"

The somber girl stared at the words penned by the stonemason. She swallowed hard before replying in a dull whisper. "It looks good." Then she drifted through the aisles of the dockside warehouse, seemingly oblivious to anything around her.

It worried Hallie. She watched her sister weave her way through the stacks of fresh-cut lumber and slabs of granite and marble. The bright morning sun caught the sheen of Dagny's bonnet, casting her face in shadow as she wandered out onto the loading dock. But Hallie knew her sister's grief still aged her face.

Hours of tears helped purge Hallie's initial sorrow, but not Duggie—she hardly shed a tear. That wasn't good. Hallie watched her sister sit, despondency encircling her like a shroud. She wondered if her young sister had the strength to deal with all that had happened to their family in recent years. Losing both parents, especially when the family had been so close-knit, was hard, but compound that with the pain of adolescence, and as Hallie well knew, the will to go on could get lost in the emotional muddle.

Hallie was convinced that the responsibility of the children kept Da afloat after Mama's death, just as her own role of substitute mother had encouraged her. But Da and Hallie were alike. She had inherited his stubborn Nordic determination and the belief that her destiny was up to her, and to God. Dagny, on the other hand, had inherited more of Mama than just her dark beauty. She was sweet, even-tempered, unencumbered by the roiling emotions that lit a fire under Hallie.

"You said Saturday, miss?" The stone carver's question broke her reverie.

"What?"

"You said the memorial services were held this Saturday, right?"

"Oh yes. That's right." Hallie forced a smile to her lips. It felt odd, out of place.

"Follow me over to that wall and you can decide the size and shape of the gravestone from those sketches."

"But sir, anything is . . ." Hallie's voice tapered off. ". . . fine." The man was already making his way across the barnlike room. He couldn't hear her.

Hallie glanced at Dagny. An empty wagon sat next to the dock, and near it, a huge, blond man stood talking to her sister, his hat in his hand. The lack of women in the city made women-snatching a common occurrence, especially here near the wharves. Acutely aware of her sister's fragile state of mind, Hallie panicked. Her fears were fueled by the sheer bulk of the man, who could snatch her dazed sister in an instant. She grabbed a brick ax in both gloved hands, just in case, and flung it over her shoulder as she marched toward the man she imagined as her sister's would-be abductor. With her adrenaline and her imagination racing in tandem, Hallie made it to the dock in time to hear the tail end of the man's words just as he reached toward Duggie.

". . . abduct you."

Hallie's fingers gripped the handle and she raised her elbows high to help heave the heavy tool at him.

"Hallie! No!" Dagny screamed, pushing the man away from the descending ax.

The solid iron smashed onto the dock, splintering the wood and sending waves of bone-ringing pain up Hallie's arms to jangle through her shoulders and resound at her neck. She squeezed her eyes closed and shook her dizzy head. When the jolts ceased and she opened her eyes, the man was sitting up, a trail of blood trickling from where he'd gashed his head on a nearby crate.

"What were you thinking!" Dagny flared. She jerked open her velvet bag, pulling out a hankie, and dabbed at the dazed man's head while she crooned an apology.

What was I thinking? "Didn't you hear him? He was going to grab you! For cripesakes! Get away from there while I get someone to call the sheriff." Hallie swirled around and slammed into the stocky chest of the stonemason.

"What's going on here?" The man looked frantic.

Hallie spoke right up. "Hurry, get some rope or something to tie him up before he gets away! He tried to nab my sister."

"Duncan?" The stonemason sounded truly amazed.

"Who?" Hallie asked.

"Oh Hallie, be quiet!" Dagny snapped. "He was doing no such thing!"

"He was too. There's his wagon right there . . ." Hallie pointed to the empty spot where the wagon had been waiting. "Well . . . it was there." She looked down the dirt street. There was no empty wagon. "Well," she looked at them, conviction flaring from her eyes, "it *was!*"

"Miss Fredriksen, there must be some mistake. Duncan is harmless. He wouldn't hurt your sister."

"But I heard him say he was going to abduct her!"

The blond man, apparently named Duncan, looked up at Hallie. "I was warning her, ma'am. I told her it wasn't safe to sit out here alone where someone could abduct her."

"Oh."

"Of course he was, Hallie! I can't imagine why you

thought he would hurt me. You see kindness written all over his face!" Dagny glared at Hallie.

Duncan looked at the older man. "Abner sent me to pick up those headstones and that order of lumber, Hank." He glanced over at the empty spot where his wagon once sat. "Looks like I'll be a while fetching after that runaway team."

Hallie felt awful. "I'm sorry, Mister . . . ?"

"Just Duncan, miss," he smiled. "And that's all right. You were just looking out for your pretty little sister." He glanced at Dagny.

"I'm sorry about your wagon," Hallie apologized.

"Don't worry, miss. I've one you can borrow, Duncan," Hank assured them. "Come on now. Duncan will look out for your sister while we finish up that order." He paused and eyed the ax, still embedded in the jagged crack that marred the dock. "You sure pack some wallop."

Hallie tried to ignore his comment, her elbows still ringing with the effects of her "wallop." She looked at her sister. "You'll be okay?"

Dagny purposely ignored Hallie, sticking her nose up in the air. She was still angry. Sighing, Hallie turned and followed Hank inside, glancing once more at her sister. It was then that she realized that Dagny had shown more emotion in the last ten minutes than she had since they got the news of Da's death. Maybe, Hallie thought as she unconsciously lightened her advancing step, just maybe, everything would be fine after all.

Abner stretched his long arms up toward the ceiling, then lolled his head back, trying to work the crick out of his shoulder. A plump, chamois bag sat on the walnut bed table. Sloping to one side with the weight of its rich contents, the pale yellow pouch rested against a hollow laudanum bottle. He picked up the rawhide drawstrings and swung the gold back and forth, as if what was inside held some special significance to the empty room.

He did it! He'd won! And it felt so good. All his misgivings faded, replaced by a sureness that convinced him he'd broken the addictive curse of his weak-minded father. He'd outsmarted them all, especially the three drunken miners who'd assumed he'd be an easy take just because he was a slow and meticulous player. He had watched, and learned, and waited, relying solely on his cunning to best those he felt were intellectually beneath him. It worked. But best of all, he had done what his feeble father, the perpetual loser, couldn't. It was this one triumphant thought that sent power flooding through his opiated veins.

Now he had the money he needed, and then some, to get that bullying group of Australian extorters off his back. There had been some talk lately of forming a vigilante group to get rid of the scum, like the Sydney Ducks, who plagued the city with their threats, setting fires and looting. Paying them off now would give him time to get together with some of the men, like Sam Brannan, who'd been pushing for vigilance.

With that pleasant thought occupying his intrepid mind, Abner washed the previous night's sweat from his face and neck, drying them with a cotton towel as he wandered over to the window. The sound of warning shouts captured his attention. Glancing out the window, he saw a wagon round the corner and career down the street. Its driverless team slowed as it neared the narrow stable path, his stable path.

"Duncan! That fool." Abner flung the towel into a corner. "Now what's happened?" He grabbed a striped neckcloth and furiously buttoned his collar as he stalked from the room.

A short time later Abner pulled the errant wagon up to the Battery Street Supply Company. He wrapped the reins around the brake lever and eyed the loading dock. Leaning against the side beam of the open freight door was his dim-witted assistant. The wide expanse of Duncan's brawny shoulders was unmistakable, and Abner couldn't see his head, which was shadowed by the doorway overhang. He could tell from the man's stance he was lollygagging around while Abner's team and wagon took off for parts unknown.

As he stormed toward Duncan it became apparent that

the idiot was talking to a woman. He could see the outline of her full skirt, and her bonnet bobbed gently as she spoke. The fool was supposed to be picking up a supply load and instead he was talking with some trull from the wharf.

"Duncan! What do you think you're doing?" Abner shrilled. He turned to give the harlot a scathing look, and was stunned to stone. It was the Fredriksen beauty. The delicate, younger sister of the troublesome virago. She shrunk back from him, and Abner quickly altered his look.

"Miss Fredriksen, I'm so sorry." Abner bowed slightly, not aware he stared so intensely. She cowered back against the pallet box behind her, and Abner thought she was repelled by Duncan's presence.

"Is this ne'er-do-well bothering you, my dear?" he asked. When all she did was shake, he assumed the poor girl was so scared of the giant that she couldn't speak.

He swirled toward Duncan. "Get away from her!" he ordered. "I'm not paying you to harass innocent women, nor am I paying you to let my strongest team run loose. You were to load those supplies"—his voice had angered into a high-pitched shriek, and its volume scratched through his taut throat—"and then come right back!"

Duncan's straw-colored hair looked even more yellow against the bright red flush of his large, square-boned face. His narrow gaze followed Abner's pointing finger and lit upon the wagon by the dock. Abner watched the hulk gulp deep breaths of air, and if he didn't know the man had more hair than wit, he'd have thought the dummy was really angry. It stopped him for a moment.

Then the most incredible thing happened. The girl stood up and placed her hand on the straining muscles of Duncan's rising arm. "Don't, please," she pleaded. "Just go on. I don't want to cause you any more trouble. I'll be fine."

Abner couldn't believe it. He thought she'd been so frightened of Duncan, and instead she was touching him! As Duncan stared silently at the girl, it looked as if they were having some kind of unspoken communication. Duncan lowered his straining fists. Silent, he turned slowly and began to methodically load the waiting wagon.

It must be pity, Abner thought. Dagny Fredriksen is young and probably compassionate. Any creature as lovely, as unspoiled-looking as she, would have to be sympathetic to someone like Duncan. The first time he saw her, well over two years ago at the burial of her mother, he thought she was exquisite. She was adolescent, and yet she had none of the usual traits. She hadn't been gangly or gawky or plump. At that young age she looked exactly as she did today, as if she were molded from head to toe out of the finest, purest porcelain. With her dark hair and eyes, she stood out among the vapid pallor of the blond Fredriksens. Just looking at her had stirred in him a wealth of emotion. He remembered feeling as if he'd discovered a finely carved piece of Singhalese ebony in a crate of sawdust.

Intending to assure her that Duncan wouldn't bother her anymore, he stepped closer. "Miss Fredriksen, I—" His delusionary bubble burst, for she looked up at *him* with dread in her eyes, and the trembling of her small, gloved hands was obvious.

"Excuse m-me, s-sir," she stammered, backing away as she spoke. "I . . . I must find my sister." She turned and rushed across the warehouse.

Abner watched, dumbfounded, as she scurried to her sister's side. She was frightened of him. He thought about the last few minutes, picturing the scene in his mind and hoping to figure out what he had done to frighten her. Briefly, he played with the absurd idea that she preferred Duncan to him, but his innate sense of self-worth extinguished that ridiculous thought. He finally lit upon the only solution he could rationalize. He must have scared her when he shouted at Duncan and then deliberately turned his angry look toward her. She might even imagine that he blamed her for Duncan's idleness.

What a foolish mistake on his part! He should have known someone young and sensitive would be repelled by his shouting. When he pondered the thought, he realized that during most of their previous encounters he'd been angry, or at least acting so. He delighted in trapping any of her young siblings in his garden because he could drag the brats home where he might have the opportunity to talk to Dagny. But the pretext never worked, because her older sister would be there every time to handle the complaint. Then he'd have to make a big show of the whole incident, and wasn't able to do much more than stare at Dagny. Thinking back, it dawned on him that she had always hidden behind her older sister, Hallie.

Abner eyed the women as they left the building. He needed a way to lessen her fear and soften her toward him. He likened her to a skittish filly of his youth, shying away from her master. He remembered how his equestrian mother had taught him that an apple or a carrot or any sweet delicacy could quench a filly's fear. It was that lesson that he'd use now. The problem was acquiring the right delicacies, for, in his limited experience, women's tastes were expensive.

The elation still lingered from his lucky gaming victory, fueled by the essence of liquid flowers tainting his blood. Abner reasoned, but the dendritic liquid dulled his ability to think rationally. Instead, it nurtured the inherently peculiar side to his logic and rooted itself to his insecure nature, planting deep within the fiber of his being a tangled, deciduous weed of confidence.

Luck be damned! He had manifested his own destiny, and he'd do so again. Thus Abner solved his problem. He strode toward home, where he would pick up his winnings and return to the gambling haven to stake a bigger venture.

Once home, he retrieved the gold, but before he left the room, he pocketed the umber bottle. Nothing, not physical pain, not anything, would hinder his goal. He left, determined to make his own destiny.

* * *

"Black Mariah. Seven-card stud, high spade in the hole splits the pot." The dealer announced the next hand while he shuffled the poker deck.

Abner watched the cards fly across the battered tabletop. His first card, dealt facedown, slid toward the table edge before it stopped, a sticky stain of spilled whiskey impeding its motion. He leaned against the wall behind him, trying to look bored. But deep inside, his guts squirmed.

Filmy light shone through the thick cloud of smoke that haloed the corner table. The sun had set hours before, and now, when his nerves sang to an unfamiliar, straining melody of tension, Abner was thankful for the concealing murk. Another card and the bet was to him. He picked up five twenty-dollar gold pieces and tossed them in the kitty. The other five players followed suit.

Again the cards flew around the circle of men, and the man on Abner's right, a merchant named Harris, had the bet with a pair of jacks showing. The pot quadrupled.

When the fifth card was dealt, Abner couldn't believe his luck. With his down cards, he had an ace-high flush, and while Harris had three jacks showing, Abner had the man's fourth jack down. Harris boosted the pot by two thousand. Two men folded and two matched the bet.

The sixth card came, and Abner tried to remember the call. *Black Mariah. Black Mariah. High spade in the hole splits the pot.* He knew Harris couldn't have four jacks, since he had it in his own down cards, so since Harris was pushing up the pot, he must have a high spade. Abner matched the bet and the two others folded.

The last card was dealt. "Down and dirty," the dealer quipped.

Sweat beads popped through the pores in Abner's forehead and the sting of smoke scratched his eyes. The last card lit facedown in front of him. By the rules of the house, neither man could look at the last card.

Harris eyed Abner's bank, then bet. If Abner wanted to call, he'd have to bet everything on this one hand. With a nonchalance he didn't come close to feeling, Abner pushed his bank into the kitty. "I call."

Harris laughed when the dealer flipped over the hole cards. He had the ace of spades, giving him a full house and the high spade in the hole.

Abner lost. Numb, he stared at the pot. Harris laughed and laughed. The sound gritted down Abner's spine.

The jeering merchant started to gather the kitty, but the dealer stopped him. "It's Black Mariah, remember? Not all the cards are up."

Abner didn't understand. Another player nodded at Abner's two remaining hole cards and explained. "In Black Mariah, if the queen of spades is a hole card, it beats both the best poker hand and the high spade. The holder takes all."

The dealer reached in front of Abner and flipped over his two hole cards. The queen of spades stared back at him.

Cheers erupted from the table; he'd won, all of it. The moisture evaporated from his mouth. He felt the others crowd around him and clap him on the back. Someone shoved a canvas bag into his hands. It was for the money.

The boisterous voices of the surrounding men made him suddenly nervous. As he scooped his winnings into the bag, he could feel their expectant stares. It was like being crushed, crowded.

A few coins were left on the table, and he waved them off. "The drinks are on me," he boasted.

The crowd swarmed back to the bar, and Abner knotted the heavy bag through the fastener on his suspenders. He jerked his sack coat closed and sighed.

A bottle of whiskey sat forgotten on the table. He was still numb, and needed to feel something, even the bitter burn of rotgut whiskey. Grabbing the bottle, Abner took a gulp.

It took about three minutes for the whiskey to create a war in his stomach. Painful cramps shot like lightning from his belly, knifing their way to his lower organs. A splitting ache ran from his rectum up his spine to his neck, and the hurt from it made him flinch.

The whiskey bottle crashed to the floor. He groped through his coat for his medicine bottle. "Water, please," he croaked at one of the nearby men.

A little Chinese man shuffled over. He picked up the laudanum bottle and squinted at it. Abner jerked the bottle from the man's small, claw-nailed hand. "That's mine!"

The man grinned and nodded his pigtailed head.

"Get away!" Abner hugged the bottle and squeezed his eyes shut when another pain gripped him. When it passed and he opened his eyes, the strange little chink stood in front of him, holding a glass of water. Abner uncapped the tincture and tried, with shaking hands, to pull some of the liquid into the dropper. The bottle was almost empty, so in desperation he dumped the small amount of remaining medicine into the glass. Instead of tinting a rich ruby, the water barely turned pink.

The grinning Chinaman shook his head while Abner pounded the heel of his hand against the bottle, trying to jar loose any hidden drops. He slammed the bottle onto the table and grabbed the glass, inhaling the contents as if he were smothered and the glass held air.

"You come. You come." The little man nodded, still wearing that toothy expression. He tapped a curved nail on the dark brown silk tunic that covered his frail torso. "Chi Ho. Chi Ho."

Abner grunted in pain. He had to get out of there while he could still walk. He pushed himself up and the Chinaman, Chi Ho, repeated, "You come, Chi Ho."

Putting his arm around Abner's bent waist, he helped him into the alley through a small side door.

The medication hardly dulled the sharp pain. Abner was so consumed by it that he wasn't even aware of where Chi Ho took him, nor did he care. All Abner wanted was the relief of a sweet, medicated sleep.

It seemed like timeless hours later when Abner choked on a strange-smelling smoke. He opened his eyes, and the little man stood over him waving a long skewer with a smoldering ball. Abner tried to push it away from his face, but the man persisted. Abner was weak and drained and he could barely hold Chi Ho's arm. He just wanted to sleep. "Let me sleep . . . please." The smoke continued to drift at him, and Abner laid there, somnolent, as the black ball of opium paralyzed the pain in a way the laudanum couldn't.

Chapter

Seven

"Ohhh-ohhh, here's to the man who darts a whale
And lives to 'poon an-nah-ther-r.
Here's to the man who irons a whale
And lives to 'poon an-nah-ther-r.
He's a hook-ker, yes indeed!
He's a hook-ker, yes indeed!
He's a hook-ker, yes indeed!
Ex-χ-actly like his mah-h-ther-r!"

"Shut up, Lee!" Kit crept a little higher in the dirt ridge. He peered over his shoulder, giving the famous Howland evil eye to Lee, who was now humming his drunken ditty.

Kit tightened his gripping hands on the rough edge of the rock ledge. His reflexes slowly, very slowly reacted to the commands of his brain, both being greatly dulled by the quantity of rum he'd consumed. His right leg inched higher up the steep, sandy cliff, until his knee was almost touching his nose. His damp trousers smelled like dirt and crushed grass and . . . he sniffed once—dead fish, old dead fish.

The wobbly shoulder on which he was standing hiccuped, and Kit almost slipped from his precarious perch.

"Dammit, Lee! Hold still!"

"Can't. Got th'iccups."

"Then hold your arracky breath! You were the one who had to have these damn eggs!"

"Um . . . hic . . . um."

"Murre eggs, for Christ's sake," Kit grumbled. "Now give me a boost, I've almost got 'em." He reached up and felt around the nest until his hands touched the cool eggshells. He carefully handed them down to Lee.

"Now you've got your precious eggs." Kit jumped off Lee's shoulders and landed with surprising grace for someone whose breath was strong enough to crack a mirror. He looked down at his clothes. They were filthy, and soaking, and damn cold. Why he'd let himself get smooth-talked into this escapade was beyond him. He was tired, frozen, and his head was blooming with the seeds of what felt like a real hummer of a headache. He looked at Lee, who clutched his egg-filled hat to his chest like a greedy child holds his first toy. He was still humming.

"Come on, let's get back to the skiff and off this hellhole of an island. It's going to take forever to row back to Sausalito." Kit shoved his icy hands in the pockets of his wool coat and walked along the water's edge, muttering, "How the hell did they come up with a name like Angel Island? This place is so cold, no angel'd come near it. Or better yet, tread on it." Kit let loose with a scornful laugh. "I guess we know who the fools are. Right, Lee?"

"Hic."

Well, at least I know he's still behind me. Kit stood on one side of the small boat while he waited for his wobbly friend to help him shove off. The snapping cold and the hurt in his head had done a great job of sobering him up. He watched through pain-squinted eyes as Lee gently placed his plunder in a safe corner of the boat.

"Ready?" Kit asked.

Lee nodded, and from his chipmunklike cheeks, Kit assumed he was holding his breath again. They shoved off, both men sprinting into the skiff with a mariner's ease that even a few pints of rum couldn't blot out.

"You . . . hic . . . row first. I've . . . hic . . . got to ge—hic—et rid of the—hic—ese."

Kit rowed, thankful for the warming action. It lessened his headache. The only sounds were an occasional hiccup and the quiet swish of the rowing oars.

Suddenly, Lee started to chuckle.

"What's so funny?"

"I was th—hic—inking."

"About what?"

"'Bout your face."

"God, you're drunk."

"No . . . hic . . . really! You look jus—hic—st like ya did at Millie's. Hic."

"And you find that funny?"

"No." Lee grinned, still hiccuping. "But did you see, hic, Hallie's fa—hic—ce when the chowder came?"

"Well, it sure was something. She was as red as a snapper, and I couldn't help but feel sorry for her. That Fredriksen brood is sure a handful."

Lee's face lit up. "Hey, my hiccups are gone. Thinking about that sweet girl cured me!"

Kit's headache rushed back in full force and throbbed whenever he thought of that "sweet" girl. His hands tightened on the oars and his rowing sped up.

"Who'd have ever thought that awkward girl would flower like she has?" Lee clucked his tongue a few times. "Those are some petals."

"And that's one flower you're not to pollinate." The small boat lurched through the water with a sudden burst of speed.

Lee pulled out a flask and toasted Kit. "I'll leave that to you." He took a swig, straddling the short bench that sheltered his murre eggs.

"Knock it off, Lee, or I'll throw those damn eggs of yours overboard. The last thing I need right now is a damn woman—girl, whatever—and remember, she's Jan's daughter!" Kit shoved the oars deep into the swelling ocean and pulled as hard as he could.

"Unload your muzzle, Kit, I was only pestering you a bit.

The way I feel about Jan extends to his family too. You know that. Here," he shoved the flask toward Kit, "have a swig. You need to lighten up. You were almost your old, fun-loving self a while ago. Drink up!"

Kit couldn't believe Lee was sucking up more of that godawful stuff. He wouldn't dare touch it. As it was, his head felt like it would explode any minute. "Is that more of that rotgut? Sweet Jesus, Lee. How can you swill any more of that piss?"

"Hell, old buddy, this is great piss rum. Guaranteed to put hair on your chest!" Lee took one last chug and recapped the bottle with a drunken flourish. He leaned back with his eyes closed, resting his head on the side of the bow. It wasn't too long before all Kit heard was a soft snore.

The last day or so his snoring friend had helped clear Kit's clogged mind, at least, about the Taber-Fredriksen contract. The rum had helped him forget about his aunt. Like Lee had said, "Why get so upset before she gets here? There'll be plenty of opportunity for that after she arrives."

But when he'd found thoughts of Hallie constantly creeping through his mind, he'd forced himself to relive every vicious moment of his marriage to Jo. The shattering memories of his wife screaming that she didn't want or need his love. All she needed was for him to hop on that precious ship of his and sail off into the blue, then she wouldn't have to suffer his touch or listen to his claims of love. She really couldn't have cared less whether he loved her or not.

He had entered that marriage with the naive surety that his marriage would fulfill his dreams of a loving woman, one with whom he could share the fantasies of his heart. He'd had that heaven with Jo those first few years, until that one long, fateful voyage that kept him away from his wife. He had thought the separation was hell until he got home, then he really knew what hell was. Jo didn't love him anymore; he'd been gone so long he had lost her.

Those remembrances provided a painful cure to the symptoms that had been plaguing him lately. Ever since Hallie backed into his office, flashes of her kept triggering his mind and his body. The only protection he could use to guard his crumbled heart were the humiliating memories of his dichotomous marriage. And then, miserable, he'd stupidly try to cover his pain with a blanket of rum. The next thing he knew, he and Lee had left the warmth of Richardson's supply shack and they were rowing toward Angel Island to get those stupid eggs.

As Kit neared the shoreline, a gust of frigid wind hit his damp back. His teeth started to chatter. He rowed harder, picturing warm, dry woolen blankets, the melting glow of a blazing fire, and a tall blond woman whose touch sent heat blistering through his skin. The skiff slapped into the sandy shore. While Lee slept on, Kit tugged off his boots and damp coat and flung them onto the beach. He turned and dove into the icy swell, surfacing a few feet from shore. As he bobbed in the freezing water, he justified his impulse with the rationalization that he needed to think about something other than Hallie Fredriksen.

Early Saturday morning Kit sat across from Lee, watching him consume the last two eggs.

"Ummmm . . . perfect." Lee shoveled another heaping forkful of the red delicacy onto a thick slab of bread. His red-whiskered cheeks bulged when he stuffed enough for three men into his mouth.

Kit shook his head in amazement. "I've never seen anyone who can put it away like you. The way you've been hunched over plates of food lately, it's a wonder you're not the size of a whale."

"I've been doing other things besides eating. And it doesn't matter how much I 'put away,' I work it off." Lee wiggled his eyebrows. "Remember last night?"

Kit groaned. "I'd like to forget it."

"You probably would, since you weren't exactly what I'd call lively. I haven't seen you look that bored since you lost that bet and had to spend three hours at Pastor Treadwell's prayer meeting. You know what you need?"

"Yes. But no doubt you're going to tell me anyway."

"You need to relax a little. All work and no play makes Jack a dull boy." Lee put a heaping forkful of his precious eggs under Kit's nose. "Here, try some."

The smell of eggs and onions, mixed with some bloody-looking thing called a tomato, was enough to make Kit ill. He pushed Lee's hand away. "God no, you couldn't pay me to taste that foul-smelling concoction."

Lee shrugged. "It's your loss, old friend." He took a couple more bites and then set the fork down. "What was wrong with you last night?"

"Just tired," Kit lied. He wished he knew what was bothering him. Last night he'd sat there, in a room full of frolicsome people, half of whom were friends, and he was suddenly overcome with the feeling that he didn't belong there. He felt conspicuous, and of all things, lonely. It was the oddest feeling. But then, he'd been antsy and itchy since they'd arrived at Richardson's Landing.

He drained his coffee mug. The crowd in the small wooden shack was getting to him, along with the smell. He stood up abruptly. "I'm going to get some air. I'll meet you outside when you're finished." Lee gave an egg-muffled reply, but Kit had already woven his way toward the door.

It was a relief to taste the wind, even though it blew so hard along this stretch of Rancho Sausalito that the locals called it Hurricane Gulch. Kit shoved his hands into the deep pockets of his coat and walked away from the clustered shacks toward the solitary shelter of a group of willow trees. He leaned against a gnarled trunk and watched the activity below.

Water from a wooden cistern gurgled down a trestle pipe that angled past the trees. The sound was a welcome respite from the ruckus of the supply and bedding shanties. The buzzing itch that had plagued Kit, like bees swarming in his blood, lessened with the soothing sound of springwater rushing and winding its way to the waterfront. Breaking into a melody was the discordant creak of an unoiled pump as men tapped water from the tressle's basin into large barrels and loaded them into a water junket docked pierside.

Another ship dropped anchor in the deep water beyond the short pier. It looked familiar. As the sails dropped, Kit straightened, straining to see if the ship was indeed the *Sea Haven*.

Lee walked toward him, pointing at the newly moored ship. "Do you see that?"

"I sure do. Let's go." Kit started down the hill. "I don't understand why Jan's anchoring here. He always puts in near Central Wharf so he can head right home."

The two men watched from the pier for signs of a launch. When none came, they commandeered a dinghy and rowed out to the ship. As they neared her, a crewman shouted something, but the loud barking of seals on a nearby rock drowned out his words. A rope ladder fell over the ship's portside, and the men climbed aboard. Kit swung over the railing and noticed a few crewmen standing together. He looked past them, searching for their captain. When Jan didn't appear to greet them, he glanced at Lee, whose shrug echoed his own bewilderment.

A small, sea-baked whaleman stepped forward hesitantly. "Mr. Howland. Capt'n Prescott." He wrung his hands nervously. "I—"

"Where's your captain, seaman?" Kit cut in. "Go tell'm to get off his old duff and come greet his friends."

"Mr. Howland, sir, I'm a-tryin' ta tell ya. The capt'n . . . he went an' got himself killed, right outside o' Magdalena Bay."

"Oh, God." Kit slumped back against the hard ship rail. His hands massaged his forehead and his mouth bit into an anguished grimace.

Lee's face flinched with the same pained look. "How did it happen?"

"We had one o' them devilfish ironed, an' the capt'n, he said this 'un'd bein' his last, he'd be damned if'n he'd not be a part o' it. He upped an' got in with the boat crew. He 'pooneered her himse'f, he surely did, but when the foul line busted, well . . . he tried ta grap it. That she-devil of a whale rolled an' crushed the boat an' crew." The sailor's shoulders sagged from reliving the gruesome sight. He looked up. "Ya see, the sharks was so bad, sir, well, ya know what I'm a-sayin'? Not a one o' them five men made it."

Silence and grief for the men lost in this death tale weighted the atmosphere with a cumbrous sense of loss, and of guilt, for although not even one of the men lacked sorrow for their mates, each man still left alive was forced, by the death of his crewmen, to remember his own fragile mortality. Deep within each survivor's gut, a thankfulness prevailed, making every man secretly glad it wasn't he who laid in a watery grave.

The poor man looked unsure and a little lost. "Mr. Howland, sir, the capt'n said I was ta come ta ya if'n anythin' ev'r happan'd ta him. I thought I should come to ya right away. We heared ya was with Capt'n Prescott in Whaler's Bay, so we figgered ta find ya."

There was no time now for mourning, Kit had too much to do. His head was filled with conflicting notions of what he should do first, until the most important of his duties pushed any other plans right out of his conscious mind.

Break the news to Hallie.

With that thought, Kit took command. "Haul up the anchor, men, and get her ready to sail about. We're going across the bay. You coming, Lee?"

"I'll be ready as soon as I send a message to my repair crew."

"Fine. I need to check the logs and cargo tallies. I'll be in the aft cabin." He started toward the steerage, and then, as if in afterthought, he stopped and turned back to the sailor. "What's your name, seaman?"

"Smalley, sir. Amos Smalley, second mate."

"And the first mate, where's he?"

"Dove in after the capt'n, sir."

After a prolonged silence, Kit asked, "You sailed her back to port fully loaded?"

Smalley nodded.

Although the man was uncommonly jittery, Kit knew he

must be competent if he had managed to get the *Sea Haven* back home. "Okay, consider yourself first mate and get this ship ready to sail." Kit turned and headed toward the small aft cabin he knew Jan used for his quarters.

When Lee entered a short time later, Kit was immersed in a pile of papers. He slumped into a nearby chair and scratched his beard while Kit added a column of figures. "So what's the haul?"

"A little over fifteen hundred barrels and"—Kit scratched some figures on the ledger—"looks like twelve thousand or so pounds of baleen. No gris."

Kit picked up a heavy sheet of paper that sat in one corner of the desk and handed it to Lee. "Read this and tell me what you think it means."

While Lee read the paper, Kit listened to the active scurrying aboveboard. The aft anchor was hauled up and the anchor chain rattled and banged against the outside wall of the cabin.

"Where was this?" Lee asked, still reading, or maybe rereading the paper.

"In the drawer with some other documents." Kit squirmed a little in his chair. "How would you interpret that?"

"I think, my friend, that you are now proud owner of the *Sea Haven.*"

"That's what I thought, but read on."

"I did."

"And?"

"Well, the way I see it, you appear to be legal guardian of the Fredriksen brood."

"I was hoping I read it wrong." Kit pinched the bridge of his nose. He slapped his hands down on the desk and stood up. "Damn! I owe Jan so much, but I don't need this heavy a responsibility." He began to pace back and forth across the narrow room.

Lee looked down at the document. "I don't see that it's all that different from what you've been doing."

Kit stopped. "What do you mean?"

"Think about it for a minute. Jan's only been home a few months out of each year. Who takes care of them while he's gone?"

"Hallie."

"You sell the cargoes and see that the money's transferred into the bank, right?"

Kit nodded.

"Who paid their accounts when Jan was gone?" Lee asked.

"Either myself or the accounting clerk at the bank."

"Then tell me how anything has changed? The house is theirs free and clear, so you don't have to supply a roof over their heads. I don't see that there's really any difference. I'll check on them whenever I'm in port, and you'll be here in case they need you. Financially, the sale of this cargo and the last will leave them with no worries. I don't see where there's a problem."

Kit realized that what Lee said made sense, but somehow he couldn't imagine his guardianship of three females—one being Hallie, and two little boys—as a problem-free relationship. He voiced as much to Lee and then added, "Before I—we—do anything, we've got to break the news to his family. At least to Hallie and Dagny."

"God, I hate that. It's always been hard for me to notify the families of lost men. Luckily, I've only lost four, but—"

A hard knock on the door interrupted the two men. Lee turned and opened the door, and Smalley entered the cabin. "We're not far from the wharf, sir, an' this bein' Saturday, the crew was a-wonderin' if'n they could go to the services?"

Kit looked startled. "What services?"

"The memorial services for the capt'n, sir. Ya see, his girls sent word that they was ta have a service today and—"

"You mean his family knows already?" Kit shouted, as his mind flashed with the picture of a distraught Hallie. To have to handle the death of her only remaining parent had to be crushing, but then, having to explain, all alone, to the younger ones, well, that thought really made Kit's chest ache for her. If there were to be services, then Hallie and Dagny

92

must have handled those alone too. He didn't feel like much of a friend to Jan Fredriksen right now, even if he hadn't been notified in time to share some of the agony and burden that must have been piled on those poor girls.

Smalley appeared to shrink four inches in the face of Kit's anger. "I thought they should know right away, they being his family and all."

"When did you tell them?" Lee asked.

"Late Wednesday night," the mate answered.

"Over two days ago!" Kit paced again.

"Calm down," Lee said, turning back to Smalley. "What time's the service?"

"The note said it'd be at Telegraph Hill at one o'clock this afternoon."

Kit pulled out his pocket watch. It was almost one now. "How far are we from the wharf?"

"'Bout ten minutes, sir," Smalley answered, before repeating his question, "Me an' the crew would like ta pay our respects, if'n that's all right with ya."

"Of course, of course, tell the men that's fine, but I want them to start unloading the haul as soon as possible. I'll make arrangements for the load to be added to the storage in DeWitt's. Can you handle the unloading later today?"

"Yes, sir."

"Fine. Get us into port as fast as you can so we don't miss that service." Kit looked at Lee. "Now what was that you said about not foreseeing any problems?"

Chapter

Eight

Hallie stood in the cool murk of the afternoon air as Pastor Treadwell read from his book of scripture. She didn't listen to the words he spoke over her father's empty grave because she knew those words of comfort would probably break the tight rein she'd kept on her emotions. Her stoic gray eyes had no sparkle. They were dry and dull, as if mirroring the dismal shade of the overcast sky. Her breath formed small, dew-laden clouds in the dank air, and she inhaled deeply, hoping that some of the hollowness within her would escape with each breath. But it didn't. Instead, it seemed to seep into her bones and lie there thick and misty, like the fog floating on the bay.

Apparently, death's touch didn't become more bearable each time it tainted your life. It played a hiding game. The bruising pain of grief would dim with the passage of time, appearing only as an occasional flicker of loss. Life would go on, until the next time, when death's sneaky fingers invaded the pocket of your heart and picked another loved one from deep within. And then it burned through you, this lonely feeling of being left behind and forgotten. Alone. But she wasn't alone. Dagny, Liv, and the twins were now her sole responsibility.

Lordy, but she was scared.

Her fingers were suddenly squeezed so tightly that Hallie had to bite back a yelp. She looked down at Liv, the family warrior, whose small hand grasped her own so fiercely. Her little sister's shoulders were stiff and she stared straight ahead, her gaze fixed upon the small granite marker wedged into the slope of the cemetery. Her stubborn little chin quivered under the strain of holding back her tears, and Hallie knew that defiant Liv wouldn't cry.

With a pure, youthful cussedness, Liv fought her emotions as she fought anything she considered a weakness. Hallie watched as determination battled with sorrow in her young sister's expression, and the only thing that kept her from shielding Liv with an embrace was knowing that her sister's pride wouldn't welcome any gesture of comfort.

Liv's white-knuckled fist clutched at the fabric of her woolen dress, pulling the hem up just enough to reveal a dirty, bare toe. The urge to smile warmed its way through Hallie, and in one of those odd quirks of irony, she was the one comforted. Her worry and doubt were replaced by the familiar vision of Liv's shoes, swinging from the forbidden branches of Abner Brown's apple tree.

A chunk of rock skidded across the damp grass and hit the pastor's boot with a solid thud. His flood of words stopped immediately and he turned his disgruntled gaze toward the small boy who held Hallie's other hand. She looked down at Knut, whose face wore a goggle-eyed look of guilt. Gunnar stood quietly between his brother and Dagny. Both of them stared at Knut too. Hallie frowned her disapproval and shook her head slightly. After a few more long seconds, the pastor resumed his eulogy.

Hallie knew the twins didn't understand their loss. To a four-year-old, death was only a word; its consequences wouldn't be felt until they next wondered when their da would be home. Only time would teach them that death meant their father wouldn't ever be back.

Hallie was sure they were bored with this strange ceremony. It was amazing that they'd been quiet so far. Children were keen ones, and Hallie'd had enough experience to know they could sense the moods of those around them. She felt sure that was the reason they had been so subdued the last few days, and she was thankful.

"Donnn't!"

The whispered whine raked Hallie's ear. It sounded as loud as cannon fire, so she was surprised when Pastor Treadwell continued.

The whiner, Knut, glowered at Gunnar, and Hallie squeezed Knut's hand to capture his attention. He'd barely looked up at her when he tattled, "But he's touching me!"

"Shhh," Hallie reprimanded. She started to lean toward Gunnar, intending to give him a quick talking to, but Dagny was already whispering in his ear.

The boys were having one of those weeks. Hallie assumed they were reacting to the confusing emotions displayed by the other family members, but whatever the cause, she kept an eye on them. Gunnar waited a few moments and then leaned his shoulder toward Knut, who saw it coming and stepped out of his brother's range. But apparently, besting Gunnar wasn't enough. Knut's tongue slipped past his lips and wiggled a taunt at Gunnar. It was a gesture that dared him to do something about it. His eyes narrowed and he moved his nose closer to Knut's, ready for attack.

Hallie snapped her fingers right in front of their glaring faces. It worked. With both boys staring up at her, she frowned and shook her head. They settled down, and soon both boys were innocently staring straight ahead. Hallie sighed in relief.

Dagny still held Gunnar's hand but appeared absorbed in her own thoughts. Hallie noticed that Dagny had been more responsive since the incident with that giant, Duncan, but she was still awfully quiet. The speed with which Dagny scolded Gunnar was not that of a dazed person. No, Hallie thought, each of them had his own form of strength, and the realization gave her morale a boost.

A peaceful warmth replaced her earlier doubts. Unfortunately, the peace lasted only about halfway through Pastor Treadwell's reading of the Twenty-third Psalm.

"Yea, though I walk through the valley of the shadow of death, I will fear no evil . . ."

Before Hallie could blink, Gunnar's devious little fingers reached behind his unsuspecting brother's back and pinched the tender skin of Knut's forearm. In reflex action, Hallie's hand smothered the yell from Knut's mouth and she pulled him back into the muffling fabric of her skirts. Knut's foot kicked out, aiming for his brother's shin, but before he could kick Gunnar, a masculine body stepped between the boys, separating them before the ruckus could turn into a gravesite brawl.

Hallie looked up, intending to give the man—this heaven-sent angel—a smile of thanks.

Kit Howland stared back at her and she quickly looked the other way. He was no angel.

Her little brother's muted words vibrated against her palm. As her hand fell from Knut's mouth, Kit placed his own tanned hand on the little boy's shoulder. The last time she'd seen him, the hand that was now holding her brother at bay had squeezed her waist, in the guise of checking her gussets.

One of her hands still held Liv's, but her empty left hand felt all clammy. Automatically, she rubbed it against the wool of her skirt fabric. Then she remembered she wore gloves and her hand stilled. It was a nervous habit of hers, and she wondered if anyone caught the gesture.

Hallie tilted her head slightly to the right. The wide bow on the brim of her hat flopped back, giving her a clearer view. Just on the other side of her brother stood Kit, staring at her with a worried expression.

The bow flopped back and she stared straight ahead. If she didn't know better, she'd almost believe he could read her thoughts, and that was intimidating. She decided the best thing she could do, for her own peace of mind, was to ignore him. At least for now.

Kit knew Hallie was doing her best to ignore him, and a large part of him was relieved. He hadn't known what to expect from the Fredriksen children, and he'd envisioned Hallie and Dagny as frail, grief-stricken young girls. He had assumed they'd arrive and find that the girls had succumbed to vaporish fits which only hours of coddling and a good dose of laudanum would cure. Instead, he found the three females, stiff-backed and dry-eyed, and the twins up to mischief. Maybe Lee was right about his fostering of Jan's children. It might not change his life at all.

Two wagonloads of whalemen pulled up just as the minister closed his bible and moved toward the family. Surprise lit Hallie's face when she saw the whole crew climb down and silently approach her. Kit wondered how she'd handle this.

Amos Smalley led the group, and Kit noticed the man's hat was, once again, crushed in his fidgeting fists. He wondered briefly if the covering ever graced the man's gray head.

Smalley stepped forward. "Miss Fredriksen, I'm sorry 'bout your father . . . 'ven sorrier I had ta be the one ta tell ya."

Hallie held out her black-gloved hand with a graciousness that surprised Kit. "Don't apologize, Amos," she said, nodding toward her chalk-faced sister. "Both Dagny and I thank you for telling us right away. We know it wasn't easy." She even gave him a small, reassuring smile.

Smalley twisted his hat. "Thank you, miss." He started to turn away but paused, adding, "Ya know, miss, your father, he was the finest capt'n a whaleman could set ta sea with. Never asked a-one of us ta do what he wouldn't do hisself." He swiped briefly at his damp eyes and walked in back of the mulling crew.

Kit stood back beside Lee as each of the men spoke to Hallie. With every one of them she had a kind word, and she didn't hesitate to shake each man's hand and thank him. In spite of her youth, not one tear did she shed and her voice never cracked. He wondered if maybe he'd used her age as a defense. Where before he thought of her as immature, now he realized she had an unspoiled freshness about her. He saw a whole different Hallie. She was poised, controlled, and surprisingly mature. She possessed a strength seldom found in one who had lived so few years. And for some perverse reason, Kit felt proud.

Hallie would occasionally include Dagny or one of the children when she thanked the men, and Kit used those moments to watch each one of the Fredriksen offspring. They stood like statues; the twins, their attention turned to the large group of whalers; Liv, tight-lipped, silent, and rooted to Hallie's side; and Dagny, who appeared to be looking right through everyone.

As the last crewman walked off, Kit approached Hallie. He touched her elbow and she looked up. Her expression, for once, was unreadable. "Hallie, we need to talk. How are you and the children getting back to the house?"

"The Treadwells brought us in their carriage. It's right over there." She turned and pointed. It was tied to a split-rail fence that separated the semaphore telegraph station from the slopes of the cemetery.

Pastor Treadwell intervened. "We'll take them home, Mr. Howland. Will you be coming too?"

"Captain Prescott and I came on horseback," Kit answered.

One of the twins came rushing over and began to jump up and down. "Can I go with you? Can I? Can I?"

"I wanna go too! Hallie, pleeease," the other identical one whined.

"Boys, come on," Hallie ordered, but the twins just kept pleading and leaping.

Kit squatted down face level with the twosome and they turned their hopeful faces toward him. He could not, for the life of him, tell them apart. He looked at the one he thought was the first to speak. "Which one are you?"

"Gunnar."

"All right, Gunnar." Kit poked the other boy gently. "Let's see, then you must be Knut?"

"Uh-huh. Can I go too?"

"Hold on, boys. I think you should go with your sisters."

"But we never got to ride a horse afore," Gunnar argued.

"Well, I'll tell you what. If you two go with your sisters and the Treadwells today, I'll come by on the next warm day and take you both for a ride. How's that?"

The boys looked at each other and then at Kit. They appeared to be judging his integrity, with their serious little faces eyeing him so thoroughly. Apparently, he had an honest look, because they whispered for a moment and then agreed.

The boys scurried off to the carriage and Kit straightened. Hallie stepped forward. "Thank you. You don't have to keep your promise. I'll make some excuse for you."

She wouldn't look at him, and though he resented talking to the top of her bonnet, he answered anyway. "Don't be silly. I know I don't have to. I want to."

"Oh." She raised her head, and it looked as if she now stared at his collar.

"I'll be along as soon as I talk to the crew."

"Why?"

"What do you mean 'why'?" Kit snapped. "We need to talk about your father's plans for you."

"For me?"

"For all of you." Kit was getting irritated.

"You don't have to worry about us, we can take care of ourselves." Hallie started to walk away, but Kit grabbed her arm.

"Hallie," Kit gritted, "don't be pigheaded."

Her head shot up and she stared right at him. "Pigheaded?" she repeated.

Kit remembered where he was. "Look, I'm sorry, but we've got some things we need to settle as soon as possible."

"Not today," she stated.

"Why not?"

"Because I don't feel like it." She jerked her arm out of his grasp and marched toward the waiting carriage.

Kit watched her walk away. "She doesn't feel like it!" he mimicked under his breath. Frustrated, he joined Lee, who waited by their horses. The carriage went by and Kit glared at its back, hoping that Hallie could feel the burn of his eyes.

He mounted, feeling like he wanted to ride through the city, hell-bent for leather. Instead he scowled at Lee.

"What's wrong with you?" Lee asked.

"Nothing. Nothing at all. Come on, let's go."

"Kit, wait!" Lee leaned over and grabbed the reins Kit clutched in his fist. "You need to talk to the men about the cargo."

"Goddammit, I know that!" Kit shouted. He jerked the reins out of Lee's hand and galloped toward the waiting wagons.

Lee pushed his cap back and stared at his friend. "You could have fooled me," he muttered.

Less than five minutes later the two men were forced to slow their pace by a group of heavy teamsters. Lee eyed his brooding friend. "You want to talk about it?"

"No," Kit snapped.

"That's good. It's much better to just let it eat at you. That way when you're really mad, you can clamp your jaw so hard that you bust your nuts. That'll put an end to all your problems. The way I see it—"

"She ignored me."

"Uh-huh. And that bothers you."

"Quit smirking! She was being ridiculous. I told her so too."

"Exactly what did you say?"

"I told her she was being damn pigheaded!"

"That was politic of you."

Kit sighed. "You can cut the sarcasm, Lee, I know I was out of line."

"Considering what Hallie has gone through in the past few days, I'd say you were more of an ass."

"Well, she has a bad attitude. All I wanted to do was talk to her about their welfare. I wanted to reassure her that I'd handle everything. I had thought to put her at ease."

"So you told her she was pigheaded."

"She was. She sure had me fooled. I thought she was fine. It looked like she handled her grief real well. There were no tears, and did you see her with those men?" Kit shook his head in disbelief. "I couldn't believe the mature way she handled them."

Lee halted his mount and he stared, dumbfounded, at Kit.

"What's the matter with you?" Kit asked.

"I can't believe my ears. Do you really think that Hallie was fine? My God, man, she was ready to break any minute. Any fool could have seen it. Every one of Jan's girls was straining to hold her emotions. The boys are too young to understand, but those poor girls have lost both their parents in less than four years. If you think Hallie's fine, then you're an ass."

Kit didn't respond. His first reaction was to punch Lee, but his friend's words rang true. Hallie had been pale and tight-lipped. And now that he thought about it, her voice had had no life to it. Like someone who'd gone without sleep for days, it had been dull and strained. Lee was right.

As they rounded a corner, Kit decided it would be prudent to drop the subject of his rotten handling of Hallie. "Do you want the *Sea Haven?*"

"Why would I want two whalers? The *Wanderer* is enough ship for me. What are you going to do with her?" Lee asked.

"I suppose I'll see if Smalley wants to buy her, but somehow I doubt it. He seems a bit old, and he doesn't appear to be captain material."

As they came to a crest on the hilly street, Lee looked out at the clutter of abandoned ships in the harbor. "Doesn't appear to be a seller's market for ships right now."

"That's changing." Kit saw the doubt on Lee's face. "No, really. I've been hearing about the sale of the water lots. Land speculators have bought hundreds of acres of water lots and they're filling them in. The problem is, there's not enough fill dirt, so they're using garbage, debris, and some are now buying up the ships, breaking them up and using them as fill base."

"God, that's a waste of a damn good ship."

Lee's comment put Kit immediately on the defensive. "Lee, what the hell am I supposed to do with a ship? I have a business to run. I can't and won't sail her myself. With all those ships available, do you really think I could find someone who wants her?"

"You're right, but it still seems like a bit of sacrilege. Jan loved the *Sea Haven.*"

"I know that, but if I can get a good enough price for her, then I can add that to the cargo sales, and the future of Jan's children will be set," Kit reasoned. It made sense to him. He'd get rid of the burden of owning the ship and make some money for Hallie and the children. It was a sound business decision.

"Are you going to tell Hallie?" Lee asked.

"Of course. Why would she care about the ship? She's a woman."

At that instant a supply wagon filled with iron mining tools rattled past. The ringing racket of metal scraping against metal echoed through the narrow street, completely drowning out Lee's prophetic groan.

As Hallie pushed hard on the heavy oak door, the swollen doorframe protested, emitting a deep noise that sounded like a groan. She stared at the door and thought, I've got to get Da to fix that. Then she remembered.

She untied her bonnet and hung it on a hook near the door. Unbuttoning her short cape, she flung it in the vicinity of an old corner chair. She missed. Retracing her steps, she bent to pick up the cape and spotted a small, milky-colored object. It was a scrimshaw lion.

Hallie put the cape on the chair and looked at the whalebone animal. It was one of a pair that went with the toy ark. Each stroke of her father's carving knife carefully detailed a feature of the lion. Two little knicks in the nose were nostrils, curved slashes formed the slanted eyes, and wide, deep, liquid strokes formed the animal's flowing mane. It must have taken her father hours to carve it.

After every voyage he would bring the twins another set of animals, one male and one female. His homecomings always seemed a bit like Christmas, what with the whole family together laughing, opening gifts, and listening to Da's whale stories. Her fingers closed tightly around the lion, and for a brief moment she felt a treasured bit closer to Da.

The sound of voices from the front parlor reminded her that the Treadwells were still there. After one last, quiet look, Hallie put the lion in her dress pocket and went to join the others.

Not more than fifteen minutes later Hallie was sorry she wasn't the fainting type. If she had to listen to Agnes Treadwell's profusions of sympathy and advice for one more minute, she would scream. Dagny had gone to the kitchen to make some more tea, and judging by the amount of time she'd been absent, Hallie expected they'd have enough tea to flood the British parliament. A yawning Liv sat on a chair behind the woman, and every time Hallie looked at her youngest sister, she had to stifle her own yawning reflex.

Agnes paused and looked across the room where the twins were showing her husband their ark. "You know, my dear, Pastor Treadwell and I will be happy to have the young ones, and little Liv, spend some time with us. They're such fine children, especially Liv." She turned and smiled at the young girl, who had just finished her latest yawn. "She's so well-behaved. We would just love to have them come for a nice long visit."

Liv began to crack her knuckles, loudly.

Agnes looked around. "What is that sound?"

Hallie tried to get Liv's attention, but when the young girl ignored her and started on her left hand, Hallie tried to cover the obnoxious sound by answering in a loud voice, "What sound? I don't hear anything. Do *you*, Liv?" She narrowed her eyes at Liv in an unspoken warning.

Liv stopped. But when she began to purposely swallow big gulps of air, an act Hallie knew Liv would do just to make herself burp, Hallie stood up and walked to her sister. She pulled her out of the chair. "Liv, please go see what's keeping Duggie. Now."

Hallie pushed Liv from the room. Just as Hallie started to sit down again, a huge belch echoed from the hall.

Agnes Treadwell looked shocked. "Now, Hallie, don't tell me you didn't hear that! What on earth was it?"

I'll kill her! "Oh that. Uh . . . sometimes . . . the water pump sticks and . . . and the air makes that horrid sound when it escapes the pipe."

"My, that is horrid."

"I can't imagine what's keeping Dagny." Hallie stood up. "I think I'll go see."

The pastor stopped her. "That's not necessary, my dear. We must be going. I've got to write tomorrow's sermon. Hallie, you and the children should get some rest."

He turned and helped Agnes up. Hallie walked them to the door. "I'm sorry about that tea. It shouldn't have taken Dagny so long. I should have gotten it myself. Duggie's been hit harder by this than the others."

"Don't apologize. This is a terrible thing for all of you. Just remember that if you need anything, come to us." They gave Hallie's hand a pat of reassurance and walked the short, foggy distance to their carriage.

Hallie stormed down the hall, bound for her sisters. She didn't care if this was a day for patience, she'd lost hers. Besides, nobody in this family seemed to care that she was hurting too. As she passed the parlor, she poked her head in to check on the twins, but the room was empty. She pushed open the kitchen door and there they sat: Duggie, with Gunnar on her lap; Lee Prescott, holding

Knut in his; Kit Howland, with that obnoxious pipe crammed between his teeth; and Liv, reenacting her deafening burp.

Their laughter stopped when they saw Hallie. No one said a word. It was the unnerving silence, hanging like a guillotine above her, that severed her last shred of control.

Chapter

Nine

Don't let me interrupt your performance, Liv." Hallie waved her hand dramatically. "Please, go on. Show us how well-behaved you are."

Liv plopped into her chair and stared at her lap.

Hallie walked over to the stove and lifted the cold, empty pot used to heat extra water. She made a point of looking inside it and then stared right at Dagny, who was nervously biting her lower lip. Hallie held the copper pot in two fingers, as if it were a dead rat, and then she let go. The metal crashed and bounced noisily on the stovetop. Hallie gained as much satisfaction from the loud racket as she did from watching Dagny cringe.

The tea tray and pot were sitting abandoned on the sideboard. Hallie crossed the room and picked up the pot. She tilted it over a delicate china teacup. Nothing came out, so she held the lid tight and shook the pot. A few drops fell into the empty cup. Setting the pot down, she picked up the cup and served it to Dagny.

"I think it's a little weak." The cup clattered on the tabletop. Hallie spun around, but Kit grabbed her arm.

"Don't blame your sister, Hallie, it's not her fault. Lee

and I came in the back way on purpose, and we kept Dagny so busy, she forgot to make the tea."

He had that stupid pipe still stuck in his mouth and she could barely understand his garbled excuse. She had to listen closely. She was still angry and didn't feel like listening to him at all. His hand still held her forearm, so she glared at his knuckles. "That's the second time today you've grabbed me." Her angry eyes met his. "Let . . . go . . . of . . . me."

His hand remained. Her laugh was forced, its pitch high, almost hysterical. "You called me pigheaded!"

Kit pulled his hand away, but the pipe remained in his bite. He started to rise. "Now easy, girl—"

"Now easy, girl?" she repeated, spitefully. "You sound like you're talking to your horse!"

Hallie rammed her balled fists onto her hips and leaned over toward him. "I am not a horse! Don't talk to me as if I am! I'm a human being, with feelings and a brain. I'm not some silly toy put on this earth for you to laugh at!"

She turned and looked daggers at each and every one of them. "I hurt just like all of you!"

She moved her face right in front of Kit's. "And take that confounded pipe out of your mouth so I can understand you!"

Fueled by anger, she paced back and forth in front of the stunned and subdued group. A moment later she spun around right in front of Kit. "On second thought, leave it in your mouth because I don't care to hear anything you have to say!

"And you." She pointed an accusing finger at Liv. "If you ever do something as rude as that again, I will send you to Agnes Treadwell's for a month!"

As if pleading for an answer, Hallie threw her hands into the air. "What is wrong with all of you? Don't you think I feel pain? I loved Da with all my heart, but I set aside my grief and absorbed all yours. I worried about each and every one of your ungrateful little hides. I wondered how we'd live, whether I could raise you right and give you the things Da and Mama would have. You think it's easy being the oldest? Well, it's not! I love you, but right now I don't like you very much!"

Hallie shook so hard that her vision blurred, so she raised her fists in front of her, tightening them to help control the wave of emotion that welled in her body. Tears of rage flooded her eyes and streamed, unchecked, down her burning cheeks. She swiped at them with a fist and then held it out in front of her. "See these? They're tears, real tears. And you know why I'm crying? Because I think you're selfish, an-and m-mean, and right here and now, I don't want to be in the same room with you!"

She could no longer control the sobs that welled in her hoarse throat, so she ran through a doorway into the back bedroom. Leaning against the door, she bolted the lock and threw herself on her father's bed. Hallie laid there, hurt, drained, and tearful. And nothing, not yelling, not crying, not shaking, could stop her helpless, crushing ache.

The room was narrow and dominated by a large walnut bed. Carved across the headboard was an arched design that looked like a crown of wooden swirls. It had reminded its owner of the eddying waves of the sea. A ribbed coverlet of deep maroon velveteen was spread atop the bed, and on it laid the owner's daughter, curled in sleep.

The intense glow of the afternoon sun glared through the bare west window when Hallie opened her puffy eyes. She blinked at the brightness, seeing that the fog had finally melted away. Turning over on her back, she rubbed at her scratchy lids and wondered how long she had slept. She sat up, remembering her hysterical anger, and felt awful.

Absentmindedly, she picked at the curly snags on her black woolen stockings. What had come over her? To lose control like that wasn't something she was proud of. She sure hadn't set much of an example, screaming and hollering like she had. And the twins. Those little boys were probably scared to death. They wouldn't understand her hysterical display. She was the one who had acted selfish, wallowing in self-pity.

Thoroughly ashamed of herself, she got up and walked to the door, cupping her hand to better hear the quiet voices. There were no familiar kitchen sounds. She paced nervously for a moment and then paused. Maybe they were waiting for her before they fixed supper. She started to unbolt the door but stopped. She wasn't ready to face them.

Hallie walked to the walnut highboy and rested her elbows on its top. She looked into the oval mirror. Her reflection showed the ravages of her fit. Hanging down over her chest was one loose, blond braid. Bent hairpins stuck out at odd angles from the tangled plaiting. She pulled out the pins and wound the braid back into a looped bun. Leaning a bit closer, she squinted, hoping she'd look less ravaged.

She didn't. In fact, she looked . . . piglike. Her eyelids were swollen, like boiled peaches, and they made her wide gray eyes appear half their normal size. Pig eyes, she thought.

Rubbing her fingers over her dry lips, she could feel the ribboned cracks. Her cheeks were sleep-puffy, and the skin on one side of her face bore plum-colored creases from the corded pillow. In a fit of whimsy, she placed her finger on the tip of her nose and she pushed upward, so her nostrils came into full view. She resisted the urge to snort. *Add a few hairs to your chin and they could pickle your feet.*

Hallie looked toward the pitcher and bowl. The porcelain was dull, from sitting unused for so many months, and the film blurred its intricate bird and floral design. The pitcher would be as dry as her lips. Da hadn't slept in this room for months. Her gaze returned to the mirror. Maybe if she waited a few more minutes, she'd look less porcine. She drifted around the room, here and there, touching small remembrances of her father. And stalling.

Sitting atop a corner bureau was an old gimcrackery box, its varnished finish faded orange with age. Hallie lifted the lid and rummaged through the contents. She fingered her father's shirt studs, his broken watch and fobs, a key and a ring. Removing the wooden tray, Hallie looked in the bottom compartment. The miniatures were gone—Da always took them with him—but the daguerreotype of the *Sea Haven* lay brown against the muted velvet lining.

Her father had loved that ship. The whaler had been more than the means by which he supported his family. It had been his spirit. One of her earliest memories was aboard the *Sea Haven* as a five-year-old when her father spent hours showing her each facet of the whale bark. From the depths of the vessel's immaculate hold to the sparkling brass of the ship's bell, young captain Fredriksen had lovingly introduced his firstborn—the child of his heart—to the ship of his soul.

Replacing the tray, Hallie closed the lid; she had been dawdling long enough. It was time she faced her family. She walked to the door and slid the bolt. With a deep breath, she turned the knob and left the room.

The kitchen was empty but the back door stood wide open. Hallie walked onto the small wooden porch and peered down in the small plot of yard. Nobody was there either. As she turned to go inside, she spied Liv, sitting on the bottom step.

She walked down the stairs and stood next to her sister, who was bent over her slate. "Can I sit down?"

The chalk paused but Liv didn't look up. "I suppose." She scooted over, making room for Hallie.

Hallie sat down. "What're you doing, sweatpea?"

"Don't call me that."

"Why not?"

"Jus' 'cause."

"Oh." Hallie nodded as if she understood exactly why. Liv was so sullen lately, and now Hallie seemed to have made it worse with her outburst this afternoon. "Did I embarrass you earlier?"

Liv shook her head.

"Even when I yelled at you in front of everyone?"

"Nope."

"If I did, I'm sorry."

With chalk in hand, Liv began to add numbers on the slate.

Hallie sighed. "Where is everyone?"

"When the sun came out, Gunnar and Knut started pestering the men for a horseback ride."

"Where's Duggie?"

"She went too."

"Why didn't you go?"

"Didn't want to."

"I see." Hallie looked around, hoping for some help from somewhere. None came. "Why didn't you want to go? You like horses."

Liv shrugged.

Hallie peered at the slate. "That's very good, Liv." She reached for the slate. "Here, let me write some numbers and you can add them up. Like we used to do."

As she began to write, Liv stood up. "I don't feel like it. I'm going upstairs. I'm tired."

"But Liv—"

It was too late. She had run up the stairs and closed the door before Hallie could stand up.

She felt like a failure. She couldn't even handle her nine-year-old sister. How was she going to care for the bunch of them? *Oh Da, I'm not doing very well.* She looked down at Liv's slate, abandoned in her lap, and those stupid tears clogged up her throat. She was going to cry again. Crossing her arms on her bent knees, she laid her forehead on her arms and let the weakness flow.

Kit found her later, hunched on the back step, defeated. "Hallie?"

"Oh God, not you," she wailed.

He just stood there, grounded by the wealth of emotions squirming through him. Lee was right. Hallie had been ready to crack. His stomach turned with each whimper and choke. He couldn't stand it. Grabbing her elbows, he pulled her into his arms and held her head against his chest, trying to absorb some of her pain. "I'm sorry, Hallie-girl, so, so sorry."

She started to pull back, but he held her fast. "No! Hallie-girl, get it out. Cry all that hurt out. I'm here, let me hold you. Let me help you." He patted her shuddering back gently.

A mishmash of words rumbled against his shirt front and he bent his head to hear her better. "I didn't hear you, sweet."

"H-how can y-you help me? Nobody c-can help me!"

Kit rubbed his hand over her back to try to quiet her.

"Liv hates me!"

"That's not true. After you ran out, she kept eyeing the door, and not with hatred. She looked about as worried as a guilty nine-year-old could. And Dagny didn't feel much better. Lee and I took the twins for a ride to give you some time alone."

"You d-did?" Hallie sniffed.

"Sure we did. Hallie, you can't be everything to everyone. Not when you're hurting too." His hand smoothed the loose tendrils of hair off her neck. With each stroke, he could feel her shudders weaken. "You know, Dagny went along, but Liv wouldn't leave."

"She wouldn't?"

"No." He marveled at the delicate texture of her skin. It seemed to stroke at his fingertips in return, titillating an invisible silken nerve coupled right to his awakening groin.

Hallie sighed, defeated. "I probably shamed her so that she was too embarrassed to go."

"I think, Hallie-girl, that she was afraid to leave you all alone. Liv didn't act ashamed; she looked concerned, about you. Although from what I've seen of her, I doubt she'd be one to admit it." Kit spoke spontaneously, truthfully, and he was only half aware of what he said. His mind couldn't think clearly when his immediate existence rested solely on his sense of touch.

"You really think so?"

"Um-hm." His hand slid down her long spine, slowly, and

then moved across her waist to travel up again, along the back of each rib. She twitched when his fingertips brushed the sensitive juncture of her arm, and he moved his hand back to safer territory. With small circular motions he rubbed his palm against her shoulder blade, imagining that his hand was filled with the soft fullness of her breast.

Kit and Hallie were silent, wrapped in a cocoon of dual sounds: the rustle of her dress fabric as his hand played across it, and her soft, slow, wistful breath.

"I'm scared," Hallie whispered.

Those two words, so helpless and pleading, ruined him.

"I'll take care of you, sweet. Don't be scared, let me help you." He tipped her melancholy face up toward his. "Let me worry for you, let me . . ." Her breath, warm and sweet, grazed his chin, stroking his lip and chilling his spine. "Let me . . . kiss you."

Hallie felt his lips, warm and dry, as they gently swept hers. His hand surrounded the back of her bare neck, and his thumbnail etched a sensual pattern on the tactile skin beneath her ear. She opened her lips, freely, remembering the kiss from before and dying to feel the luscious friction of his tongue searching her mouth. He licked the edge of her teeth, teasing at the entrance to her mouth, but his arm pulled her hard against his chest, as if he was compelled even closer.

Still his tongue teased. So she stretched on tiptoe and wrapped her arms around his neck, instinctively pressing her lips harder against his, hinting of her need.

He took the hint. The shock of his hand closing over her breast caused her to suck in air, and at the same instant she received the full force of his tongue, thrusting into the yearning hollows of her mouth.

She was trapped by her need, and once again she swirled under the spell of his intimate kiss—and a new compulsion, the intense desire to be held in the palm of his hand. That magic hand; it kneaded, while his tongue pumped, melting her being to the root of her womanhood.

Low, she tingled, itching with a natural need she had yet

to know. Unconsciously, her hips rotated forward. As if in answer, Kit's hands cupped her bottom and lifted her higher. Her arms tightened around his neck, holding tight while her feet dangled free.

His knee pushed a forbidden path between her upper thighs, shoving yards of fabric through her legs while his hands held her hips. His tight thigh nudged upward as she straddled it, saddlelike. She rode his parrying body movements, guided by his tutoring hands. The hard, bulging muscle of his thigh slid upward, against the center of her tingling womanhood. It scratched her primal itch.

Her body soared, as if the very spirit of her being was dancing, round and round in a fast circle. At the same time her nether region drummed toward some lofty peak that hung right above her, almost within reach. Awe of what lay beyond kept her hovering near some unknown, frightening edge. And her body drove her movements—movements she couldn't seem to control.

The swirling drive within her shifted from chilling hunger to fear. Panic churned in her rising stomach. Surely she was going to die! She needed air! Inhaling deeply through her nose, she tried to fill that need.

It was her last conscious thought.

Hallie went limp. She sagged against Kit's chest. The first thought in his passion-muddled mind was that she peaked, but he was wrong. Her breathing was slow and in no way resembled the urgent pant of repletion.

Kit grabbed her shoulders and pushed her back to see what was wrong. Her head lolled forward, rocking lightly like a cork at sea.

Alarm throbbed in his head. His sense moved from within his taut body back to his mind. He grasped her under the arms and lifted her off his leg. Bending, he picked her up and sat down on the stairs with her draped across his lap. Her head rested on his supporting arm, he stared at her pale face.

"Hallie?"

Nothing happened.

"Wake up, sweet." He stroked her cheek.

Still nothing.

"Hallie!" Kit raised his voice, patting her cheek with rapid but gentle little slaps. "Wake up!"

Her head moved from side to side.

"Oh hell! Hallie, come on, wake up!" Kit shook her shoulders.

Her lips moved but he couldn't make out the words. He rubbed her cheeks, hard. "What? I can't hear you."

With her eyes still closed, Hallie whispered, "I'm a pig."

She thinks she's a pig? He uttered a vile curse and Hallie came around. She opened her eyes and blinked up at him.

"Do I still have my feet?"

Her feet? Kit leaned closer to examine her dazed eyes. He watched her expression clear and knew the moment she was fully conscious.

"What happened?" she asked.

"You fainted," he answered, trying to see how much she remembered. He wondered about that pig business. Did she think she was soiled because their kiss exploded into touches more intimate? Good Lord, how was he going to explain? And what about her feet? Kit looked at them. He didn't see anything wrong.

"Can you wiggle your toes?" he asked.

"Of course. Why?"

Kit sighed. "You asked me if you still had your feet."

Hallie frowned for a second and then giggled. He smiled, too, he couldn't help himself. He found her giggles infectious, and those childlike dimples did strange things to the pit of his stomach.

"I was confused," she explained. "You see I thought I was a pig—"

"Wait!" Kit ordered. "Hold it right there. I need to explain some things to you." He couldn't look at her innocent face when he explained that what happened wasn't her fault. "Hallie, it's no reflection on you. There are some things we can't control. What happened was a spontaneous reaction. I just wasn't thinking clearly. Since I'm older and more experienced, I shouldn't have let myself go like that."

Hallie's joyful face fell. She looked so disappointed, so abandoned. He felt like hell.

She looked down at her fidgeting fingers. "I guess you didn't really mean it?" she quietly asked.

How was he supposed to answer that?

"It's all right. You don't have to feel obligated. I can take care of the kids. I don't need any help, really. I understand how you must have felt sorry for me and promised something that you can't do. Don't worry, I understand. You're a busy man—"

"What are you talking about?"

"You promised to help, to take care of us. Earlier, before the . . ." Hallie colored slightly, "the little kiss."

Little kiss? Any more little kisses like that and his blood would evaporate. Then her words registered. She jumped at his bark of laughter. She thought he was abandoning them. She didn't feel soiled. Her eyes narrowed at his laughter, and he wanted to explain but he needed a moment to stop laughing.

"I don't think it's funny, Kit!"

"Hallie, wait. Don't get all fussed up. I meant what I said about helping you. That wasn't what I was talking about."

"It wasn't?"

"No, sweet. I'll do anything I can for you and the children. Your father left some documents naming a guardian."

"He did?" she asked, apprehension cracking her voice. "Who?"

"Me," Kit answered with a spark of pride.

She appeared horrified. "You're our guardian?" She pronounced the last word as if it sickened her.

"It's mostly for financial reasons. I'll handle the last consignments and transfer the funds, pay any bills, handle the sale of the *Sea Haven,* you understand, the business end of things."

"Sell the ship?" Hallie sat erect. "You're going to sell Da's ship?"

Everytime he tried to talk sense to Hallie, she twisted things all around and started questioning his judgment. He was damn tired of it. "Of course. He left it to me. I have my own business to run. What would I do with a ship?" Up went his defenses and his temper. "In case you haven't noticed, there isn't a big market for whaleships. You *have* looked at the bay recently, haven't you?"

Hallie ignored his sarcasm and spat her question. "To whom?"

The collar on Kit's shirt suddenly shrunk, a good inch.

"No one you would know," he evaded. "Now let's decide what to do about the children. Don't worry about the ship."

"I asked you a question. To whom are you selling the ship?" One at a time, each word was ejected past her pursed lips.

His jaw ached from clenching it. "Dickson and Hay."

"They're land agents. What would they want a ship for?" Hallie was thinking, and Kit could almost smell the smoke. "They're selling water lots, right?"

"What do you know about that?"

"I can read, Kit Howland! It was on the front page of the *Alta*. I know those men are making a lot of money selling water acreage. All they have to do is fill the shallow lots and—" Hallie clamped her mouth shut and her eyes narrowed suspiciously.

Her look made Kit want to disappear.

"You wouldn't," she denied, shaking her head and glaring at the same time. "Fill! You're going to sell the ship for fill! And you call yourself my father's friend? He loved that ship. There is no way I will let you destroy the *Sea Haven!*"

"You have no choice. The ship belongs to me, and I'll do anything I damn well please. No eighteen-year-old girl is going to tell me what to do!" Kit bellowed, standing up and half dumping the thankless brat on her sweet little butt.

Hallie leaped to her feet, prepared to fight him nose to nose. "You weren't treating me like a *girl* a little while ago, now were you?" Her words were syrup.

Kit stepped toward her. His hands knotted into fists as he kept himself from popping her. He was afraid he wouldn't be able to control the urge much longer.

"You . . . you heartless bastard!" Hallie egged.

"Shut up, Hallie!" Kit gripped the stair rail with his right hand.

"Don't you tell me to shut up, you Judas!"

"You're hysterical again. No one could reason with you when you're like this. I'll talk to you later." He stomped past the ungrateful witch, knowing he had to get away. Never, never had he been so bloody mad. He rounded the corner, seeing nothing but a red haze.

Hallie's last words screeched all the way out to the street. "How much will you get for it, thirty pieces of silver?"

Four hours later Hallie was still so mad she felt like kicking the stove barefoot. Instead, she pulled out the fire box under the black range and shoveled out the coal ash. Dumping the chalky powder into a tin pail, she stopped now and then to rescue a salvageable chunk of fuel. Clouds of soot puffed around her while she worked with a vengeance.

The frenzy of cleaning felt good and helped to vent her spleen. Her latest chore finished, she disposed of the ashes and cleaned up the dirty floor.

Lord, what a day. Hallie sank back against the welcome support of the stove, pressing her sore shoulders against its water reserve. Still half full of hot water, the metal tank radiated soothing warmth right through her tired muscles. Savoring the warm solitude, she planted her bottom on the hard floor and stretched out her long legs. Numb for an instant, her limbs suddenly flooded with swarms of tiny pinpricking sensations. She wiggled her feet awake, and once the tingle died, she brooded.

Her heart had gone through so much today that it felt cold and dark, like a burned-out lantern. She was exhausted, and deep within her, completely disillusioned. When God handed out judgment, she must have been in line for a second helping of stupidity. How could both she and Da have been so wrong about Kit's character, or lack thereof?

Obviously, *she* thought with her heart instead of her head, but Da, well, he always knew exactly what he was doing. He

119

seldom made mistakes. But he sure made one this time. There was no way she would let Kit Howland, her father's traitorous ex-friend, sell that ship for fill. The *Sea Haven* would be broken into masses of splintered wood and bent metal. Then it would be buried under piles of garbage, dirt, and sand. Hallie wasn't sure what she'd do about the ship, but she'd darn well do something! She snuggled closer to the comforting warmth of the water reservoir, and her heavy eyelids drifted closed.

She awoke with a start. Her nose twitched at a charred smell, and her first thought was that she'd gotten coal ashes up her nose. Wiping at it with one finger, she sniffed, but the odor was too strong, too fumey.

Hallie smelled smoke.

Chapter

Ten

Bolting upright, Hallie ran to the back door. As she jerked it open, clamorous shouts rumbled up from the street. Thick smoke sat like fog in the cool night air. Wind mixed with the fumes, shooting a wave of hot air and cinders right at her. She slammed the door and, clinging to the knob, paused to wipe the ash from her eyes. The knob suddenly heated, burning her fingers. She turned to a small window where an eerie orange glow swelled from the west. Once again, San Francisco was on fire.

Racing upstairs, Hallie flung open her bedroom door. Its loud crash awakened both Liv and Dagny. As soon as Hallie yelled "Fire!" both girls scurried through the room, randomly grabbing possessions.

"There's no time for that!" Hallie shouted. "Just grab your shoes—you'll need 'em." Hallie turned to get the boys just as flames exploded through the roof like an incandescent tornado. Red light and blasting, undulant heat tore through the crumbling roof, buffeting her face as she charged across the small hall toward the twins' bedroom.

Inside the room, one wall was on fire and the flames spread upward, devouring the thin wall as if it were paper.

Smoke spewed forth and wrapped its choking fumes around the small, squealing bundles huddled together in one bed. The boys' cries sounded hoarse and were almost instantly deafened by the rumble of flames and the shattering of window glass.

With a strength fed by fear, Hallie lifted a twin in each arm and fled the fiery room. Roof beams had crashed through the upper floor, leaving a gaping crater in the path to the other bedroom. The remaining floorboards splintered and the finish blistered and bubbled like a caldron's liquid. Hallie screamed toward the girls' room, calling her sisters' names and praying that they'd had the sense to get out of the house. There was no way she could get to them now.

The boys' fingers pinched her neck, and their small heads were wedged up to her chin. Hallie could barely see around them. She smashed her right hip along the stair railing, using it to help guide and support her. Tossing the sobbing boys slightly, she repositioned her numb arms under the twins' bottoms, holding them as close to her sides as possible.

While she descended the smoke-filled stairway, Hallie prayed the rail wouldn't give out. Cinder-filled smoke rushed up at her through the open front doorway. Hot embers singed her skin and brought cries of hurt and panic from the small boys. The banister held, and a thankful Hallie was just thinking that her prayers were answered when something seared her left leg. The pain sent her staggering through the door. She could feel flames licking an agonizing path up her leg, so she locked her fingers around the boys and rolled down into the street. As she tumbled, she pressed her hands to the ground, pushing her weight upward to keep from crushing the small, sobbing boys.

Her rolling stopped when she rammed into a hard wagon wheel, but she held the boys to her ribs, unwilling to let go even though the searing burn continued to cremate the skin on her leg. Someone tried to pull the boys from her arms but she held on, screaming, "No! Oh God, Nooo!"

Someone beat at her petticoats, and each swat crushed torturous wads of hot, scratchy fabric against her tender leg.

She looked up. It was Dagny who knelt over her, beating the flames from Hallie's smoldering skirts. Her leg felt on fire, as if it were blistering like the paint on the floorboards. She couldn't hold back her sobs, and she heard Duggie's pleading voice. "Put it out! Please, you've got to put it out!"

The wooden wheel vibrated against her temple. *Oh no, the wagon! It's going to run over us!* She let go of the boys, but before Hallie could order her own body to move, the vibration increased. Suddenly, her legs and torso were doused with a powerful spray of cool water.

Relief was instantaneous; relief from the hot pain, from the horrid fear of the crushing wagon wheel, and from the worry for her sisters' safety. Hallie knew that since Dagny was here, helping her, then Liv had to be all right too. Dagny would not have abandoned Liv. But just to be sure, Hallie forced herself to sit up despite the pain.

The blond giant, Duncan, clad in the leathern cape that proclaimed him a volunteer fireman, stood right in front of her. His hand held the now limp hose of the fire wagon—the one with the death-crushing wheel—and Duggie still gripped his forearm. Liv stood alongside, holding Gunnar and Knut by their small hands. All three were crying.

"Hallie, don't move. Your leg's burned," Dagny warned when Hallie started to rise. But Hallie stood up, slowly, with Duncan's strong hand helping to ease her ascent.

Hallie hugged the great big man who'd helped to save her and repeated her thanks over and over. He stood in awkward stiffness, as if he didn't know how to respond to her hug of gratitude. Then she stood back, wobbling a bit on her bad leg, and she smiled, but a shout shattered the moment.

"Hey, you! Get that engine pumping on those flames!"

Duncan turned to Hallie. "I have to get back. Can you make it on that leg, miss?"

"She's burned," Dagny cried. "Can't you help her?"

"It's all right, Duggie, I'll be okay. Let him get back to work." Hallie waved him off before ordering, "We've got to get out of here."

Dagny looked skeptical, but she nodded as Duncan and

his wagon pulled away. Hallie looked up and down the street, trying to see through the smoke which way looked the safest.

Although the flames appeared less intense toward the north end, that area was overflowing with people rushing down the long blocks toward the waterline. Hallie knew that if she couldn't get them near the bay, then her best bet was to seek high, barren ground. Telegraph Hill was the closest, but they'd have to travel south, where the fire still blazed. "Duggie, you'll have to carry Gunnar, I'll carry Knut. I couldn't get to their shoes. Liv, you hold my hand tight and don't let go no matter what."

Dagny picked up Gunnar. "But Hallie, what about your leg?"

"Don't worry, I'm fine. It's not that bad." Her leg hurt like the dickens, but she refused to slough off her responsibility on her younger sister. If she was going to head this family, then she'd start now. Besides, if her leg looked anything like it felt, the sight of it wouldn't ease the panic in the younger ones. She settled Knut on the flare of her hip and grabbed Liv's hand. "Stay as close as you can, Duggie, and hold Liv's other hand. If we get separated, we'll meet at the semaphore wall on Telegraph Hill. Okay?"

Dagny nodded, and they started up the grade. The farther they walked, the more crowded their path became. Wagons filled with store goods and carriages strewn with belongings were jammed together in the hazy street. At the crossroads packs of people flooded into any open street space. Horses, spooked by the smell of fire and the milling of the crowd, jostled and reared, one carriage overturning onto innocent prey trapped by the immobile mob.

The bone-chilling sound of screams raked the raucous air, and in the distance, explosions reverberated like Thor's hammering as the incendiary path met some combustible matter. Hallie and the others threaded through the mass, sometimes able to travel a few yards, and at other times the small group was smashed and pitched in the frenzied crush. Most of the victims had fled their homes with little or nothing and were clad in only their flimsy nightclothes. Others, with their hoarded belongings piled nearby, were digging shallow holes with their bare hands, creating dirt vaults for their precious possessions.

Hallie couldn't count the number of times the raw skin of her injured leg was battered and scraped. When they moved uphill, her limp eased, the angle of the slope making the climb less strenuous.

The fire grew more intense at the crest of the hill. Flames fanned into the night sky, appearing to coronate some of the majestic three-story buildings with a devastating crown of blue-orange brilliance. Almost a third of the city was ablaze, dominated by the reign of despotic fire, and the city's ruling power, the entire business district, lay in state, smoky and snuffed out, while its subjects, like the Fredriksens, trudged to the safety of the wet or barren borders.

When Hallie and the children finally reached the semaphore wall, volunteers were there to hand out blankets and help the injured find aid. A section of the hill was roped off to serve as a temporary hospital, and Dagny insisted that Hallie have her leg checked.

The twins had small burn blisters smattered across their exposed cheeks. Both Liv and Dagny had ash and black cinders covering them, and Hallie, like the twins, was beginning to swell with blistered burns where her fragile skin had been exposed. They clustered together in line, waiting for treatment. When they reached the tent opening, their angel of mercy appeared in the form of Agnes Treadwell.

"Landsakes, look at all of you!" Agnes hustled them just inside the crowded shelter to a small table near the canvas flap. Two lanterns swung from a roof pole, pouring their swaying streams of light onto the small area. The medicinal smell of antiseptic tainted the air, and volunteers nursed the disabled all around. Through the crowd Hallie caught a glimpse of shadows moving in a brightly lit area cordoned off with sheets. Moans and sobs welled from behind the translucent sheet, the sounds louder than the noisy chatter and cries in the open area. One loud wail had the twins clinging to her, and Knut unknowingly squeezed her burned leg. Hallie sucked in a pain-whistled breath.

Agnes was too occupied rinsing cloths in a bucket of water to notice Hallie or her reaction. "Set the little ones up here and I'll fix those burns." She wrung out the cloth and came at Knut.

He eyed her suspiciously. "You're not gonna hurt me are you?"

Agnes paused. "Of course not. I'm only going to wash off this dirty soot and then put some medicine on those blisters."

Hallie had been holding her breath, knowing the twins to be especially leery of anything remotely painful. Agnes apparently had more experience with four-year-old children than Hallie had imagined.

Agnes picked up a large brown bottle of antiseptic and poured it on a clean cloth. "Now, dearie, this might sting just a little, but—"

"What's a sting?" Knut demanded.

"Bees sting, dummy!" Gunnar stated. "And it hurts real bad!" The argument began.

Hallie shifted her weight off her bad leg, and Dagny must have noticed. She elbowed Hallie to get her attention. "Get your leg tended first," she whispered. "The boys' burns are minor, and they'll fight Mrs. Treadwell all night if they think they'll get away with it."

"Shhh! I'll get my leg looked at later." Hallie no more wanted the scatterbrained Mrs. Treadwell tending her hurts than did the boys.

Dagny lifted her chin to apparently tell Hallie a thing or two, but she was too late. Liv, the picture of innocence and goodness, approached the minister's wife.

"Mrs. Treadwell, Hallie's hurt real bad. Much worse than these two. Please help her." Liv's sweet little plea worked. She pointed a tattling finger at Hallie's leg.

"Well, Lord Almighty, why didn't you say something before? Let me see, Hallie." She plucked a lantern off the pole and leaned down to get a closer look. "My eyes! Sit up here right now while I go get a doctor."

Resigned to her fate, Hallie sat on the table. If the truth be told, ridding the leg of her weight relieved the aching throb. Four anxious, dingy faces stared at the angry red flesh of her exposed leg. Dagny looked worried, Liv was the color of pea soup, and the twins' identical faces mirrored their curiosity.

"Hallie?" whispered Knut.

"Hmm?"

"Does it . . . sting?"

"No, love. A sting isn't so bad, you know. It's just kind of a strong tickle." She took her first gander at her leg. It was horrid. The white skin on the inside of her calf and lower thigh had mottled into ridged bubbles of transparent sacs. Rims of the burn were charred to a dirty black crust, and the centers oozed blood and liquid. It was odd seeing the damage. She felt detached, impartial, as if she were only viewing the cankerous injury instead of experiencing it.

"My, my, what's this, young lady?" A harried man examined the burn. He noticed the fretful faces surrounding her. "I think, if this wound continues up as far as I think it does," he said, "that we'd better fix you up in the back area." He helped her off the table and led Hallie away from the others.

Cots lined the back wall of the tent, each bed filled with severely charred bodies. Women dipped toweling in buckets of milk and saturated the burned areas. Antiseptic couldn't conceal the stench of burned flesh that tainted this air. The doctor led Hallie to another sheeted area and helped her onto the table. "Lie flat, young lady, and let's have a look at this."

Hallie laid silently while the doctor worked, cleaning her burn and piercing the festering blisters.

"I'll just be a moment more, you're doing great. Better than most men I've seen. I'll need to put this salve on it and then wrap it to keep it clean." He walked to the head of the table, and Hallie wiped the quiet tears from the corners of her eyes.

His smile was kind, and he patted her hand. "You know, you'll have a scar from this."

Hallie nodded.

"Well, not to worry, my dear, any girl as pretty as you needn't worry about scarring. No one but your husband will ever see it. Now you'll need to change this bandage every few hours for a day or so, and then at morning and night for a week. Pop any blisters that fester up and apply this salve. Once it scabs over, you can stop wrapping it, but keep the salve on the scabs to keep them from cracking. The itch will drive you crazy, but it'll pass."

He finished his doctoring and helped her up. "You can use this salve on those facial burns too. Oh, and if there's any sign of infection, you come see me right away. Second floor, Brannan Building, California and Stockton, Dr. Jim."

Hallie found Agnes awaiting her at the entrance. The woman toddled toward her. "Are you all right, my dear? I got the others settled there on the hill. How's that leg? Do you need some help?"

"No, I'm just so tired. How were the boys? Did they give you any trouble?"

"Heavens no! We got them all fixed up and they're bedded down right up here." Agnes followed a narrow trail through the throng of homeless, tired people that covered the lower slopes.

The women reached a small group snuggled sleepily near the gate to the signal house. Blankets and precious pillows were piled high for their comfort, and Hallie knew this was Agnes's doing. "Thank you, Mrs. Treadwell. They've all been through so much today."

"It's nothing, my dear. I feel just terrible about this whole thing. The reverend and I lost the rectory, the church, and the school. We're staying up here tonight and with my sister until we can rebuild." Agnes placed her small hand on Hallie's arm. "I feel just dreadful. We can't offer you a place to stay right now."

"Don't you go worrying yourself over us. I'm sure I'll have no trouble finding a place." Hallie knew this was one of those times when a little lie would make things easier for everyone concerned. Although, she wondered briefly if it was a greater sin to lie to a preacher's wife. "We have a place to stay if we need it. My father made Mr. Howland our guardian, and he'll provide us with a home." *And pigs fly!*

Agnes couldn't disguise her relief. "Oh, that kind man! I'm sure the reverend will be as pleased as I am, my dear. We'll check on you soon. Take care now." She walked down the path a few feet before she turned. "Be sure to give Mr. Howland my best."

That man needs someone's best, Hallie thought. He was the last person on this earth she'd turn to now. Her injured leg pulsed painfully beneath the bandage. The area behind her knee hurt the worst. As Hallie laid down by her exhausted family, she stretched her leg out carefully, thoughts of the despicable Kit Howland absorbing her mind.

Just the idea that he'd sell the *Sea Haven* for fill was enough to recharge her fury here and now. She would stop him somehow. She leaned back against the incline of the hill, so tired she couldn't sleep.

Somewhere out there they'd have to find a place to live. But from the hundreds of sleeping bundles scattered in front of her, Hallie knew finding a new home wouldn't be easy. Part of the city now glowed like cooking coals, and other sections still raged with flames.

From here on the hillside the view was expansive, and she watched the fire spread toward the bay. At the water's edge smoke rose upward and hid the stars from view as it floated over the harbor. She could see all the ships abandoned in the bay. They were crammed together like herrings, and their masts spiraled into the air, creating a spiky forest against the horizon. Somewhere in that forest was the *Sea Haven*, awaiting its fate.

Just like us.

Why, it was the perfect solution! She would move the family on board the *Sea Haven*. They'd have a comfortable place to live and Kit wouldn't be able to sell the ship. After all, possession was eleven points of the law. And if it wasn't, she'd be able to keep an eye on Da's ship *and* his traitorous ex-friend.

For the first time in days Hallie smiled, a truly satisfied smile. Then she chuckled. She hadn't lied to Agnes Treadwell after all. Kit *was* providing them with a home. She snuggled contentedly into her blankets and closed her eyes, finally ready to sleep a sweet, contented sleep, for Haldis Fredriksen had another surefire scheme.

"We're going to lose it!" Kit shouted as flames engulfed another wall of the DeWitt warehouse. He ran past the laboring men of the bucket brigade to where Lee Prescott and some of his crew worked feverishly on a jammed water pump. Both men pulled on the pump crank but nothing happened. Lee jumped onto the bed and pried open the pump casing, while Kit planted his boot against the wagon bed to get better leverage and tried the crank again, straining and pulling on the metal bar with such exertion that his muscles quivered. "What the hell's wrong with it?"

"I can't tell," Lee yelled back, leaning down to poke around inside the mechanism.

Kit wedged his body between the wagon and a brick wall and kicked at the crank to loosen it. Finally it moved and the pump kicked in, but no water came through the hose. Lee hopped down and followed the hose to the water tank near the dock. He cupped his hands and hollered, "The tank's empty!" He pointed toward the bay. "It's low tide!"

Some of the men ran over and began to bail from the ebbing waterline into the tank, but Kit knew it was a lost cause. The whole city could burn before they could fill the thing pail by pail, especially with a receding tide. He paced the loading dock. "Goddammit, Lee! What can I do?" Kit shook with frustration. "This is useless! Look at that." He gestured to the group of men heaving bucket after bucket of saltwater on the flames. The water didn't douse the fire, it only turned to clouds of steam that billowed skyward with the smothering smoke.

The fire spread to the neighboring brick building. It was supposed to be fireproof, but the iron shutters and doors glowed red from the trapped heat, and within minutes they melted as the supporting walls crumbled like month-old bread.

"Can we get any barrels out through the waterside doors?" Lee asked.

Kit shook his head. "There's no way to get to them. The wharves were broken up to keep the fire from spreading out to the ships. Apparently, munitions and gunpowder are stored in the two barks at the end of the wharf."

The wind picked up, fanning the flames like giant bellows. Havoc and noise from the blaze filled the air, forcing Kit to move closer in order to hear Lee shout, "Where's the oil stored?"

"Near the back section." Kit pointed to a wall of flames.

"Jesus!" Lee swore. "What about the baleen?"

"The warehouseman handled the storage on it. That bone could be anywhere." Kit was about ready to give up. In a last effort, he searched for the warehouseman and found him bailing water out of the bay, into the shallow water reservoir. "I'm Howland. Where's the bone from the *Sea Haven* stored?"

"On the wharf side behind those barrels of vinegar."

"Vinegar? What vinegar?" Kit asked.

"There's eighty thousand gallons of vinegar stored in the front section."

"Christ, man! Why didn't you say something before now!" Kit raced back to the engine, firing orders along the way. He pulled men off the bucket line and had them roll out barrel after barrel of vinegar and dump it into the water tank. Lee cranked up the pump, and Kit and some others aimed the hose at the fiery building.

The sharp odor of vinegar filled the air, more acidic and suffocating than just the smoke alone. The flames lessened and began to die when a thunderous blast torched the fire a good twenty feet into the air as half the warehouse ignited. Winds fanned the blaze and flames lit the area like full sunlight. The right rear section of the building burned like hell, and along with it went all of Jan Fredriksen's whale oil.

A blast soared in the distance, its deep bass timbre drummed out over the bay. Waves lapped at one of the many neglected ships, rocking it, and the wind blew, the masts creaked, and deep within the dank hold, Abner awoke.

Old, slivered wood from the overhead bunk stared back at him. Sitting up, he rubbed his sleep-numb fingers into the sockets of his scratchy eyes and then peered into the room. The other bunks were empty, but an aged Chinese woman sat against a center beam, rocking with the ship's movement and rolling something between her long, clawed fingers. Square bricks of black, claylike opium were piled beside her, and she plucked small wads of the drug and rolled it into olive-sized balls, placing the black pellets in a reed basket.

Abner stood, his hand grasping support from the upper bunk. "Where am I?"

The woman rolled another ball.

"Answer me! Are we at sea?" His sharp voice tinged with panic.

She rocked, autistically, as her skillful fingers rolled. Then the woman turned her sunken, glazed eyes at him, staring blankly before she returned to her task.

God, what time is it? Abner felt for his pocket watch, but it wasn't there. *The gold! All his winnings!* He searched his pockets frantically and ripped the shabby linen from the bunk. They were gone.

He turned on shaky legs just as Chi Ho scurried down the steerage steps. Abner grabbed the man's silk tunic in his tight fists, and with a strength driven by drugged anger, flung the Chinaman onto the empty bunk.

"You thieving little bastard!" Abner's hands closed around the small man's fragile neck and his thumbs pressed into the chink's throat, garbling the foreign chatter that cackled from his mouth. His long, mandarin nails dug pits into Abner's wrists before the terrorized man miraculously pulled a silken pouch from beneath his clothing. Abner stopped choking him and grabbed it, jerking open the strings and dumping its contents on the bunk.

All his belongings, the gold, his watch, a few coins, and his door key, fell onto the dingy flat tick.

"You try kill Chi Ho!" The Chinaman cowered against the ship's wall. "I keep safe for you. No thieving bastard!" He turned and pointed to some bunks hidden in the deeper caverns of the hold. Three of the four beds were occupied, and one of the bundles awakened, turning his fathomless features toward them before he reached a long, filthy arm toward the old woman in a beckoning gesture.

"They steal if Chi Ho not keep for you."

Abner watched the woman pick up a tinder box and walk to the man's side. Sliding open the lid, she roasted an opium ball posed on a needle-shaped holder until the smoke drifted upward in a steady stream. Pulling a wooden crate from nearby, she stood on it, slowly waving the kindled ball under the man's nose. A sweet, searing smell filled the narrow cubicle.

Chi Ho pulled on Abner's coat. "You understand! No steal! Chi Ho help! Understand?"

"Sure, sure." Abner shrugged off Chi Ho's pestering hand and turned back to the bed, shoving his possessions into his pockets. He plucked up the gold bag and heaved it in his palm to check the weight. Having no idea how long he'd been here, he flipped open his watch. It was almost five o'clock. He had to get home before sunset to meet that slimy Duck. He pocketed the watch and headed for the short companionway, went out through the steerage and then up the last few steps to the deck.

There was no sunlight, but it wasn't night.

It was a smoky, gray dawn.

On shaky legs Abner slowly made his way to the rail, staring in silent horror at the sight before him. Light from the eastern sun cast the city's hills into smoldering shadows. The heart of San Francisco was destroyed, devoured by a carnivore of fire.

Something batted against the portside, capturing Abner's attention. It was a small dinghy tied to the ship's ladder. He had to get home! He climbed down the ladder and fell into the rocking boat. Sitting at the row bars, he grabbed the oars and rowed the few hundred yards to shore.

Within ten minutes he reached the devastated square behind his home. People pushed and crowded toward a guarded barrier, while others wandered aimlessly in circles, as if they had no direction. He elbowed his way to the front of the barrier and started to climb over it.

"Hey there, now. Where do ya think yer a-goin'?" A burly guard gripped Abner's arm and waved a pistol in his face.

"I'm Abner Brown, the undertaker. I live there and have to get home!" Abner tried to pull away from the man, but he was held fast.

"I've me orders. There's been plenty o' lootin' here tonight. Have ya got any proof who ya are?" he asked.

"Find Sheriff Hayes or one of his men. Any of them can identify me! And hurry up!"

At that moment a fire wagon rolled down the hill toward the barrier. Duncan was driving.

Abner grabbed the guard's arm and pointed. "Over there! That man on the wagon can identify me. Duncan!" Abner jumped up hollering. "Duncan!"

Pulling the wagon to a stop, Duncan slowly climbed down. The guard started to speak, but Abner interrupted. "Duncan, tell him who I am! He won't let me pass."

Duncan spoke to the guard. "He's who he says. The funeral home is behind this square."

The guard released Abner and he raced to the wagon. "Come on! You can drive me there faster!" Abner hopped onto the wagon seat, demanding that Duncan hurry.

They drove the few blocks to his home. The entire area was charred into burnt rubble. When they pulled up to the remains of his home, Abner was in shock, unprepared for the sight that greeted him. No walls were left, just piles and stacks of blackened wood. He jumped down and stepped over the debris scattered where the planked walk once paralleled his bustling street. He kicked at a beam and it slid down to the ashy ground. Cracked pieces of his mother's most valuable urn were scattered through smoldering remnants of his burl desk. The same one that scummy Duck had run his finger across. Abner's stomach churned, his head ached, and he lost control.

Duncan stood near the front wall, and Abner bent down and gathered the jagged pieces of the rare porcelain urn. He turned to Duncan and started flinging them at the huge man's pitying face. His look made Abner sick! "Get out! Get out!" he screamed hysterically. "You stupid, dumb son of a bitch! I don't need you!" He fell to his knees and scrounged up more ammunition, now throwing it in any direction. "It's gone! Everything . . . all gone." His voice, already high-pitched and frazzled, cracked.

He grabbed a scorched metal box, still hot from the fire. It sizzled in his hand. But he didn't let go. Instead, he grasped it tighter, gritting his teeth so hard his head and neck shook. He squeezed his eyes shut and tears edged through the corners. Finally he dropped the scalding box and stared at his hands. The hot, sharp corners charred vees into his palms, like Christ's nail holes. He threw back his head and screamed, a howling, pain-filled scream that rent the air as it expelled his soul—and his sanity.

Chapter

Eleven

"What a night!" Lee sat on an empty vinegar barrel and wiped his blackened hands on his filthy trousers.

Kit, who was just as smudged, slumped against the hard hub of a wagon wheel and stared at half the DeWitt warehouse. The other half, the one that housed his storage, was gone. "I lost it, Lee."

"I know, and I'm sorry. There wasn't a damn thing we could do, Kit. Don't stand there looking as if the whole loss is your fault. It's not."

"Oh yes it is. If I hadn't been so blasted anxious to make the Tabers pay through the nose, Jan's load would have been sold elsewhere." Kit turned to his friend. "You questioned my choice yourself, remember?"

"Oh hell, I didn't mean—"

"I know you weren't criticizing. Don't you start feeling guilty too. It was my doing, alone. But you were right, I wanted a taste of revenge so badly that I jeopardized Jan's entire shipment and his children's future." Kit leaned his head back and stared at the sky. "God, what an ass I am. When I think of how I rushed the crew to get the shipment unloaded and stored. Jesus." He shook his head in ironic disgust. "What time did the fire start?"

"Around midnight."

"Two hours. They finished only two goddamn hours earlier. If I had only waited until tomorrow, the second cargo would have been saved."

"Look, Kit, I know you're feeling pretty bad right now, but remember, you've still got my load to commission, and it's three times the size of Jan's. Substitute it to Taber. You'll still have your profit."

"And what about Hallie!" Kit snapped. He was tired and moody, but most of all he was damn mad at himself, so he lashed out at the only other person around, his best friend.

Lee looked startled, and then angry. Kit instantly regretted his outburst, and while he could blame his lapse on exhaustion, he still had no right to bite Lee's head off. Fool! His friend had worked just as hard as he had. But before he could apologize, or cover himself, Lee spoke. "I haven't forgotten about her." He looked directly at Kit and added emphatically, "Or the rest of Jan's children."

Kit gnawed on the side of his tongue, resisting the urge to bite the damn thing in two.

"You'll make a bundle from the sale of my load, if Taber's paying what you say. You'd be able to support them." Lee's wry expression changed to one of concern. "Or is there something you're not telling me? If you need money, Kit, or you're in some kind of trouble, I'll help out."

"No, that's not it. I'd have made enough from Jan's contract to build my warehouse and still live well. With the profit from your load, Christ, I'll be frigging loaded," Kit said, unable to keep the disgust from his voice. He pushed himself away from the supporting wheel and rubbed his hand over his tight neck muscles as he paced. "It's just different now. I feel even more responsible for them. I told myself you were right about my involvement with those kids, that I could just dole out the funds and occasionally check on them. My duty would end there. Well, I could no more do that now than I could have spit on that fire and put it out."

"Does Hallie have anything to do with your change of heart?"

Kit stopped pacing. "You know, you should have been a lawyer, not a whaler. Your questions shoot right to the quick."

"You didn't answer me."

"All right. Yes, it has to do with Hallie. When I went to check on her, I found her crying so damn hard. She looked helpless and pitiful, and in a moment of weakness I promised to help her. I told her I'd take the burden of the children. She tries to do everything herself, and . . ." Having admitted this, Kit suddenly felt the urge to justify his reasoning with an excuse. "I figured I owed it to Jan, anyway, since he entrusted them to me, but the next thing I knew, she was being unreasonable." Kit stopped speaking before the path of his words trespassed into forbidden territory—that of his less than paternal reaction to Hallie. And, too, Kit wasn't all too keen about admitting to Lee how wrong he'd been about her reaction to the sale of the *Sea Haven*. Lee would have trouble hiding his "I told you so" look, and then Kit would have to hit him. And he was just too tired, especially when he knew he still had to talk to Hallie, the hellion.

He turned back to Lee. "I really should go by the Fredriksen place and check on them. You want to come along?"

"Naw. I'm starved."

Kit chuckled. "Naturally."

The hint of a smile quirked Lee's lips too. "I think I'll make my way back to the ship." Standing, he examined his filthy clothes. "I need to clean up."

The two friends parted. Lee headed toward the bay, and Kit walked up the street, hoping to locate the nearest livery. But the one they frequented was no longer standing, and neither was anything else on that block.

People roamed through the rubble, gathering what they could salvage. As Kit walked farther, several wagons passed by him, carting away the massive amounts of burnt rubble.

Then more wagons loaded with fresh lumber and brick flooded the streets. The district was already rebuilding, and the smoke hadn't even cleared the bay.

It was probably natural, since this was the fifth fire in two years. San Francisco was experienced, and like the mythical phoenix, the city would rise, bigger and better, from her ashes. The more he walked, the more he realized how bad the fire had really been. Working all night on the warehouse had kept him too busy to know the extent of the damage, but now he was seeing it firsthand, and it was frightening. The number of horse-drawn vehicles traversing the area told Kit that his chances of finding a horse or a team and wagon would be nil. It looked as if every conveyance in the city was being put to use in the burned district.

A quarter of an hour later he rounded the corner of Serra Street. In each direction blocks were demolished, to the degree that not one building, wood or brick, still stood. As he neared Hallie's home, the destruction continued. Kit had assumed they would be safe since no fires had ever spread into the Happy Valley district. But now he was struck by the possibility that Hallie and the children might not be safe. His tired legs moved faster as he raced toward the Fredriksen home. Wagons blocked his path, so he wormed his way through, stopping finally in front of the heap that had once been Jan's home.

Looking at the devastation made his gut wrench, and he turned, pale-faced, toward the swarm of wagons. Just beyond, a group of men dug through the powdery heap of a brick building that had stood across the street. One man shouted, "Here's two more!"

The men began to pull debris away, uncovering the dead bodies of the fire's victims. The sight made Kit break out in a deep sweat. Afraid to ask the question but knowing he must, he walked to where one of the men stood, fastening a canvas tarp over a wagon. "Have they searched that house yet?" Kit pointed to Hallie's home.

The man stared at him briefly. "Nope, they was some of the lucky ones; they got out."

"Thank God." Kit breathed a sigh of relief. Of course, he still had to find them. "Did you hear where they went?"

"I was here, fighting the fire, when they escaped." He straightened the tarp and checked the rope ties. "One of 'em, a tall blond, come barreling outta the door, burning like the hubs o' hell. I thought she was a goner for sure. Heard tell someone put the fire out, but next time I looked up," he spun around to face Kit, "they was gone—" The man scratched his head in bewilderment and searched the empty spot where Kit had stood only moments before. The man shrugged and then continued his work.

Beyond the work crowd, Kit raced up the steep street, stopping every so often to question someone, anyone, who might have seen the Fredriksens.

Five hours later Kit still hadn't found them. He'd been to three volunteer centers and every makeshift hospital he could find, and still he had no news. Most of those who might have known Hallie and the kids had been displaced by the fire. He'd checked all the places he'd thought they might go, and though he'd heard there had been a shelter on Telegraph Hill, someone said the victims had been moved out by noon. Before he checked out this last lead, he made his way toward Oatt's, thinking that they might have gone there for clothing or supplies.

But when he arrived, the mercantile had a line so long it looked like the Pike Street Post Office on mail steamer day. Men stood in their knit underwear, barefoot, with blankets or coats flung over their shoulders, and women, dressed in assorted nightwear, wrapped their makeshift coverings tightly from neck to foot. From the adjacent alley a clerk wheeled out a cart heaped with articles of clothing, and the victims of the fire clamored to purchase garments of any kind from the mishmash of goods available.

Kit edged into the alleyway, trying to be as inconspicuous as possible. He hurried to the side door and whipped inside. The storeroom appeared ransacked. Trunks, boxes, and crates were upended from one side of the small room to the other. He stepped over the mess and made his way to the draped doorway. The store's interior could only be described as absolute chaos. There must have been over fifty people sardined into the place, and everything from stockings to bags of coffee beans flew through the air like goose feathers on plucking day.

A small, harried, bald man plowed through the doorway, stopping to catch a panicked breath. He jumped when he saw **Kit**, but recognition lit his face almost immediately. "Whew. Kit, you startled me! What're you doing back here? As you can see, there's not much left."

"I'm sorry, Charles, I just need some information. Have any of the Fredriksen bunch been in here? They were burned out and I can't locate them. I heard Hallie, the oldest, was hurt."

"They were here earlier, bought a few things, and I've a larger order to fill and deliver as soon as I can. Miss Fredriksen looked all right to me, considering the circumstances. They looked like everyone else. Half dressed and a little scorched, but not hurt badly."

"Thank God," Kit murmured, relieved. "Where are they?"

"On their father's ship, the *Sea Haven*. I'm to have the goods delivered to the east end of the Broadway Wharf."

The *Sea Haven*. Of course! "Thanks, Charles. By the way, I'll be handling everything for them now. You heard Jan was killed on the last voyage?"

"No, I hadn't heard. Too bad, though, he was a good man." Charles Oatt pushed away from the doorjamb and shook his head. "That's quite a brood. I don't envy you, Kit." He cringed when the clatter from the other room rose a full octave higher. Eyeing the doorway with a look that was part fearful and part disgusted, he added, "Well, I've got to get back in there. Do you need anything?"

Kit shook his head. "No."

"Good. I doubt I'd know where to look." He walked to

the side door and opened it. "I need to bolt this after you. God forbid if some of that hoard were to come through here too. They'd demolish the place."

Kit moved down the alley and onto the street, his worries relieved after talking to the store owner. Hallie and the children were alive, and contrary to what he'd heard, she was unharmed. Now that he thought about it, he really should have guessed their whereabouts. It made perfect sense for them to go to the ship. The *Sea Haven* was familiar and should be relatively safe. By now the crew would have signed on elsewhere. They'd understood Kit's plans, and experienced, able-bodied seamen had no trouble securing a place on another ship. Gold fever still lured sailors from their ships, and finding replacements for them was a burden that plagued most sea captains.

Locating Hallie on the ship would be so much easier than combing the streets, as he had been. Yes, it was a smart thing to do. Hallie had really used her head. That thought stopped Kit dead in his tracks. Somehow, the idea of Hallie using her head was just too premonitory.

"Here, let me try," Dagny said, pushing Hallie's frustrated hands away. She wedged her fingers under the little, black satin shoulder ribbons and tried to pull upward. Nothing happened. Well, something did happen. The burgeoning swells of Hallie's large breasts wiggled in the dress bodice like a jellyfish atop the sea.

"Oh drat!" Hallie looked down at the dress, the scarlet silk and black beaded lace gawked right back. "How am I supposed to wear this in public?"

"Just don't speak any French and you'll be fine," Dagny teased.

But Hallie, forced into a low-cut and gaudy dress, wasn't amused. She was just mentally translating a scathing French comeback when Liv pranced through the cabin door.

"Why shouldn't she speak French?" Liv asked.

The two older sisters eyed each other, both seeking some fabricated answer because they knew they couldn't explain to Liv that in San Francisco being French and being a prostitute were synonymous.

"Never mind!" Hallie and Dagny responded simultaneously.

"Hmmp! I thought so. Whenever I hear anything really *good,* you two tell me to never mind. How am I ever supposed to learn anything if you won't tell me?" Liv plopped her impudent little bottom on a bunk. "Next time Reverend Treadwell asks me what I've learned, I'm going to tell him nothing, and that it's all your fault. You're stippling me!"

Hallie frowned. "Stipple?"

"I think she means stifle," Dagny clarified.

"Oh. Well, young lady," Hallie looked at Liv with a nonchalance she was far from feeling, "since the school burned down, you won't have to worry for a week or so. Agnes said it will take that long before the reverend can start classes again. So you needn't concern yourself with all that learning. And I would hate to think either Duggie or I were 'stifling' you. If you're really afraid of falling behind, I could make sure you *learn.* I would teach you myself, all day, every day, in this cabin . . ."

Liv's open mouth clamped shut. After a few pregnant seconds she rested her elbow on her swinging, gangly legs and watched her sisters fiddle with the low-cut dress.

In the mirror above her father's ship sink, Hallie caught Dagny's reflection as she examined her, somewhat futilely. Hallie was envious. Dagny wore a lovely, pale blue dress with deeper blue stripes which seemed to accentuate her petite and delicate form. When they had left the volunteer station that morning, Hallie herded them straight to Oatt's to get clothing and supplies. For Hallie, the available clothing was limited.

There must have been thirty dresses that would fit petite Dagny, but there were only three pieces that would accommodate Hallie's bust, and only two of the three were dresses. One dress was made for someone under five feet. Hallie could have worn her mother's ruffled pantalets with it, and she would have looked like a shepardess guiding her little lambs.

This red thing she had on was the other dress, and while it covered her long legs, it didn't cover much of her chest, and the color was blinding.

"Hallie?"

"What, Liv?"

"I think you've got your dress on backward."

Hallie dropped the dress bodice. That did it! She ripped at the dress hooks and in a frustrated voice asked, "Would you two please go check on the boys and dig up something in the galley for supper?"

Dagny pulled a protesting Liv from the small cabin, and when the door closed, Hallie tore off the dress. She couldn't wear this. She walked over to the other bundle of clothes, unfolded them and laid them out on the bunk. She took off the one petticoat she'd bought and tossed it and the red dress onto a heap of rope in the corner.

Hallie put on her corset cover and heaved a relieved sigh. Now her deep cleavage was safely concealed by the high neckline of the linen undergarment. Then she picked up the frilly, white chemisette and slipped her arms through its sleeveless armholes.

Sitting on the bunk, Hallie looked at the remaining pieces of the reform dress. She set the short, blue jacket aside and tried to understand the fit of the lower two pieces. She reached into the brown wrapping paper and pulled out the sketch Mr. Oatt had given her from a past *Godey's Ladies Book*. Strange though the billowy bottoms were, they really did look comfortable. And the seams would better protect her bandage. The bulk of the wound dressing was knotted high on her thigh, and when she walked, it chafed her tender skin. She pulled aside the inside seam opening on her drawers and eyed the bandage. It covered her leg from ankle to upper thigh, and despite the soothing salve, underneath the cloth strips it still felt like her skin was being eaten right through.

Hallie wobbled slightly as the ship creaked and rocked

from a sharp gust of wind. Although her leg was hot, she was chilled, and with good reason. There was no coal in the small cabin brazier, and the late afternoon breeze was whipping its way across the bay, chilling the damp ship and turning the interior air downright cold. Hallie picked up the other garments and began to dress, hoping that the advertisements hadn't lied about the practicality and warmth of Amelia Jenks Bloomer's healthful but bizarre new attire.

Chapter

Twelve

Kit swung his leg over the side of the *Sea Haven* and leaped onto the deserted deck. The northwest wind blew in short spurts, whipping flecks of ash from his dark, unruly hair. He brushed it aside, and as he walked toward the steerage and down the companionway, he could smell the stench of smoke from his gritty clothes. He needed a bath, but first he needed to see for himself that Hallie and the others were unharmed.

"Hello! Is anyone aboard? Hallie? Helloo!"

The two small cabins in the aft were empty. Jan's cabin was just beyond, and Kit opened the door.

Hallie was inside, and she was all right. At least he thought it was Hallie. She was bent over tying something around her ankle, and that fanny sure looked like hers, even if there weren't any leaves on it this time. "Hallie?"

She shot upright and spun around, obviously taken by surprise. "Kit!" she sputtered, clutching the waistband of the strangest garment Kit had ever seen. It looked like huge, billowing drawers, but the fabric was heavy trouser fabric instead of the fine stuff used for underwear. He couldn't help but stare, trying to figure out what the hell she was wearing.

"You're the rudest man. You could have knocked."

She looked ridiculous, standing there bare-armed, scolding him in those . . . things. Kit had to laugh.

"What are you wearing?" he asked between guffaws.

She looked down and then quickly spun around. "I'm dressing. Get out."

"You mean there's more to that . . . that getup?" Kit pushed away from the doorjamb and sauntered over to her father's desk. He pushed aside a scrimshaw paperweight and hitched his hip on the edge of the oak top. Dusting the ashes from his trousers, he rested his arm on his leg so he would be nice and comfortable while he was entertained. "This I've got to see."

"I said, get out!" Hallie's face was blood-red.

Kit spun the paperweight. "Why should I? Your modesty is covered." He pushed away from the desk and walked slowly around her, scrutinizing her from head to foot. He had a hard time keeping a straight face. "Covered by what, I don't know, but you are covered."

"This is a reform dress," she informed him in a tone that indicated her superior knowledge.

"As in reformatory? How appropriate. That would be a great place for you."

"No," she retorted, "as in abolish—you know, correct evils. And your plans for this ship are definitely evil!" She stomped her foot, apparently to emphasize her next words. "I won't let you do it!"

"Oh?" Kit picked up a piece of clothing from the bed. It looked like half of a skirt—the top half. He held it up and looked at her through the hole he assumed was the waistband. "How do you intend to stop me?" he asked, turning the thing this way and that, trying to understand its purpose.

Hallie jerked the overskirt out of his hands and threw it behind her. "We're going to live here."

"Oh?"

"Yes. You could call it—" She stopped.

Kit could see her mental search reflected on her face.

"Homesteading!" Her eyes lit with naive pride. "We're going to homestead the *Sea Haven*."

"There's only one problem." Kit brushed the gray ashes from the shoulder of his dark coat.

"What?"

"The *Sea Haven* is mine. You can't homestead someone else's property."

"Oh." Her prideful face fell. Then, with a casual wave of her hand, she dismissed that theory and turned to her female ammunition, stubbornness. "Well, we're still not leaving."

Kit had crossed over to the open porthole, and he stood staring at the bay, not because he wanted to look at anything in particular, but to avoid looking at Hallie. Her facial expressions touched something deep within him, something he didn't want touched. He shoved his hands in his pockets and rocked back slightly on his heels, still staring outside. "Hallie-girl, you'll leave if I want you to leave. I can cart your sweet fanny off of here faster than hell could scorch a feather."

"Try it!"

He spun around, ready to do just that, but instead of facing an insolent, stubborn, beautiful blond brat, he faced the barrel of her father's Navy Colt, in the shaky hand of that same blond brat.

"What are you doing?" Kit bellowed. "Put that thing down before you hurt someone." He stepped toward her.

"Don't move! I mean it, Kit. You will not carry me off this ship and you will not sell it for fill!" She now held the gun in two shaky hands.

Prudence stopped him, that and the look of utter fear on her face. If she was as scared as she looked, his best bet would be to humor her. Waving that gun around when she was so frightened could be disastrous, especially from his point of view—centered on that long, dark, quivering gun barrel.

"Get off the ship!" Her aim dropped an inch. "Now!"

Kit held his hands out in front of him and slowly backed out of the cabin. He needed to think of some way to get that thing away from her before she hurt one of them. She followed him out the door into the narrow companionway. He backed up the stairs and contemplated slamming down the hatch door, but he discarded that plan because the gun could blow the door and him clear to Kingdom Come. Maybe he'd be able to get the weapon when Hallie maneuvered the stairs. Women always had trouble with shipboard stairs. Lack of space forced ship companionways into little more than steep, narrow ladders, and women's huge skirts would—dammit!—she had those prison-pant things on.

It irritated him even more when Hallie ascended the stairs. The freedom of movement must have surprised her, too, because she looked down at her attire as if astounded. That gave Kit the opening he needed.

His long arm shot out and grabbed her wrist, forcing her arm and the gun barrel straight into the air. His body pinned hers to the locker wall just as the gun discharged, sending a shower of wood splinters raining on them. He could feel her head burrowing into his chest while he coughed from the descending cloud of sawdust. The cloud settled but neither combatant moved.

And it was quiet, so quiet that you could almost hear the sun set.

The gun dropped from Hallie's numb hand into a tin bucket, and the resulting clatter rang clear through every tooth in her head. She was afraid to look up, but Kit's fingers released their tight hold on her wrist, and his hand slid, slowly, down the bare skin of her inner arm, over the sensitive hollow of her armpit; and his palm, hot and damp, closed over her hard-tipped breast.

Hallie could feel his eyes boring their heat into the top of her head, but still she fought the overpowering urge to look up. She was afraid, and though Kit Howland angered her—though he didn't give a fig about her father's ship, though he was arrogant, demanding, and even though he laughed at her—Hallie couldn't deny that he still owned her heart. It was no different today than two years ago. Only now she wasn't a gawky young girl; she was a woman. And when he touched her, oh Lord, she became weak, malleable.

Her body was like clay, his hands were the sculptor's, and passion between them became that magic creativity—the force that forms a priceless work of art.

The action of his hand as it held her, and felt her, was now something she craved, like the intimate friction of his tongue in her mouth. When his lips whispered across her temple, her own lips parted instinctively, and she had no choice but to surrender and look up into the dark, verdant depths of him. With eyes open they kissed, tonguing and watching, in a silent, sensual duel. Once again Kit wedged his knee between her legs, but this time, when her burned leg needed the protective barrier of her petticoats, that protection wasn't there. Hallie shoved Kit away, spurred by the excruciating pain that shot through her. It dissolved the passion that had only moments before ruled her body and her mind.

Hallie turned her shoulder into the wall, waiting for the pain to pass. The wall was cool against her fiery skin, and its support felt heavensent. She could hear Kit mumbling, and she looked up.

"For Christ's sake, your face is green." Kit's angry expression changed to one of panic. "You're not going to faint again, are you?"

Before Hallie could answer, Kit picked her up and carried her out the afterhouse door. "Breathe!" he ordered the second they were out on the open deck.

"You can put me down, Kit," Hallie responded. The pain in her leg had lessened to a slow throb.

"Can't you do anything I say? Breathe!"

"But—"

"Breathe, dammit!"

Her pain dimmed, replaced by the irritation of Kit Howland's words. He had no reason to shout at her like that. She surely didn't need *him* to tell *her* what to do. She just hated it when people started telling her—an adult—what *they* thought *she* should do. It made her feel . . . stupid, and she was not stupid! *So, he wants me to breathe, does he?*

Hallie leaned her face right into his and started panting as hard as she could.

"Hi."

Both Hallie and Kit looked down at Knut.

"Whatcha doing?"

"Breathing," Hallie said in an exaggerated tone.

"Pushing her luck," Kit shot back with equal meaning.

"Put . . . me . . . down," Hallie ordered through her locked jaw. She glared at Kit when he jostled her slightly, for she knew the gesture was calculated to emphasize his power over her. When he pulled her closer to his big chest, her temper burned all the hotter. "I said, put me down."

Kit didn't budge. Instead, he willingly joined her in a stubborn stare-down.

"Hallie? Know what?" Knut asked.

The child's question forced her to bow out of the battle of wills, but she couldn't resist giving Kit's chest one hard shove. It put her a few safe inches away.

"What?" Hallie responded absently. Kit finally set her down, and that made her feel better, until she caught a gander at his face. It was bathed in a confident "I won" smile.

"Gunnar has a gun."

"What!" Hallie shrieked.

Kit sped past her into the afterhouse. He returned seconds later with the gun in one hand and Gunnar tucked safely under his arm. He set the boy down, none too gently, and put the gun on the tool shelf above his head.

When he turned again, he paused, and then his eyes narrowed at the twins, who were now standing side by side.

"Guns are not toys," he said, his angry voice holding fast the twins' attention.

"But we don't have any more toys," one boy announced.

"They all burnt!" finished the other.

"But playing with a gun is dangerous!" Hallie scolded. "You two are nev—"

"Let me handle this, Hallie," Kit interrupted.

"Wait just a minute—" Hallie said, wondering who the heck he thought he was. They were her brothers.

"I'll handle it!" Kit picked up Hallie and plopped her down on the nearby hatch hood.

She felt like a pesky fly that he'd just swatted away. All right, mister, she thought, you want to handle this? Fine.

Hallie sat back, wondering what Kit would do. While her heart went out to the bored twins, guns were not something to play with. She shuddered at the thought of what might have happened. Da would have tanned Gunnar's hide, toys or not, and even she had to admit that she'd have probably given the little boy a swat. But with Kit, she just didn't know how he'd handle Gunnar, and that bothered her. She had been the boys' authority figure for months now, and suddenly here was Kit Howland trying to supplant her. Just who did he think he was?

Kit stepped closer to the twins, still staring intently, and then he looked at Knut. "Which one are you?"

The twins looked at each other and smiled. Hallie could see their plans register all over those devious and identical little faces. She had to smother her own grin, knowing from the look they exchanged that neither of them would pass up a chance to fool someone. With the family, they would tattle and argue, but with others, the twins had an unbreakable bond of loyalty, especially if it meant that one of them was going to get in trouble.

Hallie chewed on her cheek to keep from laughing at Kit's frustrated expression. When he turned to her for help, she got immense satisfaction out of her exaggerated shrug. "You were going to handle this, remember?" she reminded him.

His green eyes narrowed.

Hallie took great pleasure in thoroughly examining the nails on her left hand before she asked, "What do you intend to do?"

"Teach him a lesson. Now tell me which one is which." Kit crossed his arms and waited, arrogantly, expectantly.

"How?"

"Just never you mind."

"Are you going to hit him?"

"I want to teach him a lesson. What do you think your father would have done?" The volume of Kit's voice grew.

"That doesn't matter since you're *not* our father."

"I'm your guardian, hand-picked by your father. You all had better get used to doing as I say." Now he was shouting.

"Then don't look to me for help. You'd better learn to tell them apart yourself." Hallie heaved a sigh and smirked just a little. "Since you're going to be doing all this ordering around."

Kit stooped down, eye level with the boys. In utter silence he stared at them, appearing to be memorizing every pore, every freckle, every burn mark on their suddenly serious little faces. "I'll tell you both this just once. Guns are not for children. Never, never are you boys to touch any gun, do you understand?"

They nodded.

"Our toys were all burnt up," Knut repeated, and then both boys began to whimper.

Kit put his hands on the boys' shoulders. "I understand, and I'll try to do something about that, but no more playing with guns." He straightened and glowered at Hallie.

"Yoo-hoo, Christopher! Yoo-hoo, over here!"

A look of true horror replaced the menace Kit had been wearing. Hallie turned toward the high-pitched voice at the same time Kit did. Lee Prescott stood on the deck, helping a short, middle-aged woman climb on board. Her hair, a mass of curls the exact color of a ripe persimmon, waved from beneath the wide, flat brim of her straw bonnet. But to Hallie the most astounding thing was the woman's apparel She was clad in an emerald-green version of Amelia Jenks Bloomer's reform dress.

Like Queen Victoria with her scepter, she raised her green parasol imperiously. "Get over here, young man, and greet your aunt properly!"

It amazed Hallie that a man over thirty could actually look like he was a nine-year-old in trouble. Kit slowly walked toward his aunt. As he passed Hallie, she dismissed that thought, for no child could mumble such an inventive string of curses.

Not wanting to pass up such a prime opportunity, she whispered, just loud enough for him to hear, "Now I understand where you get your obnoxious habit of ordering everyone around. It runs in your family."

Hallie could tell exactly when her words penetrated his blue mumbles because he paused and his shoulders stiffened.

His aunt placed her gloved hands on Kit's forearms and she looked up at him. "Humph! Don't look suicidal to me. Could use a bath, though." She shoved her parasol into Lee's stomach. "Here, young man, make yourself useful and hold this."

She dug through her purse, pulled out a pair of spectacles, and held them up toward the sun. She helped herself to the handkerchief in Kit's top pocket and snapped it open. Ash and soot flew through the air. Tossing the linen square overboard, she used her overskirt to polish the lenses. Then she pushed the frames on her noble nose and studied her towering nephew, looking him up and down.

"Still smoking that godforsaken pipe, are you young man?" Before Kit could answer, she went on, "Filthy habit, gets ash on everything!"

"Aunt Maddie, there was a fire. Didn't you see it when you docked?" Kit stared at his aunt.

"A fire? Oh, that's right," she said absentmindedly. Then her expression changed. "Good heavens! Don't tell me your house burned down. If I have to stay in a hotel after spending four extra weeks on that floating vermin den Charles Taber calls a ship, well, you can bet—"

"Calm down, Maddie, my house is fine," Kit interrupted. "Only a third of the city burned, Happy Valley and the business district. My place is on Fern Hill, that one over there." He turned and pointed to one of the unburned hillsides. "Come on, I'll take you home."

"Just a minute, Christopher. Who are they?" Maddie

pointed at Hallie and the twins, and again without giving
Kit a chance to answer, she drew her own conclusions.
"Well, good for you! It's about time you forgot that flighty
Taber girl you were stupid enough to marry. I'm glad you
picked a strong one this time. Just look at her! She's tall
and . . . good God, are those twins? Never mind, don't
answer that, I can see they are! That's all the better, means
she's fertile too."

Hallie heard Lee's laughter, and if she weren't so stunned,
she probably would have been laughing too.

Kit grabbed his aunt by the arm. "Hold it, Maddie. I'm
not married."

"Oh." Maddie's exuberance deflated.

Kit led her over to where Hallie still stood, flanked by her
twin brothers. She had never seen anyone quite like Kit's
aunt. While she felt overwhelmed and somewhat uncomfortable about the woman's assumption, something told
Hallie that, mouthy and bold as she was, Kit's aunt would be
a friend.

"Aunt Maddie," Kit said, "this is Hallie Fredriksen and
her two brothers, Gunnar and Knut."

"Which is which?" Maddie asked.

"I'm Hallie."

Maddie laughed, a hearty deep laugh that sank in decibel
a full octave lower than her scolding voice. Her laughter
petered out, but she still smiled warmly at Hallie. "I love
your ensemble, my dear. Shows extreme good taste."

Hallie grinned. "Thank you. I like yours too." She felt one
of the twins fidgeting with her pants leg. "Oh, this is Knut."
She put her hands on the little boy's shoulders and then
turned to the twin on her right. "And this is Gunnar." Hallie
smiled directly at Kit as she identified the boys for Maddie.

Kit wasn't smiling. "I've been named guardian of the
Fredriksens."

Maddie perked up. "Really?"

"Hallie has two sisters too," Kit added, completely oblivious to Maddie's sudden brightness.

"How old are they?" Maddie asked, with what Hallie thought to be exaggerated indifference.

"Dagny's sixteen and Liv's nine—"

"Oh, that's good, they're too young," Maddie said.

Hallie grinned, and Maddie, who had removed her spectacles, gave her a sly wink. Kit looked confused.

"Well, Christopher, I want to get settled, and you need a bath! Haven't changed much in twenty years. I still have to tell you when to bathe." Maddie started again. "You know what he used to do?"

"What?" Lee asked, his grin wide and his blue eyes sparkling.

"Never mind!" Kit broke in. "Come along, Maddie, I'll take you home."

Lee handed Maddie her parasol, offered her his arm, and as they walked back toward the gangway, Hallie could hear him pumping Maddie about Kit's childhood antics.

Kit looked at Hallie. "I'll be back tomorrow."

He followed the others. Hallie waited until Lee and Maddie were over the side. Then Hallie called out, "Oh, Kit?"

He stopped and looked at her. Smiling, she dangled the gun from her fingers. "I'll reload."

"Good God in heaven! The bottom of a baby pram is cleaner than this . . . this hovel!"

Kit cringed at Maddie's assessment of his home. He looked around the dingy interior and had to admit that it wasn't particularly clean. Cobwebs hung from the parlor's high ceiling, and boxes and crates were piled on the bare and dusty wooden floor. "Now, Maddie, I never use this room."

"Don't you 'now Maddie' me, Christopher Howland. It's little wonder you don't use this room. It's not fit for human use!"

Maddie pulled off her gloves and marched down the hall toward the other rooms. She shoved the kitchen door open, looked inside for a moment, and then turned back around. "How long have you lived here?"

"Three years," Kit answered, walking to the kitchen doorway. "Why?"

"What's in that crate?" Maddie pointed at a huge wooden crate that took up most of the left side of the room.

"The range."

"Did you just order it?"

"Uh . . . no. It came with the place."

"I see." Maddie walked past the crate and threw her gloves onto the sinkboard. She plucked a pail off the floor and set it beneath the pump. Grabbing the black pump handle, she worked it up and down. After a few chugs, rusty red water flowed in bursts from the spigot. "Humph! At least you have water." She scanned the room, obviously looking for something in particular. "How do you heat the water if the range is still crated?"

"I don't. I use the public bathhouse, and when I'm at home, I use cold water."

"Well, *I* won't use a *public* bath! Lord only knows what one would catch. And," Maddie shivered with disgust, "I refuse to use cold water." She grabbed her gloves, slapping them impatiently on her palm. Her action reminded Kit of a childhood incident with a hickory switch. Suddenly he felt as if he were ten and about to get a licking.

"Show me the other rooms," she ordered, and walked out. Kit sighed and followed her out of the kitchen, knowing that his bossy aunt was going to give him hell for the condition of the remaining rooms, all six of them.

Three hours later he had the range together and the flue pipe secured. A loud thud sounded from the room above him, and he shook his exhausted head. She was still at it. He'd given his aunt the tour she wanted and gotten his ears chewed off. She declared the downstairs study and his bedroom the only rooms that were livable, and then she commandeered his bedroom, telling Kit he could sleep on the sofa in the small downstairs study until she cleaned up the rest of the place.

He stifled a yawn. Here it was Sunday evening, and he hadn't slept since he'd been at Rancho Sausalito on Friday night, and then it had only been for three or four hours. He was tired, his muscles ached from exhaustion, and he was starved.

He went over to the pantry and began to rummage through its narrow cabinets. Then he opened the flour bin and a bottle of whiskey banged against the tin lining of the drawer. A drink wouldn't help his stomach, although it might lessen the pain of his aunt's chaotic presence. Kit thought that he might just take it to bed with him. Of course, with his aunt here, the bottle of whiskey would probably be the only thing he'd be taking to bed for a damn long time.

In the top cabinet he found a tin of soda crackers, and he stuffed them into his mouth, two at a time, while he continued his famished search. Sitting behind an empty lard container was a forgotten crock of berry jam. He grabbed it like a dying sinner grips the Good Book, then tugged at the seal. It wouldn't budge.

"I know there's a knife around here somewhere," he mumbled aloud, or at least as loud as he could with a mouthful of dry crackers. He opened and slammed shut a few drawers, still searching for the knife, and then he looked up.

"Ah-hah!" Kit spotted it on the windowsill under a large, yellowish chunk of lye soap. Grabbing the knife, he cut through the waxy cloth seal on the crock, dipped the crackers into the dark jam, and savored the sweet taste and the satisfying feeling of food plummeting to his empty stomach.

With the cracker tin shoved under an arm and the jam in one hand, he grabbed the bottle of whiskey and went into his study. He set down his meal and eyed the torturous shape of the sofa. Unbuttoning his vest and wadding it into a tight ball, he stuffed it against the hard wooden sofa arm and then settled back, feet up and head resting on the makeshift pillow. He took a long swig of the whiskey, enjoying its fiery trail to his stomach.

He looked around the room. It wasn't filthy, a little dusty maybe . . . The rich mahogany furniture was covered with a gray film that seemed to jump out at him. He dipped a cracker into the jam, shoved it into his mouth, and thoughtfully chewed. He knew this would happen. His aunt arrived, and his life, which was going along just fine, became all complicated.

Of course, if he were honest with himself, he would have to admit that most of his complications preceded Maddie's arrival. Maybe he could blame his father, since everything in the letter was the beginning of Kit's trouble. Nah! He couldn't blame his father or Maddie for his problems with Hallie, or for the fire, or for the loss of Jan's shipment, but she was destroying his only refuge. He liked his messy house. Kit scanned the room. It was a *man's* home.

He took another swig. He didn't have to worry about where he put his feet. He'd even rented out the upstairs rooms to some seamen he'd known, and no one ever complained. And hell, the public bathhouse was great! He could bathe and get a haircut and a shave, all for twenty-five cents. He didn't have to heat the water, or lug it back and forth, or dump out the tub, or uncrate the massive iron range. He'd managed to get along fine. He didn't need household help, not that it mattered, because help was impossible to find in this city. The lure of gold was still fresh, so no one was willing to work for the small salary received by servants. Why should they? Most people unrealistically saw gold mining as a way to make a fast fortune.

He had gotten along just fine until Maddie came, and then suddenly he felt like a little boy who'd forgotten to pick up his toys.

Toys. Kit sat up, suddenly remembering the twins. He set the whiskey bottle down and walked over to his desk. Pulling open the bottom drawer, he dumped its contents on the floor and rummaged through the pile of papers. A dirty brown bag sat buried under some old contracts, and deep within that precious brown pouch was what he sought—his old clay marbles.

Kit picked up the bag and went back to the sofa. He untied the drawstrings and poured some of the marbles into his hand. The first three to fall out had been his favorites, his blood alleys. He had used them as taws, shooter marbles, and he'd always won with them.

It was amazing how twenty-four years hadn't changed them. They were pale pink and still had the same dark red veins marbling through them, and they were just as special now as when he'd won them from his older brother.

Kit smiled. Thomas had been so mad. It must have been hell for Tom to lose those rare marbles to a brother who was three years younger. Now that Kit looked back on it, Tom's pride was probably more wounded than anything else.

The cool, pink marbles rolled over Kit's palm and something twisted, deep within him. He'd always thought he'd give these to his own sons. He picked up the whiskey bottle and started to drink, but then stopped. What good would it do to get drunk? That wouldn't change things. He set the bottle down and fingered the marbles, imagining briefly what it would have been like to teach his own son to play ringtaw.

His hand closed tightly around the marbles; there would be no son because there would be no marriage. He'd made that mistake once, and he wouldn't make it again. He could never give his heart to another woman because he didn't think there was a woman alive who could love him with equal depth. For Kit, love was his weakness, the tool to his destruction, because when he loved, he loved hard and so, so deep, and the betrayal of that love had almost killed him.

He put the marbles back into the bag and tightened the strings. He'd take these to Knut and Gunnar and teach them to play the games he would have taught his own flesh and blood. Maybe this guardianship was a Godsend. He could purge this rising need for fatherhood that had been flickering through his thoughts lately. It was unsettling, this nesting spirit that he just couldn't seem to shake.

Kit closed his eyes and soon his breathing was deep and even. One arm was bent, its hand resting behind his neck, and the other cradled a bag filled with a young boy's memories.

Chapter

Thirteen

Hallie spent the next morning ordering her family about the *Sea Haven*, since she had decided that keeping them busy would also keep them out of trouble. Dagny was in charge of supplies and had been busy organizing the food-stuffs that were delivered to the ship the evening before. Hallie coerced the twins into believing that they were doing her an invaluable service by removing all the nails, in small handfuls, from a huge barrel in the fo'c'sle to an empty barrel in the afterhouse. Since the fo'c'sle was in the bow of the ship and the afterhouse in the stern, Hallie knew that her morning would be unhampered by the boys chattering. Liv, naturally, was another matter.

When Hallie sent her to help Dagny, it had only taken about a half an hour before Dagny was chasing Liv around the deck, trying to get an expensive bag of raisins out of the nine-year-old's hands before she ate them all.

Next, Liv was to remove all the ship's bedding and take it topside to air. When Hallie checked on her, Liv was leaning over the edge of a whaleboat, with a long spade hook, trying to catch the blankets that were fast sinking into the salty depths of the bay. Finally, Hallie sent her to pick up the trail of nails that ran from bow to stern.

Now Hallie was back in her father's quarters, changing her bandage and trying desperately to think of some way to handle Kit Howland. As she rubbed the salve into the crusty burn, she thought of his words. He had said he'd be back today, and she honestly didn't know what she'd do. Her quick jibe about the gun was only an empty threat. Having held that cold, metal weapon certainly convinced her that it wouldn't do much good where Kit Howland was concerned. Even if she could dredge up the nerve to pull the trigger, her foolish heart wouldn't let her harm him.

She snapped the tin cap back on the salve jar. She should absolutely hate and despise that man. He was obnoxious and he laughed at her and teased her, and most of all he betrayed her beloved father's trust. Hallie unfolded the linen sheet she'd been using for bandages. Da wouldn't have given Kit the ship if he'd thought Kit would destroy it. The only thing Da loved more than the *Sea Haven* was his family. It was up to her to make sure that the ship remained intact and safe from Kit's heartless and money-grubbing plans.

Picking up each end of the sheet, she began tearing bandage-sized strips. Yesterday, when she should have found some way to throw his traitorous hide off the ship, she'd ended up in his arms, all melting and mushy. She dropped a piece of sheet on the bunk.

How could her heart betray her like that? She gripped the fabric and tore off another strip. She should have fought him, root hog or die. Instead, when his aunt assumed she was Kit's wife, she had felt like preening. Last night she had fallen asleep imagining what it would be like to be Mrs. Christopher Howland. She groaned. Lord, she had even practiced kissing, on her dry pillow. What a silly fool!

Hallie stood and ripped strips of linen while she paced. What she needed to do was to concentrate on all his bad traits.

First, he was insensitive, so much so that she'd hidden from him for two whole years. She flung a shredded strip onto the bandage pile. Second, he made fun of her in public—she grabbed the cloth in her fists and pulled as hard as she could—and he called her a *girl*. The sound of rending fabric scraped the air. And he really thought she was stupid too. Three more cloth strips landed on the growing pile. Then he had acted so surprised when she knew about the landfill, as if understanding the land business was too complicated for her, and her pretty head. Hallie gritted her teeth and ripped off a five-foot-long piece.

Humph! She glanced at the leftover swatch of sheet, shrugged, and tossed it on the mound of bandages. Maybe she was stupid. How could she fall for someone like that? Well, it didn't matter, because now she intended to make herself fall out of love with him.

Besides, he was unpredictable, and that was a terrible trait. Hallie plopped down on the bunk, plucked a piece of sheet off the pile, and wrapped it around her burned leg, from the tender area to just above her knee. She knotted the cloth as a small smile played on her lips. She'd recalled Kit inspecting the twins' faces, obviously looking for some way to tell the boys apart. And that was another thing. Instead of helping her, he just barged right in and took over, as if she weren't capable of handling the twins.

Criminey! She'd been doing it for three years, and where was he? Hallie pulled her dark stocking over the bandage and stepped into her bloomers, mumbling about Kit's lack of sensitivity. He wouldn't know the first thing about handling small, orphaned children. Why, if his aunt's arrival hadn't distracted him, he probably would have done something awful to the twins.

Then she realized she hadn't heard a peep out those two imps in quite a while, so just to be safe, she left the cabin and went to check on them. All the way to the bow she thought of all the horrible, heartless things Kit could have done to the boys. The thoughts stoked her anger, which she hoped would help kill her feelings for Kit. She rounded the corner of the tryworks and stopped cold.

"I got your toe!" Knut yelled, jumping up and down with excitement.

Kit reached out and tousled the little boy's blond head. "You sure did. But it's called a *taw,* not a toe." Kit picked up a pink marble that rolled nearby and he dropped it into Knut's open palm.

"Now," Kit instructed, smoothing Knut's spiky blond hair, "it's your brother's turn."

From where Hallie stood, she could see Kit as he bent over and patiently helped Gunnar position his pudgy little fingers on a marble. With a flick of Gunnar's little thumb, propelled by Kit's strong one, a pink marble shot into a group of brown and yellow ones, sending three of them out of the chalk circle.

"Gosh! I got three! Did you see? Did you?" Gunnar grabbed the marbles and held them, cupped like fallen stars in his small hand.

If Hallie had really hated Kit, at that very moment her hate would have turned into love. As it was, her love became something so powerful that it frightened her. This was something over which she had absolutely no control.

She felt such an ache in her heart that she had to reach out and grab the mizzen for support. When Knut threw himself into Kit's broad chest and hugged him for all he was worth, she felt the rising burn of her silly tears. Just before she turned away, through her blurred vision, she saw two little towheads snuggle on the broad shoulders of the man she knew she could never hate.

A week later Kit paced the cabin of the *Wanderer.* "What the hell am I supposed to do?"

Lee propped his feet on his desk. "You could bunk here. Let your aunt do whatever she wants to do to your place. You would be here where she couldn't bother you."

Kit ran his hand through his hair for the third time in two minutes. It didn't help him think. "No, I can't abandon her. She's my mother's sister, and no matter how much she irritates me, I just can't up and move out. Besides, Maddie would probably find me."

He walked over to Lee's desk and slumped into an empty

chair. He looked at the stack of papers and logs piled on the desktop. Charts were rolled loosely and strewn from one end of the desk to the other, and Lee's booted feet rested on the open spine of a copy of *Barry Lyndon*. Two amber-crusted glasses sat next to a brandy decanter, and a coffee mug, ringed with cold coffee, weighted down the recent consignment contracts for Lee's cargo.

Kit eyed the familiar clutter while he pulled out his tobacco pouch. Filling his pipe, he said, "Of course, I could bring Maddie over here." He lit the pipe, drawing on the stem and expelling the pipe smoke in small puffs. "One look at this place and she'd be in hog heaven."

Lee pulled his feet off the desk and sat up. "Oh no! I don't want that cleaning dervish on my ship. Don't you try to pawn her off on me. She's your aunt."

"Thanks for reminding me. I really needed to be told that, since she begins every sentence with, 'Any nephew of mine . . .'" Kit mimicked her screechy falsetto.

"Just tell her you've got some business to tend and that you'll be gone for a few days. You could stay here and she'd never be the wiser."

"I can't do that." Kit sighed. "I need to check on Jan's family, and Maddie has always had an uncanny ability to tell when I'm stretching the truth. No," Kit shook his head, "if I were to stay here, she would come looking for me. And it wouldn't take her long to find me either. I swear that woman is part ferret."

Kit chewed his pipe thoughtfully. "I need to find something to keep her busy . . . busy enough to leave me alone."

"Ah," Lee said. "Then she needs another lost cause."

"I suppose . . ."

"You could suggest she join the movement to clean up the city." Lee laughed facetiously. "Even the authorities can't do that. It's a cause that ought to keep her busy."

"Might get her killed too. She might be bossy and domineering, but despite the trouble she causes, I do care about her. Hell, she taught me how to fish. Those sneaky brothers of mine ran off without me because they didn't

want some little kid tagging along. So, Maddie took me."
Kit smiled at the memory. "We came home with twice as
many fish each as Thomas, Nathan, and Benjamin had all
together. She's a spry one, and just like my mother, when
she gets an idea in her head, she doesn't give up until she's
had her way. Considering her strong views on women, I'd
say she would set her sights on cleaning up the bawdyhouses
in Frenchtown. Then what would *you* do whenever you
came to port?"

"Same thing I'm doing now," Lee retorted. "Which
reminds me, I've an appointment this afternoon with a
certain señorita." Lee's grin became a leer. "You'll have to
think of a way to keep your aunt busy on your own. I can't
think of anything, unless you want to loan Maddie to Hallie.
I'm sure she could use the help handling those twins. Why, I
had one helluva time keeping up with them the other night.
All those questions would keep your aunt busy."

Kit shot out of the chair, pulling the pipe from his mouth.
"That's it! It's perfect!" He traversed the room again, only
this time he was driven by excitement. "I'll send them—the
twins, Hallie, and the girls—to live at my place with
Maddie." Again he paced, expounding with exuberance the
answer to his problems—all his problems.

"It's brilliant! I can use one problem to solve another. I'll
stay with you until I can find another place." Kit stopped
and spun around to face Lee. "I don't know why I didn't
think of this before."

"How are you going to get Hallie off that ship?" Lee
asked, his voice filled with skepticism.

"I'm thinking . . ." Kit stuck the pipe back in his mouth
and considered his alternatives. He could try to order Hallie
off the ship, or carry her off bodily, but in the past week he
had learned that such actions only served to make Hallie
resist all the more. She wouldn't even talk with him the day
after his aunt arrived. He'd given the boys his old marbles
and taught them how to play before he'd searched her out.
When he found her, Kit had a one-sided conversation with a
locked cabin door.

Of course, there was always bribery, and the one thing he could use to bribe Hallie was the *Sea Haven*. While it ran against his grain to give in to her, he knew that he really didn't need to sell Jan's ship. Now that he thought about it, he had to admit that if Hallie hadn't made him so goddamn mad in the first place, he never would have forced the issue of the sale. And he wasn't really giving in to her, he was making a deal. He'd give Hallie title to the ship if she, along with her brothers and sisters, would move in with his aunt. That high-spirited group would occupy Maddie, and she, in turn, would take care of his wards.

This plan would also solve another problem—his uncontrolled, physical reaction to Hallie. With his aunt guarding Hallie, Kit would be forced to control himself around her. And that was certainly something he needed. Hallie had managed to break through the hard-won barrier he'd built around his heart. It had been a long time since a woman's arms felt like home, all warm, soft, and secure—almost comfortable, like family. He didn't need thoughts of family and marriage mucking up his life.

"I'll bribe her with the ship," Kit stated with resolve.

"Ah-ha! She won," Lee teased.

"No, I have," Kit said, reasoning that he'd given up little to set his life back in order.

Dagny stepped from the wooden planks of the wharf onto the gravel of the street. The soft dirt muffled her purposeful steps as she marched up the steep hill, heading for Oatt's, which was ten blocks and another hill away.

"She's being ridiculous!" Dagny muttered. "It's full daylight. Nothing's going to happen to me." She continued walking, and thinking about the argument she had with Hallie before she'd slipped away. The whole thing was silly. Hallie was just being overprotective again. It was perfectly safe for her to go alone to get the supplies they needed. Why should she wait for the rest of them? Hallie certainly never did. She used to take off alone all the time.

Dagny looked up the street. There were only a few people

coming her way, and just to reassure herself of her safety, she glanced back. There was no one behind her. She crossed another street and was once again on a wood-paved walk. As her heels clipped along the raised wood, Dagny saw that this street, like the last, was almost deserted, but it was darker. She looked up at the high brick buildings, noticing how their added height shadowed the street. A little splinter of fear pierced her, but she dismissed it, rationalizing that Hallie's dire warnings had stirred her own imagination.

Another set of heels, sounding heavier, deeper, echoed up from behind her. Dagny stopped. So did the sound. She quickened her pace and the heels drummed faster. She looked over her shoulder, but no one was there.

Dagny sighed, relieved and a bit amused by her silliness. She walked on, and within minutes the heavy heels sounded again. She looked again, but still no one was there. The whole thing was making her awfully uneasy. At the crest of the hill Dagny crossed the street. She needed to ease her mounting fear, and she could see a small crowd a few blocks down the street. She was almost running toward the safety of the crowd. Her anxiety swelled, so she looked back once again. From seemingly nowhere, someone grabbed her arm in a grip so strong that she was suddenly lifted off her scurrying feet.

"You shouldn't be out alone."

Duncan! "Oh, thank God," she breathed, trying to still her galloping heart. She glanced up. Concern cloaked his plain, oversized features, until all she saw was the blue softness in his eyes. "You frightened me."

The softness hardened a tinge. "You should be frightened. This is not a good place for a woman to be walking alone. See that group up ahead?" Duncan pointed to the group she had targeted as safe.

She nodded.

"Those are Hounds. You know who they are, don't you?"

Dagny nodded again, fear reflecting from her wide eyes. The Hounds were a notorious gang of thieves who were not above killing to get whatever they wanted. They rivaled the

Sydney Ducks for status as the worst bunch of criminals to ever plague a city.

Hoping that he had been the owner of those heavy heels, she asked, "Have you been following me?"

"No. I just came out of the livery and saw you coming this way. Is that why you were running? Was someone after you?" Duncan looked down the street.

Dagny didn't want any trouble, and now that Duncan was here, she knew she had no reason to be frightened, so she decided not to tell him what she heard. It probably was her imagination anyway. "No, I'm going to Oatt's and I'm in a hurry."

"I'll go with you. You shouldn't go alone." He offered her his arm and led her through a side street. "I'm surprised your sister would let you go alone."

Dagny grimaced with guilt. "Well, she didn't. I sneaked out." She kept her eyes pinned to the ground, wondering what he would think of her admission. She waited for a lecture, but he said nothing, although she could feel his stare. He muttered something and then took her arm, and soon they were in a well-traveled and bustling section of San Francisco.

While they walked, Dagny explained where they were staying. When he told her he'd looked for her family after the fire, she was warmed by the knowledge that this sweet, kind man cared.

A shout brought them to an abrupt halt. Across the narrow street a carriage had overturned, trapping its occupants. The fallen carriage horse whinnied and screamed, trying to get free of the broken shafts and tangled reins.

Duncan pulled her across the street. "Stand back here, out of the way. I'm going to help free that horse."

Dagny stood back and watched. The crowd of spectators grew. Duncan freed the horse and then tried to help right the carriage. She smiled when she noticed how Duncan's strength made the impossible task look more possible. The rescuers, now a large group of men, pushed and rocked the heavy brougham as the spectating crowd grew.

Dagny stepped away from the milling group so she could get a better view of Duncan, but she still couldn't see. She lifted her skirt and stepped off the walkway, craning around the people.

A clammy hand clamped over her mouth and jerked her into a dark alleyway. She tried to scream, to fight, to bite, but her assailant was dragging her backward, and she couldn't strike out from the awkward angle in which she was held.

The man said nothing, but his panting breath grew stronger and deeper as it swished past her head. He stopped in a dark doorway and his arm gripped her by the neck as he fumbled with what sounded like the jangle of keys. His arm tightened and she had no air. She tried to breathe, but his arm pressed painfully into her throat. Her chest hurt, and his hand now covered her nose, making it burn for air. Racing stars flickered on her closed eyelids until, suddenly, a curtain of black killed the light.

Chapter

Fourteen

Abner dragged the unconscious girl into the tiny room. He laid her on an old tick in the corner and tied her hands together. Looping a rope around her right ankle, he secured the free end to the handle of a heavy trunk. Now she couldn't run.

Shuffling across the dirt floor, he picked up a candle stub that sat on a broken crate. He lit the stub and then let the wax drip onto a small pewter saucer, watching it through his sunken, opium-teared eyes. Like some nocturnal animal, he blinked at the light, his drugged state making the small flame appear blinding. He stuck the candle into the well of cooling wax and he sat by Dagny, waving the saucer near her porcelain face to wake her. Her eyes opened and instantly filled with horror. He could read the scream coming, so he shoved his wadded handkerchief into her open mouth. Her scream was muffled.

"You must be quiet." Abner patted his pockets, searching for the gold he'd won for her. "I've something to show you." Smiling, he pulled out the gold bag and showed her. "See this?" He opened the strings and looked inside the bulging bag. "It's full." He tilted the bag toward her frightened face, and she jerked her head back.

He frowned at her reaction. "This is for you." He poured the gold coins and nuggets into his palm and held them out to her.

Then she did the oddest thing. Her eyes narrowed and she butted his hand with her head, scattering the gold. He watched, detached, as the coins rolled in the hard dirt.

Looking up from the gold, he examined her face. It was strange. He had thought he didn't want Dagny to be afraid of him, but now it was different. His blood rushed from the preylike fear he read in her eyes. She shook, and his hand reached out to brush a lock of shiny black hair away from her face. His fingertips grazed her skin and traced the path of perfection that edged her hairline. He gently rubbed the struggle marks marring her throat. Her hard swallow contracted under his hand, and he supped power.

When he touched the throbbing pulse in her neck, she twisted away from him and faced the wall. Her foot pulled at the ankle bond; it gave no slack. Abner swelled from the thrill of a captor's power, and suddenly he ached to see her struggle.

The buttons of her dress were so easy. One by one they slipped through their loops, and with each button she struggled more. Her frantic movements drove him to release the next, and the next, until they were all undone.

But then she stilled. His hands shook violently with the need to feel the helpless, futile fight in her. He grabbed both sides of her open dress, and rising to his knees, he ripped it in two. She flopped back on the tick.

There was no struggle.

Abner dropped the fabric and rolled her onto her back. She had fainted again. Panting, he shook her. "Fight! Fight me!" He drew back his hand and slapped her. Nothing happened. Again and again his hand, open and stinging, cracked against her face, but she remained unconscious.

His breathing slowed and he felt suddenly drained. He stood, closing his eyes to control the rolling, the shaking within him. And he stared at her. Her pale cheeks were now blood-red with the manna of imprints—angry marks from his own battering hand. Blood leaked from a split in her cracked lips, and it trickled from her mouth's corner. He turned his open, scarred palms up and examined them. Had they done this?

Something rammed hard against the door and he looked up. Again the door shuddered, and sharp, creaking sounds came from it as the wood began to splinter. He scooped up handfuls of dirt and gold and shoved them into his coat pockets. The door cracked again and he glanced back at Dagny. The sight of her beaten face and her torn clothes snapped some sanity into his teetering mind. He needed time to escape! He raced over to the locked door and pulled down the wooden bar.

A ladder hung from the storage loft, and he climbed the rungs. Just as he reached the loft, Abner heard the door shatter. The crash sent him bounding over the crush of barrels and containers until he reached a tall shipping crate that stood under the trap to the roof. He scaled the crate and jumped up to grab hold of the trap edge. He pushed open the trapdoor and pulled himself through. Squatting, he looked back to see if he was being pursued. Duncan's familiar blond head appeared from the ladder below.

Abner stood and ran across the flat roof, climbing up onto the neighboring one. He scurried up the sloping shingles of the street's last house, and as he grabbed hold of the roof peak, the shingles gave way. He slid down the steep roof, clawing at the wooden tiles with his scraped and splintered hands. His hands grasped the roof edge and held, even as the weight from his swaying body jarred through his arms. He looked over his straining shoulder to the roof next door. No one followed.

He peered down at the alley, some twenty feet below. Again he looked up, but the sound of a slamming door sent him plunging to the ground. His ankles buckled with pain when he landed, but his mind still spun with hunted fear, so he crawled into the shadow of the building and rocked with the pain. Footsteps echoed from above, and Abner pushed himself up the wall. His right ankle held but his left one pierced with sharp pain. Still, he limped down the alley, dazed but driven, and escaped into the dark and shadowed maze of the city's back streets.

Hallie grabbed Liv's shoulders. "Are you sure you haven't seen her?"

"Uh-uh," Liv answered, shaking her head.

Hallie stormed out of the ship's galley and again searched for Dagny, with Liv following right on her heels. They had just reached the upper deck when Hallie heard a cry for help. She looked up, and there were the twins, hanging from the ratlines just under the lookout nest.

"Oh, my God! Hang on!" Hallie ran to the mast and started to climb the rigging, Liv right behind her.

"No, Liv! You stay right here," she ordered, gripping the wobbly ropes as tightly as she could.

Hallie climbed on, taking in deep, calming breaths with each rung of rope. The higher she climbed, the more she swayed and that old familiar light-headed feeling resurged. But she had to go on.

She heard a shout and looked down. Kit stood far below, yelling, but she couldn't understand him with her ears buzzing so loudly. She looked up. The boys were only about four feet higher. Knut was closest to the mast, and Gunnar hung from the end of the yardarm. She tried to grab at the next rope, but her hands were in a frozen grip. She willed them, and her feet, to move, but they wouldn't. Her panic grew. She couldn't do this! She looked down and Kit was right below her, scaling the ropes. He grabbed the lines on either side of her and climbed up until she felt the warmth of his body against her back.

"I've got you. Don't worry." His calm words helped. "Can you hang on? I've got to get the boys in the nest."

Hallie nodded, and through wide eyes watched him pluck Knut off the footage and drop him into the crow's nest. Kit wrapped the shrouds of rope around his wrists and leaned out at an angle so ungodly that Hallie's stomach lurched. Instinctively, she clutched the rope tighter. He pulled Gunnar to safety.

"Hallie?"

At the sound of his deep voice, she looked up.

"I'm going to put you into the nest, too, and then take you each down one at a time. Okay?"

She nodded.

"Give me your hand."

She stiffened. He wanted her to let go. Her hand wouldn't budge. "I can't."

"Yes you can. I won't let anything happen to you."

"I can't," she pleaded.

"All right, sweet. Just hang on."

Hallie felt the ropes sway, and her hands gripped them so tight that she could feel her nails biting into her palms. His warm hand closed over her wrist, holding it firmly.

"I've got you now, Hallie. Grip my wrist and I'll pull you up."

"My hand won't move."

Kit pried her hand off the rope and lifted her onto the lookout platform. Her arms wrapped around the security of his chest and she wept sobs of relief. He tilted her face upward and their eyes met. He searched her face. There was no censure in his expression, and no ridicule, just honest concern that calmed her like a mother's touch.

Hallie took a deep breath. "I'm all right. Go on. Take the boys down." She leaned back against the wooden wall of the nest. "I'll sit here and wait."

He nodded, and then quietly explained to the twins exactly how he would get them down. He took Gunnar first, holding him to his chest, and Knut sat down in Hallie's lap, waiting and watching as Kit showed Gunnar how to hold on. Placing Gunnar's arms around his neck, he had the boy lock his small legs around his waist, and then the two disappeared over the side of the nest.

Hallie hugged Knut to her, brushing his hair off his forehead and rocking him in her lap. It soothed her just to hold him and feel his warm little body next to her own.

The fall would have killed them. This was not the first brush with danger they'd had. Since they'd moved onto the *Sea Haven,* the children had had one close call after another. In one short week Hallie was fast realizing that a ship was no place for small children, or for young girls. The scum of San Francisco hovered around the wharf area, so she refused to let any of her family run free. She and Dagny had argued over that very thing earlier, and now Dagny was nowhere to be found. Although a small bit of her hoped it wasn't so, she had a feeling that her sister had traipsed off on her own to get the supplies they needed.

Kit climbed into the nest and spoke to Knut. "All right, son. It's your turn. Can you hold onto me like your brother did?"

"Sure!" Knut hopped up, the danger from minutes before forgotten in the excitement of his new adventure.

Kit settled the boy on his chest and turned to Hallie. "I'll be right back. Will you be all right?"

"Yes," she said, and he disappeared again.

In what seemed like no time, Kit climbed back onto the platform. "Let's go." He wiped his hands on his trousers and offered her his hand.

She let him pull her up, then she tried to glance down, but the drop made her so dizzy she had to grab the side of the lookout wall to steady herself. She knew her face screamed vertigo, but she didn't care. She was too darn scared. "Wh-what do I do?"

He didn't respond right away; he just watched her. She felt like a specimen. Then his expression changed. Kit paused and let his gaze roam slowly, from the top of her head down to her feet. All that sweet concern and kindness she'd seen before disappeared, replaced by his cocky, male grin.

"You can grab my neck, Hallie-girl . . . and then wrap your legs around my waist, just like your brothers . . ." He looked, purposely, at her bloomers, and with feigned innocence added, "Those prison pants ought to make it simple."

She wanted to smack him; and she would have if she'd had any other way to get to firmer ground. Hallie glared at him instead. "They are not prison pants. I told you before. It's called a reform dress or bloomers." She stuck her nose in the air. "And you'll have to think of some other way to get me down."

Kit crossed his arms and then appeared to be estimating her weight, like one judges a side of beef. Rubbing his chin thoughtfully, he suggested, "Well . . . you could grab onto the ratlines and then step out on the rope webbing. I'll climb on behind you and we'll descend together . . ." his grin widened, "sort of . . . spiderlike."

Sure, Hallie thought, and I'm the fly. She eyed the ropes. They weren't tight, so she would have to grab hold and then get her feet on them while they swayed. She didn't want to do that. "No."

"Well then, I guess we'll stay up here." Kit sat down on the platform and crossed his legs at the ankle. He patted the empty spot next to him. "Have a seat. The afternoon breeze should come up soon, and it will get good and cold up here." Kit smiled, wolflike. "But don't you worry, I'll keep you— and your bloomers—warm."

The hunger in that smile set Hallie's mind spinning, and the thought of spending any time with Kit, especially in the small confines of the *Sea Haven's* crow's nest when he had that goat-randy look on his face was just the catalyst Hallie needed.

"Get up," she said, none too graciously. "I'll go."

Hallie inched nearer the edge of the platform while he got up.

"Don't look down," he ordered.

Hallie swallowed and obeyed; her fear superseded her pride.

"Here," he said, "give me your hand."

She placed her left hand in his and instantly felt a bit better. Taking a deep breath, she grasped the ratlines and stepped onto the rocking ropes, keeping her eyes scrunched shut. Immediately she felt Kit's warm body against her back as he straddled her frame on the ropes.

"Good girl." His breath was hot against her ear. "Now move one hand down to the next rope, and then the other—that's right."

Hallie followed his commands.

"Now you can step down. I'll be right behind you so you can't fall."

She knew he was right behind her. With each step his body, male, hard, and protective, brushed against her own. The breeze picked up, sending the rich, exhilarating scent of tobacco swirling around her. Caught in his magnetic web, she continued to do as he patiently instructed, not realizing that his voice had lost all its cocky tone.

When her feet touched the solidity of the deck, she finally opened her eyes. She sat down on the main hatch, relieved and exhausted. The children huddled around her, and she met Kit's gaze over their excited blond heads. She smiled her thanks, then voiced it and made the boys do the same.

"I have to talk to you," Kit told her.

God, not again. Hallie got up. "Kit, I don't feel like arguing over the ship, and I have to find Dagny." She started to walk away.

"I'll give you the *Sea Haven.*"

She spun around. "What did you say?"

"You can have the ship. But there's a condition."

Hallie was skeptical. "What condition?"

"I want you and the children to move to my home."

"Live with you?" Hallie asked, amazed, appalled, and a little excited.

"With my aunt. I'll stay on Lee's ship until I can make arrangements somewhere else," Kit explained.

"Why?"

Kit shoved his hands in his pockets and stalled. He looked everywhere but at her. Finally he opened his mouth to speak, but a commotion captured their attention.

Duncan, the blond giant, was walking toward them. He carried Dagny, lying limp and frail, in his beefy arms.

Hallie raced to him, with Kit and the others right behind. Dagny's face was marked and puffy and her lips were crusted with dried grains of blood. "Oh God, what happened?"

Duncan's pale eyes turned a colder blue when he answered. "Abner Brown nabbed her. I tried to catch him but . . . I . . . I would have had to leave her. I couldn't, so he got away. I, uh . . . don't know what he did . . ."

He looked past her to Kit, and Hallie saw the look that passed between the men. She read the gaze and looked at her battered sister.

Rape. They thought he might have raped her. Hallie grabbed her sides as she fought the urge to vomit. Then she turned, stunned and drained, to Kit. "Get a doctor. Please, Kit, hurry."

An instant later he was gone. Hallie grabbed Duncan's arm. "Bring her this way." She pulled him toward the captain's cabin, and then remembered the children. "Liv, bring your brothers along." Hallie opened the door for Duncan and turned back to her little sister, brushing back the girl's straggly bangs from her worried eyes. "I need your help. Can you keep the boys busy out here while I see to Duggie?"

Liv bit her bottom lip and nodded. Hallie entered the cabin and closed the door. Duncan had laid Dagny on the bunk, and his huge gray sack coat still covered her pale sister. Hallie went to the basin and poured some water, taking it over to the shelf by the bunk. She paused, afraid of what she might uncover, then pulled back the coat.

Dagny's neck was marked, and though the bodice of her dress was torn, Hallie noticed that all Dagny's underthings appeared untouched. She checked her sister's petticoats and drawers and was sure no rape had occurred. She bathed Duggie's battered face with cool water and whispered soothing words to her.

Duncan came to Hallie's side. "I'm so sorry, miss. She's special, too special to have to go through something like this."

"I know." Hallie wiped off the dried blood. "Why would he do this? It's insane."

"He's insane."

"What?" Hallie turned, shocked. She always thought of Abner as only a strange priss.

"The fire left him devastated. The last time I saw him, he was kneeling in the ashes of the funeral home, screaming and carrying on something fierce. I don't know where he's been since the fire, but . . ." Duncan tightened his powerful hands into fists. "I'll find him. I promise you, I'll find him."

Kit entered with the doctor right behind. It was the same man who had tended her burn. While he examined Dagny, Kit and Duncan waited outside and Hallie joined them.

She shut the door quietly and glanced down the companionway to where Liv was confusing the twins with a game of cat's cradle. Hallie sat on a wheel housing. "The doctor said she wasn't molested."

Duncan slumped back against the wall with his eyes closed, and Hallie could see his tension wane, just like her own. "But he said her face and head have been struck awfully hard, and he's concerned because she's been unconscious for so long." Hallie rubbed her hands over her burning eyes. "Oh, God. Why her?"

Kit squatted down beside her. He took her hand, and the shock of his warm fingers against her icy ones made her thread her fingers through his.

"Hallie?"

She heard him but didn't answer. She stared at his hand. It was so hard and strong, yet it had held her own so gently. Oh, why was everything so confusing? She wasn't sure if he was her enemy or her friend. Would he hurt them or help them? He spoke her name again, and his voice was as gentle as his hold. It made her instinctively tighten her hold around his. Her gaze met his, needing to see if those deep green eyes betrayed the kindness of his tone. They didn't.

"I think you need to get off the ship, sweet. My offer still stands. It makes sense, now more than ever." Kit nodded toward the children. "They'll have a safe home. Maddie's great with children, and she can help with Dagny too. It would be best, for all of you." He gave her hand a reassuring squeeze.

He was right. And now, it didn't matter what her feelings were for Kit, she had to think of the family's welfare. They needed a stable home, and God knew she needed some help. Nothing but bad, horrible things had happened to them since Da had died.

His fingers touched her chin, lifting it upward so she was forced to look at him again. The honest concern in his face was her undoing. She closed her eyes, hating the tears that dripped onto her cheeks. "We'll move."

Chapter

Fifteen

Hallie straightened and stretched her tired arms high over her head. Her muscles ached like the very dickens. She rolled her shoulders to work out the kinks. Pressing her hands against the small of her back, she arched backward until a satisfying crack eased her tight spine.

She eyed the parlor, thinking that no one, not even Maddie, could find one speck of dirt in here. The dark walnut furniture glowed from Maddie's polishing concoction, a mixture of candle wax and oil of almonds, and the rich, nutty fragrance made the room smell delightful, like Christmas marzipan.

Lordy, she was tired, and her leg itched. She sunk into the soft pillows of an overstuffed chair, scratched her healing leg, and took a break. They'd been in Kit's home for five days, and she had yet to get a good night's sleep. The boys were having trouble sleeping in their new surroundings, what with all the recent upheaval in their lives. The large bedroom Maddie had given them was right across from Hallie's, but apparently that wasn't close enough for them. For the past few nights either Knut or Gunnar, or the two of them together, had crept into her room and crawled into the big feather bed. Those imps did more roving in their sleep than they did awake.

The first restless night, Hallie had repeatedly trotted them back to their own beds. It had done no good. Like magic seers, those boys had the uncanny ability to discern exactly when Hallie would finally fall back to sleep, and then they'd sneak back in, fall asleep, and pummel an unsuspecting Hallie with a small fist or a flailing foot. Her nights spent sleeping with the twins had her feeling as if she'd been beaten.

Like Dagny.

The thought of her sister's bruised face and puffy lips sparked guilt in Hallie. She was responsible for the welfare of her family, and in her eyes, she had failed. Dagny's beaten features and catatonic state proved it. If Kit hadn't provided for them, they would still be struggling along, on board the *Sea Haven,* unprotected. Of course, she would still have her pride. Lucky her. But then who else would she sacrifice for it?

A whistle of appreciation pierced the quiet room, making Hallie jump.

"The place smells like home." Kit walked into the room. He stood before Hallie, who was slouched in her chair. "Has Maddie been working you too hard?"

"Not really. I was just sitting here . . . thinking," Hallie answered, her voice sounding distracted.

"How is she?" Kit walked over to the sofa across from her and sat on the arm.

Hallie frowned at him. "How did you know I was thinking about Dagny?"

"A good guess."

She averted her eyes, staring at his knee and wondering if her face would forever tell the world what was on her mind. She only hoped her face didn't reveal what was in her heart, but just in case it did, she looked away. "There's no change. She just stares, dully, as if we don't exist. The doctor was here again this morning, but he still couldn't get any response out of her. He said there was no surefire way to snap her back, and he has no idea how long this will last."

Silence hung in the room. It was awful for her, sitting there, feeling responsible and helpless yet not knowing what to do or say. There was nothing Kit could say either. No words could ease her sister's pain. He knew it too. She could feel it in the awkward air.

"I just came from talking to Sheriff Hayes," Kit said. "No one's seen Abner Brown. He's either left town or he's holed up somewhere. The sheriff seems to think he's left, but I'm not sure. If he's as crazed as Duncan thinks, well, I don't want to take any chances." He leaned on his knee, and the action brought his face closer to hers. "Hallie?"

Silent, she returned his stare.

"I don't want to take any chances. I've hired Duncan as a bodyguard, and he's moving into the downstairs bedroom this afternoon. No one, not even Maddie, is to leave without him accompanying them. He can handle the carriage and will take any of you wherever you need to go. I've spoken to Liv and the twins, while Maddie was present, but I need you to help me enforce this."

"Fine," Hallie said, standing. "I'll make sure the children understand." She fidgeted with her hands. "Thank you, Kit. For all you've done."

Kit stood and tilted her head upward so he could see her face. "I meant it, Hallie, when I promised to take care of you, all of you."

Hallie nervously tucked some strands of loose hair behind her ear. It gave her the chance to do something other than ogle him. The air in the room took on a sudden thickness, and when Kit stepped even closer, she felt that same familiar, consuming thrill. His hands rested on her upper arms, and he rubbed them slowly, up and down. Ever sensitive to his touch, she shivered.

His breath whispered past her temple. "Are you cold?"

Her eyes drifted closed. "No."

His hands rubbing her arms lulled her right back into that

sweet world of sensation. His shoulder was just inches away, beckoning. Her cheek moved to rest on the rough wool of his coat and she settled closer, breast to chest. She gazed up at the dark stubble shadowing his jaw, and when his lips descended, slowly, toward her own, she met him halfway. The taste of him, of their kisses, drove the feeling from her legs. Her hands roved his shoulders as his hands stroked her back, and she opened her eyes again, wanting the eye contact that heightened their last kisses. His eyes were closed but she willed them to open. They did, but an instant later he pulled back and pushed her hands down and away from his back.

"What the hell am I doing?" he muttered, stepping back to put a few feet between them while he stared at her as if she had made him hold her and kiss her.

His look carried no love, just censure, which Hallie assumed she directed toward her. She shivered with the need to get away. "I am cold," she blurted, knowing that the word cold was too mild a term for how she felt.

"Hallie, wait." Kit reached out to stop her.

She sidestepped his hand and rushed out of the room, her good-bye echoing in the wake of her need to get away.

"What have you got there?" Maddie studied Liv, who hovered by the back door.

"Nothing." Liv was wedged into the corner, and every few seconds her shoulders would wiggle as if she were struggling with something behind her back.

"Liv!" Hallie scolded. "Don't you fib." Hallie pulled her hands from the tub of dishwater and wiped them on her apron.

"Let me handle this, Hallie," Maddie said, setting down the dinner tray she had just brought down from Dagny's room. She crossed her arms. "Let me see your hands, young lady."

Guilt filled Liv's face, then she leaned back against the wall. It was obvious that whatever she held was now pinned between her skirts and the corner wall. She stuck out her hands, one at a time.

Hallie and Maddie exchanged knowing looks, but before either of them could move, Liv's eyes widened with shock and a loud, ear-piercing screech erupted from her skirts.

"Ouch! Oh cripes!" Liv jumped away from the wall. "Get her off!"

Clinging to the back of Liv's dress was a huge, muddy cat.

"Ah! Hallieee. Get her off!" Liv hopped in a circle, trying to dislodge the clawing cat.

"Hold still, Liv!" Maddie grabbed Liv by the shoulders to steady her while Hallie plucked the frightened cat from her sister's back.

Hallie cradled the muddy cat in both arms. It was so big it spanned from one of her elbows to the other.

Maddie still held Liv by the shoulders. "Why were you trying to sneak the cat inside?"

Liv averted her eyes before she whispered, "I didn't think you'd let me have her. She's so dirty and all, and you've been cleaning everything, and I . . . I just couldn't leave her all alone. She probably got burned out just like we did, and I . . . I just wanted to help her."

"You know that sneaking is the same as lying, don't you, young lady?"

Liv nodded solemnly.

"You should have asked first." Maddie's voice was stern but kind, and she had Liv's full attention, which was not always the case with Hallie and Liv.

"Where did you find her?" Maddie asked after a long, silent pause.

"Out back. It's so cold and she was hiding under some bushes, all alone . . . crying. I had to do something or else she'd starve."

Hallie's arms were numb from holding the heavy cat, which was now purring in her arms. "Starve? This thing's too heavy to starve."

"Maybe she has big bones, then," Liv argued.

Maddie gave Hallie an exasperated look, then scrutinized the cat and Liv's tragic face. After a pregnant pause, Maddie relented. "I'll let you keep the cat this time, but you are not to try to sneak anything again. Is that understood?"

"Oh yes!" Liv promised.

"And you'll have to take care of her. Starting right now with a bath."

"Oh, thank you, Aunt Maddie! I'll take real good care of her. You'll see." Liv's smile beamed from ear to ear.

"And for sneaking," Maddie added, "you will do each of your multiplication tables ten times."

The start of a groan escaped Liv's frowning mouth. Maddie's look stopped the protest that always followed one of Liv's groans. To Hallie's amazement, instead of arguing, Liv held out her arms for Hallie to hand over the cat.

A few minutes later Liv was happily scrubbing the squealing cat in a tub of dishwater. Maddie brought out a flannel towel and set it on the drainboard. "What are you going to name her?"

"I don't know." Liv looked thoughtful.

The kitchen door banged open and the twins galloped into the room, doing their best to mimic a tribe of Indians. They were followed by Duncan, cast in the role of Great White Father. The boys stopped their whooping the minute they saw the cat peek around Liv's shoulder while she dried its back.

"Golly! It's a cat!" Gunnar rushed over to get a closer look, and Knut followed.

"It's mine." Liv clasped the cat to her chest and the animal meowed a protest.

Knut turned around. "Hallie. Liv's not sharing."

Maddie took over. "You boys go over to the table and we'll set the cat down so you can look at her. But remember, she's frightened, so don't scare her more. And Liv found the cat so it's hers. When you boys are older and can take care of animals, you'll be able to have a pet too." Maddie leaned down toward Liv and whispered, "Let them pet her and then they'll leave you be."

"All right," Liv relented, but not too graciously. She lugged the towel-wrapped cat over to the wooden table and set it down. Duncan stood quietly by the boys, and Hallie watched as Liv unwrapped the damp cat. The animal was all black, except for a little white around her whiskers and the wide strip of white that covered her huge belly.

"She's expecting," Duncan stated.

Maddie groaned.

Knut looked up. "What's she 'specting?"

"Kittens!" Liv exclaimed, thoroughly delighted.

The cat laid on her side and started cleaning her paws. She didn't look the least bit frightened. In fact, Hallie thought she looked completely contented. The twins were studying the cat's bulging stomach, obviously looking for the kittens.

"She looks like a skunk," Knut announced.

"No she doesn't!" Gunnar argued, his voice full of scorn. "A skunk has a stripe on its back."

"That's what I'll call her," Liv interjected. "Skunk. Mrs. Skunk, because she's going to be a mother." She picked up the cat and announced, "I'm taking her upstairs to my room. So she can rest." She walked out of the kitchen with the twins close behind her, both of them arguing over the cat's new name.

Maddie shook her head. "What have I done?"

"Probably kept her out of trouble for weeks. The cat will keep her too busy to pull any of her usual antics." Hallie smiled at Duncan. "Did you get all settled in?"

"Yes, miss."

"Can I get you something? Some coffee maybe?"

"No thanks, miss. I think I'll check the locks and then go to bed." Duncan walked over, bolted the back door, checked the kitchen window and then left the room.

Maddie glanced at the closed door. "He's a quiet one."

"He's so big. The first time I saw him, he scared me to death. But he's really very kind."

"He asked me earlier if he could visit Dagny. He appears concerned. What do you think?" Maddie asked.

"The man saved me from burning up, and Dagny from

Abner Brown. He wouldn't harm her. There seemed to be something special between them, before. Maybe he can reach her. I remember when they met, right after Da died, Duncan was the first person she responded to. I had been so worried about her then, and now . . . oh, Maddie, I didn't think things could get any worse, but they have, and it's all my fault."

Maddie grabbed Hallie's hand. "Now don't you go getting all upset. Everything's going to be just fine. It is not your fault that Dagny was hurt. Casting blame won't change things, and it won't heal your sister. In fact, your moping around like this could make her worse. She needs our strength. And young lady, you are one of the strongest young women I've ever met. So knock it off!"

Hallie smiled. Maddie was good for her.

Maddie added, "We'll take good care of Dagny. She's much safer here; all of you are."

"But we're a bit of a handful, wouldn't you say?"

"You stop that kind of thinking right now. If you and the children weren't here, I'd be rambling around this place with no one to harp at but that nephew of mine. Which reminds me, did you two have an argument?"

"No." They hadn't argued. Hallie had thrown herself at him once again, and because of that she ignored his call and ran out of the room. She didn't want to face him or talk about him.

"Oh." Maddie looked puzzled. "Then something else must have set him off. The last time I saw him, he was blustering out the front door, wearing his scowl."

Hallie didn't want to think about Kit, let alone discuss him with Maddie. She stood. "I'm exhausted. I think I'll go up to bed."

"Of course. I'll see you in the morning." Maddie tried to hide her knowing grin, but Hallie saw it anyway, and chose to ignore it, like she had ignored Kit.

Bidding Maddie a good night, Hallie left the warmth of the cozy kitchen and hurried upstairs, where some of the day's warmer air still lingered. She entered the bedroom and took her nightgown off its hook behind the door. Shedding her clothes, she pulled the gown over her head and then walked to the dressing table. She opened the top drawer to get her hairpin box, and stopped. The scent of Kit's pipe tobacco filled the air, reminding her that this had been his bedroom. She didn't want to be reminded.

She jerked the pins from her hair, threw them into the drawer and slammed it shut. Grabbing her hairbrush, she pulled her long hair over her shoulder and furiously brushed out the tangles. She could still smell him.

Dropping her brush, she went over to the night table and picked up the small vial of perfumed oil that Da had brought her from a voyage to Lahaina. She removed the cork and poured the sweet smelling plumeria oil onto her hankie. Some of the oil spilled onto her fingertips, so she dabbed the excess behind her ears. She walked over to the dresser, opened the drawer and dropped the perfumed hankie inside, muttering, "So there!"

Returning to the huge feather bed, she blew out the lamp and crawled under the mounds of covers. She *was* exhausted, and her body ached. She only hoped she was tired enough to forget the intoxicating, tobacco scent of the man in whose bed she slept.

"Do you want another round?" Lee picked up the empty rum bottle.

Silence.

"Kit, do you want another bottle?"

Silence.

Lee eyed Kit. "Did you know there are seven gorgeous, naked redheads walking this way?"

"That's nice," Kit answered.

Lee rattled on with his lascivious lie. "One of them is carrying a sign."

"Uh-huh."

"It says, one dollar a lookie, five dollars a feelie, ten dollars a dooie."

"Dewey who?"

"Fredriksen," Lee answered.

Kit blinked once and turned to Lee. His friend was watching him with a wry look on his face. "What are you talking about?"

"Obviously nothing of interest. I should have made them tall blondes," Lee muttered before he pointed to Kit's empty glass. "Do you want another round?"

Kit glanced at the empty bottle in Lee's hand. "Oh hell. Why not?"

Lee banged the bottle on the table. "Hey, more rum over here!"

An hour later Kit lifted his head from the table and stared at his half-empty glass. "I'm an ass."

"Me too," Lee agreed.

"I can't keep my hands off Hallie," Kit announced.

"You are an ass."

"I know." Kit lifted his glass and swilled down the rum. "You know this whole thing is my fault."

"Yup." Lee poured more of the dark rum into Kit's glass. Half of it poured onto the table.

"I should have contracted Jan's cargo sooner. I was greedy."

"Yup." Lee closed one eye to better his aim and tried again to fill Kit's glass. He poured the rum into his friend's smoldering pipe instead.

"I lost the fortune intended for his children's future. I have to take care of them. They have no one else." Kit sighed.

"Do you like rum tobacco?" Lee asked.

"Sure. That's the blend I smoke."

"Good."

"Why?"

"Just checking," Lee said as he scrutinized the mouth of the rum bottle.

"Hallie's really changed," Kit stated.

"She sure has."

"I don't think I've ever seen hair that shade. Have you?"

"Never." Lee gave up on the glass and brought the bottle to his lips.

"She really is lovely."

"Gorgeous," Lee agreed, wiping his mouth with his sleeve before handing Kit the bottle.

"But she's so young. I feel like a lecher."

"I am a lecher." Lee scanned the room. "I thought you wanted to cut your wolf loose? We need some ladies!"

Kit finished off the bottle. Maybe Lee was right. He needed a woman. Then he would be able to keep his hands off Hallie. He was her guardian, after all, so he should guard her, even from himself.

Another bottle thumped onto the table, and suddenly a woman sat on Kit's lap. He looked at her but he couldn't make out her features. He squinted at her blurred nose—noses—while she snuggled up to his chest. Her perfume was strong and it did nothing for him. Her lips met his and parted. Instinctively, he accepted her kiss and invaded her mouth with his tongue. It didn't belong there.

"I'm sorry, love." Kit pulled away and lifted her off his lap. "You'll have to share your charms with someone else." He shoved a handful of money into her hand. "It's not my night."

The woman's eyes roved over him like a prospective buyer. "No sugar, it's not *my* night." With that, she strolled off.

Kit stood, and the room rolled like it was at sea, during a storm—a big storm. He leaned on the table for support. "Lee?"

"Hmmm?"

Kit couldn't see Lee's face with that brunette wrapped around him. "I'm going home."

Lee came up for air and waved him off.

Kit grabbed his coat and hat, and the bottle, and left the saloon. Shrugging on the coat, he hummed Lee's whaling ditty while he walked up the street, but he stopped when he

193

reached the corner. He remembered his horse. Walking back to the animal, Kit crammed his hat onto his head and the bottle into his pocket, untied the reins and mounted the horse, sipping and humming on his way through town.

When he reached home, he dismounted, throwing the reins over the hitch post. He walked up the stairs and tried the door. It was locked.

"Damn!" He searched his pockets. "Where is that key?" Then he remembered he kept a spare in the band of his hat. Feeling around the rim, he located the key and unlocked the door.

He headed straight for the stairs, realizing that he had better scale them now or else he'd pass out on the floor. He entered his room and felt for the lamp. It wasn't near his dresser. Oh hell, he didn't need it.

Kit shucked off his boots and clothes, casting them behind him as he headed for his soft feather bed. He pulled back the blankets and climbed in. He closed his eyes and turned over, slinging his arm over the extra bed pillows. Breathing deeply, he drifted to sleep, dreaming of the sweet tropical smell of plumeria blossoms.

Hallie awoke, stirring slightly. One of the twins was in the bed again. She tried to turn over but the weight of a leg across her ribs stopped her. She wiggled to dislodge it, but it flopped back. Irritated, she opened her eyes so she could move the boy off, but it wasn't a leg that had her pinned. It was an arm, a hairy, adult, male arm. Hallie screamed and twisted around, using both her hands and her feet to push the man out of the bed.

Kit, in all his naked and hungover glory, hit the hard wooden floor. Stunned, he looked up at Hallie, who knelt on the edge of the bed, staring in shock. He realized he was naked and grabbed the sheet to cover himself. He grabbed her nightgown by mistake. And when he tugged, Hallie flew off the bed, landing right on top of Kit. His arms closed around her and they rolled on the floor, trying to get untangled.

"Oh, my God!"

Both Kit and Hallie looked up at the sound of Maddie's voice. She stood in the doorway, spreading out her skirts to block the scene from the twins' curious eyes.

Chapter

Sixteen

My sister's getting married," Knut informed Agnes Treadwell.

She smiled at Knut. "Yes she is, and it's wonderful. That handsome Kit Howland just swept her off her feet. It's so thrilling." She turned to Hallie. "Isn't it, my dear?"

Hallie nodded, not knowing if she would be able to keep up this charade.

"Tell me, my dear, how did he propose? Wait! Let me guess." Agnes gazed upward and her eyes looked dreamy. "I bet it was during a romantic walk in the moonlight, right?" Agnes turned her expectant face back to Hallie.

"Well, uh, no. Actually, it was this morning." Hallie picked up the pillow from the sofa and began twisting its fringed tassels.

Agnes clapped her hands. "Oh my, that boy's in a hurry, isn't he?"

"Aunt Maddie made him," Knut announced.

The tassel came off into Hallie's hand.

Maddie walked into the parlor. "Knut dear, would you please go find Liv for me?" Turning to Agnes, she explained, "I suggested that since Hallie didn't want a large ceremony, they might as well get married today. That is, if Pastor Treadwell is available."

"Well, of course he's available. We just love doing weddings. And this one, well, I must say I've been expecting it. Why only last Sunday Mary Oatt said that Charles said that Kit Howland was just frantic with worry after the fire. Well, I'll tell you, when I heard that, I just knew something like this would happen."

While Agnes rambled on, Hallie kept twisting the tassels. For some reason, she couldn't still her hands—or her stomach. She was miserable. And this was her wedding day. It should have been the happiest day of her life, but instead it was humiliating.

After sending the twins away, Maddie had told both Kit and her, in no uncertain terms, that Kit would marry her . . . today. So the one thing Hallie used to dream of, her proposal of marriage, took place on the bedroom floor, with her reluctant future husband garbed only in a sheet. Instead of hearing words of love, Hallie got: "I guess I have to marry you." These were not words of devotion.

"Hallie?"

She looked at Maddie, who was staring at the three torn tassels in her hand. "Yes?" She jammed the tassels under the sofa cushion.

"I think you should go up and get ready. The ceremony will be at four o'clock." Maddie nodded slightly at Agnes, who was still grinning as if she were the bride.

Maddie was giving her an escape, and Hallie took it.

"You look lovely, Hallie." Maddie closed the bedroom door.

Hallie sat on a small stool in front of the dresser and looked down at her dress. It was one of the four Maddie had insisted be made for Hallie when she had first moved in. Maddie had delighted in clothing them all. "Do you really think so?"

Maddie walked across the room and placed her hands

gently on either side of Hallie's face. She tilted her face toward the mirror. "What do you think?"

Hallie bit her lip and stared at her reflection. The sleeves and the gown's huge skirt were made of deep emerald-green silk embroidered with white, long-stemmed flowers. The skirt split in front to reveal a white silk panel embroidered with the same long flowers, only done in the deep green. The snug-fitting bodice was also done in the white. Hallie took a deep breath. "I think it's the most beautiful gown I've ever seen." She looked in the mirror at Maddie. "Thank you."

"You're welcome. Now what are we going to do about your hair?"

Hallie pulled the pins from her wad of hair. "Cut it all off!" She held up bunches of her straight, fine hair. "It never does anything but hang."

Maddie bent over the dresser and grabbed the brush. "Let me see what I can do."

For the next few minutes Maddie worked silently while Hallie tried to shield her hurt from the older woman. Maddie had her best interests at heart when she had insisted on the marriage, Hallie knew that.

"You know it's best, don't you?" Maddie asked.

Hallie shrugged, not wanting to disagree, but feeling it was worse for everyone, not best.

Maddie twisted another thin braid high on her head. "You have so much love to give, Hallie, and if ever there was anyone who needed loving, it's my nephew."

Hallie said nothing; she just handed Maddie another hairpin.

"Don't give up on him. Men need us women to make them aware of what's best for them. Have you ever known a man who didn't need a woman's guidance?"

"Kit," Hallie answered.

Maddie frowned in annoyance at the response. "That's not true. He needs you more than most."

"Why?"

Maddie pinned the last braid into the intricate cluster of

interwoven plaits. She acted as if she hadn't heard Hallie's question.

"I said—"

"I heard you." Maddie set the brush down. "I know my nephew, and I can tell that he already cares, Hallie." She set down the last pin. "There. How do you like it?"

"It's . . . perfect," Hallie answered, unable to believe that she could look like this. Maddie had her flyaway hair in at least twenty intertwined braids that softened her square, Nordic jaw.

Maddie smiled. "I have some silk leaves that I think are the same shade as the dress. Let me go get them and we'll weave them through the braids."

Hallie stood, lifting her full skirts so she could stand in front of the mirror. She was still tall, pale Hallie, but the mirror said differently. It said she was beautiful, and no longer did she appear girlish. She was a woman.

Just what Kit needed. Maddie's words sounded so familiar. Then Hallie remembered. Her own mother's words had been much the same. *Men needed women to teach them to love.* Hallie wondered if she could make Kit love her. She was still wounded from when she had tried to make him realize she was a grown woman. She glanced back at the reflection. Of course, she hadn't really thought of herself as a woman until now. Before, she'd just fought against being labeled a "girl." Common sense told her that if she didn't believe it herself, how could she convince anyone else? Hallie didn't have much choice anyway. She and Kit were getting married in less than an hour, whatever the circumstances, so what did she have to lose?

Maddie entered with the silk leaves and pinned them into Hallie's hair. They were the perfect touch. Maddie went off to see to the children, and Hallie went downstairs to wait for the ceremony. As she descended the stairs, the weight of the heavily embroidered silk trailed behind her, making her feel regal, lovely, and confident.

When she reached the foyer, Hallie started toward the

parlor, but then remembered Agnes. She wasn't *that* confident. She peered down the hall and decided that Kit's study would probably be the safest place to wait, and it would be quiet so she could plot her next siege on Kit's unsuspecting heart.

Her hand grabbed the doorknob, but she heard voices from inside the study. It was Kit; she'd recognize that bellow anywhere. Hallie turned to go to the kitchen when she heard him say her name. Curious, she leaned closer to the door, wanting to hear what he had to say. After all, she reasoned, husbands and wives shouldn't have any secrets between them.

"Jo's dead, Lee!" Kit snapped.

"Oh Christ, Kit. I didn't mean to open old wounds," Lee responded. "I'm sorry . . ."

Joe? Who was Joe? Hallie leaned a little closer.

"Forget it. It's me," Kit said. "Just the mention of her name can still gut me."

Her?

Kit went on. "You know, it's as if that lovely, passionate wife of mine can reach her deceitful hand all the way from the grave and twist her Brutus's knife a little deeper into my back."

Hallie sagged against the cold door. *A wife. He had a wife!*

"Sometimes I still blame myself for the change in Jo. Maybe if I hadn't left her for so long, maybe . . ." The anger left Kit's voice, and in its place was what sounded like the quiet, wistful tone of a confused man.

"But I really thought the bond between us was strong enough to survive one voyage apart. I loved her, Lee, and she stopped loving me. Tell me, how can you leave a warm, loving wife and come home a year later to a cold stranger? She killed something in me, and so help me God, it still hurts. I spent two months trying to find some spark of love in her. Two months of swallowing my pride and almost begging her to stay home and give us a chance. She wouldn't even try."

"There must have been some reason," Lee speculated.

"Oh, she had a reason." His bitter tone returned. "A reason named Jonathan Hicks. I remember the last time I tried to talk to her. I suggested we take a trip, anywhere she wanted to go. When we were first married she had wanted us to see Paris together. She had been so insistent; she said you had to go to France with someone you loved, because when you were there, you fell in love all over again. That morning I tried to rekindle that excitement, fool that I was. God, when I think of how I almost begged her to go . . ."

A thud sounded from inside, and Hallie could picture Kit slamming his fist on the desk while he spoke the hurtful, purging words that killed her dreams.

"Do you know what she did? She laughed at me! I'll never forget that laugh; it was unnatural. Even now it makes me feel empty. Then she made up some lame excuse about visiting her cousin in Boston. She said she didn't care where I went as long as it was far away from her."

"Kit, you don't have to tell me this," Lee said.

"Yes I do. I need to talk about it. I haven't told anyone except my family, and for five bloody years I've let it burn in my gut. Jo left for Boston, and I took the ship out for a few months. When I came home, part of me still hoped that maybe by some miracle the old Jo would be waiting. But she wasn't. She was dead, killed in a carriage accident in Boston along with her lover, Jonathan Hicks."

The room was silent, like the tears that streamed down Hallie's blotched cheeks.

"Don't ever fall in love, Lee. Love is a disease. It sucks the life from your veins and the warmth from your soul. Then it wraps your mind in chains from which you'll never be free."

A glass clinked. "Here," Lee said, "you need a drink."

"God no! That's what got me into this mess. Marriage, shit! Just what I need. It was bad enough when I was married to someone I loved. But with Hallie . . . I don't feel anything."

"That's not what you said last night," Lee reminded him. "You said you couldn't keep your hands off her."

"I was drunk."

"Oh, I see."

"I don't love her, Lee."

"Okay, but maybe you'll feel differently in time. She's a lovely girl. You said so yourself."

The clock chimed four and Hallie pushed herself away from the support of the door. She didn't want anyone to see her hurting. She turned and ran to the kitchen door. Just as she pushed it open, she heard Kit's final words.

"It's four o'clock. Come on, Lee, let's go on to this farce of a wedding."

Chapter

Seventeen

The clock chimed on the half hour.

"What the hell is keeping her? It's four-thirty." Kit crammed his hands into his trouser pockets and paced the foyer.

"Calm down, man. She's probably nervous." Lee turned at the sound of the door closing and an appreciative hiss escaped his lips.

Kit turned and caught his breath at the sight that greeted him. Hallie stood in hallway, and the glow from a wall sconce shimmered behind her, making her appear haloed. The image was so beautiful that for an instant his anger disappeared. She forced her chin a notch higher, which only made her appear more regal. She stepped toward him and her silk gown rustled.

Maddie passed Kit on her way to the parlor. "You can escort Hallie in, Kit. Pastor Treadwell's been waiting long enough."

Hallie stepped into the light, and Kit tightened his fists. She was pale, overly so, and radiated a winsome, lost quality that made Kit remember he wasn't the only one hurt by the marriage. This knowledge was not comforting; in fact, it deepened his anger—self-anger that made him want to lash out at whomever was available.

She glanced from Lee to Kit and her expression changed. "Yes, by all means, let's get on with the wedding farce . . ." Her eyes filled with scorn. "Excuse me, I meant wedding fest."

Kit heard Lee groan under his breath before he left them alone in the hall. Knowing that she must have overheard his earlier words made Kit even angrier at himself for getting into this mess, and at Hallie for making him feel guilty.

"Fine," Kit said, grabbing her hand and almost pulling her through the doorway. Once inside, he trapped her fingers in the crook of his elbow. She tightened them until she was pinching his forearm. He turned his angry eyes to hers and flexed his arm muscle until she slackened her grip. Then he covered her hand with his own. It wasn't a loving gesture, but one of self-preservation. Her disgruntled face glowed with the need to pull something else, like digging her nails into him.

He led her to the gathering near the fireplace, only slowing his long stride when they faced the pastor. The children, Agnes, and Lee stood by Maddie, whose disapproving look forced Kit to avert his eyes. He knew he wasn't making this any easier, but he had never been able to hide his emotions for very long. He scowled at the pastor. "We're ready."

The ceremony began, and it was just as hard as Kit thought it would be, listening to the marriage vows for the second time. In his youth he'd thought these vows meant something. His mind flashed with the memory of his first wedding and how he'd been filled with love and pride. His marriage had stripped him of both. And here he was, once again entering the *bonds* of matrimony, but this time he was older, wiser, and stronger, because his heart wasn't ruling his head.

When Pastor Treadwell asked if he would love, honor, and cherish Hallie, her unladylike snort brought him back to the present. The minister was frowning at them, and Lee, who stood on Kit's right, prodded Kit with his elbow. Kit realized it was time for his response.

"I will."

The pastor turned to Hallie and repeated the vows.

"Whatever," Hallie said with a curt wave of her free hand.

Kit tightened his grip on her hand, but she refused to speak again. "She means yes," Kit snapped.

The minister shrugged and asked for the ring. There hadn't been time to buy a ring, and besides, in all his blustering around, Kit hadn't thought about it. He worked his grandfather's signet ring off his finger and shoved it on Hallie's. It swam on her finger, and in his anger, he'd put it on the wrong hand. She stared at it with such hurt on her face that he had to look away.

The room was thick with tension, making everyone, including the pastor, acutely aware of the antagonism between the bride and groom. He abruptly ended the ceremony. Hallie pulled her right hand from Kit's, and the ring slipped off her finger and fell to the floor. She watched it roll with what Kit could only describe as a numb, blank look, and when the ring hit a table leg and spun to a stop, Hallie stared pointedly at it and then at Kit before she turned, with her head held high, and walked out of the room.

Hallie slammed the bedroom door as hard as she could. All the way up the stairs her breathing fumed, until now her shoulders heaved with each pant. She didn't deserve this. She hadn't trapped Kit into marriage; he had been the one who had drunkenly crawled into bed with her.

Sure, she felt somewhat guilty, she thought, because everytime he was close to her, she had all but thrown herself at him. Well, she'd be damned if she'd do that again! She kicked her shoes off her feet and sat down on the bed to think.

The door burst open and Kit stormed in. He held his ring in his outstretched hand. "You forgot this," he said through gritted teeth.

"I don't want it."

He stepped toward her, seething. "Well, you've got it, and me." He shoved the ring into her hand and tightened his own around it.

"Lucky me."

"It's nice to see that you're not going to change my opinion of the married woman."

"That could be because my 'husband' is so kind and loving. After all, I've got your undying love, don't I?" She tried to jerk her hand free, but he wouldn't let go. Instead he pulled her against his chest.

"Is love what you want, Hallie?"

Hallie knew her face mirrored his anger. "Let go and get out."

"When my 'wife' wants loving? Never." His hand left her back and spanned the back of her head, forcing her mouth to his.

Hallie kept her lips tightly closed and she pushed at his chest. He kissed her harder. She drew back her foot to kick him, but her shoeless feet could do no damage. She tried to knee him, but he must have sensed her intention, because his hand gripped her lower thigh, right on her healing burn. She gasped, and his tongue penetrated her mouth while his other hand moved from her head to hold her jaw so she couldn't bite him. His tongue plundered her mouth and her pain dwindled, superseded by what his kiss did to her. Her thought process stopped the minute his tongue touched hers. She loved it, loved the feel of his tongue in her mouth. So much so, she couldn't stop her own response. Her tongue joined his and he softened the kiss. His hands roamed her body, stroking the tension from wherever he touched her. Soon his lips left hers to drift softly across her cheek. He brushed aside her braided loops of hair so his lips could play with the outside of her ear.

"I want you," he whispered. "God help me, but I want you."

His tongue laved her ear, making gooseflesh bubble on her skin.

You're doing it again. Oh, but she couldn't stop, not when it felt so good.

His palm inched in slow circles over her cloth-covered breast. Her nipples tightened, and with each motion of his hand, they scratched against the fabric of her corset. She pressed into his hand and he kneaded her. His other arm tightened across her back and his hand worked the buttons of her dress free. Hallie felt her corset loosen, and suddenly her breasts were free. His hand closed over her and he bent her back over his arm, giving his mouth access to her other breast. He suckled her and she moaned, because with each pull of his mouth, Hallie throbbed deep in the crevice between her thighs.

He lowered her to the bed and removed the support of his arm. The coolness of the coverlet now lay against her back. She opened her eyes and looked up at him, standing there coatless, tieless. His hands tore open his white linen shirt, sending the onyx studs scattering to the floor. The shirt split to reveal dark body hair swirling thickly across his exposed chest. Her curious gaze followed the path of hair from just below the hollow of his neck to where it disappeared into the waistband of his trousers.

Then he was laying atop her, his hips pressing in hard rotation against her skirts. His open mouth met hers and again his tongue plunged, keeping rhythm with his moving hips. His chest hair rubbed against the breasts he'd licked to the peak of sensation. Her mind, overpowered by the sensory response of her body, was vaguely aware of her heavy skirt moving down and off.

Kit rolled with her until he laid between her and the bed. His hand tore at the ties of her petticoats. He shoved them down her legs and kicked the yards of fabric free. The petticoats rustled loudly in a room filled only with the sound of heated breathing. His tongue moved from her mouth to her ear and plunged inside. At the same time, his hand moved between their bodies, scooting down to the open seam in her drawers. He touched her.

"No," she gasped in shock, closing her legs tightly on his fingers.

His tongue, damp and warm, left her ear, but his lips pressed against it, whispering into the damp interior. "Yes."

His knuckle, held tight by her tense thighs, pressed against her woman's bud, making her cry out, half in protest, half in pleasure. Her legs relaxed, and deep within her she melted. His hand left her throbbing center and he lifted her so her melting moistness rested on the cloth-covered bulge of his pants. Again he rotated his hips, slowly, pressing upward to push his hardness against her most sensitive point. He rocked with her, and the friction of the movement made her moan.

Kit drew the laces from the last eyelet of her corset, and the garment separated. He pulled it from between their bodies and flung it on the floor. He rolled over with her again, shedding his shirt and mumbling against her ear. "Give me your body, sweet. I want you . . . want you . . ."

His mouth traveled up and down the cord of her neck while he undid the buttons on his pants. Everywhere their torsos touched there was hot skin against hot skin. His mouth assaulted her taut nipples, first one, then the other. His hand drifted over her ribs, stroking in soft, caressing circles, and then moved downward, into her drawers, where his fingers tangled through her woman's mound and circled the center of her pleasure. Her thighs parted more and he lifted them until her knees bent. The inner seam of her drawers gaped open and he rose up, pushing down his pants and poising the tip of his hard, male length at the entrance to her body. Still his finger circled, driving her higher while he inched inside. He paused, both his entry and his finger, and she moved against them both, not wanting to lose that elusive thing her body strived toward.

His lips met hers, soft and drifting, and they teased across her own. His finger started again and he filled her a little more, stretching into her until he touched her barrier. His tongue filled her mouth and his finger rubbed faster. She was dying and she didn't care, because his finger gave the last stroke she sought. She cried her pleasure against his tongue, and he thrust through her, the painful tearing of her maidenhead eased by the drumming of her release.

He stopped, embedded tightly within her. Then, after her pulsing ebbed, his hips rotated, each upward movement pulling him to the edge of her just as the downturn of his circle pushed him back inside. Again she felt the drive, only it was faster, deeper, but before she reached the peak, Kit groaned and plunged painfully deep, making Hallie cry out.

He rested heavily against her, his ragged breathing slowed. "Are you all right?"

"You're hurting me."

He used his elbows to lift his chest from hers. "Is that better?"

"No. It hurts . . . inside." She was going to cry.

He pulled out. "Okay?"

The sobs burst, and she cried so hard she couldn't get her breath.

"Hallie, don't, please."

He tried to hold her, but she turned away, crying and shamed.

"Hallie, listen to me. It can hurt a woman . . . at first. I tried to make the loving easier . . ."

Love?

I don't love her, Lee . . . His words echoed in her mind, and she cried harder. What had she done?

His hand stroked her shoulder.

"No! Don't touch me!" she wailed, grabbing at her drawers. Her body, half naked and exposed, curled into a protective fetal ball. His weight left the bed and she heard the rustle of clothing.

"Hallie?"

"Go away."

"Goddammit, talk to me!" Kit grabbed her shoulders and pulled her up to her knees, forcing her to face him.

She sucked in a breath. Her burn ached from the pressure

of kneeling, but its throbbing was nothing compared to the crushing hurt inside her heart. She crossed her arms, hiding her breasts, and twisted in his grip. "Don't touch me! Don't you ever touch me!"

"What the hell is the matter with you?"

She was angry, she hurt, and she was ashamed because she'd given the gift of her body to a man who didn't love her. And worst of all, she hadn't done one thing to stop it. She stared at the clothes, her clothes, scattered nearby, and then looked down at the white, bloodstained drawers and stockings that still covered her.

"I just let it happen." she whispered aloud.

Kit let go of her and shrugged into his shirt. He watched her and then ran an impatient hand through his hair. "It's okay. We're married."

"No. You don't understand." Hallie kept shaking her head, as if by doing so she could erase what had happened.

"Look, Hallie, it's bound to happen again. A man and a woman can't live as closely as we will," he gestured to the room, "without some sort of physical . . . encounter. I realize you're hurt and angry, but there's nothing either of us can do about it. We're married and that's that."

"It's all your fault!"

"What?"

"I didn't crawl into your bed drunk. I didn't want you there then or just now!"

Her words, spat in anger, made his face pale. He looked angry enough to hit her.

Kit crammed his shirttails into his pants and buttoned them. In two long, angry strides he reached the dresser where only hours earlier he had returned his personal belongings. He jerked a drawer out of the dresser and dumped its contents into his valise.

Numb and teary, Hallie watched him. "What are you doing?"

He shoved the last drawer closed, grabbed the valise, and turned around. "Giving you your wish. I promise I won't crawl into bed with you again, Mrs. Howland. You'll have to beg."

Without another word, Kit grabbed his coat and walked out the door, leaving Hallie alone, just as she had asked.

Chapter

Eighteen

At first Kit thought it was the tight pain in his neck that woke him up. He was wrong. Something was stroking his chest. Still half asleep, he stirred under the covers. The stroking stopped. He sighed and was almost back to sleep when the petting began again, very lightly, first one long brushing stroke and then another. He willed his heavy lids open and stared at Liv's cat.

Kit groaned and flung an arm over his eyes. "Damn cat," he muttered before he forgot himself and began to scratch the cat's ears distractedly. The cat settled her hefty self onto his chest and began to purr.

He lifted his arm and squinted at the cat. "What day is this?"

She turned her furry black head to the side so he could get the right spot.

"Right. It's Thursday," Kit answered. "Ten days . . . I should say nights. For ten nights I've been contorting myself to sleep on this"—he looked at his bare feet, propped on the carved arm of the sofa—"bed of torture, while everybody else sleeps in a bed—in my house!"

The cat opened one eye.

"Now I ask you, is that fair?"

Kit's fingers rubbed her ear, and she shook her head, nudging slightly at his hand.

"Good. I'm glad someone is on my side." He moved, and then winced at the sharp pain racing up his neck. "Damn women!"

The cat meowed, as if in protest.

"Sorry."

The clock in the hall chimed six times, and Kit knew he'd better get up if he wanted to shave and wash up in peace. Soon Maddie and Hallie would be in the kitchen, making breakfast and doing their best to ignore or irritate him.

"You know, cat, I don't think those two have, together, spoken over ten words to me. Hell, Maddie still hasn't stopped glaring at me, and Hallie—" Kit stopped. Conflicting emotions shot through him like those old marbles.

He felt guilt when he wanted to feel anger. He wanted to blame her for everything that had happened, but he couldn't. He could only blame himself. He didn't want a wife, but he'd married her and then gone and made her his wife, physically. He was a mess, a living, breathing, dichotomous fool who had better damn well decide what he wanted.

But not today.

Kit got up and placed the ponderous, loitering cat in the heap of warm covers. Naked, and rubbing his sore neck, he walked to the gun cupboard in the corner and opened the door, eyeing the stack of underwear and trousers that sat on his Colt case. He pulled out a clean pair of striped trousers and stepped into them. Plucking a towel off a rifle hook, he slung it over a shoulder and opened the ammunition drawer to gather his shaving paraphernalia and toothbrush. With everything in hand, he left his study and padded barefoot into the kitchen.

Within minutes he had filled a pitcher from the range reservoir. He recapped the reservoir spigot and walked over to the dry sink, thinking about how nice it was to have warm water every morning. He should have uncrated that range ages ago. He washed, and humming away, faced the mirror while lathering his face. He was just brushing the soap on his chin when he saw Hallie's reflection in the mirror. She wore her nightclothes, but that sight wasn't what stopped his breathing. It was her hair. He'd never seen it unbound. Pale and silvery, it hung in tangles clear down to her hips. His shaving brush stilled.

Her startled expression turned icy, and she purposely ignored him, walking over to the range with a pottery pitcher in her hand. Kit dropped the brush into his shaving mug and picked up his straight razor, trying to ignore her. His effort failed; he couldn't keep his eyes off all that hair. When she bent over the reservoir to open the spigot, her hair pooled like a waterfall to the dark wooden floor. He shook his head, trying to forget the sensuous image that had flashed through his mind. Pulling his razor strop away from the wall, he slapped his blade across it. When she tossed some more hair over her shoulder, his eyes locked on her mirrored image and the room reverberated with the sound of his razor flapping rapidly over the strop. Finally, in a last ditch effort to distract the dangerous path of his thinking, Kit drew the razor across his cheek.

"What is wrong with this thing?" Hallie eyed the spigot, and Kit leaned closer to the mirror so he could see her better, blindly shaving his face. She set the pitcher on the floor and straightened so she could open the reservoir lid.

"It's empty." Hallie scowled at him.

"Oh?" Kit drew the blade across his other cheek.

"You hogged all the warm water."

Kit raised his chin to shave the heavy stubble along his jaw. He completed the stroke and dipped the razor into the water basin. "Then I guess you shouldn't lounge around all morning . . ."

Hallie slammed down the iron lid. Pitcher in hand, she marched over and filled it from the water pump. She vigorously pumped the handle, using two hands in a chokelike grip. He knew exactly what she was thinking.

Then she lugged the filled pitcher to the range, stomping at random along the way.

". . . in bed," he added, watching in the mirror as she repeated her angry motions.

She muttered as she dumped the water into the reservoir, so he couldn't make out what she said, which was just as well, considering her expression. She returned to the water pump and pumped away.

He poised the razor below his nose and let loose with his final dig. ". . . my bed."

"Maddie gave me that room, after *you* demanded we move here!"

"I realize that!"

"Then why did you bring it up?"

"Because I'm damn tired of sleeping on that crooked sofa!"

She slammed her filled pitcher on the dry sink and turned to face him. "Why do you have to? Just go out, get drunk, and crawl into some poor innocent's bed."

"Damn!" Kit dropped the razor and pressed the towel to the cut on his upper lip. It hurt like the devil. Turning toward her, he pulled the towel away and eyed the blood spot. He reached for her, but when he saw where her gaze rested, he stopped. She stared at his naked chest, her look curious, yet for all its innocence, cloaked with sensuality. Then her stunned gaze roamed downward and his body responded.

Her eyes widened and she grabbed the pitcher, holding it in front of her, shieldlike. He could tell she wanted to flee the room, and any other time he might have tried to stop her, but now he saw the fear in her eyes—real honest-to-goodness fear. Her anger or her sarcasm he could have dealt with, but realizing that she was truly afraid of him—and his body's response—well, that bothered him. So he turned back to the mirror, masking his hurt with a bored look of dismissal.

She fled the room. Kit watched the door close, and then

he dumped the basin and refilled it with fresh water from his pitcher. He bent over the bowl and splashed water on his soapy face.

"Dammit!" Kit gasped. He opened his eyes and stared at the water—the icy, cold pump water. She'd taken his pitcher.

He leaned against the sink. "Well, wife, you've stolen my bed and my water." He turned back to the mirror. "What the devil is next?"

"At Sacramento City a Reverend Mr. Hummer has been arrested for an attempt to murder his wife, by suffocation, under the pretense of driving the devil out of her. She was rescued from his hands by neighbors. A strong desire was shown to lynch the reverend gentleman . . . Humph. Looks like things aren't any better there than they are here." Hallie closed the newspaper and folded it in her lap. "Well, Duggie, that's all the news for now."

Hallie followed her sister's dull gaze and sighed. Dagny stared at a blank wall. Hallie placed the paper on a night table and bent over the bed. She turned her sister's face toward her and looked into her dazed eyes. "Please hear me, Duggie . . . I'm sorry, so, so sorry—"

"Aunt Maddie wants you to find the boys and get them washed up to eat." Liv had burst into the bedroom with her cat clamped to one shoulder.

"Oh?" Hallie asked, not liking Liv's bossy tone. "And what, pray tell, are you going to do?"

"Brush Mrs. Skunk." Liv pulled a silver hairbrush from her skirts and began to brush the pregnant cat.

Hallie walked over to Liv. "Where did you get that brush?"

"I found it."

"Where, Liv?"

"In the kitchen. It was wedged behind the dry sink."

"Did you ask Maddie about it?"

"Yes. She said it wasn't hers and I could have it if it didn't belong to you or Duggie."

Hallie eyed the brush. "It's not mine."

"I know."

"How do you know?"

"I looked in your room."

"Liv, how many times do I have to tell you to stay out of my things!"

"I wasn't in your things."

"You just said you looked in my room."

"I did." Liv drew the brush along the cat's furry back, and the animal melted her girth farther into the feather bed cover. "But I wasn't *in* your things. Your brush was sitting on the night table, in plain sight. So . . ." Liv looked up, the word "there" half formed on her sassy lips.

Hallie waited, glaring, but Liv wasn't stupid. She clamped her lips shut and turned back to brush her cat. Hallie started to leave, but remembered Dagny. "Who's going to feed Duggie?"

"I've got her supper right here." Maddie shouldered the bedroom door open, her hands filled with a tray of steamy food.

"Here, I'll get the door." Hallie grabbed the doorknob.

"Thanks. How is she?" Maddie asked, with a nod in Dagny's direction.

"The same."

"Give her time, Hallie," Maddie advised, carrying the tray to Dagny. She set the tray on the table and sat down. She glanced at Liv. "Well, Livvy, I see you've made good use of that brush."

"Yup." Liv kept brushing the cat, but she looked at Hallie long enough to give her an "I told you so" look.

"When you finish up there, Livvy, you can go wash your hands and set the table for me, please."

Hallie paused, awaiting Liv's usual argument. She wanted to see how Maddie would handle another one of Liv's inventive excuses.

"Sure." Liv agreed.

Hallie shook her head as she left the room. Liv never obeyed her without an argument. Belligerent little Liv was obviously different with Maddie. Apparently, for the younger Fredriksens, moving here was best. But Hallie was miserable. She hid it well enough, but at night, she would lay crying on the bed—the same bed where she'd made the biggest mistake of her life. She'd fought so hard, thinking in her silly mind that she could make Kit love her, never knowing the feat was impossible. His heart was locked in an old grave, cold and dead.

As she'd listened to him through the door, Hallie's hopes had died, and it hurt. So she'd hid in the kitchen while her pain swelled into such anger that she couldn't cover it, even for the sake of salvaging her own wedding. Oh God, that wedding—it was just awful. Hallie grabbed the newel post at the base of the stairs. She needed something to hang onto when she thought of the ceremony—and what transpired afterward. She sat down on the bottom step, her knees suddenly as weak as her will had been that evening. She had always thought she was a strong, willful person, but she had no strength when Kit held her or kissed her. Even her anger, hot and true as it had been, drowned in the sea of his arms.

With her wedding a mockery, and all her youthful dreams of love destroyed, a strong woman would have stood her ground. But she hadn't. Instead, she'd dissolved into him like sugar into hot coffee—all because her body craved the sweetness of his touch. Only when she emerged from the shock of what she had done did she find the strength to keep him, and his touch, at bay.

It had been easy at first. Since she felt nothing, her icy role had come naturally. But as each day went by, she found it harder and harder to ignore Kit, and this morning it had been nigh on impossible. The memories triggered by the sight of his bare chest were downright consuming. They ate right through her will and her common sense. Suddenly her skin was tingly and her body had started to rule her thoughts. If Kit had touched her then, she'd have been lost.

"You're supposed to be helping Maddie," Liv accused, standing right above Hallie with her hands on her hips and her bossy mouth puckered.

Hallie snapped back to the present, where her mood was not tolerant of her sister's obnoxious lip.

"Liv?" Hallie said, standing up and walking down the hall.

"What?"

Hallie pushed the kitchen door open. "Just shut up."

Kit grabbed the back of his neck for the third time in as many minutes.

"Hurt your neck?" Lee asked.

"It's just stiff." He stretched his neck, grimacing at the soreness before muttering, "I need a bed."

Lee slowed his mount so he could stay even with Kit's plodding pace. "How long are you going to keep this up?"

"What?"

"Blaming Hallie for every mistake you ever made."

Kit scowled at Lee. "Since when are you her champion? I thought you were only interested in her . . . petals."

"Ah-ha!" Lee grinned. "The old Howland counterattack. You really do that rather well, you know it?"

"What?"

"Avoid the question by launching your own verbal assault."

"God, I hate it when you start that sarcastic sh—"

"Attack evade, attack evade . . ." Lee interrupted.

"You harp like a woman."

"If I were one, we wouldn't be friends. You'd find some reason to hold me responsible for Jo's actions."

Kit turned in his saddle. "Just what the hell are you trying to say?"

"You want it in plain language?"

Kit nodded stiffly.

"I'm saying that you're making Hallie suffer because your first wife was an unfaithful bitch. Is that plain enough?" Lee looked Kit right in the eye.

Oh, that was plain enough. The truth of Lee's words clawed at Kit, and he didn't like it, because Lee reminded him of what an ass he was being.

"So what am I supposed to do about it? Forget my past experiences and magically turn into the loving husband?" Sarcasm dripped from his words.

"You could apologize and try to make the best of the situation. Hell, Kit, how many marriages are based on love, or at least remain love matches?"

"Not many," Kit answered.

"Right. So you're making it difficult for yourself. If I were in your shoes, I'd accept the situation. Look at what you have."

"No bed. That's what I have," Kit interjected.

"You have a bed and a pretty, young wife to share it with. For Godsake, this town is filled with men who would give up a gold claim to have what you're hell-bent on throwing away."

With each word Lee spoke, Kit's guilt became stronger. Rigid in his saddle, he stared straight ahead as they rode on.

They turned the corner and Lee reined his horse in. "Stop for a moment, will you? I want to see when this place is opening."

Kit had hardly noticed the building, yet it took up half the block. The building was red brick with only a few narrow windows, which were covered with decorative iron shutters. Workmen stood on a scaffold while they attempted to hang an oversized sign announcing the opening of the new Jenny Lind Theater.

Lee dismounted, and after a quick glance at Kit, decided to roll out the cannons. "I won't be long, but while I'm gone, you might think about how Jan would feel. You professed to owe him so much, and then you repay him by making his daughter miserable."

"Ah crap," Kit mumbled, frowning at Lee's back.

But he mulled over his friend's words, and it didn't take him long to admit Lee was right. He had treated Hallie badly, and she didn't deserve it. She wasn't Jo.

He crossed his arms and relaxed in the saddle. A fly buzzed around the head of his horse and landed. Distractedly, Kit watched the bay's ear twitch as he thought about his recent actions with a less jaundiced frame of mind. It was true. He hadn't repaid Jan. Sure, he'd done his guardian duties. He'd given the Fredriksen children shelter and provided for them, but he hadn't given much of himself, at least not since they'd moved into his home. Since then, he'd pawned off the responsibility for them on Maddie and Hallie.

He swatted the fly away. Despite the fact Hallie was Jan's daughter, Kit owed her too. She had moved to his home as he'd asked, she'd handled the children, and she'd been a great help to his aunt. He was the one who had caused all the problems. He was attracted to Hallie, and he couldn't deal with it. What it boiled down to was, the almighty Kit Howland, tower of self-restraint, had thought he'd become immune to women. The realization that he wasn't as strong as he thought was as emasculating as his lack of control where Hallie was concerned. So he'd blamed her.

He was a fool. Also, he knew deep in his craw that there was no way he could wipe Hallie from his mind, especially after the other night. They were bonded together, both lawfully and in his lusty head; and now that he admitted that bond, it wasn't so bad. After all, Kit mentally justified, he wasn't in love with her, and that kept him safe. Why shouldn't he make the most of his mistakes? Hell, it would be better for Hallie, he reasoned, and he'd be doing his duty to her both as Jan's daughter and as his wife. He could view this marriage as a business partnership, and maybe they could become friends. He would like that, because he really did like her. A small smile simmered around his lips. Hallie's lopsided way of thinking intrigued him, and she made him laugh. Lee was usually the only one who could do that.

Lee returned, grinning as if he'd just struck gold. "They open tomorrow night, and guess who got the last box?" Lee waved the tickets under Kit's nose.

Kit eyed the tickets. "How many seats in the box?"

"Four."

Lee was enjoying this; Kit could read it in his friend's devilish eyes. "You're not going to make this easy, are you?"

"Nope." Lee smiled.

"All right. Mind if we join you?"

"We?"

"Hallie and myself!"

"Sure." Lee remounted. "It's good to see you've come to your senses."

"Well, I need a good night's sleep in a real bed," Kit admitted, rubbing his sore neck. Even now it wasn't easy to admit aloud that he'd been wrong.

"Uh-huh," Lee agreed with a smirk.

Kit rode on, absently thinking aloud. "Moving into the study wasn't smart. Now I've painted myself into a corner. I've got to get back in Hallie's good graces, Maddie's, too, and still save face."

"The theater tickets should help."

"Maddie will appreciate that I'm taking Hallie to the theater," Kit acknowledged. "But I'm not sure about Hallie. She's afraid of me," he said quietly, remembering their encounter this morning and the fear he'd read in her eyes.

"I'm sure we'll think of something," Lee added with a laugh, "and still manage to save your ugly old face."

Hallie glanced across the table. The twins' heads were bent together and they chattered to each other behind their cupped hands. "What are you two whispering about?" she asked.

Both boys looked up, their eyes wide. They glanced at each other and replied in unison, "Nothing."

Hallie exchanged a knowing look with Maddie before she continued dishing up the boys' plates. She buttered their biscuits, and the boys' eyes lit up. They loved any kind of bread, as long as it was soaked yellow with butter.

She handed them their plates. "You boys eat now, and no more whispering."

The meal continued in silence, at least until Gunnar

finished his third biscuit. "Hallie, how do I know when I'm older?"

It amazed Hallie how much knowledge she took for granted. She smiled at Knut. "When you have your next birthday, in November, you'll be another year older."

Gunnar looked thoughtful, and then he asked, "Can you only get older in years?"

"What do you mean?"

"Am I only older on my birthday?"

Liv snickered, bringing a glare from Hallie and a negative shake of Maddie's head. Liv returned to her food, and Hallie was sure her own glare had nothing to do with her sister's obedience.

Turning back to Gunnar, Hallie explained, "No, you don't just age on your birthday. Every minute, every hour, or every day, you get older. Like right now, you're older than you were this morning because you're closer to your next birthday."

Gunnar appeared to be soaking all this in.

"Me too?" Knut asked, his little voice threaded with excitement.

"You sure are," Hallie assured him.

Knut looked at Gunnar. "Did you hear her? We're older now!"

Gunnar frowned thoughtfully and then turned to Maddie. "Are we really older now, Aunt Maddie?"

Maddie smiled. "Yes you are."

"Remember when you said we could have a pet when we got older?" Gunnar recited.

Maddie and Hallie had been had.

"I meant a lot older," Maddie explained. "Like six or seven."

"But that's not what you said," Knut whined, and then he spilled the beans. "We found a pet and we want to keep it like Liv. You just said we were older."

Maddie and Hallie exchanged looks, and Gunnar added, "You did." He nodded his bright little head. "You really did."

"Wait till you see'm!" Knut jumped down from his chair and ran to the back door. He pulled it open and dragged a sack inside before Hallie or Maddie could do a thing. He bent over the sack and opened it, lifting out their pet. Turning, he carried it toward the kitchen table.

"Look!" Knut said, holding up the animal.

"Good Lord!" Maddie screamed. "It's a skunk!"

At Maddie's scream, Knut dropped the skunk and it ran under the table.

Maddie grabbed a broom and yelled, "Catch that thing before it sprays!"

"How?" Hallie shouted, standing on her chair, as was Liv, who was pinching her nose, just in case.

"I don't know, just do it!" Maddie waved her broom in the air.

The boys were peering under the table, and Knut kept calling, "Here skunky, here skunky . . ."

Maddie started poking her broom at the table, and Gunnar ran and grabbed the brush end. "Don't hurt him, Aunt Maddie!"

"We're not going to hurt him, Gunnar, we just need to catch him!" Maddie turned toward Hallie. "Get on the other side of the table while I shake the broom around . . . Gunnar! Let go!"

Hallie wasn't going to touch that thing for the life of her. She'd had enough bad luck lately. She called out to Maddie, "I can't catch it!"

"Thunderation! Where in the blazes is Duncan?" Maddie yelled, trying to get Gunnar to let go of her broom. "Duncan! Duncan!"

The door burst open and Kit, Lee, and Duncan came running into the room.

"What the hell is going on?" Kit bellowed, staring at his aunt, who was shouting while she played tug of war with one of the twins. Kit turned around. Hallie and Liv were huddled next to each other, on chairs.

Liv's voice caught his attention. "There's a skunk under the table!"

His worried gaze shot beneath the table. "Don't scare it!" Kit ordered.

At that instant the skunk raced from beneath the table right toward Duncan and Lee. Duncan stepped aside and the animal ran right through Lee's legs and out into the hall.

"Don't let it upstairs!" Maddie shouted, wresting the broom from Gunnar and waving it frantically in the air.

Lee and Duncan ran after it. Seconds later a door slammed so hard the candles in the ceiling lamp shimmied. Kit pushed open the kitchen door while the women and children huddled behind him, peeking like nosy ferrets through any open space left in the doorway.

Lee leaned casually against the wall, with a silent Duncan by his side. "I locked it in the study," Lee announced with a cream-whiskered grin.

Hallie waited for Kit's bellow of anger, but it never came. He looked at Lee for an intense moment, and then Lee said the strangest thing.

"I just saved your ugly old face."

And all Hallie heard was Kit's ringing laughter.

Kit pushed open the bedroom door. Hallie sat in the overstuffed chair, her face blanched with fear. Her eyes darted to his loaded arms. "What are you doing?"

"Moving back in," Kit answered, pointedly ignoring her gasp.

"Why?"

He dropped the folded shirts onto the dresser top. "I can't very well sleep in the study. It'll take days to air out." The horrendous smell still lingered in Kit's nostrils. He glanced at Hallie, noting the dread in her pale face. Maybe if she were kept busy she'd forget her wariness.

Raising a shirt to his nose, he sniffed. "Hallie, would you see if these smell like skunk? I can't tell."

She stared a moment then nodded. Kit handed her his clothes and she sniffed at the shirts and then handed them back. "They're fine," she said, still looking at him with quiet fear.

He bent and picked up his woolen stockings. "You didn't check these," he said, frowning to mask his smirk.

Hallie shot out of the chair. "I will not smell your socks!" She crossed her arms and glared at him.

This Hallie was much better than the frightened rabbit she'd been a few seconds before. He bit back his satisfied smile. He had to admit he enjoyed teasing her. "You're shirking your wifely duties."

"I did not promise to smell your socks! Besides, the wedding was a farce. Your exact words, remember?" She plopped down on the bed.

Kit turned to face her. "I'm sorry you heard that, Hallie."

"I bet you are. Sorry I heard, not sorry you said it." Her chin lifted.

"That's not what I meant, dammit!" Kit ran a hand through his hair and took a deep breath. "I am sorry I said those things, and that I hurt you." He walked to the bed and started to reach for her.

"Stay away, Kit." Hallie scooted back on the bed. "Don't touch me."

He stopped. "Hallie, please, I won't touch you. I just want to talk about this."

She crawled around to the other side of the bed, stood and went back to sit in the chair. She looked him right in the eye and waved her hand in the air. "So talk."

"I'd like to start over and try to forget what happened."

"I'd like to forget a lot of things," Hallie muttered.

Kit sighed, looking for patience. Then he sat on the edge of the bed. "Okay, Hallie. You tell me, what can I do? I didn't want to hurt you, and I still don't. There's nothing you can say that I haven't already heard, either from Lee or from my own conscience."

Silently, she watched and waited.

"We've gotten ourselves into this—"

"We?" she interrupted.

"Okay, me. I'm the one who made the mistakes. I'll take the blame, but can't you meet me halfway? I'd like to pick up the pieces of this marriage, and maybe we can reach some compromise."

Hallie looked away, but she appeared to be thinking over his words.

"The damage is done, Hallie," Kit reminded her.

When she turned back to him, her eyes revealed her pain. He knew he'd hurt her, but the knowledge didn't make viewing the deep hurt any easier. His shoulders sagged and he tried again. "I'm sorry." The words sounded empty and shallow, even to him.

Her eyes filled with tears and she looked away, but Kit could see her biting her lip in an effort to hold them back. She was trying to hold her own, and her show of strength touched something in Kit.

"You make the terms, Hallie. I'll agree."

She stood, picked up a hankie from the table and twisted it in her hands, seemingly unaware of her nervous action. "Where will you sleep?" she asked.

"Here."

"In the bed?"

"Hallie, I'm tired of sleeping on the sofa."

She appeared thoughtful. For long seconds her eyes looked everywhere but at him. Then she said, "Okay, Kit. We'll try, on my terms, right?"

"Right."

"And you don't have to sleep on the sofa anymore." She smiled, the first smile he'd seen on her lips in weeks.

Kit smiled back. It had worked!

She walked over to the armoire and opened it. She turned around with a blanket in her hands and she threw it at him. It hit him right in the chest. "You can sleep in the chair."

Chapter

Nineteen

Hallie pulled the coverlet over the pillows. She walked over to the chair and folded Kit's blanket. His pipe and tobacco pouch sat on the small table, and some colored paper stuck out from beneath the pouch. Hallie strained to read the writing, but it was too small. She glanced at Kit. He was delving through the dresser drawers, cursing under his breath.

She used the folded blanket to block his view, and slid one of the papers out from under the pouch, straining to try to read it.

"They're theater tickets, for tonight."

Hallie jumped at the sound of his voice, reading into the depths of her devious mind. He had a perfect view of her actions because he was on his hands and knees, looking at her while he felt around underneath the dresser.

"We're going with Lee."

"Who's going?"

"We are, you and I, husband and wife." He leaned into the dresser, still searching.

The theater. Hallie'd never been to a theater, not ever. She watched for a moment, both stunned and excited.

"Where the hell is that thing?" Kit straightened and immediately grabbed his lower back, groaning.

"Are you all right? What thing?"

He grabbed the dresser and stood, slowly and stiffly. "I can't find my brush." He started opening and closing the drawers again.

His brush? Hallie's mind flashed with the picture of Liv, using Kit's brush on her cat. While he slammed around the room, Hallie walked across the hall and retrieved the brush. She walked back into the room and held it out to a grumbling Kit. "Is this it?"

He spun around, scowling. He glanced at the brush and then grabbed it, drawing it through his thick curly hair before Hallie had a chance to warn him.

"Where was it?"

Hallie stepped closer, automatically brushing the cat hair from the shoulders of his white shirt.

He stopped brushing. "What are you doing?"

Hallie smiled. "Brushing the cat hair off your clean shirt."

He examined the brush. "Liv?"

Hallie nodded, biting back her grin. She plucked the brush out of his hand and walked away. "I'll clean this for you. After all, I wouldn't want to be accused of shirking my wifely duties." She left the room laughing.

"I'll be right back." Kit jumped down from the carriage and loped up to the door of a narrow brick building.

Leaning away from the lamplight, Hallie watched him wait at the door of the house. He looked so tall, in the silk high hat, and so impressive, cloaked in black except for the stark collar of his white dress shirt, which caught the light from the narrow windows. Though his face was shadowed, she could picture every fine, masculine feature, and she squirmed, her thoughts making her uneasy and more nervous than she already was.

Hallie stared at the white lace of her gloves. They made her hands look softer and more pink—at least Maddie had said so when she had helped button her into the white lace gown. Pushing aside the deep rose velvet of her cloak, she fingered the silk lace. It shimmered in the soft carriage light, and she knew this wasn't a dream. She was really here, dressed like a princess and on her way to her first play, and she was with Kit, her husband.

Her stomach fluttered. She wasn't sure if this was good or bad. Her truce with Kit was new and tenuous. She had no idea what he expected of her. Furthermore, she didn't know what she expected of herself. Was she smart for making the best of her situation, or was she weak for giving in to Kit, whom she loved so hopelessly?

The carriage door opened and the wind blew a spicy, exotic fragrance into the vehicle's already tight interior. A woman was lifted through the door and she sat right across from her. Her midnight-blue silk skirts and matching cloak took up almost the entire carriage seat.

Lee poked his red-bearded head inside and smiled a hello. "Hallie, this is Miss Sabine Dolan." Lee smiled at the woman. "This is Mrs. Howland."

His words sent Hallie's head reeling. The only other time she'd been called Mrs. Howland was by Kit, the night they were married, and somehow, hearing it again made Hallie feel strange and even more jittery, until she sensed the woman's penetrating gaze.

Hallie looked up and really noticed Sabine Dolan. Her features were perfect. She had flawless white skin and eyes the exact shade of her dress, but it was her hair that rang a warning in Hallie. It was red, not the lively orange red of Maddie's, but a deep, dark mahogany red, the same color as her Norwegian *kusine,* Anja, the one who used to pinch her. Hallie decided she was being silly, associating her mean, pinching cousin with this woman just because they had the same hair color. Then Hallie caught the woman's frosty smile and she changed her mind.

Suddenly, Kit sat down beside her and the carriage took off, rocking its way through the narrow, hilly streets. Sabine dominated the conversation, just like she dominated the carriage seat and the men's attention. She made Hallie feel inadequate, so she sat quietly, listening to Sabine's flirting and trying not to consider her evening ruined. Kit reached over and threaded his hand through hers. When she looked up, he winked, and Hallie no longer gave a fig about Sabine or her chatter.

As they neared the theater, the street was thick with other playgoers. They inched their way forward, and once in front of the theater, Kit opened the door. He and Lee got out to help the women down. The crowd at the entrance milled about, filling the night air with noise and laughter. Kit pulled her to his side while he spoke to Duncan, and then they joined Lee and Sabine as they made their way inside. Tobacco smoke and musky sweat laced with strong perfume hung as densely as fog in the air of the foyer. Hallie's eyes teared in reaction.

Kit's hand held her close to his side as they moved with the crowd. Finally, the space widened and Kit led her into an open section cordoned off with gold-braided rope. There were no grubby, sweaty miners here, only the well-dressed members of the city's burgeoning affluent class. Kit helped her off with her cloak and handed them, along with his hat and gloves, to a waiting attendant.

The man then assisted Lee, and when Sabine removed her flowing cloak, Hallie had to stifle her shocked gasp. The woman's dress had no bodice, only a lacy ruffle that barely lapped over her nipples and then plunged in a deep vee ending just above her tightly cinched waist. At least Hallie assumed it was cinched; even Liv's waist wasn't that small. Then she stared, trying to figure out what type of corset Sabine wore beneath so scant a dress.

"Put your eyes back in your head, sweet. You'll only give her the reaction she wants," Kit said, unable to keep the smile from lilting through his voice.

Hallie turned away from Sabine and moved closer to Kit. "What do you suppose she's wearing underneath?" she whispered.

Kit laughed out loud and then leaned down to her. "Skin, lots of skin."

Another attendant passed by, this one carrying a tray filled with glasses. Kit helped himself to two, handing one to her. She eyed the pale, bubbling liquid as if it were witches' brew.

"It's champagne," Kit explained, before he sipped his own glass, watching her over its brim.

Hallie slowly brought the glass near her lips. The bubbles sprinkled her nose, and it smelled . . . odd, dry yet tart. Then she tasted it and her face puckered. "It's like rotten cider that's been watered down."

Kit choked on his drink. He took the glass from her hand and set it and his own on a ledge. He took her arm again. "A wife with simple tastes. What more could a man ask for?"

Simple? "Wait, Kit. I changed my mind." She plucked the glass off the ledge and downed the champagne in one huge gulp. She held out the glass. "More, please."

"I thought you didn't like it." He scrutinized her.

"It grows on you," she replied.

Kit looked around. "I don't see him anywhere. You've had enough anyway, for your first taste."

The waiter came from Hallie's direction. "Oh! I was just thinking about you," she said, smiling sweetly at the man while she took two glasses off his tray and guzzled them down. She hardly had time to set the glasses back on the puzzled man's tray when Kit pulled her down the carpeted corridor.

Hallie felt delightfully light. She glanced at her surroundings, eyeing the tiered chandeliers and the dance of their flickering candles. Etched glass wall sconces lined the stairway and gilt mirrors hung from the richly flocked wallpaper. She tried to see her reflection in the mirrors, but there wasn't time to focus and keep up with Kit's long stride.

"Where are we going?" she asked, swallowing a burp that would rival Liv's.

"To the box," Kit said, his tone brooking no argument.

"Oh. That's nice."

He pulled her through a draped doorway, and he paused, apparently letting his eyes become accustomed to the dim theater. Lee and Sabine were seated on the right, in the rear chairs. Kit pulled her around and pushed her into one of the front chairs. She should have been irritated at Kit's manhandling, but she didn't really mind; right now, she liked everyone. Sabine tittered. Well, Hallie thought, not everyone.

She blinked and looked around the cavernous room. The stage was draped with the same rich material that secluded the box. The high ceiling rose another two stories above them, and the area below the elevated stage was jammed with people, sitting or standing wherever there was a small space. Hallie weaved slightly and she felt that queasy vertigo feeling.

Kit pulled her back. "Are you all right?"

She shrugged, her face contorting a bit.

"Oh Christ! I forgot about the height." Kit pulled her chair back, next to his own, and pulled her against his side, letting her rest her head on his shoulder. "Is that better?" he asked.

It was wonderful! Hallie nodded, snuggling closer to his warm body. The curtain rose, and soon she was immersed in the actors and their play. Kit's arm held her comfortably against him, and she relaxed, leaning her head against his neck. The rich scent of his tobacco began to work its magic, and then his hand softly caressed her bare arm. Hallie sighed, and then suddenly hiccuped.

Her hand flew to her mouth, trying to stifle the next one. It was louder than the first, and they seemed to pop out of her like champagne bubbles. People began to "shoosh" at them, and in a flash Kit was kissing the breath right out of her. Her hiccups left, her sense left, and she just let herself taste him. His tongue played havoc with her own, filling her mouth thickly and then retreating to beckon her mimicry of the kiss.

It was the applause, loud and cheering, that finally made them sever the kiss. With slumberous, passionate eyes,

Hallie gazed at Kit. His look was as hot as she felt. She looked down, aware of his hand resting on her breast. She watched as he slowly drew his fingertips across the sensitive skin of her collarbone. Her breasts swelled and tightened, and she shivered from the soft stroke of his fingertips as they whispered across her skin. The activity around them broke the spell, turning her passion into embarrassment.

Moments later Kit stood, stretching his long legs. "It's intermission. Do you want something? Lemonade, not champagne."

Hallie shook her head.

"Stay away from the balcony rail, will you? I'll be back in a few minutes. You'll be all right here?" Kit nodded in Sabine's direction.

"I'll be fine." Hallie was getting a headache. Her chair was well away from the railing, and she could care less about Sabine.

After a few peaceful minutes, in which she tried—without success—to understand her ripening sensuality, she felt something poke her shoulder. It was Sabine's ivory fan prodding for her attention. She swallowed her dislike and decided to give the woman a chance. She turned around with a friendly smile plastered on her face.

"When are you due?" Sabine asked, staring at Hallie's waist.

Her smile died. "Pardon me?"

"The baby, my dear, when is it due?"

"There is no baby due," Hallie blurted.

"Really? How odd. Your marriage was so . . . hurried, that I assumed . . . Well, my dear, you must know that Kit Howland has always been considered unattainable. Since he's never associated with any particular woman, I suppose I expected that he had . . ." Sabine must have seen the rising anger in Hallie's look, because the woman shut her mouth. She snapped open her fan and prudently changed the subject.

"My, but the air is close in here." Sabine fluttered her fan while her piercing eyes darted from one group to another.

Sizing up the competition, Hallie thought, watching the burgundy-haired witch position her exposed body to where it would draw the most attention. It irritated Hallie, having to sit by while this woman preened in front of the ribald males in the mezzanine below. The whistles and jeers forced Hallie to glance down. Suddenly, her embarrassment, her anger, and her headache vanished, replaced by pure panic. Through the raucous crowd, one face stared back at her. It was Abner Brown.

She tried to memorize his position before she raced from the box in search of Kit. She worked her way down the crowded stairway and then paused, trying to locate Kit or Lee. To get through the swarm of people, she had to finally edge her way along the wall of the corridor. She came to where the hallway split, and as she edged blindly around the corner, a hand jerked her into a dimly lit nook.

"What the hell are you doing out here alone!"

Kit's angry voice forced a breath of relief from her lips. "Abner Brown's here. I saw him," she blurted.

Kit grabbed her shoulders. "When? Where?"

"About five minutes ago, down in the far gallery, near the pillar under the front box."

"I'm sending you home with Duncan."

"But what—"

"Don't argue with me!" Kit bellowed, dragging her, cloakless, out of the theater.

Hallie's teeth chattered from the cold, wet air. "I c-can't ar-argue if I—I fr-freeze to d-death," she grumbled, hugging her bare arms.

Kit shrugged out of his coat and wrapped it around her just as their carriage pulled up. He all but threw her inside, gave Duncan some garbled instructions, and then disappeared through the theater doors. Hallie huddled against the seat, wondering why they weren't leaving.

The carriage door opened and Duncan helped Sabine inside. Hallie stifled her groan; she had forgotten about Sabine. As the carriage snapped into motion, the woman ranted about Lee and her ruined evening. Hallie shivered in silence, thinking that Lee was lucky, since Sabine would most likely have pinched him.

Abner moved through the crowd, pushing and shoving at anything in his hurried path. He turned his pasty, sunken face around and scanned the room.

She had seen him, and he had to get away. He clawed his escape, his mind flashing, one moment with the picture of Dagny's beaten face, and another with the look of horror on the older sister. As he neared the rear exit he spotted that friend of Howland's, the whaling captain named Prescott. He was pointing right at Abner and shouting. Abner's anxious eyes darted to the other doorway. Howland looked straight at him, fighting his way toward him. The man's look was rabid.

Abner stooped to the floor, hiding his escape path from the two men, and crawled toward the stage. When he neared the front, he stood, looking for his pursuers. He heard a commotion a few feet away. Sheriff Hayes was there and had spotted him too. Abner looked around and ran through the drapes near the wing of the stage, not stopping until he was hidden behind a huge wooden crate.

His heart throbbed in his ears and his breathing was ragged and shallow. He could hear them following, tracking, ordering his hunt. The sounds of the play began again, but still Abner could feel the men closing in. Along the open framing of one wall stood a row of trunks with costumes scattered around them. Abner peered around the crate and then ran for the nearest open trunk. He shoved the musty clothing aside and crouched inside, pulling the trunk closed.

He hid in the dark interior, panting and feeling like a hunted animal. He, Abner Brown, who should have been viewing the play from a private box, cowered in a trunk. He rocked with contempt.

Nothing was left. He had nothing; his heritage was long ago sold, and his name no longer meant anything. His business and home were destroyed, and he was a fugitive, forced to hide in the depths of a floating opium den, where his gold had bought the sweet oblivion his body craved.

Abner closed his burning eyes, and his mind—in a rare, lucid moment—savored an old dream. The same one he had tried to live tonight. Dreams of play openings, of gaiety, of respect, of position—the dream of the successful man he thought he had been.

Kit closed the door and slid the bolt. On the small table near the staircase, a pale light still burned. He removed his cloak and hung it on the hall tree, hanging Hallie's cloak alongside. He walked over to the table and turned up the lamp wick. It was after four, and he was exhausted. They'd searched the theater and the surrounding area, but somehow Abner had slipped away. It ate at Kit, knowing that lunatic was still lurking around.

Using the lamp to light his way, he went upstairs. He entered the dark bedroom and set the lamp on the nearest table. His blanket sat on the chair—the one he'd been sleeping in.

The sound of Hallie's even breathing drew his tired gaze. She slept soundly on one side of the bed, huddled in a lump underneath a mound of covers. Over half the bed was empty. He eyed the chair. Not tonight, he thought. He sat down and pulled off his dress boots, wondering just how mad Hallie would be when she found him in bed with her.

He sank back into the chair, releasing the studs from his shirt before reaching over to drop them on the table. He missed. The studs bounced and rolled, scattering on the wooden floor and reminding him of the last time they had done that, on the night he made love to Hallie. That sweet night when he'd learned that his passion hadn't died, and the moment he admitted to himself that he wanted her, craved her, and needed to bury himself deep within her. And he had. But it had also been the same day he'd hurt her, both emotionally and physically.

While their marriage arrangement was improving, she

was still frightened of him, and that was not something he was proud of. He needed to erase the hurt and her sensual timidity. It was there, her fear, hovering around them whenever their passion flared. He'd felt it tonight, when he had kissed her hiccups away.

The memory of that roaring case of hiccups made him smile. He never knew what to expect from her. Just when he thought he had her pegged, she'd do something that blew his theory to hell.

On the way to the theater she'd sat quietly, as if intimidated, but later, when he'd teased her about the champagne, she'd plucked up and done exactly as she pleased, and he had a hunch that she'd done it just to defy him. Of course, as he well knew, liquor could make one do stupid things, whether out of false courage or, as in his case, crawling into the wrong bed. And crawling into bed was exactly what he was going to do right now.

Kit unbuttoned his trousers and pulled them off, adding them to the pile made by his discarded shirt and his thin boot socks. He started to remove his flannel small clothes but stopped. Maybe Hallie wouldn't be as angry if he weren't in bed buck naked. It was worth a try.

He walked around to the empty side of the bed and drew back his end of the covers. Slowly, he got into the warm, soft bed. It was heaven, and the muscles of his neck and back relaxed. It was almost as if they sighed with the forgotten comfort of a real, honest-to-goodness bed. An instant later he was sound asleep.

Abner opened his eyes. He had fallen asleep, crouched in the costume trunk, and had no idea how long he'd slept. The muscles of his legs were asleep. He listened intently. There was nothing but silence.

Very carefully, he wedged open the trunk and peered out through the crack. As the crack slowly widened, inch by inch, he watched, praying he wouldn't be caught. The room was almost as dark as the interior of the trunk. No stage lamps were lit and there were no windows backstage to let in light or give him an idea of the time.

The theater appeared empty. He crawled out of the trunk, willing his tingly legs to support him. After a few moments respite, allowing the feeling to return to his legs and making sure he was truly alone, he walked over to the draped doorway, and peered into the black theater. It, too, was empty. A narrow el hid a small door. Abner carefully slid the bolt, and opening the door a crack, saw that it led outside, into the alley. He left, making his way to the street, where the pale glow in the east signaled dawn.

Twenty minutes later the pain was back. Abner leaned against a pier post, grabbing his middle in reaction to the stabbing ache that knifed up from deep in his bowels. He stumbled forward as the sharp pain subsided, but within seconds another consumed him.

Stooped, he moved along the barrel pier that bobbed its way to the opium ship. Wave after painful wave ripped through his addicted body, and he grasped the rope rail, pulling himself past the storage ships out to the end of the wobbly pier where, in a dank hold, smoldering, black balls of relief awaited him.

His nose began to run, and he wiped it with the grimy sleeve of his woolen coat. Grasping the rope ladder, he climbed to the deck, and that was when he sneezed, over and over, as the recurring fit took control of his deteriorating body. Sneezing uncontrollably, he stumbled into the hold, heading for the brazier guarded by the old, hollow-eyed woman. Through eyes raining with tears, he grabbed the long needle that held the drug—his drug.

Again the pain came, starting at his rectum and serrating upward until his head throbbed with it. He sucked up the smoke, taking in quick, panting sips of the narcotic vapor that governed his mood and decayed his mind. He moved to a bunk, still drawing on the smoke, and laid down, sticking the needle into a hole whittled into the rough wood of the bunk. Then he stared, unseeing, while his mind painted rich, chimerical images that surpassed anything he could view with his watery eyes.

Automatically, he turned his head and inhaled, the deep needle holder having positioned the gummy ball conveniently near his musty pillow. He dreamed of wealth, parties, and balls; he dreamed of success, social acceptance, respect; he dreamed of his maternal estate, of his mother and the horses she loved, of the hunt.

And he remembered the trunk.

His teeth ground together until his jaw shook with anger, and his long fingers rolled into rock-hard fists. He was the hunted, the fox. Abner Moffatt Brown, forced to hide like a hunted animal. The dream metamorphosed into a nightmare where red-coated hunters surrounded him, screaming, "His father's son! His father's son!" Their screams became a chant, "Weakling . . . coward . . . failure . . ." The hunters' hands held pistols, the butt end of each gun facing him as he cowered and the hunters egged him to use the gun, as his father had.

Abner opened his mouth and sucked in more smoke, and then the image changed. The small, cowering fox bared his teeth and the animal's jaw grew. The fox became a lion, roaring his rage and charging the hunters, who now had faces: Hayes, Prescott, and the man who was being crushed in the lion's jaw, the man who'd cornered the fox—Kit Howland.

Abner laughed, for the fox had grown into a lion and exacted his revenge.

Chapter

Twenty

Kit awoke with a start. His muscles didn't ache. He was in a bed, a soft, warm, heavenly bed. Then he remembered Hallie. He was on his side, facing the edge of the bed, so he couldn't see if she was awake. He stared at the wall for a minute, trying to decide how he could turn over and not wake her. She was liable to clobber him—or kick him onto the floor, as she had before. Closing his eyes, he groaned and rolled over, flinging his arm up above his head so he could open one eye and peer from under his arm. The bed was empty.

He sighed with relief and then scanned the room. She wasn't there. He gave in to the luxury of a yawn, and laid there savoring the feel of the bed. His home life had gone well since he'd applied his work ethic. When he decided to treat the marriage like a business partnership, he'd made amazing progress, from sleeping in the study to the bedroom, from barely speaking to a halfway companionable—even entertaining—evening out with his wife, and his latest progress, moving from the chair to the bed.

Now he needed to quell her fear. If he could just catch Hallie unaware, apply a little seduction, he'd be able to show her that physical loving wasn't always painful. He'd teach her pleasure, even if the control killed him.

Throwing back the covers, Kit got out of bed. From all the light shining through the bedroom windows, he knew it was late. He washed and shaved with the tepid water left in the pitcher and then dressed. He descended the stairs, feeling better than he'd felt in a damn long time.

The mouth-watering smell of bread baking and fried ham made his stomach growl like Lee's. He entered the kitchen where the bread, tantalizing and yeasty, sat cooling on the kitchen table. He poured some coffee from the tin pot, picking out the eggshells that floated on the top of his mug. He must have reached the bottom of the pot. Grabbing the butter crock from its cool home in the water tub, Kit crossed over to the kitchen table, sipping distractedly on his black coffee. It was strong and gritty from the grounds, but this morning he didn't care.

The *Alta* sat folded near the bread. Sitting down, he tore off a chunk of warm bread and rubbed it in the white butter, then folded it in two to better shove it into his mouth. He opened the paper and chewed while he read.

"Did you catch him?" Maddie stood in the doorway.

He shook his head. "I don't know how that bastard got away. Lee and I thought we had him."

"I'd love to be alone in a room for about five minutes with that scum—"

The twins raced into the room, cutting off Maddie with their arguing.

"It was your fault!" one accused.

"Was not! You let him out of the bag. That's when he got loose," the other retorted.

"You two stop your arguing," Maddie ordered. "The damage is done, and you promised—no more pets."

"But it looked just like Liv's cat," one of them said.

"That's enough! You two sit down and I'll get you something— Christopher! What are you doing to my bread?"

"Eating it," Kit said, ripping off another chunk and swabbing it across the crock. "Isn't that what it's for?"

Maddie glared at him. "Don't you get smart with me, I used to wipe your nose when you were no bigger than these two!" She spun around and started banging around the kitchen.

The twins sidled over to Kit with looks of wonder on their faces. The one on Kit's left spoke first. "You used to be little?" His eyes grew more.

Kit laid down the paper. "Yup. 'Bout your size."

"Really?" the other one asked.

Kit smiled at him and then looked back and forth between the two. For the life of him, he could not tell these boys apart. "Which one is which?"

The boy on his left scrutinized Kit.

Ah, Kit thought, this must be Gunnar, the thinker.

"Are you mad at us for the skunk?" he asked, his eyes still trying to read Kit.

Kit hid a smile, knowing these two little boys had no idea how indebted he was to them.

The one on the right piped up. "It was his idea. I just opened the bag."

Knut, the tattletale.

"No, I'm not mad, this time . . ." Kit said, forcing a stern tone into his voice. "But don't pull something like that again, okay?"

Gunnar looked relieved. "Okay," he agreed, and the imp grinned. "I'm Gunnar."

"And I'm Knut!" the other boy said, following his brother's suit.

Kit tore off some more bread and handed it to the boys. They sat down next to him, mimicking his butter dipping.

A butter knife clunked onto the table, along with three plates and some cloth napkins. "Use the knife, Kit, you're teaching these two bad habits," Maddie ordered, and then returned to her work at the dry sink.

"I like you," Gunnar admitted, making Kit smile.

"I like you too," Kit said. "Both of you."

Knut smiled with his mouth full. He swallowed and then added his two cents. "Even if you are old."

Kit choked on his coffee.

"Will we be tall when we're old like you?" Gunnar asked.

"Probably," Kit answered, adding under his breath, "if you live that long."

A snort came from Maddie's direction.

"I'm sorry our skunk smelled up your room." Gunnar mimicked Kit and ripped off a chunk of bread.

"But it doesn't stink anymore," Knut added. "Maddie said so. Huh, Maddie?"

"It's aired out," Maddie replied, wiping her hands on her apron and checking the other batch of bread in the oven.

"Now you don't have to sleep with Hallie anymore," Gunnar reasoned.

There was sudden quiet from Maddie's direction, and Kit tried to think of something to say. Finally, he resorted to logic. "I married your sister, and married people sleep together."

Both boys were thoughtful. Then Gunnar said, "But you didn't sleep with Hallie at first. You sleeped down here, remember?"

Maddie leaned against the range, crossing her arms. "This one I've got to hear."

Kit scowled at Maddie. Then he turned to the boys. "I . . . uh—"

The door burst open and Liv came running in. "She had her kittens! My cat had her kittens! Come see."

The boys raced out of the room, and Kit relaxed.

Maddie walked over. "You've more luck than any man deserves. I'd have paid a pretty penny to hear you explain your pigheadedness to those two boys."

"I'm trying to make up for it, Maddie. Just give me time."

Maddie started to leave the kitchen, but she paused at the door. "As far as this marriage goes, you've had an angel on your shoulder, Kit Howland, and from the way you've treated Hallie, I don't think you deserve it. All I can figure is that you're a prime example of how the Lord protects dumb animals."

With that, she left the room.

Duncan helped Hallie down from the carriage, and she turned, waiting for him to get Dagny. The huge man lifted her sister and carefully set her down, as if Dagny would break in two. Hallie took her sister's arm and helped her ascend the stairs. Duncan opened the door and followed them inside.

Hallie untied Dagny's cloak and removed her gloves, while her sister just stood there, staring. There was no life in her eyes and she never spoke, nor acknowledged that she heard or recognized anyone. Hallie had hoped that Dr. Jim would have some suggestions, some diagnosis, or a cure. But this visit was the same as the others—hopeless. He said she could snap out of her dazed world at any time or . . . never. They would have to wait, and waiting was not something Hallie did well. She was a doer, not a waiter.

"Are you going to take her up to her room?" Duncan asked.

He seemed anxious, as if her answer was critical.

Hallie removed her own gloves and cloak before she replied. "I thought she might like to sit in the parlor for a while." Hallie glanced at Duncan, whose eyes gave away his thoughts. "Would you like to do me a favor and keep her company for a little bit?"

His eyes lit up.

"The doctor said we should spend time talking or reading to her. He thinks it might help her come out of this thing."

"I'd like to help, if you don't mind?"

A small smile played at Hallie's lips. "I think Dagny would like that."

Duncan smiled shyly. "Yes. Thank you, Mrs. Howland."

Hallie's stomach twisted. She turned to Duncan, who had just taken Dagny's arm to guide her into the parlor. "Call me Hallie, Duncan, please."

The huge man nodded, then gently guided her sister into the other room, talking to her softly.

Hallie walked down the hallway. The door to Kit's study was open, and Hallie could hear the sound of Liv and the twins' voices, arguing. She looked into the room. Liv, the twins, and Maddie were stooped over something behind Kit's massive desk.

"What's going on?" Hallie asked.

Maddie smiled and waved her in, and Knut's head popped up. "It's kittens, Hallie! The cat had her kittens!"

"My cat," Liv corrected.

Hallie walked over to the desk, and there, settled deep in the bottom drawer of Kit's desk, was Mrs. Skunk and five little newborn kittens.

"Oh, they're so cute, Liv." Hallie watched the kittens squirm blindly around their mother's belly.

"They look like wet rats," Gunnar decided.

"So did you," Liv retorted. "I remember."

Gunnar stuck his tongue out at Liv, but Knut looked horrified. "Me too?"

"That's enough," Maddie warned.

"Do we get to keep them?" Knut asked.

"That's up to Liv. They're her responsibility," Maddie answered, drawing Hallie out of hearing range.

"What did the doctor say?"

"Same as before," Hallie told her. "He did say we shouldn't keep her shut up in her room. He suggested that she be around the family as much as possible, and he thought that reading and talking to her was a good idea. He said he felt she wouldn't be able to block us out of her mind forever, but we have to be patient."

"Where is she now?" Maddie glanced into the hall, looking for Dagny.

"Duncan is with her, in the parlor."

Maddie nodded and then placed her hand gently on Hallie's arm. "Abner got away, Hallie. Kit told me."

"Damn," Hallie mumbled.

"They'll catch him," Maddie said with conviction.

Hallie nodded and then glanced at the children, who were huddled around the drawer, whispering like conspirators.

Maddie called out to them, "Come on you three, it's time to let the new mother alone for a while."

Hallie wondered if Kit was still home, but she wasn't sure she wanted to ask Maddie. It seemed like every time Hallie mentioned his name lately, Maddie started in, listing his faults. Hallie didn't need to listen to them because she knew them all. She mentally recited them herself whenever she couldn't get him out of her head, and those times were increasing to the point that she wondered if she were obsessed with him.

It was then that her obsession stuck his handsome head in the room. "Where's the new mother?"

"In your bottom desk drawer," Maddie told him as she left the room.

Kit groaned and went over to inspect the damage, squatting just behind Liv. "Those are my contracts," he said.

Liv patted his shoulder gently. "They made a wonderful bed for her, see?" She glowed with pride and a tenderness that Hallie hadn't seen in Liv since the death of their mother.

Kit covered her hand with his, patting her in turn as he shook his head at the drawer and its new occupants.

Knut jumped up. "Liv's gonna keep 'em all, an' she said we get to help her take care of them, an' Kit, y'know what?"

"No, what?" Kit asked, his undivided attention focused on Knut's excited face.

"Liv's gonna give one to Hallie for her birthday."

"Knut!" Liv cried. "That was a surprise, and you ruined it!"

He hung his head. "Sorry."

Kit pinned Hallie with a heated look.

The room was suddenly very warm, and Hallie began to sweat, almost as if her body were melting under his scrutiny.

"What day?" he asked, his eyes never leaving Hallie's face.

She was silent, but Liv answered. "The twenty-seventh."

"Then she'll be older. Almost as old as you," Knut said.

Kit chuckled. "Nineteen? Boy, that is old."

It was hard for Hallie to watch this side of Kit. It reminded her of the marbles, and that memory always made her heart sing. When he was kind to her, it was all she could do not to throw herself into his arms and declare her love, and when he showed a vulnerable side, as he had when he asked her to help him make the best of their marriage, the strength of her love for him was frightening.

So, here she was again, needing to put some distance between them to keep safe the secret of her heart. She murmured some excuse and started to leave, but Kit straightened and used his tall body to block her exit. She could feel his eyes boring into the top of her head, as if he could stare her into looking up. She fought the urge to do so with every bit of her willpower.

"I wanted to thank you," he said.

It was the last thing she expected to hear. "What for?"

"Letting me sleep in the bed."

She turned away, embarrassed and uncomfortable. "I, uh . . . it's a big bed." Her words seemed to echo in the heavy silence that followed. Uncomfortable, Hallie searched for something else to say and finally blurted, "Besides, you were . . . clothed." Then she ducked under his arm and fled to the kitchen.

Hallie went straight to the table and busied herself by clearing it. Then Kit came in, whistling. She ignored him as best she could, treating the cleaning job as if it were tantamount to her existence. She grabbed the paper, but Kit plucked it from her hand.

"I need this," he said, looking excessively pleased. "Well, I'm off. I've got something to take care of, so I'll see you both later."

He was looking at her when he spoke, but Maddie, who was busy baking, muttered a "humph," her usual good-bye. Hallie picked up the butter crock as Kit reached the door. Out of the corner of her eye she caught his hesitation.

"Hallie?"

She looked up at his grinning face.

"You looked."

What was he talking about?

He leaned a little farther into the room and whispered, "Under the covers."

The door closed, shutting out the sound of the butter crock as it crashed onto the wooden floor.

"Ohhh no, not again!" Hallie bent down to pick up the pieces of the teapot. It was the fourth thing she'd broken today. She bundled the broken china in her apron and stood up, intending to throw them away before Maddie saw her latest accident. Unfortunately, Maddie stood by the back door with a heavy laundry basket wedged on her hip, surveying the mess.

"Oh Maddie, I'm sorry." Hallie dumped the pieces into a waste barrel near the dry sink, then grabbed a cloth from a wooden peg and sopped up the tea. "I don't know what's wrong with me today. I'm—"

"A mess—a nervous wreck," Maddie finished, setting the basket on a table and walking over to help Hallie to her feet. Maddie took the wet cloth, tossed it near the pump, then grabbed Hallie's hand and led her to the table. "Sit!" she ordered.

Hallie sagged against the chair slat, folded her arms and felt completely useless.

Maddie sat down across from her. "Now, what's bothering you?"

"Everything." Hallie stared at the dark wood grain of the tabletop, distractedly running her finger along the lines.

"Hallie, please, talk to me." Her hand covered Hallie's and gave it a reassuring squeeze. "I thought things were better between you two. Why, in the past couple of days you've been smiling, and yesterday you were so excited about the play. What has that idiot nephew of mine done now?"

"He slept with me." Hallie stared at the wood again, and missed the knowing smile Maddie valiantly hid with a cough.

"Hallie, I'm well aware that the two of you have been . . . intimate. It goes along with being married. You know that."

"Oh, but we haven't been intimate," Hallie declared, and when she saw Maddie's startled face, she clarified. "Well, not since just after we married—you remember, when Kit moved into his study?"

"I remember, but he's moved back in, and you both seemed to be getting along better, so I assumed you had worked things out. Today you're acting like you did right after the wedding."

"When he moved back in, I made him sleep in the chair," Hallie admitted quietly.

"That's better than he deserved," Maddie said firmly.

"But I woke up this morning with him in the bed, and he's been really nice, and that makes it so much harder to ignore him."

"Why do you want to ignore him?"

"Because if I don't, we're going to end up—" Hallie averted her eyes.

"You're married, Hallie, it's all right for you two to . . . end up, as you put it."

"But I love him," Hallie wailed. "And he d-doesn't love me, and he never will. He l-loved his first wife and then she hurt him and l-left him and died and he can't love me a-and I f-feel horrible!" Hallie swiped at the stupid tears running from her eyes.

"Good Lord! Did that mule-headed man tell you all this?"

"I heard him talking to Lee, in the study, just before the wedding."

"Ah, the wedding fiasco. Now I understand," Maddie murmured.

"Oh Maddie, I'm so miserable."

"I can see that." Maddie rubbed her hands over her eyes as if she were struggling with a decision. She took a deep breath. "I guess I'd better tell you the whole thing, as I know it."

Hallie sniffed. "Is it a different story?"

"No," Maddie replied. "But I think if I tell you what I saw and how Kit used to be, then maybe you'll be able to understand why he's the way he is now."

She started with Kit's childhood, telling Hallie of the competition that existed between the three brothers, and how Kit, being the youngest, fought so hard to keep up with his older brothers.

"Oh, they are a handsome lot, those boys, but somehow Kit has always had a special place in my heart. Maybe I was removed enough to see how hard he struggled to be like the older two. I think that was what sent him out on the whalers when he was only sixteen. The older two took their places— Ben, the eldest, ran the Howland fleet of whalers, and Tom handled the Meecham shipbuilding after his grandfather stepped down—but Kit found his own niche on the whale ships. He was determined to know every facet of whaling, and he loved the sea. You could see his face light up whenever he was near the wharves. His father saw it, too, so when Kit had a chance to go on his first voyage, the only one who tried to stop him was my sister. Kit finally convinced her himself, and it turned out to be the best thing for him. He'd come home from a voyage, and it wasn't long before he'd get unsettled and off he'd go again. It was special to him, so much so, he earned his master's papers before his twenty-second birthday."

That surprised Hallie, since twenty-two was an extremely young age to have earned the captaincy of a whaler. Usually, the crew needed someone older, stronger, and more experienced to earn their confidence and respect.

Maddie smiled. "Oh, if you could have seen him when he came home, he was a sight, so proud and self-assured. I couldn't have been prouder if he'd been my own son. And his father, well, he about bust his buttons."

Hallie saw Maddie's eyes cloud with regret.

"It wasn't too long after Kit'd earned his papers that his

relationship with Josephine Taber changed. It went from childhood friendship to something . . . much stronger. The Tabers and the Howlands were almost like family. Jo and her brothers grew up with Tom, Ben, and Kit. Jo and Kit were forever shadowing the older ones. I think that's why she and Kit were close. They were always left behind by the others. Jo used to come up with some wonderfully original ways to get even with the older boys, and she and Kit got into more scrapes.

"Whenever there was trouble, Jo was around. She was a wild little thing. Her father used to laugh about her antics. He'd say she did the first thing that flew into her head. I always thought she was overly reckless, but then I think her parents did, too, because they were quite relieved when she and Kit married."

It was difficult for Hallie, listening to her husband's past, especially the parts about Jo. But Hallie needed to know about this, as hard as it was, because while she listened, she could feel some obscure void within her being filled.

"I'm not going to sugarcoat this, Hallie," Maddie told her.

Hallie knew this was going to hurt.

"Those first two years, they were inseparable, and very much in love."

It did hurt—the thought of Kit's loving marriage—but Hallie appreciated Maddie's honesty, because she *had* to know, everything.

"I never could figure out what went wrong, none of us could." Maddie's face reflected the bewilderment of her words. "Jo had always gone with Kit on his voyages, and then, just before they were to leave on another one, she got a terrible case of influenza and the doctor wouldn't let her go. She didn't like it much, but with the doctor, Kit, his parents and hers, all in agreement, well, she couldn't fight them all. He was gone sixteen months, and I thought she was going to wither up and die without him. She was withdrawn, and quiet, and completely unlike her usual spunky self. We all wrote it off to loneliness and just plain lovesickness, but then Kit came home and all hell broke loose." Maddie paused, shaking her head at the memory.

Then she continued. "Within a week they were sparring like the worst of enemies. Jo was awful. She picked at him, she belittled him in front of everyone, and she left him for days on end with no explanation. It was almost as if she were punishing him for leaving her for so long; at least that's what we all finally decided. Kit tried everything, and he put up with more than anyone should ever have to, but finally she broke him."

Hallie's stomach tightened with the pain-filled picture Maddie painted. Kit must have been so hurt.

"She went off on one of her jaunts, and Kit readied the ship and left. He cut the voyage short and came home three months later, but by then it was too late. She'd been killed in that carriage accident in Boston. When he found out about Jo's lover, he told both families, together, and Jo's father came unglued, calling Kit a liar. He said his daughter wouldn't do that and that Kit must have driven her away. God, what a scene! Ben and Tom had to pull them apart before they killed each other. Her father was sorry later, but by then Kit was on his way out here and he'd changed. It was as if any love he had was sucked dry. The only emotion in him was an intense hurt and anger. No one could reach him. That boy erected a wall around him that was so hard, a cannon wouldn't break it."

Hallie's fists were as tight as the knot in her stomach. She could only imagine Kit's pain. While she had lost both parents and the loss hurt, at least she had known they died loving her and her brothers and sisters. But to lose someone you loved when you knew they hated you had to be a helpless feeling. Kit was a proud man, and as such, that sense of failure would haunt him.

"He needs someone to shatter that wall, Hallie. I think someone who loves him can do it." Maddie sounded much more confident than Hallie felt.

"I don't know how, Maddie."

"It's not going to be easy, Hallie, don't think I'm saying it is. There's going to be tons of giving on your part, and not a lot in return, at least at first." Maddie grabbed her hand again. "You've got a few things in your favor. First of all, Kit cares about you."

She groaned in disbelief.

"Stop that!" Maddie ordered. "He does care, I can see it. The seeds are there, but you'll have to be the one to make them grow. You are married, and while I'm almost sorry I forced that, I still believe it was best for both of you. What has Kit said about the marriage? You must have talked some."

"He said he was sorry he'd hurt me, and that he'd like to forget what's happened and maybe we could reach some sort of compromise." Hallie looked sheepish. "He said I could name the terms, and that's when I told him he had to sleep in the chair."

This time Maddie's laughter wasn't covered up. "Oh Hallie, you really are good for him. I wish I could have seen his face."

By this time Hallie was smiling too. She couldn't help it when she remembered Kit's stunned face. It had been almost comical. "He was . . . a little surprised."

"I can imagine." Maddie laughed harder, and it was contagious.

"He did look awfully silly with his long legs hanging over the arm of the chair." Hallie grinned, and then her own laughter sang out.

Maddie finally controlled her mirth. "If you love him, Hallie, you'll try to help him forget the past. Use all that love of yours to help my nephew." She squeezed Hallie's hand. "Please."

Hallie wanted to try again, even without Maddie's plea. She just didn't know if Kit could ever love her. It seemed so hopeless. Of course, if she didn't give it one last try, she would probably always wonder whether she could have done it. The doubt would haunt her to her grave.

"I'll try," she told Maddie. "After all, what have I got to lose?"

Hallie got up and left the room, under the pretext of checking on the children. She reached the hall and then mentally answered her own question. She could lose her self-respect, her happiness, her dignity, and her heart. But then, hadn't she already lost her heart? Besides, she mentally argued, while the stakes were high, the prize was everything she could ever want; if Kit could learn to love her, it was worth any risk.

Chapter

Twenty-one

Kit was late, much later than he'd expected when he sent the note home. But it was unavoidable, and what was one missed supper when he'd just made such a good deal? The papers were signed and the last of his burdens lifted. It was perfect timing. Now, if he could just keep Hallie from finding out.

Once home, Kit went directly to the study so he could hide the agreements in his desk. He lit the desk lamp and automatically reached down to open the bottom drawer. It was already open and still filled with cats. He put his papers in another drawer.

He spied his pipe sitting by a small tobacco holder. A smoke would be relaxing, and the smell of burning tobacco might help dispel the lingering essence of skunk that still subtly flavored the room. As he puffed on his pipe, Kit thought about the radical changes in his life over the last six weeks. Despite the smell, his study was as immaculate as the rest of his home. While he had groused about Maddie, he had to admit that his life had taken a change for the better.

The kittens stirred, bringing the memory of the looks on the children's faces when they hovered over the animals. The twins had been examining those cats with so much curiosity and awe that for once they were quiet. It was then that Kit suddenly saw the difference between the two boys; it was in their eyes—a look—and the minute he saw it, he knew he would never again confuse the two. And then there was Liv, whose pride-filled face caused him to smile even now. He would bet that at nine, Hallie had looked just like Liv. When she patted his shoulder and thanked him, any thoughts of his damaged contracts had disappeared as fast as the food on Lee's plate.

The children had changed his life, given him a purpose, and really made him feel as if he had a home. He had always thought that kids were okay, but never knew how rich life could be until he saw it through the fascination of a child's eyes. Marbles and kittens, even skunks, were no longer just toys and animals, but instead, each became a special wonder that colored the way he viewed things. Nothing seemed quite so urgent or so crucial, and it was a nice feeling.

However, there was one new aspect of his life that was not simpler. His marriage to Hallie. Kit Howland, who had vowed never to marry again, had done so under pressure, and to a girl who was thirteen years younger. Of course, he hadn't wanted to marry Hallie, but he'd done enough fool things to make the marriage a just punishment. Then again, it would be a punishment only if he spent his entire marriage sleeping on a sofa or in a damn uncomfortable chair.

Until Hallie, he had forgotten what it was to want a woman—one certain woman—so badly that it haunted you, day in and day out. While he had fought that very desire, it hadn't done a bit of good. He still wanted her.

When they made love, it had been the worst possible time. She was hurt and he was angry. She was a young virgin, and her hysterics afterward were probably milder than he deserved, considering his belligerent attitude. Now he was paying for it, and he wondered how long it would be before he could hold her without reading a glimmer of fear in those expressive eyes of hers, or before he could teach her how gently his body could love her.

Kit drew on the pipe, but it had burned out. He emptied it, laid it on its wooden stand, then stood up. After foolishly saying good night to the damn cats, he turned down the lamp and left the room. A clatter sounded from the kitchen, drawing his attention to the light spilling from beneath the door. Someone was still up.

He walked in, and there was Hallie in her nightclothes, and, God help him, her hair was down.

"Hello," she said so quietly he wondered if he'd imagined it.

"It's late."

"I thought you'd be hungry, so I kept some things warm for you." She walked over to the stove and grabbed one of the aprons hanging nearby. She tied it around her waist, and the ties tangled in her hair. "Can you help me, please? I've got this awful hair caught."

Awful? Kit went to her aid, and touched the curtain of her hair. It caressed his fingertips. He parted it and tied the strings.

"I'm sorry about this," Hallie said over her shoulder. "I should cut it off, but—"

"No!" he shouted so loud she jumped.

She looked at him like he was crazy.

"There, you're all fixed up." He was a fool. All it took was the whispering brush of her hair across his skin and he was burning up.

"Are you hungry?"

"Starved." Kit spun around in self-defense and got a mug from the shelf. Then he froze. It was a bad tactic. He had to go back over to the range to get the coffee.

"Go sit down and eat so it doesn't get cold. I'll bring the coffee and some bread and butter." She dished up some stew and handed it to him, taking the empty mug out of his hand.

Kit sat down and stared at the food. He didn't have any silverware.

Hallie brought the coffee and looked at his untouched plate. "Oh! How silly of me, I forgot the fork."

She—and her hair—spun around.

He took a huge gulp of hot coffee, which burned his mouth and throat, and probably the inside of his stomach.

"Here," she said, holding out a fork and napkin.

He took them and dug into the stew. Just as he had his mouth open over the fork, she walked across the kitchen, her hips swaying in the same rolling, undulant motion of her hair.

Damn, it was hot in here.

Her dressing gown was some pink thing that belted around her waist. Her waist was so small for such a tall woman, and her hips were just wide enough to cradle his own.

Kit shoved the tasteless stew into his burned mouth and chewed. He was in bad shape tonight.

"There," she said, setting a plate of bread and some butter on the table.

He shoveled more stew in his mouth.

She sat down, put her chin on her hands and smiled at him.

He stopped chewing and stared back. *What the hell was she doing, watching him eat?*

She picked up a slab of bread and spread butter on it. "Here, have some bread. Maddie just baked it this morning."

She's buttering my bread?

Kit forced his mouth into a grimace. It locked his jaw and kept his mouth from gaping open.

When he didn't take the bread, she laid it on the rim of his plate.

"How is it?" she asked.

Hard. Very, very hard.

"The stew. It's okay?" she repeated, still sweetly staring at him.

"Fine." He stuffed the bread into his mouth and concentrated on chewing the hell out of it.

She eyed his half-empty mug. "I'll get you some more coffee."

Kit raised his hand, intending to stop her, but she was

already at the range, coffeepot in hand. Why didn't she leave? She was acting skittish enough so he knew she was nervous. He could grab her and kiss her. That ought to send her running, except he knew if he touched her, he'd lose his finely held control and then never get near her again.

She refilled his mug and put the coffee back. "Well, I guess I'll go upstairs."

Thank God!

"Do you need anything else?"

Don't say it, his conscience warned. Kit swallowed his first answer. "No, I'm fine." His voice cracked, and he held his breath.

"Oh. Well, I'll see you upstairs?"

He didn't look at her. He just nodded, and when he heard the door close, expelled his breath and sagged against the chair. His food rolled around his belly like a cannonball. Kit tossed his fork on the table, knowing he couldn't touch another bite. His consuming hunger had nothing to do with food.

A door closed in the room above him. Hallie was in their bedroom. He sat looking at the ceiling and listening to the sounds she made. She kicked off her slippers. He could hear them thud lightly on the wooden floor, and then she padded across the room. She stood in the middle of the room above, right next to where he knew the bed sat. The bed creaked softly, and Kit envisioned Hallie cloaked in a fine veil of hair and sitting on the edge of the bed, right where he wanted her. He closed his eyes and groaned.

He pacified himself with the knowledge that before long she'd be asleep, and then he could go up without worrying about this intense desire. If he gave in to it, the way he felt right now, he would probably scare her to death, and then he would never get near her. No, what he needed was patience and timing. He would wait.

It was quiet up there, and Kit took a deep, relaxing breath. Not long, he thought. He picked up his plate. The stew was cold and the meat juices were starting to congeal. He put the bread on top of the stew, covering it so he didn't have to look at it.

Not much longer.

Picking up the coffee, Kit sipped it, and then he heard her. His gaze shot upward as the sound of her pacing seeped down from above. He groaned and waited. The pacing continued. What the hell was she doing? Maybe she couldn't sleep; it was a possibility, even if the steps pattered with the beat of impatience.

He stood and carried the plate toward the waste barrel while the pacing continued. No, he thought, shaking his head in disbelief, she wouldn't be waiting for him, would she?

Ah damn, she was. Kit changed directions and headed for the back door. He flung it open and heaved the plate into the backyard. It was a stupid and rash act that did nothing more than make him feel good, for about two seconds.

He slammed the door so hard the wall screamed, and he walked in the middle of the kitchen and stood, glowering at the ceiling.

Hallie rushed into the room, and at the sight of him, skidded to a stop. Her hand grasped her robe and she said, "Oh! I thought you'd left!"

Kit looked at her, then glanced at the door, then looked at her again. She was panting, he assumed from running down the stairs so fast. Why should she care if he'd gone? Why was she being so . . . agreeable?

She wants something, he decided. That was why she was buttering his bread, serving him coffee, and waiting up for him . . .

He crossed his arms. "What do you want, Hallie?"

She shifted from one bare foot to the other. "Want?"

"Yes, want. All this sudden *wifely* care must be for a reason, right?"

She shifted again and nodded.

"What do you want?"

She bit her lip in hesitation.

Growing impatient, he prodded, "Fallen out of any trees lately?"

Her face registered hurt, shock, and then anger. Her eyes narrowed and she took her belligerent stance. "Crawled into any strange beds, lately?"

They squared off.

"It was not a strange bed," Kit said through gritted teeth. "It was my own bed."

Hallie's hands plopped onto her hips. "Oh yes, *your* precious bed. How could I forget it? Especially when I was foolishly trying, with all this wifely care, to lure my husband back into it!"

"What?"

"You are the most stubborn, bull-headed, inconsiderate man I have ever met. Why I would even try to make this marriage real is beyond me!" Her hand waved in the air with each shouted word. "I don't know why I was thinking you—"

Kit crossed the room and had a grip on her waving wrist before she could finish. His eyes bored into hers. "What were you thinking?"

"Nothing! Let go."

"Hallie, what did you want?"

"Forget it!" She tried to pulled her hand away.

He wasn't going to let her go, not until he heard her say exactly what she meant by "luring" her husband. She pulled her hand again, and he wrapped his arms around her, pinning her to his chest so she couldn't get away. Her hair fell over his arms. She wiggled like a hooked worm, forcing him to tighten his hold. She looked up at him, glaring, and her hair spilled downward. He was lost.

His lips met hers and she stilled. He released her hands, and suddenly they were around his neck, clinging to him the same way her lips clung to his. His hands closed over her bottom and he lifted her higher, held her even tighter against his body. Her soft breasts pillowed against his chest and her lips parted, an invitation to his tongue, so he tasted her.

As they kissed—deep, tongue-stroking kisses—he reveled in her flavor and his hold relaxed, letting her slide in slow, slow inches, back to the floor. Her arms wrapped tighter around his neck and her tongue mimicked his, swirling in the recesses of his hot mouth, licking and sending his want of her to new heights. Against his ribs her breasts rubbed slowly with the motion of their kiss, and hot, sweet desire bolted through him. His kiss moved from her sweet mouth to her ear, where he knew his tongue could make her quiver.

"You want me . . . don't you? I can feel it." His tongue flickered into her ear, dampening it, and then he whispered, "Tell me, sweet, tell me you want me. Tell me you're not afraid. . . ."

Hallie moaned, and pressed her ear harder against his open mouth.

"Tell me with words. I need to hear the words," he said, breathing his plea into her ear.

"I want you . . . but I didn't know how to show you. I—"

"Show me now," he murmured against her damp lips, and kissed her with a kiss so powerful he ached with need. He filled his hands with clouds of her hair. He filled her mouth with his tongue, stroking her teeth, her mouth, her tongue. Her hands moved, tentatively, into small, stroking circles on the tight muscles of his back. Her tongue joined his and she rubbed against him. He was in heaven.

No, he was in the kitchen. Kit pulled his mouth away and tilted her head up to his. Her eyes, closed in passion, opened as his thumbs lightly stroked her jaw.

"Are you sure?" he asked, praying that she would say yes.

Her eyes, misty and moist, gave him the answer he wanted, but as if to create no doubt, Hallie's lips melted against his, her body moved against him, and her hands, wedged between their bodies, rubbed rhythmic circles on his chest.

Kit stilled her teasing hand, threaded it through his own and pulled her from the room. They ran upstairs, and once in their room, he pulled her against him, kissing her hard and using his back to shut the bedroom door. His hands covered her bottom and he lifted her, pressing her against his aching, hard length. Holding her against him, he walked to the bed and sat, draping Hallie over his arm while his mouth closed over a cloth-covered breast.

She moaned and threaded her hands through his hair, instinctively pulling him closer while she pressed her breast against his open mouth. He kissed her neck and laved a trail to her mouth while his hands pulled the clothing from her shoulders.

He pulled away, driven to see her breasts bare. She saw the direction of his gaze and tried to cover herself.

"No," he said. "Please, you're beautiful. Let me look at you . . . all of you." He set her on her feet and his fingers fumbled with her belt. He loosened it and shoved her clothing down to the floor, seeing for the first time the wonder of her bare body. Her beautiful white breasts were so full, he would have to use both hands to hold one. Never, never would he think of her as a young girl again. Her body was a woman's body, and so stimulating that he could almost feel his blood run thick.

His eyes roved downward, past her small waist and full hips, to her legs, and he stopped. The inside of one thigh was scarred a bluish-red, and the mark ran from mid-thigh all the way down to her calf.

His eyes met hers. "What happened?"

Tears streamed from her eyes and she turned to the side, hiding the scar from his view and shaking with shame.

"I'm sorry," she whispered, and bent to try to pull up her clothes.

"No!" Kit tore the fabric from her hands, and pulled her to his chest just as her tears burst into sobs.

"The f-fire. I b-burned it." Her fists knotted against his shirt front. "It's s-so ugly. I'm sorry," she whispered between crying breaths.

Kit brushed her tears away with his thumbs. "No, Hallie, it's not ugly. It caught me by surprise, that's all. I thought you came out of the fire unharmed. Why didn't you tell me you'd been hurt?"

"Why? The doctor said no one but my husband would see it." Hallie tried to pull away, but Kit held fast.

He was her husband, but he sensed that logic wasn't what she needed to hear. She needed to know that he didn't care one whit about the scar. She needed reassurance.

"It doesn't matter, sweet. I'd want you if you had a hundred scars." He kissed her, long and deep. His hands roved over her, soothing the tension from her taut muscles, and his mouth moved down to the tip of her breast, closing over it and flicking his tongue against her distended nipple until she was again limber with passion. He laid back on the bed, pulling her with him while he drew the tie from his collar.

"Help me, sweet," he asked, struggling between kisses to remove his shirt. He moved her hesitant hands to his shirt studs, and while she removed them, he held her face in his hands and buried his tongue in her mouth. Her skin touched him as his shirt opened, and he turned with her, onto their sides, so he could get free of the cloth barrier.

In passion, he turned again, pressing his chest against her and feeling her nipples bead through his chest hair. When the hard tip of a breast brushed his own nipple, desire shot through him like a bullet.

He sat up, removing his boots, and then tore free the buttons of his trousers, pulling off the last of his clothes. Then he was kissing her deeply while their naked legs tangled. His hands stroked lower and lower with each caress, until his fingers threaded through her pale body hair. She moaned and turned her head to lave his own ear with her small, flicking tongue. His fingers teased over her, grazing lightly against the point of her desire. She cried out, and the sound was so sensual, so exciting, that he touched her over and over again just to hear it.

In invitation, she pressed against his hand, and his finger entered, buried to his knuckle. She moved against it, her damp tightness wanting more. Her tears of desire wet his cheeks as he kissed her mouth and moved his finger in the very core of her. His hips burrowed between her legs and his hand left her body and grasped her thigh, pushing it outward and spreading her leg wider for his entry. He rose up on his elbows, poising at her entrance, and he looked at her. "Open your eyes, sweet. I don't want to hurt you again. Your eyes will tell me if I am."

Her lids opened and their gazes met. Kit inched inside, slowly, watching for any sign of pain with each enveloping penetration. He took two deep, controlling breaths and penetrated more. When he was fully seated, he threaded his fingers through hers and bent to kiss her softly, with eyes open.

Her eyes drifted closed and he pulled back. Her eyes opened.

"Watch me, sweet, watch me." With gazes locked, Kit's hips began the slow beat, drumming in and almost out of her hot core until the friction drove him faster and faster. Crying with passion, she strained toward him, innocently signaling her need, and he thrust hard, touching that elusive trigger that sent her release throbbing so hot around him that he came.

He lay there, spent and drained, but still looking at her. He unthreaded a hand and brushed a bit of hair away from her damp temple.

"Did I hurt you?" he asked, his lips feathering her hairline.

"No," she whispered, her voice raspy from her cries.

Her chin and cheeks were bright pink from the dark stubble of his beard, and he traced the rashes gently with a finger.

Then she smiled, the sated, sensuous smile of a woman well-loved.

He looked at the love there on her expressive face, and something deep within him called out, as if his soul were crying. He closed his eyes tightly, fighting the emotion, fighting the feeling, and fighting against the chains that would bind his heart. Instead, he bent and kissed the deep crevice between her breasts, laying his head on her breast while her hand tentatively stroked his head. He laid there, wrestling with the hopeless feeling that he was no longer in control of his life.

Her fingers grazed his cheeks, his nose, and then his chin, feeling the dark, rough growth of his thick beard before those same slender fingers traced his lips. Her touch was so innocent, so gentle, that his desire quickened.

He opened his lips and stroked her fingertips with his tongue, which must have surprised her, for she lifted her head to better see him. He raised his head and his lips closed over hers as his hands held her ribs, stroked her breasts, and once again he was deep within her, driving their bodies over the edge. Again, and again.

Chapter

Twenty-two

Hallie floated down the stairs, smiling. It was something she did a lot lately. She paused near the walnut hall tree to pinch some color into her pale cheeks, but it wasn't necessary. The face in the mirror glowed from something that went much deeper than her skin.

Three weeks, Hallie thought. It had been three weeks since the night in the kitchen and, she smiled, in the bedroom. Every night since had been more and more wonderful.

She looked in Kit's study, but the room was empty, except for the cats, who had made the study their home. Liv had moved them, at Kit's request, into the back room of the kitchen, but it hadn't been a successful move.

Hallie grinned at the memory of Mrs. Skunk, parading past the dinner table, carrying a kitten in her mouth over and over, as she methodically moved her babies back into the study. After that display, Kit relented and shared his study with the cats.

She entered the kitchen, but Kit wasn't there either. Maddie sat at the table, braiding Dagny's hair and talking away to her just as the doctor had advised, but still there was no change in her sister. Liv was at school, but the twins were there, sitting with their noses wedged into separate corners. It was Maddie's latest punishment.

She glanced from one to the other. "What did they do now?"

Maddie looked at Knut and called out, "Knut, turn around and show Hallie what you did."

The little boy swirled around on his fanny and looked innocently at his oldest sister—as innocently as he could without any eyebrows.

"How?" she asked Maddie, biting back a laugh.

"Kit's razor. It seems they've watched him shave and asked him why he did it—"

"He said lots of men shave the hair off their faces," Knut interrupted. "But we don't have any hair 'cept out the hair on our eyebrows, so Gunnar shaved them off me!"

"You did it too!" Gunnar turned around. He was only missing one eyebrow.

"Turn around, boys, your time's not up yet," Maddie commanded, and the twins immediately obeyed.

Hallie had just poured herself a cup of coffee when the back door opened and Duncan came in. He went straight to Hallie.

"Captain Prescott sent his man over with a message that you were to come to his ship right away. Some kind of emergency, I gather. I've got the carriage out front so we can leave as soon as you're ready."

Hallie looked at Maddie as she got up. "You think it's Kit?"

"I don't see how. He just left here himself a few minutes ago. He said he had a meeting with some banker at ten."

Hallie ran and got her hat and cloak. She stuck her head back into the kitchen. "I'll send a message if it's anything urgent," she told Maddie, then left with Duncan.

Half an hour later Hallie and Duncan boarded the *Wanderer,* and while Duncan waited on deck, she was taken to the captain's quarters. They entered the small cabin and her gaze met Lee Prescott's.

"I found something of yours," he said, nodding across the room.

Hallie turned, and there was Liv, sitting on a bunk, dressed as a boy.

"What in the world . . . ?"

"She tried to stow on board a clipper leaving for the Orient this morning," Lee informed her.

"You did what!" Hallie ran to Liv and grabbed her by her ridged little shoulders. "You could have been killed, young lady! What are you doing, stowing on ships?"

"Running away," Liv announced, obstinacy radiating from her face. "And I don't care if I do die!"

"For Godsakes, why?"

Liv was silent.

Hallie looked to Lee, but he shrugged.

"I'll leave if you want to be alone," he offered.

"No, thank you, Lee," Hallie said, grabbing Liv's grubby hand and pulling her to the door. "I'll take care of this at home. But thanks for saving her ornery little fanny."

He waved them off, and Hallie continued to drag Liv behind her, ranting at her along the way and walking so fast that even Duncan had trouble keeping up with them. They walked down the ramp, heading toward the carriage, when Hallie stopped. She looked over to the next wharf and saw the empty mooring.

The *Sea Haven* was gone.

She looked at Liv. "Isn't that where Da's ship was moored?"

"Yes," Liv answered, then clammed up again.

Hallie marched toward Duncan, dragging Liv along. "Duncan, do you know anything about my father's ship?"

"No. Why?"

"It was moored right there," Hallie pointed to the empty mooring. "Would you put Liv inside the carriage? Oh, and watch her, she's got some fool notion about running away. I'll just be a few minutes. I want to ask some people about the *Sea Haven.*"

Duncan helped Liv inside while Hallie went to question some of the dock workers. After a few minutes she located a warehouseman who was said to know everything about anything that happened near the Broadway Wharf.

When Hallie asked him about the ship, he answered her immediately. "Oh, the *Sea Haven,* that's the Howland ship, right?"

"No," she corrected. "It's the Fredriksen ship."

He tipped back his hat and scratched his forehead. "You don't say. Hmm. Well, some feller named Howland and some other feller, can't remember who, had her hauled away."

"Hauled away?" Hallie whispered, hoping that what she was thinking was not true. But something deep down inside told her Kit had lied and sold the ship for fill.

Heartbroken and confused, she ran away from the stunned warehouseman, not stopping until she reached the carriage. Sobbing, she begged Duncan to take her right home, jerked open the carriage door and crawled inside.

Liv looked at Hallie's tears and turned her stubborn face away, as if she couldn't stand the emotion in her sister. On the silent ride home Hallie tried to tell herself that it wasn't true, that the man she loved and had married hadn't done this to her. But it was the only answer. That bastard had lulled her into a sense of acquiescence with his lovemaking, then turned around and sold the ship—her ship—for fill.

The carriage pulled to an abrupt halt in front of the house, and in the blink of an eye the carriage door flew open and Kit blocked the doorway. "I heard what happened." His angry glare was directed right at Liv, who scooted even farther into the corner.

"You're coming with me!" he ordered, and lifted Liv out, carrying her up the stairs before Hallie could get out of the carriage.

"Don't you touch her!" Hallie yelled, but the front door had already slammed shut.

"Come with me," she ordered Duncan, and ran into the

house with him following close behind. When she reached the hallway, she heard Kit shouting at Liv in his study. She tried to open the door but it was locked.

"Open this door!" she shouted, banging on the thick wood.

"I'm taking care of this, Hallie. Go away!" Kit answered.

"No!" she yelled back, but no sounds came from within. She banged harder on the door and still heard nothing. She turned to Duncan, who was standing by Maddie and the curious twins.

"Break it down, please, Duncan."

"What?"

"Come along, boys. This doesn't concern us," Maddie said, herding the twins back into the kitchen.

"Break it down," Hallie repeated.

"I don't think Kit's gonna like that—"

"I don't care." Hallie interrupted. "Either you break it down or I will." She grabbed a lead doorstop and raised it above the doorknob.

"Wait!" Duncan said. "I'll break it down." He stepped back and kicked the metal plate just above the lock. With a loud crack the door popped open.

Hallie was inside in a flash. Kit sat behind his desk, holding Liv as she cried her soul out. Her sister's sobbing story froze Hallie in her tracks.

". . . and she died because I killed her!" Liv wailed.

Hallie put aside her anger at her lying husband. She could tell Kit off later, but right now Liv was crying hysterically, something she never, ever did. Hallie went to the chair and knelt by the sobbing girl, touching her hesitantly on her shuddering shoulder.

"Come here, sweetpea, tell me what's wrong." Hallie pulled her from Kit's lying, traitorous arms. "What is it? Please tell me."

Liv clung to Hallie. "I killed her, Hallie. It was me. I killed Mama . . ." Liv wailed into Hallie's shoulder.

Hallie rocked her sister slowly, as she hadn't been able to

since Liv was three. "No you didn't, sweetpea. Mama died from a disease."

"I'm not sweet, don't call me that! Sweet people don't kill their mothers!" Liv cried.

"That's not true, Liv!"

"You don't have to lie to me, I know Mama caught it from me! Remember how sick I was, and then Mama got sick and then sicker and then she died. And none of you ever said anything, but I knew it. I knew that if I hadn't got sick, Mama wouldn't have died. It's my fault, a-and I need her, Hallie. I need her—" Liv broke into more heaving sobs.

The chair creaked, and Kit, who had been absorbing this whole scene, stood and quietly walked over to the door. Hallie watched it close behind him, thankful that he'd left them alone. She rocked Liv while the miserable young girl cried so hard she could barely catch a breath.

"Liv, look at me." Hallie forced her sister's chin up. "Mama died of peritonitis. Do you know what that is?"

Liv shook her head.

"You didn't give it to her. You just had a cold. Mama had tuberculosis, and it came on so fast, she only had the symptoms for a few days. Before anything could be done, she had developed peritonitis, and she died less than a day later. These diseases are not contagious Liv. That means you can't get it from someone else. Mama had the sickness growing inside long before you were ever ill."

"Really?" Liv whispered.

Hallie nodded, hugging Liv's thin body against her own. "Now where did you get the foolish notion you had killed Mama, and why didn't you talk to me about it? You used to come to me."

"You were so busy all the time. I thought you didn't have time for me like you used to," Liv admitted.

Hallie felt hellish. Everything had been so chaotic after the death of their mother. It had come so suddenly, and Da had been gone. With the twins just babies, there hadn't been time for Liv. So her little sister had become withdrawn. This also explained all the trouble Liv seemed to create—it was a way to get Hallie's attention.

Hallie pulled Liv to her, holding the young girl and trying to make up for the hurt. "I love you, Liv, and I'm so, so sorry. I'm here when you need me, I promise. Don't ever think I don't have time for you, please."

"I love you, too, Hallie. I really, really do." Liv clung tightly to Hallie's neck.

Brushing the tears from her sister's cheeks, Hallie settled Liv on her knees. "You won't do something silly like stow on ships or some other method of running away again, will you?"

Liv shook her head.

"I need you, sweetpea. Don't ever forget that." Hallie rubbed Liv's back with a soothing hand. "Feel better?"

"Uh-huh." A small, untroubled smile lit Liv's tear-streaked face.

Hallie stood, setting Liv down and taking her hand. "Come on now, we'd better get you cleaned up."

As they entered the hallway, Hallie spied Kit deep in conversation with Duncan. She gave Liv's hand a reassuring squeeze and paused in front of Kit. "I would like to talk to you, privately, as soon as I'm done."

"Fine. I've got some contracts to go over, so I'll be in there when you need me." Kit nodded toward the study and then watched Hallie with a hungry look—the same look, she thought, that had fooled her into thinking that their relationship was at least honest and trusting, even if it wasn't based on mutual love.

She left with Liv, planning exactly what she would say to the bastard she had married.

An hour later Hallie stood at the base of the stairs, staring at the broken door. It was half open, and she could see Kit bent over the desk, working while he puffed on his pipe. She took a deep breath and entered the room.

Kit looked up, took the pipe from his mouth and smiled —that wonderful smile that had the ability to make her melt. But not this time. She steeled herself against the love in her heart and concentrated on his betrayal.

"Where's my ship?"

Shock registered on his face, only to be quickly masked by a look of absolute indifference. He bent back toward the papers and mumbled around his pipe. "What ship?"

Hallie marched over to his desk. "Don't try to act like you don't know what I'm talking about! You know damn well I mean the *Sea Haven!*"

"What's the matter, Hallie, did you lose your ship?" Kit leaned back in his chair and puffed arrogantly on his pipe.

"You sold it for fill, didn't you?"

Kit's gaze narrowed. "Do you really think I would do that?"

"Isn't that what you were going to do before? Why should I think you would be any different now?"

"Why . . ." Kit's face was suddenly very red. "If you can't answer that, then I'll be damned if I'm going to tell you. I thought we at least had some trust between us." He puffed harder on the pipe, and his hands gripped the arms of his chair.

"So did I! Until I heard that you had my ship hauled away. You gave me that ship. It's mine!" she shouted, banging her fist on the desk in frustration.

Kit pushed the pipe to the other side of his mouth. "You sound like a child, Hallie."

"Don't you dare change the subject, you . . . you lying bastard!"

Kit shot up and stood across the desk from her, glaring and puffing. He was trying to intimidate her. She would show him!

"How could you be so mean and awful!" Hallie leaned over the table, her face only a foot from his. "I want you to stay away from me, do you understand? Stay away."

"Fine," he spat around his pipe stem.

In an instant she grabbed the pipe from his mouth and flung it into the fireplace. "And I'm sick and tired of trying to understand you around that stupid, damn pipe!" She spun away from his stunned face, ran upstairs to the bedroom and slammed the door shut. Hallie looked at the door through her teary, furious eyes, then slid the bolt closed, locking Kit out of the bedroom and out of her heart.

Hallie closed the book and placed it on the night table. She turned down the wick and snuggled farther under the fluffy covers of her lonely bed. Closing her eyes, she willed herself to sleep. Her effort failed. She pushed up and stared down at the pillow, frowning. It smelled like Kit, so she flung it across the room and plopped her head onto the other pillow.

For three long, torturous nights she'd slept alone. She hadn't seen Kit for two days—no one had—and some perverse part of her wondered if he was all right.

Don't do that, she mentally scolded. Don't think about him, don't worry about him, and don't you dare love him!

She glanced across the dark room, her eyes adjusting to the darkness enough for her to make out the door. She eyed the glass knob. The first night when she'd locked herself in the room, Kit had tried to talk to her but she wouldn't respond. She couldn't give him the chance to wear her resistance down with either his lies or his hot touch. So tonight the doorknob hadn't twisted. Tonight, Kit hadn't knocked and demanded she let him in. Tonight, she got what she wanted. She was completely miserable.

It was quiet, except for the wind that rattled around the upper story. The gusts made the tree branches scrape along the house's wooden siding. It was a terrible racket. Hallie covered her ears with her pillow and burrowed farther into bed. Sleep finally came, in small spurts, and she drifted in and out of the drowsy state.

A short while later something banged against the wall so hard the windows shook, and Hallie sat up, trying to adjust her sleepy eyes. She stared at her open window just as a hand closed over her mouth, cutting off her scream. She fought hard, but the intruder pinned her to the bed, stuffing a cloth into her mouth, tying another around her eyes and binding her hands behind her back. He covered her with a bed coverlet, and then Hallie was thrown roughly over his shoulder.

She could feel the cold air through the blanket as her abductor hauled her out the window and down to the ground below. It was freezing cold, and Hallie shivered, both from fear and the icy air. She was thrown into a carriage, and it took off with a sharp jolt that sent her rolling onto the damp carriage floor. She squirmed and wiggled, trying to get free of the blanket, but with her hands tied, she couldn't do it.

The carriage stopped and the door creaked open. Hallie screamed through her gag, hoping the muffled noises would alert someone nearby. It did no good. Her abductor lugged her up a rope ladder, and as she struggled, she banged her head repeatedly against something hard and woodlike. She smelled the salty scent of the sea and realized her abductor was taking her on board a ship. She could hear his gasping breath, so she struggled more. Maybe she could use her weight to her favor. His shoes dragged across what sounded like a wooden deck, and then a hatch slammed open. He lugged her down another stairway and she heard a door open, just before he set her on her feet.

She kicked her foot back at random, trying to connect with whoever had kidnapped her, but she missed. The blanket was jerked from her and someone untied the blindfold. Hallie blinked her eyes to adjust them to the lamp light.

It was her father's cabin, and Kit sat on a large bunk, casually sipping some wine.

"Happy birthday, Hallie." He toasted her and then took a drink.

"Should I untie her?" a familiar voice asked.

She spun around to see that her abductor was Lee Prescott, then looked back and forth from Kit to Lee.

"Go ahead and untie her, but maybe we should leave the gag in," Kit suggested with a devious grin.

"She's your wife," Lee said, struggling to cut the rope from her wrists. "I just wish she was lighter."

Hallie ground her heel on the toe of his boot.

"Ouch!" Lee cut the bonds loose. "That does it! I've been kicked and elbowed, all because you can't get along with your own wife. I've had enough. I'm leaving. This was your stupid idea, you explain it!" Lee sheathed his knife and slammed the cabin door, leaving Kit and Hallie alone.

"Want some wine?" Kit held up a bottle and a glass.

Hallie jerked out her gag. "I—"

"Tell me, sweet," Kit interrupted, "does this room look familiar?"

He ambled toward her with a glass of wine in his hand. "Here." He handed it to her. "You haven't answered me, Hallie. Isn't this your father's cabin?"

She gulped the wine. By the tone of his voice, she could tell she was going to need it.

"What, no comments? Please notice that it's all in one piece. You can see that, can't you?"

Hallie nodded, guzzling the rest of the wine.

"Ah, I see you've finished your wine. Good. Come with me." He grabbed her hand and pulled her out of the room and up onto the deck.

"Look!" he ordered, and she did.

The ship was intact and spotless. The only difference was that a tall, narrow building now sat on the fore deck, between the mainmast and the foremast. Looming some three stories high, the plank building had a flat roof and narrow windows. Hanging from the booms and gallows were oil lanterns that spilled their light all over the ship. Hallie turned, and it was then that she saw the city, completely surrounding them. The *Sea Haven* wasn't moored in the bay, it was sitting on land, right in the middle of San Francisco.

She gaped at Kit, and he pointed to a sign leaning against a row of barrels. It read: THE HAVEN HOTEL.

She could feel the burn of Kit's watching eyes. Then he spoke. "This is San Francisco's newest hotel. It's been leased—in your name, incidentally—to a gentleman who had it hauled on shore and converted. The official opening is in a few days, but for tonight I planned for us to celebrate your birthday on board." He turned and looked her right in the eye, speaking quietly. "Do you still think I'm a lying bastard?"

"Oh God, Kit, I'm sorry!" Hallie threw herself into his arms and cried. "I mean it. I'm so sorry."

Kit held her silently.

"You're not a lying bastard," she told his chest.

"That's good to know," Kit said, his voice tinged with a smile. His hands roved over her back. He tilted her face up toward his. "I'll never lie to you, Hallie. I promise you that. I might make mistakes and make you angry, but I'll never, ever lie to you."

Hallie stood on her tiptoes and kissed him, softly and sweetly. "Thank you . . ." she murmured against his damp lips . . . "Thank you."

"Happy birthday, sweet," he whispered back. He pulled her to him and kissed her, softly and then deeply. His hand stroked her back, then he pulled her tightly to his chest and held her with such longing that Hallie felt as if she had finally, for a fleeting instant, touched his heart.

A loud catcall pierced the air and they broke apart, turning toward the shout. In plain sight, on the street below, stood a crowd of miners, jeering and whistling at the lovers.

Kit pulled her away from the railing. "Let's go below."

They went back to the cabin, and Hallie took the time to look at the room. It had been refurbished. The large bunk was covered with a deep green comforter that was so fat, she knew it must be filled with down. Jewel-toned pillows were scattered on the wall side of the bed, and a rug of the same colors covered the dark wood floor. A large screen blocked off the area where her father's desk sat.

Kit strolled over and moved the screen. The desk was no longer there. Instead, a low table and two high-backed chairs sat in its place. The table was set for two.

"What's this?" Hallie asked.

"Your birthday supper, or at least it will be in a moment."
Kit reached over and rang a brass ship's bell. The loud
clanging startled them both. "I think they might want to
change that," he said, laughing.

Within minutes there was a knock at the cabin door and
two men entered with steaming trays of food. The men left,
but the rich smell of beef filled the room, making Hallie's
mouth water. She hadn't eaten much of anything the past
few days, mostly because she'd been so angry with Kit. He
popped the cork on another champagne bottle and refilled
their glasses, then set them on the table and seated Hallie.

An hour later Hallie had cleaned her plate, his plate, and
was just finishing the last bit of food in the serving dishes,
when she became aware of Kit's smile.

"Hungry?"

"Um-hm," she mumbled with her mouth full. She swallowed. "I was starved."

He laughed. "So I noticed."

"I haven't eaten in two days," she admitted, smiling.

His smile faded, the mirth in his eyes replaced by another
look, a hotter look. "I'm starved too . . ."

His meaning was clear.

His fingers trailed along her arm while he spoke. "It's
been two long, cold nights, sweet."

His deep voice rumbled through her just as his words set
her on fire.

"Come." He took her hand and drew her over until she
sat in his lap. His lips feathered over hers. "Feed me."

His mouth, hot and open, met hers, and their tongues
parried. His tongue stroked hers with long, retreating licks
that drove her mad, and his hands worked free the fasteners
on her clothing, shoving the clothes down to her waist. His
palms lifted her heavy breasts while his tongue meandered
from her mouth, down her neck, and then traced one hard
tip and then the other.

She wrenched the studs from his shirt and rubbed her
fingers through the thick, coarse, black hair that covered his

chest. Her fingers grazed his nipples, and his mouth pulled hard on her breast, making her cry out from the heat that shot to her core. The harder he sucked, the more she melted.

Her hands wandered to the buttons on his pants, slipping the first couple through the holes. He wore no smallclothes, for the thick hair of his groin prickled her fingers. She lifted her weight, trying to open more buttons.

"Stand up, sweet, please," he whispered.

She stood on shaking legs, and he wrapped his arms around her skirts and bunched them up, at the same time lifting her to straddle him. The back of her skirts fell over them, but the fabric in front was wadded against their stomachs. He reached up underneath her skirts and grabbed the outside of her thighs, pulling her up against the hard, male part of him. He pressed upward and his hands rocked her thighs so she rode against him. Through the split in her drawers Hallie could feel the cold buttons of his trousers.

"Please," she begged, struggling to get at his buttons.

He pushed aside her hand and freed himself. Grabbing her ribs, he lifted her and slowly slid her onto him. She cried out from the depth, and he stilled.

His hands cupped her head, tilting it only inches from his warm mouth. "Am I hurting you?" he gasped.

"No," she whispered. "Oh God, no—"

His mouth stole the words from her lips. His hand pulled the pins from her hair, and he wrapped the pale silk hair around them, groaning as the hair brushed over him. His hips remained still, but he was embedded so thoroughly, so deeply rooted, that she could feel his pulse beat through his member. He pushed up once and she throbbed with release.

She sagged against his shoulder, and he pulled her forward, rubbing her seed against the base of him and sending her higher and higher. Again she peaked, crying out with each contraction.

Sweat dripped from him onto her breasts. He moved his chest sideways so the coarse hair tickled her nipples. He kissed her ears over and over, whispering how it felt inside

her, what her cries did to him. Finally he lifted her, up and
down, sliding her along his hard length, and when she
tightened into her third release, he burst into his own.

Long moments later she heard him mumble against her
naked breasts.

"Hmm?"

"I don't think I'll ever be able to look at a chair in the
same light again."

Hallie burst into laughter. She had been thinking the same
thing.

Chapter

Twenty-three

We came through that snowy pass, Dagny, and I knew I was on my way home. I could taste it in the air. It took another week to get down to Sacramento City, and then I had to wait for a steamer, but eventually I got here."

Hallie had eavesdropped on Duncan and her sister long enough. It would be embarrassing if she were caught, like some old biddy, listening to Duncan as he lovingly related to her sister the perils of his journey west.

She quietly closed the back door and went off to start cleaning the attic as she had planned. It would keep her busy. Since four whalers had docked earlier in the week, Kit was busy consigning the loads. He had been penned up in his study since early this morning.

Hallie climbed the stairs and opened the narrow door that led to the attic. The small staircase was dark, so she grabbed a lamp from the hallway, lit it, and took it up with her. She stood near the top stair, eyeing the dusty strings of cobwebs that hung from the open rafters.

Her lamp was the only light in the room, and Hallie set it on the attic floor. She was getting light-headed, peering below, so she knew she had better get up on the solid floor before her vertigo overtook her completely. She moved to the top step and crawled up onto the floor.

The room was only half full, which was a great relief. She didn't want to be up here a week, cleaning out other people's old junk—people she didn't know. Kit had told Maddie when she first moved in that most of the stuff up here belonged to the previous owners of the house.

"Well, the sooner you start, the sooner you'll be done," she muttered, and stood up, only to crack her head on a low beam. She massaged the pain and surveyed the boxes. There were five or six over in one corner, so she picked up the lamp and settled herself on the floor.

She opened box after box, weeding through musty old clothes and a variety of china pieces, none of which matched. This could all be thrown out, she thought, wondering if maybe she should just tell Duncan to trash everything up here.

The picture of Duncan with Dagny replayed in her mind. That sweet, giant man spent all his spare time with Dagny, talking to her, walking with her, just as if she had recovered. But she hadn't. She still walked in a daze, her eyes never showing any comprehension or recognition and her lips never speaking. She just stared. But that didn't stop Duncan. Wearing his love on his sleeve for all to see, he opened his heart to her sister. He told her everything about his past and all his dreams for the future. He loved Dagny, and it showed in his eyes, in his actions, and in his words.

If only Kit could love her that way, she thought.

The marriage was more than she ever imagined it could be, but still Kit said nothing of love. He was attentive, and heaven knew he was passionate, but he never said a word to her about his family, or his dreams, or of Jo.

Her love for him was so immense that she felt it in every inch, every pore of her being. She wondered what her life would have been without him, and the emptiness that thought created was frightening. She dreamed of their future and lamented their past, but did not see these feelings in Kit. How could he be free to love her if he wasn't free of his painful past? Until he opened up to her and purged his yesterday, they would have no tomorrow.

Hallie sighed and pushed aside the last box. A small chest sat in the dark corner, and she moved her lamp closer. It was a sea chest, and when she dusted off the film on top, the brass nameplate became readable. It was marked with the initials C.H. She pulled on the lock hinge but it wouldn't move. Impulsively, she pulled a pin from her hair and bent it so she could squeeze it into the keyhole. She wiggled it and twisted it and the lock popped open.

Lifting the lid, she looked inside. A pile of letters, tied with an old blue ribbon, sat on top. She scanned them, seeing they were love letters from Jo to Kit. Hallie read through the first few, amazed that she didn't feel upset or even jealous. The love words were odd and almost unreal to her. The love expressed in the letters was old and dead, cold as ashes from last winter's fire. The love between Kit and his first wife didn't have anything to do with now, only the hurt did. She felt strangely removed.

She set the letters aside while she removed the things Kit had kept from his first marriage. The wedding certificate was there. It showed they had married in late summer, whereas Kit and Hallie had married in the late spring—not that it mattered, except she now knew the date. An envelope held the torn remains of two passages to France. To this Hallie did react, crushing the envelope in her hand, for she remembered the agony in Kit's voice when he spoke of taking Jo to Paris. It had been his final attempt at salvaging his dying marriage. She threw the envelope aside. It contained the torn pieces of the hope of a hurt and confused man—the man she loved.

There were other things, items that meant nothing to her but must have held some significance to Kit: an old theater program, some jewelry, and a beaded bag. Hallie put them back inside, but as she held the bag, she realized there was something inside. She snapped it open and it was empty, but she could still feel something in the lining. She slipped two fingers into a small hole and pulled out a small, leather-covered book. She leaned closer to the lamp and opened the book. Each page was dated and was filled with writing—Jo's writing. Reading on, Hallie realized it was a diary, detailing a whaling voyage.

November 12, 1846

We left the Western Islands today, and I'm in trouble again. Kit is up on deck, brooding. He's very angry with me for traipsing off alone again. Personally, I think he's being too protective. After all, now what harm can come to me in a church, for heaven's sake?

Kit says this island is filled with sailors who have been thrown off their ships for anything from murder to greenhorn seasickness. He says it's dangerous. Well, I didn't see any danger, just the most wonderful old Portuguese church, with color-stained windows that were brought from Lisbon. Oh, they were so beautiful.

Hallie read each page, learning from Jo's words the story of Kit's first marriage. It was strange, because Hallie could read the devotion Jo had for Kit, despite their disagreements. And there were many of those, most of them over Jo's ability to get into some hair-raising predicaments. Reading some of them even gave Hallie the willies, and she could imagine how Jo's sense of adventure had frightened Kit. Even Hallie thought some of Jo's antics were foolhardy.

One entry in particular made Hallie pale.

December 15, 1846

We're two days out of the Cape Verde Islands, and yesterday we hit a furious storm. It was terribly exciting! The wind howled with such force that I was blown overboard. Kit said the only thing that saved me was the safety line he made me wear. He was probably right.

I've never seen him so pale or scared as he was when

he pulled me from the water. He held me so tight, and when we went below he said I would never know what went through his mind when he thought I was dead. He loves me. He really loves me, and that is the one thing I'm frightened of—the responsibility of his love and, now it seems, of his life. He said he didn't think he could live without me, that he wasn't strong enough to go on if anything ever happened to me.

What he said made me think about what I've done. I have to choose between his love for me and the excitement I crave so passionately. I love him. The choice is easy. I'll have to change for him. No more of the reckless spirit. I'll find my excitement in his arms.

To Hallie, these were not the thoughts or promises of an unfaithful wife. Jo loved Kit. It was here in her own words. No woman alive would doubt that love. What could have happened between them? Now Hallie was driven to find out why Jo had changed, so she read on.

She read about the remainder of their voyage, of how pleased Jo was because Kit was so happy. Jo had done a good job of staying out of trouble, and apparently her marriage was the better for it.

They returned home, and from Jo's story, Hallie got some insight to Kit's family. Then Jo was ill and she begged to go on the next voyage, but everyone was against it. It was just as Maddie had told her, except she saw everything through Jo's eyes. Every moment Kit was gone, Jo longed for him.

Then Hallie found it.

April 11, 1847

I just returned from Boston, and oh God, this is hard. I don't know what to do. Kit is gone and I'm alone . . . and heaven help me, I'm going to die.

I laughed at first, thinking the doctor was jesting. But he wasn't. Then I cried all over Dr. Hicks. The poor man, he tried so hard to make it easier for me. He held me while I cried. He thought I cried for myself, and I guess in a way I did. But mostly I cried for Kit—my love, my life.

What would he be when I was gone? His love of me was his weakness. How many times had he said so? He would hurt so badly. I wonder if it is possible that he would really choose not to go on living without me. He said as much . . .

The entry ended, and Hallie, with her heart bleeding for Jo, turned to the next page.

April 12, 1847

I laid awake last night, thinking. What do I do about Kit? Oh, I love him so much and I want him with me, but that's selfish. I really wonder if there is a Heaven. Last night I thought about dying together, Kit and I. Would we go on together through eternity? No answers came.

Am I being foolish and romantic again? All my life I've been told so, but this time I can't take that chance. My life is gone, but Kit's isn't, and I must make sure he's safe, even from himself. So I'll do it. I'll give him his life by destroying his heart. If I can turn his love to hate, he'll go on without me. His love for me is the only thing I can control, and I love him enough to kill it.

Hallie dropped the journal. Her breath rushed from her lungs and over her dry lips and she cried. She cried for Kit; she cried for Jo; she cried for herself.

What a waste! What a horrible, horrible waste. Jo was wrong. The Kit Hallie knew was not weak. To hurt Kit as Jo had, to destroy what they had, was stupid, so so stupid. Jo viewed her actions as a gift; she was giving him his life. That was ridiculous. All Jo did was kill his heart. In the name of love Jo had stripped Kit of his ability to ever love again.

Hallie wiped away her tears and stood, clutching the journal in her hand. She moved the lamp so she could see the stairs, and she left the attic, descending the stairs and walking into Kit's study without warning.

Startled, Kit looked up. She held out the diary.

"I think you should see this."

He opened it and all the color drained from his face. "Where did you find this?"

"In your sea chest, in the attic. Read it."

Kit slammed it shut. "It has nothing to do with us. I don't care what's in it!"

Hallie leaned across the desk, grabbed the book and found the page with Jo's plans. "Read this, Kit. You have to read this!"

He read it, and Hallie heard his breath catch. She saw his expression change from anger to incredible pain, and she saw the tears he tried to hide with his hand.

"Jo," he whispered.

Hallie read the longing in his voice, and her stomach turned.

His wide shoulders shook and he covered his face with both hands. "I need to be alone . . . please . . . leave me alone."

Numb with his rejection and with the knowledge that he still loved his first wife, Hallie walked from the room. She ran through the empty kitchen and outside, heading for the only person to whom she could pour out her soul.

Kit sagged back against his chair and stared at the ceiling. *God, what a mess!*

He looked back at the diary. Oh, Jo, he thought, you were so wrong. Her words brought forth the vivid memory of the night he'd told her he couldn't live without her.

He had said the words because he needed to make her understand how foolish she could be. Sure he had loved her, incredibly so, but when she jeopardized their future over and over again for the sake of some adventure, he had tried to find the one thing that would make her understand his fear. He wanted her to have a taste of what he suffered when repeatedly faced with losing the woman he loved. Kit knew Jo's adventurous nature, and he'd figured that if she thought his life rested in her hands, then maybe she would curb her recklessness.

At the time, he thought his ploy had worked, because Jo did calm down. But apparently her idealistic nature hadn't changed, because when their love was tested by fate, his wife had wasted their last precious few months destroying his faith in love, in women, and in marriage, all in some twisted, noble effort to make him stronger.

To give him his life, she had written. The pain she'd put him through had killed the life in him—until Hallie brought it back.

God, how he loved her.

He had loved Jo, too, but that love was gone, and his past had paled into a faded memory, replaced by the brilliance of his love for Hallie. And until now, until he faced the truth of what had been a painful misunderstanding long ago, he had been blind to the depth with which he loved Hallie.

He rubbed his hand over his pounding forehead. He had treated her like hell, and still she loved him. He knew it. He felt it in every look and every touch. It radiated from her like heat from a bonfire, and he, who had been singed, never appreciated the fire's heat because he was so damn afraid of getting burned.

Kit stood, suddenly needing to find Hallie, to tell her, to hold her. He left the room and looked through the house. She wasn't there and no one had seen her for hours. But she'd brought him the journal not more than fifteen minutes ago. He rechecked the downstairs and finally thought to look outside. Kit opened the back door and stopped. Dagny sat on a small bench in the back, and Hallie knelt beside her, crying. He moved closer, but stopped again when Hallie's words became clear.

"He doesn't need me, or my love. Oh, Duggie, Maddie was wrong. I was wrong. I tried so hard, but he doesn't love me. He can't when he loves Jo. Oh God . . . he still loves Jo." Her voice was loud and mournful with hurt, and the pain and agony of her words paralyzed him.

She was nearly hysterical, and her cries grew as she grabbed Dagny's shoulders and shook her. "Listen to me, Duggie! Hear me . . . please hear me. I don't have anyone . . . please, Duggie, I don't have anyone to hear me." Hallie's head fell into the crook of her arms and her shoulders jerked with her sobs.

Suddenly, she looked up at Dagny with a tormented, tear-ravaged face, and Hallie grabbed her sister's shoulders and began to shake her, over and over while she cried. "Dammit, Duggie, hear me! I need you to hear me . . . Oh God, Duggie, please, please hear me . . . help me . . . I need you . . . I need you, please . . ."

"Don't cry, Hallie. I hear you," Dagny whispered.

Hallie stopped shaking Dagny. "Duggie? Oh God, you heard me . . ." Hallie clung to her. "You heard . . . you're back, oh thank God, you're back."

Hallie called out, "Maddie! Duncan! Come, please come. It's Duggie!"

Kit moved toward them, but the children came barreling out the back door and ran straight toward their sisters. Hallie still held Dagny, and before he could reach them, Maddie and Duncan had arrived. Kit stood back, unsure and feeling as if Hallie's heart were lying crushed and shriveled in his cruel hands. She stood, and her eyes met his for an instant.

Her look was empty. There was no emotion, no life, no tenderness, and most of all, her expressive face no longer held any sign of love. So as they went inside, Kit stayed behind, feeling helpless and vulnerable. He had finally accepted what his heart knew—that he loved Hallie. But something told him he had realized that love too late, that he had waited too long. And for the second time in one day, he cried.

* * *

"I love you."

At the sound of Kit's voice, Hallie stopped splashing water on her teary face.

"I love you," he repeated, closing the bedroom door behind him.

With face dripping, Hallie spun around. "What?"

Kit shifted his stance slightly. "I don't love Jo. I love you."

"Why?"

"What in the hell do you mean, 'why'?"

Hallie grabbed a towel and dried her face. She couldn't look at him. She was too scared—scared that he might give the wrong answer or the wrong reason. She tossed the towel on the dresser and walked over to the bed. "Why do you love me?"

Kit crossed the room in two angry strides. He stood in front of her, glaring.

Hallie crossed her arms and glared back. "Well?"

"I love you because . . . because I do!" he shouted.

"That's not good enough!" Hallie raised her chin.

He paced back and forth. Then he stopped. His frustrated face became smug. "Okay then, why do you love me?"

"I asked you first."

"Goddammit, Hallie! I love you because you're my wife!"

Hallie's stomach dropped. Duty, he loved her out of duty, just because she was his wife.

He turned his eyes toward her, and Hallie saw a pained expression crease his face.

"I'm not sure if I can find the words." Kit shoved his hands into his pockets and he began to pace as he spoke. "I love you because . . . you taught me how to love again . . . because you reminded me how full life was when you loved someone . . . because you washed away the hurt in my heart."

His voice no longer bellowed. Instead, it rang with sincerity. "I love because you gave me your heart when I didn't deserve it."

He paused in front of her. "I love you because you're giving . . ."

Hallie closed her eyes, unable to believe that he was telling her what she needed to hear, and in the words of her dreams.

". . . and loving." He hunkered down in front of her and placed his hand gently on her knee.

She covered his hand with her own.

". . . and beautiful." His fingers closed around hers and he stood, pulling her up into his arms.

Hallie melted into him, and then Kit tilted her chin upward and his thumb caressed her jaw, wiping off the few water drops that lingered on her face and mingled with her tears.

". . . and because," Kit took a deep breath, ". . . because when I kiss you, my soul cries."

"Oh, Kit," Hallie whispered just before his lips touched hers. As before, their kiss flared and deepened. His tongue stroked her mouth and then retreated so he could again murmur his love against her lips, over and over.

She buried her fingers in his curly black hair and pulled him closer, wanting to meld to him, her lips, her breasts, her heart.

"I need you so, Hallie, God knows how I need you . . ." He cupped her face and stroked her with a look so full of love and desire that she cried out.

Kit's hands cupped her head as he kissed her cheeks, her neck, and her ears, and her hands moved from his hair to his neck, where she feathered her fingers lovingly over the sensitive skin behind his ears.

He groaned, and then his hands were unfastening her dress and pushing it to the floor. He pulled his mouth from hers and moved back, out of her embrace.

"Step out of it." His voice ached with want.

Hallie stepped away from the pool of her dress, straight into his loving arms. He leaned down to kiss her shoulders, his lips kindling her desire while his hands untied her crinoline and petticoats. Standing just inches away, Kit slowly pulled loose the small ties on her corset cover, his fingers tracing the curves revealed with each piece of clothing that fell away.

It was sweet torment, both of them watching as eyelet by eyelet he unlaced her corset until his hands filled with her breasts. His thumbs stroked her nipples, and Hallie kissed him, hard, using the stroke of her tongue to tell him of her pleasure.

He knelt before her, untying her drawers and pushing them slowly down her legs. His fingers feathered up and down the insides of her calves and thighs, touching with equal tenderness the puckered skin of her scar.

Hallie moaned at the exquisite tingle of his touch upon the flesh of her legs. His hands roved over and around her legs, stroking her bottom, the backs of her knees, and the hollows of her thighs, nearing but not touching her aching center.

Her hand gripped his shoulders, and he kissed her belly, slowly dragging his damp lips and tongue upward, over the creases left from her corset. Her skin felt hot, burning from the inside out. He kissed the heavy undersides of her breasts while he tore off his shirt. Then he pressed her soft thighs against the hair of his chest, and his hands kneaded her buttocks while in turn his lips closed over the large pink circlets that crowned her breasts, pulling at them with the suction of his mouth. With every touch and every breath, he worshiped her body, showing her his love in a kiss, a stroke, and a whisper, hot against her skin. He drove her wild.

When he stood, no clothing covered him. They embraced, skin to skin, and he lowered her to the bed, crawling between her legs while he settled her against the pillows. He rose above her, sipping at her lips and positioning his hard tip against her pleasure point. Then he rubbed, gently, sending wave after wave of exquisite feeling through her. Wild with need, she grabbed at his buttocks, trying to dip him into her.

"Wait," he whispered, and before his command registered, he had lifted her essence to his lips and tasted her.

"No," she moaned, her mind wanting to stop the wickedness of his tongue, but her body craved more.

"Yes," he breathed, his lips nibbling at her, over and over until she pulsed with repletion.

Then he filled her, thick and hard. His mouth lowered to her ear. "I love you . . . I love you . . ." he said, his words in rhythm with his pumping hips.

Again her pleasure rose, higher and higher, and he stopped, turning with her onto his back, letting Hallie control the movement. She stilled her hips and slowly bent forward, rubbing her hard nipples over his ribs. Her mouth kissed his nipple and she lifted her hips upward so she was linked only by the very tip of him. Then she rotated her hips, once, twice, and in an instant she was on her back again as he drove into her with long, deep strokes, faster and faster, until the sweetness claimed them both.

Chapter

Twenty-four

Hallie drummed her fingers on the arm of the chair, wondering where Kit was. He had been called away well before supper, and she had expected him to be home by now. The clock chimed eleven times and Hallie gave up.

"Well, cats," she told the animals that sat all over the furniture, "I guess that's what happens. They tell you they love you and then they stay out all night."

She laughed. She knew from the past few days that Kit would never be long from her side. He loved her with his whole being, of that she had no doubt.

Like in a fairy tale, all her girlish dreams had come true. It was still hard to believe. Sometimes at night she would awaken and just watch him sleep, knowing that he was hers, heart and soul. She would look at his hair, curly and dark against the white of his pillow, and remember how it felt against her fingers. She would stare at the muscles in his back and shoulders and would remember how they strained hard against her palms when he made love to her. And she would watch him breathe, the slow breath of sleep that was so like the way he would breathe words of love and passion into her ears. And sometimes, tears would trickle down her cheeks just because she loved him.

Hallie sighed and went to check the locks, as Kit had asked. Duncan had gone somewhere tonight. With everything bolted, she went upstairs, undressed, and got into bed, hoping Kit would wake her when he came home.

She closed her eyes, but not more than a minute later she heard a noise and opened them. Her heart beat fast when she saw the dark figure crawl through the window.

Oh, that man! she thought. He's kidnapping her again. A beefy hand closed over her mouth and nose. She gave some token resistance. After all, she wouldn't want this to be too easy.

Once again she was gagged, tied, and wrapped in the blankets. Lee could have been more original this time. She'd have to talk to him about it when he unwrapped her.

Of course, the figure had been burly, which Lee wasn't. Hallie started to wonder, but then she remembered Duncan. Kit was using him instead of Lee, just to throw her off.

They reached the ground with a jarring thud, and Hallie decided she'd have to talk to that Kit about finding a more comfortable way to snatch her. She would insist on it. She waited for the sound of the carriage door, but instead she was heaved like a sack of potatoes onto a rock-hard surface. Her mind flashed with the cold gruel she would feed Duncan at her very next opportunity.

Her protest muffled against the gag and the chill of the air disappeared when something heavy covered her. A thud vibrated from in front of her, and she realized that this was a wagon when Duncan clucked the team and the reins jangled. She bounced along the hard wagon bed, knowing she'd be covered with bruises by tomorrow. She intended to plant some bruises of her own on those stupid men!

After much bouncing, the wagon finally halted and Duncan lifted her out. She wasn't very happy with her treatment, so she tried to kick out at him, but he heaved her over his shoulder and carried her down some stairs. Obviously they weren't going back to the *Haven*, because they would have had to go upstairs first. She wondered where they were. This place didn't smell very good, sort of old and burnt.

Duncan set her down, and then he did the oddest thing—he shoved her hard and she stumbled, falling in a heap of blankets onto the cold, bare floor. She yelled through her gag, but the sound was lost because the door slammed shut so loudly. She struggled to get out of the tangle, but no matter how she rolled, she was still caught.

She heard male voices and what sounded like the clink of coins before an outer door slammed shut. The click of the door signaled its opening. She heard the sliding shuffle of shoes.

It was then that she panicked. Kit wore boots whose heels clicked across the floor. He was too confident and proud to ever drag his feet.

Oh, my God! This is real!

Someone jerked the covers from her and she rolled onto the cold floor. Hallie looked up at the drawn, sunken face of Abner Brown.

He smiled and then looped a rope around her neck, tightened it, and tied it to a thick beam. He never said one word, he just walked out a narrow door.

She pulled on the rope, but it was a noose, so as she pulled, it tightened. If she kept pulling, she'd hang herself. She quickly scanned the room. It was a dark, partially burned room with no windows, like a cellar. Broken tables and a lopsided, charred cabinet were scattered through the room, and large areas of the floor were covered with rubble of burned wood and ash. A few battered coffins sat in a corner, and she realized that this must be what was left of the funeral parlor.

Her mind raced for a means of escape. A small door was barely visible in a shadowed wall. She remembered that the building sloped down the hill, which meant that she might be able to scoot out that door if she could somehow get free from this madman.

She had no idea how long she sat there, but any hope of

escape disappeared when Abner came back, followed by a burly man with another bundle.

"Set her over there," Abner ordered in a odd, raspy voice that had lost its whine.

The man dropped the bundle, and Dagny, tied and gagged, rolled against Hallie's feet. Hallie looked at her sister's eyes, fearing they would be dull again. They weren't. Dagny stared at her before her frightened eyes darted back to Abner.

Gold coins clinked again as Abner paid the man and then closed the door, turning back toward the women. He walked over and tied Dagny as he had Hallie, again saying nothing. Then he stood back and eyed them.

"I've been waiting for this," he told them. "Waiting and watching, and hiding," he spat, "like some animal!"

Hallie mumbled through her gag, and he walked toward her. His watery eyes looked from one sister to the other. He grabbed the rope around Hallie's neck and jerked it hard. The noose closed roughly on her throat then loosened, and she fell forward onto her stomach. She lifted her face from the dirty floor, looking up at him, panicked over what he would do next. He held the rope up for her to see and pulled again. Hallie cried out against the gag as the rope burned and squeezed her neck.

"Does that hurt?" he asked.

Hallie was silent.

"I can see it does." He smiled and turned toward a table, where he grabbed a bowl and a basket and turned back around. Then he sat down on the floor and pulled a tinder from the bowl. He opened the basket and pulled a long, thin needle from inside.

Hallie tried to hide her fear at the sight of the instrument, thinking he intended to torture or stab them with it. But instead he placed a black ball on the end and then lit it, rolling it over the flame until it smoldered orange. He sucked in the smoke, holding it tightly with his head thrown back and his eyes closed. Then he expelled the air and repeated the action over and over, and the smell of the smoke, sweet and strong, made Hallie's stomach lurch.

"How does it feel to be tied up like some animal?" His eyes teared and he breathed gasping, shallow breaths.

Hallie tried to mask her fear, and she heard a muffled protest from Dagny. Turning her head toward her sister, Hallie frowned and shook her head slightly, warning Dagny to be quiet.

"I know what it's like to be treated like an animal, hunted and forced to hide." He took in more smoke.

"You sent them after me, didn't you?" He stared at Hallie as if she were dirt. "The night at the theater."

He placed the smoldering needle into the bowl and stood, walking over to a large wooden crate. He shoved it aside and then spun around, the anger on his gray face so intense that it bordered on madness.

"They chased me . . . made me run. I had to hide, like a coward . . . in a dark trunk."

He pushed and pulled at something, dragging it across the room. He moved out of the shadows, and Hallie saw what he had. It was a smoke-blackened coffin.

"But I've been watching, and waiting." He bent down, picked up the needle and he moved toward Hallie, grabbed her hair with one hand, pulled her up, and with the other waved the smoke in her face.

Hallie held her breath, closing her eyes from the burning smoke. "Breathe it!" he screamed at her.

Still she held her breath, though her lungs ached with the need for air. He jerked up so hard on her hair, Hallie gasped, and then the smoke filled her mouth, nose, and lungs. Long minutes passed and she could hear Dagny's muffled crying, but she had no will left. She was dizzy and sick from the sweet smoke.

He released her hair and she fell onto the floor, unable to move her body. He reached under her arms and dragged her across the floor. Then he pushed her up against something and shoved her inside. It was cold and she shivered, but she couldn't move her limbs.

She willed her eyes to open, but her lids were like weights. Over and over she tried to open them, until finally they lifted, just as Abner slid the coffin lid closed.

He pounded the nails and she tried to move, but she couldn't. Oh, God, she thought, do something! Move! But she was numb. All she could feel was her thick blood, flowing around and around her. The air was warm, heavy, and it tasted of smoke. The wooden box shook with the madman's hammering, but Hallie couldn't move. She was so tired, so dizzy. She had no strength, and her eyelids drifted closed.

Dagny struggled and fought at the bonds on her hands and feet. She tried to scoot forward but the rope tightened on her neck.

"It won't do any good to struggle. You can't get away," Abner said with eerie calm while he hammered the nails on the coffin lid.

"You see what I'm doing, don't you?" he asked her. "I'm the lion now, you know."

The man was mad! She wondered what he would do to her, and she remembered the last time. Her head spun and she thought she might throw up. She sucked air up her nose. She couldn't be weak, not now, not when Hallie needed her.

If Hallie were alive.

Dagny didn't know what that stuff was that Abner smoked, but she saw what it did to Hallie. She told herself it couldn't be deadly or Abner wouldn't have smoked it. Oh, God, she had to get away!

"I'll devour Kit Howland, the hunter," Abner told her. "He made me hide. He made me look like a coward. I'm not, you know. My father was, but not me. I'm stronger. I'm not like him . . . no . . ." He shook his head. "I won, and I'll keep winning. You'll see."

He shoved the table over to a cabinet in the wall. He opened the door and pushed the coffin through. "I'm going to hide your sister in a dark place. She'll hide, like I had to."

He laughed again, and the sound crawled through her. He

closed the door and turned back to her. "How long do you think she'll stay alive, hmm? An hour? Two?"

Smiling, he walked back toward her, but paused by the smoldering bowl. He picked it up and breathed the smoke again.

"These are flowers, burning, sweet flowers. You want to try them? Here." He moved toward her and waved the bowl under her nose. "See, it makes the pain go away."

Dagny tried to turn away.

Abner laughed and set the dish down next to her on the table.

"You'll want it later," he told her, then left the room.

Dagny waited and listened. She could hear him sliding the coffin from the other side of the wall. She was searching for some way to get free when her eyes lit on the smoldering bowl. She hopped as far as the noose would let her and held her bound hands over the smoking ball, hoping it was still hot enough to burn the rope around her hands. She took a deep breath and laid the rope against the hot ball.

It singed her skin but also burned the rope. After a few long, agonizing seconds, she pulled her hands free. She jerked the gag out and gulped air while working the noose open, then slipped it off her head. Bending, she untied the bonds around her ankles and tiptoed to the door.

She listened closely and heard the soft snicker of horses outside. Something banged closed, and then she heard Abner's footsteps. Quickly, she looked for something to hit him with, grabbed the hammer, then held her breath and waited. A few seconds later the wagon took off.

Dagny sighed with relief, and she cracked the door open. The back street was empty, and she ran, as fast as her bare feet would take her, praying to God that she could get help in time.

"They're gone!"

"What in the hell do you mean, 'they're gone!'" Kit yelled, trying to get Maddie to calm down.

"Both Dagny and Hallie! Their windows are open and they're gone! Someone has taken them. Liv saw the man climbing out the window with Dagny, but by the time she got me, he had taken them off in a wagon!"

Maddie grabbed his shoulders. "I didn't hear anything, Kit. Oh, God, you have to find them!"

"Abner," Kit breathed, and Duncan nodded. Kit pried Maddie's hands from his shoulders. "Calm down, Maddie, we'll find them."

He turned to Duncan. "Go get Lee. I just left him at the Thistle Inn. He should still be there. Get back here as fast as you can. I'll see if anyone recognized that wagon."

Duncan took Kit's horse and rode off, while Kit went from door to door trying to find out if anyone could give him any clues as to where the women were taken.

Fifteen minutes later Lee and Duncan rode up. Kit was waiting near the hitching post.

"Did you find out anything?" Lee asked.

Kit shook his head. "Nobody saw anything, except Maddie and Liv, and they said the wagon headed that way." Kit pointed down to the bay side of the hill. He rubbed his temple in frustration. "God, I don't even know where to start looking."

As if he weren't in enough hell, the sky suddenly poured with rain. The clouds rolled in and the rain drummed on the wooden walks. A scream echoed up from the bottom of the hilly street. The men turned and saw Dagny, torn and barefoot, running toward them, screaming and stumbling up the hill.

They raced to her, and Kit caught her in his arms. She was so hysterical and out of breath that her words were indistinguishable between her struggled breaths. He held her and rocked her, trying to get her to calm down so she could speak. She cried so hard, all she could do was gasp, fighting for air, until finally her stammers cleared.

"Abner Brown. He's b-burying h-h-her . . . in a c-coffin . . ." she gasped, and then fainted.

Kit handed her to Duncan. "Take her home and get Sheriff Hayes. We'll meet you at the cemetery!"

Kit and Lee mounted their horses and raced toward Telegraph Hill. Kit kicked his horse harder and harder, praying that they'd find her. The rain poured, turning the streets to mud. As he pushed his horse faster, his mind flashed with a picture of the mud, seeping into a deep hole and covering over any evidence of a fresh grave. It drove him on, numb with panic and racing with fear.

They reached the road to the semaphore tower. Kit jumped the gate and his horse faltered in the soft, slick ground. He landed on his right arm and rolled hard against a tree but pulled himself up, ignoring the pain, running and stumbling through the grounds.

He could hear Lee calling out behind him, but he didn't stop, he couldn't. The storm lashed around in the black night air, making it hard to see. Kit came over another rise and stopped, peering through the downpour.

Then he saw the wagon.

He closed in on it, running so hard his bones ached. He could see a figure, bent and shoveling mud into a hole. He flew onto Abner, knocking the shovel from his hands as they rolled to the ground. Kit was on top and his hands closed around Abner's neck, but Abner wedged his leg between their struggling bodies and shoved Kit backward with his foot.

Abner grabbed the shovel and Kit ducked, so the shovel only cut into his shoulder. Pain shot down his injured arm and he struggled to get up. Lee ran past him, heading straight for Abner, but the madman saw him and swung the shovel, catching the side of Lee's head and knocking him unconscious.

Kit used the wagon wheel to pull himself up. Abner had the shovel, holding it in front of him like a sword. Kit charged and Abner stepped aside, laughing loudly as Kit stumbled and fell on his back in the mud. He looked up just as Abner swung the shovel back, intending to crush his skull.

The shovel blade hit one of the wagon horses and the animal screamed and reared, its frantic hooves catching Abner like hooks and pulling him under the team. Both horses trampled and pawed until Abner's broken body was pounded into the mud.

Kit groped toward the grave, using one hand to scoop out the mud.

"Noooo!" he screamed. "Goddammit, no!" The mud flowed into the hole faster than he could get it out.

"God, you can't do this!! I can't lose her . . . I can't—" His voice cracked with the agony that he couldn't get to Hallie.

Sobbing and screaming, he slid into the hole, wedging his body between the side of the grave and the head of the coffin. He grabbed at the lid but the nails held it shut. He tried to lift it but the heavy mud and his injured arm made it impossible.

He had to get the lid off!

Frantic, he looked for something to pry at the nails. He spotted the shovel, broken from the horses' hooves and half buried in the mud. He crawled from the grave, rain splattering so hard on his face he couldn't see. He felt around for the shovel but only found mud.

Hurry, Christ hurry! Then his fingers grazed metal. He grasped the wood of the broken handle, dragged the piece into the hole and wedged the metal blade under the lid. Leaning his upper body on the handle, he forced it down with all his body weight. The lid pried open. Over and over he wedged the blade until he could kick the lid open enough to get to Hallie.

He pulled her out and held her against him, rocking with her and screaming at her to wake up. Then he sat back, cradling her head in his arm and looking at her. Her eyes were closed, as if she were asleep, or dead.

He shook her shoulders.

"Wake up, dammit, you can't die . . . you can't . . . I can't lose you . . ." he cried, his tormented words dying in the noise of the storm. "I love you . . . I love you. Oh God! Don't do this again. . . . I love her . . . I love her . . . I love her . . ."

Pulling her limp body against him, he buried his head in her neck and cried out his pain, his love.

Her hand touched his shoulder, stroking it.

He pulled back, looking down into her face, wet and spotted with mud. It was the face he loved.

Her eyes opened, hazy, drugged, and blinking against the rain. Recognition lit her features.

"I love you," he said, his voice hoarse.

She whispered, "I know." And she smiled.

Epilogue

H allie rubbed the oak banister with polishing oil. It was fall, and Maddie was on one of her cleaning binges again. A giggle sang from the parlor, and Hallie poked her head into the room. She smiled. Duncan held Dagny high in the air so her sister could dust off the window cornice. His large hands squeezed her sister's small waist, and again she laughed. Next year, when Dagny was older and Duncan's masonry business was well established, they'd be married.

The smell of cinnamon rose from the kitchen, and Hallie went to check on the bread pudding. She grabbed a rag from nail beside the range and used it to open the oven door. The dessert, a recipe Maddie had wrangled from her friend Millie, was golden brown and bubbling, and Hallie used the rag to remove the hot pan. It was heavy, like lifting Liv's cat. The pan clumped on the range top and she closed the oven door, laughing at the size of the dessert. Maddie was still cooking for Lee, despite the fact that he and his ship the *Wanderer* were off whaling again.

Wiping her hands on her apron, Hallie went to check on the twins. A minute later she stood at the back door, watching the leaves quiver from all the commotion in the tree. Kit pushed a branch aside to peer down at the children standing on the ground below.

"Are you sure you want this thing on this branch?" he asked, pointing to the small wooden platform he was trying to nail to the tree.

The twins nodded.

"Okay," Kit said, and the hammering began.

A loud screech pierced the air.

"Goddammit, Liv! Keep these cats out of this tree until I'm done!" Kit dropped two black and white cats into Liv's waiting arms. She plopped them each over a shoulder and stood back to watch Kit finish the treehouse.

The hammering resumed. Hallie had just started to close the door when a loud crack erupted from the tree. She spun around just in time to see the tree branch, platform and all, fall to the ground, along with her swearing husband.

Hallie shut the door to hide her laughter, then ran over to the window and watched Kit extract himself from the broken branches. He stood and dusted himself off, glaring up at the second story, where the sound of Maddie's laughter howled through the backyard. The children had wisely disappeared.

Kit stomped toward the house, so Hallie turned to the range, where she pretended to be busy stirring an empty pot.

The back door slammed and Hallie schooled her grin, turning around to face Kit. He stood behind her, leaves and twigs still dangling from his dark, curly hair, and he wore his famous scowl.

She let her eyes meander over him, then asked, "Fallen out of any trees, lately?"

His scowl disappeared and a devious grin replaced it. His eyes mimicked hers, roving slowly from her head to her pregnant stomach. His arms closed around her, coaxing her into his embrace. "Crawled into any strange beds, lately?"

Hallie whispered against his lips. "Only yours, my love."

Then he kissed her, so tenderly and with so much love that Hallie was sure she heard their souls cry.

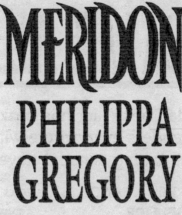